Also by Barbara Delinsky

COMMITMENTS
FACETS
HEART OF THE NIGHT
TWILIGHT WHISPERS

BARBARA DELINSKY

COMMITMENTS

WARNER BOOKS

A Time Warner Company

To Steve, Eric, Andrew and Jeremy—always.

WARNER BOOKS EDITION

Copyright © 1988 by Barbara Delinsky
All rights reserved.

Cover design by Diane Luger
Cover photograph by Nancy Palubniak
Hand lettering by Carl Dellacroce

Warner Books, Inc.
1271 Avenue of the Americas
New York, NY 10020

Ⓦ A Time Warner Company

Printed in the United States of America

First Printing: March, 1988
Reissued: August, 1995

10 9 8 7 6

· PROLOGUE ·

Derek McGill wasn't a man to waver. Once he set his mind to something, he saw it through. The industry knew him to be dogged and shrewd, self-righteous, even bull-headed when an issue hit him hard. Unanswered phone calls and untold runarounds, veiled hostility and unveiled threats—all were part of the game. He was used to them; they never stalled him long.

Yet, on the threshold of the rooftop patio, he paused. Granted, the rooms he'd passed through were posh, but he'd seen more lavish rooms in his day. The patio itself, an oasis high above the concrete maze of Manhattan, was idyllic, but he'd seen his share of makeshift Edens, too.

His hesitation didn't come from the luxury of the Fifth Avenue apartment or the greenery of its terrace. Rather, he was drawn up short by the woman standing with her back to him not far from the waist-high brick wall which lined the terrace.

She was of medium height and slender. A soft white blouse cascaded gently from her shoulders, overlapping an equally lightweight gauze skirt that veiled her in lilac from hip to mid-calf. Barefoot and oblivious to his arrival, she swayed ever so slowly from side to side. The late afternoon sun, tripping over the treetops of Central Park, gilded her blond hair and that of the small child she held in her arms, her head resting on his.

He wasn't sure what he'd expected—not that he'd had an awful lot of time to dwell on it, given his schedule. But he supposed he'd assumed this woman to be a slick city type surrounded by defenses as heavy as her Giorgio.

He'd been wrong. She was younger than he'd expected,

1

for one thing, and there was nothing slick about her. As for defenses, his radar couldn't detect any. He almost felt as though he should have brought some along for her use.

There was something awe-inspiring about Sabrina Stone as she stood in her private garden high above the city. He found himself thinking of the Madonna. With her hair loosely caught into a short, high ponytail from which stray tendrils had escaped to graze her cheeks and neck, she looked utterly unpretentious. He conjured up images of purity and goodness, both incongruous with the world around her as he knew it. Her husband was a high roller in the game of investment banking. She herself was from a wildly successful literary family.

Still, she seemed the personification of innocence, a flower child lost and alone, clinging to the one thing she cherished above all else in life.

She seemed serene. Perhaps that was what, more than anything, brought Derek to a standstill. He knew that she couldn't truly be serene, given her lot in life. Yet, the picture she presented was that, and he envied it. His own life was a rat race, a nonstop quest for the story to top all others. If he wasn't on the phone with sources or haggling with producers or assistant producers or researchers for information he needed yesterday, he was justifying his position with management or hustling for a final scoop in an eleventh-hour rush to meet the cameras.

The sight of Sabrina Stone made him pause, take a deep breath, and release it slowly and with something surprisingly akin to relief.

Over the dim clang and whir of traffic that drifted from far below, he caught bits and fragments of a tune. She was humming a song as she rocked the child. He couldn't identify it, but it didn't matter. The effect was the same, a tableau of warmth and love that touched him in strange and unexpected ways.

He was an intruder. He knew that, but he couldn't have left if he tried, and he wouldn't have tried for the world. Having set eyes on her, his curiosity was piqued. He reminded himself that this was just another story, but deep down inside, he suspected more complex forces drew him forward.

His shoes made a muted tap on the marble tiles as he crossed the terrace, but she seemed not to hear. Lost in that tiny world encompassing her baby and her, she neither looked up nor turned.

When he was within reaching distance, he stopped. "Mrs. Stone?" Her head flew around then, eyes wide and startled. "I'm sorry," he said with an odd gentleness, "I didn't mean to frighten you."

For a minute she said nothing, simply looked at him, studying his eyes as though they could tell her what she wanted or needed to know. "Who are you?" she said at last.

"Derek McGill."

She continued to study him. One of her brows lowered for the briefest instant in a frown she quickly mastered. "Why does that sound familiar?"

"I'm a reporter with *Outside Insight*. You may have seen some of my work."

She lowered her chin to the child's head, and he could have sworn that her arms tightened fractionally. Both gestures suggested protectiveness. He could understand that.

"How did you get in?" Her voice held wariness, while her eyes held his.

Their hold was strong. He'd never seen eyes quite like them, though he doubted it had as much to do with their pale green coloring as with the blend of emotions they betrayed. Among other things, he saw fear; and while he'd have been delighted to see that if he were confronting a bureaucrat with allegations of corruption, he regretted seeing it in Sabrina Stone.

So he said without pride, "I tagged along with three fellows who were visiting one of the other apartments. That took care of the doorman. Your maid was satisfied when I said that we were old friends and you were expecting me."

"That wasn't true."

"I know. But I wanted to speak with you. I've tried to call several times. Your husband is protective of your privacy."

"You've spoken with him?"

Derek caught sight of a small, almost imperceptible tic in the delicate skin beneath her left eye. It was the kind that came from being overtired, or overwrought. He suspected that with Sabrina it was the latter. "I haven't spoken with him directly. He never returned my calls, but eventually he left a message that if I tried to reach him again, he'd call the president of the network."

A flicker of hardness passed through her eyes, and she nodded.

Derek gave a lopsided smile. "He'd do that?"

"Yes." She paused. The hardness was gone, replaced by a hint of a plea, though her voice was as soft and controlled as ever. "What do you want?"

"Just to talk." His gaze dropped to the child's curls. As he viewed them closer now and from a different angle, he could see that they were more light brown than blond. "Is he sleeping?" he asked, leaning sideways to see the child's face. One view gave him his answer. The child's large brown eyes were wide open, focused on nothing at all.

Derek had seen many a tragedy in the course of his work. He'd viewed grossly deformed burn victims, pathetically spindly victims of malnutrition, severely maimed victims of war—and still he'd managed to keep a certain distance between him and his subjects. But the sight of this child, with baby-fine hair the color of pecans, a button nose, tiny lips and pale, butter-soft skin, wrenched at his heart.

"He's beautiful," he whispered.

"Yes," she said.

Derek looked up to catch the sadness in her eyes. "How old is he?"

"Sixteen months."

"His name?"

"Nicholas."

After his father. Derek should have guessed that. Nicholas Stone had never been known for either modesty or understatement. The man was a winner; he was of the breed that coupled smarts with a determination to make every venture successful.

Derek couldn't help but wonder how the man viewed his

son, whether what he'd assumed to be protectiveness had in fact been embarrassment or shame. If so, his heart went out to the woman before him.

His research said that parents of the brain-damaged suffered unimagined trials, and, up close, her face bore testimony to that. Faint smudges were visible beneath her eyes. Strain had traced tiny grooves by the sides of her mouth. And though her skin looked nearly as smooth and soft as the babe's, its pallor seemed that much more unnatural.

In spite of it all, Derek thought she was beautiful. It was as if her beauty shone from within. It was absurd, he realized, because he didn't know her for beans. But she touched him, made him ache a little. That hadn't happened to him in a very long time.

"I'm not sure why you're here, Mr. McGill," she said softly. They both knew she lied. Behind the pale green of her eyes—those telling eyes—was a glimmer of challenge.

"I'd like your help," he replied. When she didn't blink, he went on. "I'm doing a story on special children and their families—their needs, available medical resources or the lack thereof, the paucity of help, both physical and emotional."

She shifted the child, a small bundle of dead weight, and, bracing one arm under his bottom, slanted the other across his back like a shield. Opening one hand over the glossy curls, she pressed the child's head to her heart. And said nothing.

In that instant, Derek wavered. It wasn't that Sabrina Stone threatened him physically, and he certainly hadn't been put off by her husband's harsh words or he'd never have found his way to her terrace. But there was strength in the woman who stood before him, a strength that gave him pause.

For a split second he felt unsure of who he was and what he was doing. His job was to ferret out the facts, not exacerbate them, but he had the distinct feeling that his involving Sabrina in his story would compound her troubles.

He assumed it had something to do with her husband. The man had sent him a clearly hostile message. There was nothing hostile about Sabrina, though. She was cautious, as she should be. Her eyes, an emotional kaleidoscope, spoke of sadness, confusion and helplessness in turn. But he also saw in them strength.

"I was told that you've had a difficult time."

A look of hurt entered her eyes. "Who told you that?"

Knowing that he couldn't answer her question, but needing to erase that look of betrayal, he rushed on. "It doesn't matter. What does matter is that, theoretically, you and your husband are in a position to mobilize the best of resources. Few of the people I've spoken to are. Many don't recognize the handicap early on, others refuse to admit it. And then, even beyond the monetary demands, they don't know where to turn."

Sabrina tore her gaze from his and aimed it out over the park. When the baby gave a sudden weak wail, she put her mouth to his forehead, cooed softly and resumed her gentle rocking. He quieted almost instantly.

Derek smiled. "He knows a good thing, doesn't he?"

"I'm not sure what he knows, Mr. McGill."

It wasn't an admission, exactly. The most precocious of sixteen-month-olds was still a creature of sensation, an entity whose brain workings were vague. But it wasn't a denial, either, and that was what Derek homed in on.

"How long have you known that he was different?" he asked with that same gentleness he'd felt earlier, the one that was as unfamiliar to his ears as it was to his heart.

"Every child is different. Each has its own strengths and weaknesses."

"What are Nicholas' strengths?"

She thought about that for a minute, and when she looked at Derek again, her eyes were misty. "He has a heartrending smile and a great potential for love."

Invisible fingers squeezed Derek's heart. "Does he get those from his mother?"

She blinked, pressed her lips together and seemed to marshal her composure. "I try."

"But the smiles come harder these days?"

"Yes."

"Can you tell me about it?"

She took a shaky breath, then slowly shook her head.

"Why not?"

"Some things are private."

"Some things benefit from sharing."

Lowering her head, she caressed the baby's brow with her cheek. The silence went on for such a long time that Derek was beginning to wonder whether he was being tuned out as a prelude to being asked to leave; then she spoke again.

"Everyone has problems. The world is full of frustration and heartache. Some people find solace in sharing." She hesitated, and her voice lowered. "Others deal with things on their own."

"Is that what you want to do?"

"It's what I have to do."

"Why? If I can shed light on the extent of the frustration and heartache, perhaps something will come of it."

"I doubt that," she murmured, and for the first time, there was an element of defeat in her voice. "Medicine is an inexact science. Doctors aren't miracle workers. No amount of light shed on the problem will change the fact that brain damage can't be reversed."

"No, but it can aid in the coping."

She looked at him then, her eyes touched by curiosity. "Is that how you justify your work?"

"It's one of the ways."

"You're a reporter, not a politician or a therapist."

"True."

"Have you really helped people?"

"I like to think it. There are times when we've been able to publicize a problem so much that the forces-that-be had to sit up and take notice."

Her lips seemed to relax into the beginning of a smile. It was a sweet beginning, and it surprised Derek. She had every right to be bitter or cynical, yet she wasn't. *Goodness*. He thought it again. Again he was touched.

"Cheer me with one of your stories," she invited softly.

He sifted through the files in his mind. It was a large collection, comprising reports he'd done not only for *Out-*

side Insight, but for the various news programs with which he'd been involved prior to that.

"Last year I did a piece on the job discrimination faced by cancer patients. I interviewed dozens of people who, as soon as they were diagnosed as having cancer, were denied jobs or opportunities for advancement. Many of those people had been treated successfully for their illness, yet still they were regarded as futureless. As a result of awareness generated by the report, a group of patients got together and filed a class-action suit charging a violation of their First Amendment rights."

Raising her brows, Sabrina gave a thoughtful nod of approval. She was quiet for a short time as she continued to rock the baby. Then she asked, "Do you know that I'm a writer?"

"I know that you come from a family of writers."

Her lips twitched. "Quite."

Derek wondered at the momentary amusement he saw in her eyes. It softened her features and became her nicely. "Are you into Westerns, like your dad?" he teased.

She shook her head. "Nor sci-fi, like mom, nor horror, like J. B. I'm the black sheep of the family. My field is nonfiction. I've written mostly for magazines, but the one thing I'm most proud of never made it into print."

"What was that?" Derek asked.

She didn't answer at first, but seemed to be searching his eyes—much as she'd done when he first arrived. He wasn't sure if she could see the fascination he felt; but as he watched, he saw a certain calmness take her.

"It was the story of the wife of a prominent businessman who was convicted of the rape and murder of his mistress. I was interested in exploring the wife's feelings, but when it came time to submit the story to a publisher, I couldn't get myself to do it. The poor woman had suffered enough. Her name and that of her children had been dragged through the mud. The last thing they needed was additional exposure, when they were trying to keep a low enough profile to rebuild their lives."

"Couldn't you have vindicated her?"

"I couldn't change the fact that she'd been married to a

sick man, any more than I could change the fact that her children were flesh of his flesh."

"You could have established them as innocent victims."

"I could have."

"And others would have found the story interesting."

"But would the exploitation have been worth it? They'd moved to a new home in a new state. In the name of human interest, I'd have branded them all over again."

Tucking his hands in the pockets of his slacks, Derek dropped his gaze to the large marble tiles. They were variegated in shades of dark green, an urban version of a mossy forest floor. Atop their shiny finish, Sabrina's feet looked slender and graceful. With the slightest shift of his own foot, the hard leather soles of his loafers would bruise her.

The analogy wasn't lost on him. He felt rough, almost uncouth beside Sabrina. He didn't feel that way with others, but others didn't convey the kind of dignified fragility she did. Strength and all, she was fragile. She pricked his conscience.

Hesitantly raising his eyes, he asked, "Do you feel that I'm trying to exploit you?"

"Why are you here?" she countered, curious rather than impertinent. "I'd have thought that the face before the camera did little of the groundwork."

"Was incapable of doing the groundwork?"

"No. Too busy."

He shook his head. "My stories are mine. I do them because they interest me. I have people doing other kinds of legwork, but I like to interview the principals myself."

"I won't be one of your principals."

"I'm not trying to exploit you."

"There's a fine line—"

"I'm not."

"Your intentions may be honorable, but the fact is that any story you do will be broadcast from coast to coast. That won't do much for the low profile we try to keep."

"It may do some good for others in your position."

She gave a sad laugh. "Right about now, charity isn't high on my list of priorities. I have my hands more than full trying to cope with...cope with..." Though her voiced trailed off, her eyes continued to speak.

And Derek, who'd done his homework well, heard every word. She was trying to cope with endless days of constant child care, with one useless doctor's appointment after another, with the total disruption of what would, given her husband's standing, have been a socially active life. And through it all were worry and unsureness, questions without answers, a future in doubt.

He steeled himself to press his bid, but it was hard, because her eyes held that pleading again. Then a beeping sound broke into his concentration. His watch. He'd set it to remind himself of a later appointment. He stabbed at the button in annoyance, asking himself why he'd set the alarm, knowing that it was his standard practice, wondering if it was crude.

"Sorry," he muttered and took a minute to get over his confusion. Then he asked, "Do you still write?"

Her smile was sad this time, and she pressed a soft kiss to the baby's head before she spoke. "I don't have the time, much less the psychic energy."

"Perhaps it would be an outlet."

"Is that what your work is for you?"

"It's my vocation."

"But is it an outlet, too?" she asked.

"For creative energy, yes." He lowered his head and thought for a minute. "For nervous energy too, I suppose."

"What makes you nervous?"

He knew that he should be turning the questions around. He was the interviewer, and there was the business of maintaining a professional facade. But the facade seemed suddenly artificial, and Sabrina's clear gaze demanded better.

"My life," he answered. "Where I'm going. What I want."

"Why should those things make you nervous?"

"Because I'm not always sure where I'll end up and whether that'll be where I want to be."

"Where do you want to be?"

"I don't know!" he said. Then, hearing his own frustra-

tion, ran a handful of fingers through his dark hair and
forced a dry chuckle. "You're nearing the jugular."

"But you seem so . . . confident. Given your position, I'd
have thought that you'd be on top of the world." She
seemed genuinely interested, not to mention momentarily
distracted from her own woes—which was why, when she
asked if he was married, he answered.

"No. No time." He gave a crooked grin. "Like your
writing?"

"There's a difference. I don't have a choice."

"That," he said gently but pointedly, "was what I wanted
to explore."

She closed her eyes briefly, then sighed, then shifted the
child again. It occurred to Derek that the baby had to be
heavy.

"May I hold him?" he asked, offering his arms.

Sabrina seemed genuinely surprised. He wondered if no
one else offered to help her with the work. He couldn't
believe that she shouldered it all herself, couldn't believe
that her husband didn't take his turn. Then again . . .

Very carefully, she transferred the child to his arms, and
he knew a moment's panic. "Tell me what to do," he whispered with an urgency that brought a soft smile to her face.
"I'm not much good with kids." But as the bably collapsed
against him, his long arms very naturally found a hold.

"Nicky doesn't demand much," she said. "A warm
body. A heartbeat."

A warm body. A heartbeat. Raising the child higher
against his chest and securing him comfortably, Derek lowered his cheek to the soft waves and took in a long, deep,
slightly uneven breath. *A warm body. A heartbeat.* Why
did it feel so *good* to hold the child? Was it his baby-sweet
smell, or that light, lingering one of his mother? Was it the
sheer specialness of him? The total helplessness? Or was it
a need in Derek for something warm and alive and personal?

If Nicky was aware of the change of hands, he didn't
make a peep. Derek told himself that he had to be doing
something right. He knew that something felt right. Right,
and deep, and natural. When he turned his head back to

Sabrina, he found her watching him intently. He couldn't speak, because that would have been to interrupt what she was saying and he wanted to hear.

Thank you for accepting him. Most people don't, and it's going to get worse. But I love him dearly. And I'm trying to do what's right. Dear God, I'm trying.

So eloquent without a single word. He nearly melted beneath the softness of her touch.

With a hard swallow that was clearly visible, she turned her face to the park. He wondered what she was thinking, whether she wished she were a bird and could fly freely. She raised one hand absently to massage her shoulder. Then, with the abruptness of sudden remembrance, she glanced down at her watch.

"You'd better leave," she murmured as she reached for the child. "My husband is due home soon."

Derek held the baby a minute longer, peering down at his vacant expression, feeling a great sadness. When he transferred the limp bundle back to its mother, he let the back of his hand linger on the child's soft, silky hair.

"He's very special," he said.

She nodded.

Derek met her gaze. He wanted to ask whether she'd think about doing the story, but he knew better. She had her mind made up. He could cajole and badger and lobby with every bit of the skill he'd honed over the years, but he doubted she'd yield. And in a sense, he was glad. He almost felt as though Sabrina and her baby were his secret. He didn't want them spoiled. He wanted to remember them always as they'd been in their rooftop garden. Quiet. Gentle. Very special, both of them.

Tucking the memories in a special spot in his mind, he saw himself to the door.

· *CHAPTER 1* ·

Parkersville wasn't quite what she'd expected. Rising from the woods of Berkshire County, the main building was attractive in an old New England kind of way. The facade was three stories' worth of aged brick; the vast slate roof was broken by dormers and turrets. Had there been ivy climbing the walls, it might have been taken for a rural college.

But there was no ivy, and the effect was further ruined by the guard towers that stood prominently at either side.

Controlling her apprehension with an act of will, Sabrina drew her cashmere topcoat higher on her neck and, boots crunching on the snow-crusted walk, advanced toward the steps. Once up and through a pair of innocuous-looking oak doors, she found herself confronted by a trio of prison personnel who looked anything but innocuous in their starched khaki uniforms and stern expressions. The three were safely ensconced in a cubicle behind layers of bullet-proof glass.

Approaching the cubicle, she leaned toward its mouthpiece. Again in a conscious act, she projected a voice that sounded steady. "My name is Sabrina Stone. I'm here to see Derek McGill."

The guard nearest the speaker studied her. He wasn't a young man, and there was no hint of a leer in his comprehensive gaze. He studied her coolly and clinically, then asked at last in an authoritative, emotionless voice, "Is he expecting you?

"No."

The guard to his right began to flip through the pages of

a large loose-leaf notebook. He said something to the first guard, who repeated into the mouthpiece, "Sabrina Stone?"

"Yes."

"Are you a relative?"

She shook her head.

"Lawyer?"

"No."

"Business associate? Media?"

"Just a friend," she said.

The second guard reached the page he sought. Sabrina watched him draw a slow finger down its length, pause once, then again before going on, then speak to the first guard, who announced, "You're not on his visitors list."

She hadn't known of a visitors list. In fact she knew nothing whatsoever of prison protocol save what the visiting hours were—and that she learned through the call she'd made from a pay phone earlier that day.

Visiting Derek had been on impulse. She'd thought about him often in the eighteen months since he'd appeared on her terrace, but she hadn't envisioned having the opportunity, much less the guts, to seek him out—until she left New York the day before.

"Does that mean I can't see him?" she asked, nervously fingering the leather strap of her shoulder bag.

"It means we have to check." The guard tossed his chin toward a long wooden bench behind and to Sabrina's right. "Sit down. We'll let you know."

Sabrina envisioned a review of her character that would take hours. "But I have . . . time is limited. I have to be back in New York tonight."

The guard let the firm set of his mouth speak for him. He directed another, more pointed glance at the bench.

Short of creating a stir, which was the last thing Sabrina wanted to do, she had no choice but to obey. So she sat and watched and waited, all the while trying to calm the butterflies in her stomach.

Sitting was uncomfortable. The bench was hard, and between the drive from New York to Vermont the day before, and Vermont to Massachusetts today, she'd been sitting far more than usual. Her bottom ached.

Watching was discouraging. The building lost its charm once she'd passed through its doors, and the steady scrutiny of the guards was unnerving. Several other visitors straggled in after her; each was questioned briefly, then allowed to pass through each of three sets of bars. She forced the image of the bars from her mind and tried to do the same for the visitors. There was a similarity to them, a coarse, downtrodden air, which said something about the men they visited—Derek's current companions—which gave her a chill.

So she dropped her eyes to her lap and focused on the suede skirt she'd worn for warmth, on the hand-tooled leather of her hip-hugging belt and the gentle folds of the oversized sweater it cinched. She studied her neatly filed nails and her Florentined wedding band and the stylish gold watch that circled her wrist. These things were her link to another, more genteel world, and looking at them, she could almost block out her present surroundings.

The waiting was the worst. If sitting was uncomfortable and watching discouraging, waiting was a torment. Five minutes, ten minutes, fifteen minutes—each minute meant time to think, and thinking about what she was doing made her uneasy. Impulsive decisions were just fine as long as they could be carried out on the wave of the impulse. Having to wait, having to think diluted the impulsiveness and allowed the slow insurgence of reason.

She should have driven straight back to New York. Her son would be needing her. Her husband would be furious that she'd left Nicky at all. And if Nicholas knew that she'd stopped to see Derek, his fury would know no bounds.

She had so many doubts. About this. About everything. It seemed that lately, doubts were all she had.

"Sabrina Stone!"

Her head jerked up, eyes flying to the guard box. Seconds later, she was on her feet, being gestured toward the first of the bars to the left of the cubicle. The lock clicked loudly. As she'd seen the others do before her, she pushed, letting herself into the first of two caged areas. The door

closed and locked behind her as she focused on a flurry of
instructions from the guard.

Through a window at that side of the guard box, her
shoulder bag was searched. She removed her topcoat; it,
too, was searched. A second lock clicked loudly. At the
waggle of the guard's finger, she entered the second com-
partment. This time she was asked to step into a side room,
where she was thoroughly frisked. Once through the third
and final set of bars, she was escorted down a corridor, up
a flight of stairs, down another corridor.

Institutional was the most generous word she could find
to describe her surroundings. The halls were painted the
same bland gray-green that she'd seen in far too many hospitals of late. The look was antiseptic, and the smell would
have been, too, had not the odor of dubious cafeteria cooking wafted through the halls. And then there were the
sounds—the clanging of bars, the banging of steel, distant
shouts, not-so-distant calls. The overall effect was one of
an echo chamber—unsettling and endless.

After passing through another barred door, she was de-
livered into the visiting room. It was a large room, very
bright and very hot. Grateful that she'd already removed
her coat, she searched the faces in the room. There were
half a dozen men in standard-issue denims with their
guests, all seated in straight-backed wooden chairs that
were scattered randomly around the room. Guards were
scattered less randomly, so that no inmate was more than
nine or ten feet from reach.

There was no sign of Derek.

Unsure of what to do, but feeling distinctively awkward
after having been abandoned by her escort just inside the
door, Sabrina crossed to a pair of chairs that was removed
from the others. She sank into one, draped her coat across
her lap and set to studying the wrinkles on her palm caused
by her tight grip on her bag.

Moments later, a door opened on the far side of the
room. She looked up. Her heartbeat tripped, then sped.
Doubts crowded in, but the deed was done. She was here
and Derek had arrived. It was too late to do anything about

the impulse that had brought her uninvited to his ghastly world.

He stood inside the door staring at her. Unable to help herself, she stared right back. She was stunned and a little frightened. He looked so different.

Gone were the tailored blazer, the trim slacks, the polished loafers. He wore a blue work shirt, jeans and worn running shoes. A nondescript jacket was hooked on a finger over his shoulder. His dark hair was longer and slightly shaggy. His face seemed leaner, as did his hips. She'd have thought that he'd lost a good twenty pounds since his incarceration—except that his shoulders were broader, and where his sleeves had been rolled, sinewy forearms were exposed.

He looked taller than she'd remembered. He held himself very straight, almost defensively, in a stance made bold by the pride of a man stripped of pride. He was intimidating that way, intimidating and unapproachable, and the other changes in him didn't help. A small but jagged scar lay just beyond his right eye; it was a dull red shade, clearly a recent acquisition. The pallor of his skin emphasized the shadow of his beard, which, in turn, gave him a hardened look.

He did look hard. And he certainly didn't look pleased to see her.

Why am I here? she cried in a split second's silent panic. Then, with slow strides, Derek approached and she had no time for either panic or regret. His eyes held hers. There was something compelling in them that even the mask of control couldn't conceal.

He stopped by the chair near hers and stood with his hand on its back and his shoulders straight. "Sabrina." His voice was cool, either truly emotionless or carefully schooled to sound that way.

She nodded and held her breath.

"How are you?"

"Okay," she said, then paused before adding, "I wasn't sure if you'd remember me."

"I remember you."

"It's been a while."

"Eighteen months," he said without a blink.

Sabrina knew his exact knowledge of the time they'd last met had nothing to do with her personally. The man had been arrested three months later; he'd been incarcerated since then. She was sure that he knew to the exact day how long it had been since he'd lost his freedom.

He continued to study her. Her cheeks felt warm, but she attributed that to the hissing radiator, since his gaze was even cooler than his voice had been. His eyes were gray. She hadn't known that before. All that had registered in her memory from that long-ago meeting was their warmth and understanding. But that was gone now. Compelling eyes, indeed they were, but they were hard as flint.

She wished he would say something, but then remembered that she'd been the one to initiate the visit. So she asked, "How have you been?"

He lifted one shoulder in a tight shrug. His gaze didn't waver. He was annoyed that she'd come, and perhaps he had a right. She was nothing to him. She'd quite possibly interrupted something—whatever it was that inmates did at two on a weekday afternoon. It suddenly occurred to her that the interruption might cause him trouble.

"Is this a bad time?" she asked hurriedly, worriedly. "Am I pulling you from—"

"No."

"I wouldn't want to cause—"

"You're not."

She nodded her okay. Her teeth closed on her lower lip. She folded her arms across her middle, her right hand absently kneading her left arm. Her gaze went to the barred window—which she would have given anything to open wide—then to the nearby guard who was watching, listening. She found the absence of privacy humiliating and could only begin to imagine what Derek faced each day.

But she couldn't imagine. Not really. The gap between them was huge.

Wanting to narrow it, she whispered, "Will you sit down?"

For a minute she feared he'd refuse. He looked away

with eyes whose irritation was mirrored by the slight outward thrust of his jaw.

"Would you rather I go?" she asked, again in a whisper.

He didn't answer, but seemed to be considering his options. Sabrina didn't begrudge him that, even if there was an element of the power play in it. A sense of power was the least she could give him.

At length, he hooked his jacket on the shoulder of the chair, turned the chair to an angle that suited him, lowered himself and stretched out his legs. He ended up not quite facing her, not quite abreast of her, and a safe yard away.

Even seated, he looked large. Even lean, he looked strong. Eighteen months before, she'd thought of him purely in cerebral terms: he was a reporter who'd come in search of a story, and though he'd left empty-handed, he'd offered her a breath of support. There was nothing cerebral about him now, though. He was as blunt as the name and numbers indelibly inked on the breast pocket of his workshirt. Prison had taken away the intellectual mantle, leaving him hard and raw and physical.

Sabrina felt suddenly tongue-tied. She'd never been in a prison. The search she'd undergone, the bars through which she'd passed, the scrutiny of the gaurds—all were unsettling. And Derek—she'd only met him once before. She didn't know him. She had no idea what he was thinking or feeling, no idea how she should behave, what she should say. She wasn't even sure why she'd come.

But she had to say something or they'd sit there in silence. "I didn't think they were going to let me in," she finally managed. "They did some kind of check when they found that my name wasn't on your list. I was surprised they gave me clearance so quickly."

"They only had to make one call."

She frowned. "To whom?"

"Me."

The frown eased. "Oh."

"They wanted to know who you were, what our relationship was and whether I wanted to see you."

She considered that, then asked on impulse, "How could

they know that I wasn't an evil character trying to smuggle you something?"

"They searched you."

"Ah . . . right," she said, feeling a little dumb. And flushed. The room was so hot. She would have lifted her hair from her neck, except that she didn't want to appear to be complaining. Maybe the heat didn't bother Derek. For all she knew, his cell was like a barn, in which case the heat was a welcome change.

She cleared her throat. "Well, anyway, thank you for saying yes."

"Was it that important to you?"

She paused, nodded.

"Why?"

She didn't answer at first. He was regarding her so intently that she wasn't able to do much but think about the potential for feeling in the man and the fact that it was going to waste. Where was the warmth that she remembered? She could detect none now. Everyone knew that prison was hell but, she realized, only an inmate knew the true meaninig of the word. She couldn't comprehend the awful things that had left Derek McGill so cold and hard.

"I don't know," she said finally, then shook herself a little and asked, "Does my name go on your list now?"

"Yes." His tone grew cynical. "Does that bother you—that there's a record, written proof that you've been here?"

It did, a little, but only because she feared Nick's reaction if he knew where she was. Lord only knew they'd had enough to fight about lately. But she wouldn't tell Derek that. It wasn't why she'd come. "It doesn't bother me," she answered, thinking that Nick would never know. Then it occurred to her to ask, "Are you limited in the number of visits you can have?"

"Yes."

Her eyes widened. "Oh dear. Am I taking someone else's time?"

"No."

"Are you sure?"

"I don't get many visitors."

She couldn't believe that. He'd been in the mainstream

of life; more, he'd been in its limelight. She assumed that he'd always been surrounded by people, that he'd been recognized, stopped on the street, hailed in restaurants. She couldn't believe that he didn't have friends and colleagues who would want to visit him, to cheer him, to fill him in on the world's doings.

"In case you hadn't noticed," he stated in response to what she knew was visible skepticism, "this isn't tea time at the Plaza. Prisons are depressing, and convicts aren't good for much of anything."

"But you're not—" she began without thinking.

"A convict? I am."

"But you're not—"

"Like them?" he finished, hitching his head toward the other inmates in the room. "In the eyes of the law, I'm *exactly* like them. It doesn't matter where I've been in life. The fact is, I'm serving three to seven years for murder." His eyes held hers in a way that said he was being deliberately blunt. There was defiance in his tone and more than a little challenge.

Sabrina rose to the challenge. "Voluntary manslaughter. The prosecutor argued for a stiffer sentence, but the judge denied it."

"You followed the proceedings."

"Yes. I'm . . . sorry."

He quirked a brow in question.

"That you're here," she explained.

"It's not your fault."

"No. But it all seems unnecessary."

"Prison unnecessary? You should meet some of the guys here. You'd change your mind fast."

"I meant," she said very quietly, "that you shouldn't be here."

The sound he made was harsh and low, the bitter facsimile of a laugh. "Tell that to the judge."

She frowned, then swallowed and asked in bewilderment, "How did it happen?"

"The crime?"

"The conviction. I thought for sure that a good lawyer—"

He cut her off. "I had a good lawyer."

"But there was so much room for doubt," she argued softly. "I'm still amazed that a jury could have found you guilty."

"Maybe they were right," he declared without pause.

"No."

His lips twitched at the corners, as though he found amusement in her certainty. But it was wry amusement and short-lived. "Is that what you came to tell me?"

"No. But it's true."

"You're very naive." His mouth tightened. He turned his head and glared at nothing in particular. "You'd be amazed at what a man is capable of doing when he's properly provoked."

She didn't know what to make of that. Instinct told her that he wasn't talking of the past but of the present, specifically of his experience in prison. Glancing at the scar by his eye, she wondered how he'd come by it.

"I got the impression," she began tentatively, "that the issue wasn't whether you shot the man. The police said you did. You said you did. But the jury said that you killed him knowingly and willingly. That's what I can't believe."

Though Derek leaned forward to prop his elbows on his thighs, there was nothing relaxed about the pose. His eyes drilled hers. "The jury said there was motive. Maybe there was. The guy I killed snitched on my dad twenty-five years ago."

Sabrina knew about that. "You said you shot him in self-defense."

"Maybe I lied."

"You said that you didn't know who he was until the police identified him later."

"Maybe I lied about that, too."

She saw his hostility as a test and was determined not to fail. She kept her voice low, but made no effort to mute her confidence. "You said that he called you using a different name; that he claimed he had information crucial to a story you were doing. No reporter in his right mind would have looked a gift horse like that in the mouth."

"No reporter in his right mind," Derek countered in a

scathing murmur, "would have agreed to a meeting with a man he didn't know in an isolated place that he wasn't familiar with at an hour of the night when no other man in his right mind would be out!"

In that instance, Sabrina knew that his anger was self-directed. She felt compelled to take issue with its cause. "You'd gotten where you were in your field by being un-conventional and daring. Your meeting Joey Padilla that night was totally in character."

"Right. In the character to which I was born." His dark eyes glittered dangerously. "My dad was a crook. He killed. He served time. He died in an alley, bled to death with a bullet in his gut. What is it they say about history repeating itself—about the apple not falling far from the tree, about the leopard and its spots?"

Sabrina had read about Derek's father. She hadn't read anything of a like-father-like-son nature in print, but she had no doubt that it had been snickered about in more than one smoky corner of more than one after-hours bar. It was clearly a sore point where Derek was concerned.

"Self-fulfilling prophecy?" she asked slowly. "I don't believe it for a minute."

"Why not?"

"Because I knew you before."

"Once, Sabrina," he reminded her in a low, dark voice. "We met once. We spent all of fifteen minutes together."

She couldn't argue with the time, just the effect. "Put it down to instinct, then. You're not a killer. You were approached in the dark of night by a man with a gun. He showed every sign of wanting you dead. You defended yourself in the only way you could." She caught in a breath. "Lord, Derek, it was his gun! You went into that meeting totally unarmed!"

He stared at her for a long time, torn, Sabrina thought, between belief and disbelief. The radiator hissed, low voices droned on, distant banging echoed through the walls. At length, he thrust a handful of fingers through his hair and looked off in disgust. "It doesn't matter," he muttered. "None of it matters."

"But it does."

"No. It's done. I'm here."

"What about appeals?"

"Appeals?" The word came off his tongue sounding like a concept that was truly absurd. His lowered voice only added intensity as he continued, "When a case is rigged from the start—when bail is denied so you have to rot in a holding bin for two months awaiting trial, when pretrial motions fall like flies and evidence self-destructs and eye-witnesses lie and the judge's charge is legally faultless but royally biased—you don't put much faith in appeals."

Sabrina hurt for him. His words had spilled with low, seething force, and she suspected that they held merit. He had the air of a wounded animal. His faith in justice had been shattered. He was bruised and aching.

"You were railroaded."

His eyes said yes. His mouth remained shut.

"Do you know by whom?" she asked very, very quietly.

"You shouldn't have come, Sabrina."

"Is there anything you can prove?"

Straightening in his seat, he ran a hand around the back of his neck. "Christ, it's hot in here."

"Derek . . ."

"Why did you come?" he asked. His eyes, his nose, the faint curl of his lips, the rigidity of his jaw—all radiated anger.

Her gaze held his for a moment before sliding toward the nearest guard, who was looking directly at them and making no bones about eavesdropping. Sabrina knew there was little they could do to change that, but it put her on the hot seat in yet another respect.

"Why did you come?" he repeated tightly. "If it was to argue my case, you're wasting your time. My lawyer has developed an ulcer doing just that."

She pressed damp palms to her skirt. "I'm not a lawyer. I wouldn't know what to do."

"Then why are you here? Is it curiosity?"

"No."

"Pity?"

"No!"

Sarcasm gave his voice a brittle edge. "I can't believe

things are so slow in New York that you've come here for a little innocent socializing."

Her hand returned to her arm and began to knead that same spot just above the elbow. "Please, Derek . . ."

"Then it must be the old do-gooder instinct."

"No." *Why am I here? Because you understood . . .* "I was in the neighborhood—"

The punishing glance he shot her was an effective cutoff. "Not an original line," he snapped. "I've heard it before from my glib ex-colleagues who've traipsed out here looking for a scoop, and it doesn't hold water. Parkersville is in the middle of nowhere—par for the course for prisons."

"And homes for the severely retarded," Sabrina added with her chin tipped a fraction higher. Forthrightness seemed her only weapon against the bitterness she heard. "I've been in Vermont visiting a residential center that may be suitable for my son. Parkersville was along the way. It seemed a waste to be so close and not stop."

Derek's mask slipped, and she knew that in some fashion or other she'd reached him. She didn't know whether he would question her about the child, didn't know whether he'd give half a damn, what with the horror of his own life. He had every right to tell her to take herself and her problems through the nearest set of bars and leave him alone.

But he didn't. His tone mellowed. It didn't exactly warm, but it lost its caustic edge.

"How is he?"

She swallowed. "Nicky? Fine. Uh, okay."

"You look exhausted," he said even more quietly. "Is that what 'okay' is doing to you?"

"He's more than a full-time job." She studied her thumb as it tugged at her palm. Head bowed, she allowed for the flicker of a frown. "Your story was good, Derek. I watched that first airing. I wanted to tell you, but somehow . . ." She gave a vague shrug. "Time passed. I had other worries. You had other worries." Frowning more deeply, she turned her head and whispered, "Lord, that smells awful."

Derek followed her line of sight along an acrid trail to

the nearby duo who were smoking up a storm. "The rest of the world is giving it up. Not here. It's something to do, something to look forward to. No one cares if we kill ourselves."

Sabrina's head came around sharply. *We*. It didn't seem right that he should be one of them. She didn't see him as a criminal. But he did identify with the prison population. She was trying to figure out how closely when his scar caught her eye. Like Hester Prynne's scarlet letter or the mark of Cain, Derek had his scar. Its jagged edge disrupted the line of his face. Its color was that of subdued anger. It was the intrusion of violence into civility. It was symbolic of a nadir in his life.

It upset her. She felt an urgent need to touch it, to soften it, to wipe it clean. Riding on that impulse, she raised a hand—but seconds shy of the contact, she stopped. Derek's eyes had darkened to broadcast a warning. *Danger. Do not touch.* Curling her fingers into a fist, she dropped the fist to her lap.

Why am I here? Because you understood, and I wanted to talk. . . .

"Is the rest of the prison as hot as this?" she blurted out.

"Mostly."

She looked around at the others in the room. "I'm surprised."

"You expected to find prisoners freezing in their cells?" he asked, then took his time answering. "It doesn't work that way. Segregation units are cold, but that's to make it worse when they strip you down and toss you in. The rest of the time they figure that if they make you sweat, it'll zap your strength." He eyed her levelly. "They want docility."

She supposed she could understand that—the docility part. Trying to think positively, she asked, "Do you get outside much?"

"I get yard time."

She glanced at the window. "It's been a horrid winter."

"Have your husband send you south. He can afford it."

She smiled sadly, rubbed her arm, shook her head.

"He can't afford it?" Derek asked.

"Oh, he can, but I can't go."

"Because of Nicky."

She paused, then made a tiny gesture with her head that passed for a yes.

"How old is he now?"

"Thirty-four months."

"That's nearly three."

The smile that had been sad turned contrite. "Thirty-four months sounds better. More babylike. He's still pretty much a baby."

"No progress?"

"Progress is relative, I suppose. He doesn't choke so much when he eats."

"What do the doctors say?"

Lifting one shoulder a fraction, she spoke in a troubled tone. "The same thing as always—that his development is delayed and that they don't know why."

"Do they hold out any hope for improvement?"

"Not much."

Derek grew quiet. He leaned back in his chair, compressed his lips, stared out the window.

"Your story was accurate, Derek. It clearly depicted the problems."

"I tried to go beyond that."

"How could you? There are so few answers."

"I came up with one." He slowly turned his head and looked her in the eye. "Will you institutionalize Nicky?"

She began to deny it automatically. She gave a quick head shake—then cut it short when it occurred to her that she wasn't talking with her husband, or with their friends or relatives. She was talking with Derek. She'd taped the story he did and had watched it half a dozen times. He took great care with his words, but their gist was clear. He believed that in some cases institutionalization was the best course. He understood.

"Uh, I don't know. Yes, maybe."

"But you're not sure."

She thought about that for a minute. Then she threaded her fingers together in her lap, took a deep, resigned breath and looked down. "I'm sure. It's just not a popular position."

"It wasn't a popular position back then, either. Therapists claim that regardless of his handicap a child does best at home."

Sabrina nodded. "That is what therapists claim."

"Shows how much they know."

She looked up in surprise, because she could have sworn he was teasing. But there was no humor in his expression, particularly when he asked, "Do you have help?"

"Some. It's hard to get sitters to come back a second time."

"Is his father home with him now?"

"Not quite," she remarked. Then, feeling instant remorse, raced on in the hope that her sarcasm would be overlooked. "My husband is in Chicago on business. Nicky is with one of the two therapists who alternately work with us."

As they'd been discussing Nicky, Derek seemed to have relaxed a bit. His shoulders were still straight, but he'd slid a little lower in the chair, crossed his legs at the ankles and dug his hands into the pockets of his jeans. Sabrina was thinking that, prison garb and all, he was a very attractive man, when he took her off guard by announcing, "I don't like your husband."

Her first impulse was to laugh, because there'd been something sounding suspiciously like jealousy in the declaration. She was flattered. She was also frightened, because her feelings were uncomfortably close to Derek's, and she sensed that once started she'd very possibly laugh her way into hysterics. She compromised with a slightly uneven, "Where did that come from?"

Derek pointed to his gut.

"But you've never met him."

He shrugged.

"All that because he wouldn't cooperate on your story?"

"All that because I think he makes life hard for you."

He was looking out the window, his face as staunchly set as ever, but Sabrina felt a tiny nugget of warmth inside her.

It had been a long, long time since she'd felt that someone was thinking of her interests.

"Why ever would you think that?" she asked in a voice that was a little too high to sound nonchalant.

Derek made a deliberate, ninety-degree turn of his head and angled his chin to study her. There was suddenly something very personal in his expression, and his voice was oddly intimate. "That day I went to your place, I got the feeling that you would have talked with me if it hadn't been for your husband. You got nervous when you looked at your watch and saw the time. What would have happened if he'd come home and found us talking?"

"He would have called the president of your network, as he'd threatened."

"I think he would have done more than that," Derek pressed. "I think he would have given you hell for entertaining me. Forget the fact that I weaseled my way in. Forget the fact that you refused to be interviewed. I think he would have hit the roof. He doesn't want anyone to know there's something wrong with his son, does he?"

She hesitated for the space of a heartbeat. "I didn't say that."

"No, but there's never been any kind of public acknowledgment, and your husband's been profiled in the papers a whole lot lately."

"The condition of our son has nothing to do with Nick's career."

"Not directly. But Nicholas Stone's name carries clout. He could raise a hell of a lot of money for medical research if he wanted to go to bat publicly for the cause."

Sabrina had to struggle not to squirm. She agreed with what Derek said. She'd said nearly identical things to her husband. She wanted to tell Derek that Nicholas contributed privately to the cause, but she couldn't . . . because he didn't. He refused to believe that there *was* a cause. He preferred to pretend that Nicky was simply a late bloomer, but he carefully hid the child from the world.

Derek had been right about that. But Sabrina couldn't get herself to say so, so she answered his question in the most general terms. "He gives to charity."

Derek wasn't settling for general terms. "They say that charity begins at home. Tell me. Does your husband take his turn walking Nicky when he cries?"

She hesitated a second too long. "He has."

"But not often. How about patterning—I assume you've given it a shot?"

Sabrina had to hand it to him. It might have been a year and a half since he'd done his story, and he'd probably been working on half a dozen others at the time, but he remembered what he'd learned. The proponants of patterning felt that if you brought the child's hand to his mouth at the appropriate time and for the appropriate purpose over and over and over again, the child would eventually take the hint. Nicky hadn't.

But that wasn't what Derek had asked.

"We've tried patterning," she answered.

"Has your husband helped?"

"He does what he can, but between sixty-hour work-weeks and frequent traveling, he's just not around all that much."

Derek didn't look at all surprised. "And institutionalization—how does he feel about that?"

A tiny muscle twitched beneath her left eye. "He has to give it more thought." Which was an evasive answer if ever there was one. Nicholas didn't give institutionalization *any* thought because he refused to admit that his son was seriously impaired. He seemed content to have Nicky stay home with Sabrina—where no one could see the child and judge him retarded. Unfortunately, that left Sabrina with the full brunt of Nicky's care and the burden of silence. The strain of it was enormous. Just thinking about it strung her out tight.

Raking her teeth over her lip, she tried to divert herself by glancing around the room, but that was every bit as depressing. A couple had risen and were saying good-bye with an embrace whose fervor was nearly indecent.

"I've seen recent photos of your husband in the papers," Derek said.

Sabrina tried to avert her gaze from the couple, but kept returning to them. She kept waiting for them to pull apart

—either that, or go up in flames. They showed no sign of self-consciousness. Derek seemed oblivious. The guards were indulgent. Was she the only one embarrassed?

She cleared her throat. "The company has pulled off several coups."

"He looked fresh, full of energy, not at all tired. He's left the fatigue to you, eh?"

"He's been busy."

"He's a fool."

Her eyes swung to his. "Why do you say that?"

"Because he's got a good thing in you, but I doubt he even sees it. You're loyal. You stand up for him whether he deserves it or not. Does he deserve it?"

"I'm his wife. Loyalty is a . . . a given."

"Does he appreciate it?"

She shifted a defensive shoulder. "He doesn't make little speeches of praise, but I don't expect that."

"What do you expect?"

She didn't answer.

"He's a fool, because he'll lose you," Derek said. Swiveling swiftly and smoothly, he dropped his forearms to his thighs. For the first time he faced her fully. His voice was low, tautly controlled. His eyes flashed. "If you were mine, I'd appreciate you. But you're not mine. You're his. And, goddamn it"—his voice fell to a thick, dark rumble—"I don't know why you're here. Is it to torment me? You do, you know. It was weeks until I was able to get you out of my mind last time. And it sure as hell won't be any easier now."

Sabrina was stunned. She hadn't thought . . . it hadn't occurred to her . . . perhaps she'd misunderstood . . . *surely* she'd misunderstood. With nervous fingers, she gathered her coat to her, possibly in a prelude to leaving, more probably for the sense of security, however false, it gave. "I'm sorry," she whispered.

His voice was nearly as low, but much, much more forceful. "Don't be sorry. Just tell me why you're here."

"I don't know. I wanted . . ."

"What?"

"I wanted . . . I want . . ."

"What could a visit with me possibly offer?"

His face was close. His features filled her vision—wide-set eyes now the color of charcoal, ruggedly carved nose, firm-set mouth, tight jaw. She saw the scowl lines on his brow, the sootiness of his eyelashes, the tiny mole at his temple, the way his lower lip was fuller than its mate.

But his eyes drew her back. In them, hidden behind defiance and anger and pride, she saw despair, and she wanted to cry.

"Sabrina . . ." he prompted in a low, guttural command.

"You understood, Derek. That day. You understood. I don't know why I'm here now. I didn't plan it ahead, but it seemed the only thing to do when I knew I would be so close, and after visiting the center I felt so devastated that I was hoping . . . hoping . . ." She ran her thumb under her eye.

"Hoping for sympathy?"

"No—"

"Because I'm plumb out."

"I don't want sympathy."

"Then what?"

"I don't know!" she cried. Startled by the sound of her own voice, she shot a damp-eyed glance around the room. Several of its occupants and nearly all of the guards were looking at her. Embarrassed, she quickly lowered both her eyes and her voice. "I don't know," she whispered. "Maybe I was hoping for something . . . a fragment . . . that warmth I felt when we met and you understood how it was." Her fingers bit into her coat as she struggled for composure. "Strength. I thought maybe you'd have some. It was foolish, selfish of me, I guess."

Slowly, Derek straightened. "Any strength I have now is earmarked for survival; and as for warmth, it's gone, Sabrina. It just isn't there anymore." The words had barely left his lips when he stood.

Sabrina looked up and caught her breath, but before she could say a thing, he'd turned on his heel and was walking away. His fingers were tight around his jacket. His shoulders were stiff. He paused once at the door and looked back, forever etching in her mind the image of a man scraping for dignity, a man ultimately alone. Then he passed through and disappeared.

Moments later, Sabrina sat behind the wheel of her car, shaking. It wasn't the cold air that disturbed her; she welcomed that. It was what she'd seen and felt that caused the quiver.

Derek was angry. He was bitter, at times hostile. He was the proverbial caged animal, wounded and lashing back with a look, a tone, a word.

Very probably he'd been right when he said that he didn't have strength to spare, and she'd been wrong to ask it. But he lied about the warmth. She'd seen it during those few moments when he questioned her about Nicky. And she'd felt it after that.

I don't know why you're here. Is it to torment me? You do, you know. It was weeks until I was able to get you out of my mind last time. And it sure as hell won't be any easier now.

She'd felt the alertness of his body, had heard the thickness in his voice, had seen the heat in his eyes. And what was heat but warmth once-removed?

Oh, yes, there was warmth. It was stashed away, buried beneath crates of anger and bitterness and frustration and distrust. It had to jockey with pride and dignity for a brief showing, and for the most part it lost, but it was there. He'd lied when he said that it was gone. He'd lied.

· *CHAPTER 2* ·

Sabrina always had a thing about lying. She supposed the aversion dated to her childhood, to the times when her mother told her that if she didn't clean her room the Ardulonian enforcer would turn her ear inside out, or the times when her father forecast a showdown at high noon between her suitors if she got much prettier, or the times when her brother informed her that the nighttime shadow on her bedroom wall was the reincarnation of an ogre who had been buried beneath the oak in the courtyard nearly a century before.

It took her a while to figure out that the Ardulonian enforcer was nothing more than a figment of her mother's imagination and that, rather than being an incredibly advanced country somewhere in the vicinity of Antarctica, Ardulon was make-believe. She'd been weaned on Ardulonian lore. She hadn't realized that the nighttime stories her mother told her were shortened versions of tales that were well sold, well published and well read. Not until she was seven and studying geography in school did she learn —with considerable embarrassment—the truth, and even in spite of that, she continued to keep her room clean on the vague chance that the school map, the teacher and the other students were wrong.

By the time she accepted the truth, she was onto her father's imaginative efforts as well. Even if she'd been as pretty as her father said—which she knew she wasn't— and even if the boys were fascinated with her—which they weren't—showdowns at high noon, in the OK or any other corral, simply didn't happen in the second half of the twentieth century . . . other than in series Westerns like those her father churned out for his legions of followers. Nor were ogres reincarnated into shadows on the wall in anything but the horror genre in which her brother, eight years her senior, eventually went on to make his name.

She was a gullible child, her family said. They told stories that she believed. Fiction, they called it, and she eventually conceded that such stories, when bound and properly labeled, were okay. But the stories she was told, the warnings and predictions and dread alerts, were offered as gospel.

She'd been lied to, she decided, and for a time she was furious. Then resignation came, and with it, acceptance. Her family was her family. They were an eccentric bunch, and there was nothing Sabrina could do to change them. Amanda Monroe wouldn't be Amanda Monroe if her mind wasn't in outer space half the time. Nor would Gebhart Monroe be the same without a yoked shirt, a stetson and spurs. And J. B., who was unfairly good-looking, had always been and would always be a horror.

Sabrina rebelled. She devoted herself to being down-to-earth. She watched the evening news, majored in history in college, dressed stylishly, if conservatively. She wrote nonfiction. She liked to believe that she had a firm grip on reality, and she made it a habit not to lie.

But habits, like rules, were meant to be broken when better judgment demanded, which was why she didn't find fault with what Derek had done. She wanted to think of him as a friend. She didn't know why, but she wanted that badly. Anything beyond friendship was impossible, though, and for that reason she was grateful that he denied the heat she'd seen. It could lead nowhere.

So said better judgment.

It was this same judgment that caused her to fudge the truth a bit when she arrived back in Manhattan and received a call from her husband.

"Where have you been, Sabrina?" Nicholas demanded. "This is the third time I've called."

"I'm sorry," she answered breathlessly. She'd barely come in, checked on her son, changed her clothes and sent Pam on her way when the phone rang. The housekeeper, Mrs. Hoskins, had dutifully answered it, then passed it on when she learned who it was. Sabrina was still trying to settle a cranky Nicky on her hip. "I had to get out."

"Where did you go?"

Shifting the phone to her other ear, she wedged it between her shoulder and jaw, hoisted Nicky a little higher and belted him in with her arms. "I took a drive."

"I've been trying to reach you since noon. It's seven now. That was quite some drive."

"It felt good getting out of the city."

"I hadn't realized you were bored," he said with just enough sarcasm to set her off.

"Not bored, Nick. Tired and frustrated and wound up tight. It's been an awful month. Taking Nicky out in the slush and cold is twice as hard as taking him out normally, and we've had appointments with each of three regular doctors, and two new ones, an eye specialist and a psychologist. I needed a break."

"What's wrong with this connection, Sabrina? I can't hear half of what you're saying."

She sighed. It figured that he'd miss the message. "I'm walking Nicky, so I'm using the cordless."

"It's a lousy cordless. You'll have to pick up a new one next time you're out." That settled, he blithely moved to the next item on his mental agenda. "How did the meeting go with Naholy?"

Joseph Naholy was the manager of the Westchester country club where Nicholas golfed. Once upon a time, Sabrina had enjoyed an occasional afternoon at the pool, but that was before Nicky. She only went to the club now for dinner, and only then when she couldn't beg off. She and Nicholas were hosting one such affair in two weeks' time, and she was to have met with Joseph the day before to make the final menu selection. She'd canceled that meeting to drive to Vermont.

"I couldn't make it yesterday—"

"Why not?"

His imperious tone made it easier for her to say, "Because Nicky was acting up." She didn't want Nicholas to know she'd visited the Greenhouse—as the residential center in Vermont was called. It was exclusive and expensive. She wanted to make sure that it was the right place for the child before she launched a crusade for his admission.

"Nicky is always acting up," barked his father, "but life has to go on."

Sabrina closed her eyes and took an unsteady breath. She didn't want to argue. Not now. Not when she was feeling just that little bit refreshed after two days' freedom. "When I talked with Joseph, he said we still had plenty of time."

"You could have stopped there today, as long as you were out. That really was a long stretch you were gone, Sabrina. Are you sure you should have left Nicky with Pam all that time?"

Sabrina kept her voice low and calm. "Pam is a trained therapist. She's perfectly qualified to care for him."

"But he needs you."

"No, Nick. He needs someone, but whether it's me or you or Pam doesn't matter." The child chose that moment to stiffen up and wail. In her attempt to soothe him, Sabrina lost her grip on the phone. It fell to the carpet. She knelt down to snatch it up. "Sorry," she told her husband. Still on her haunches, she gently bounced Nicky on her knee. "Just dropped the phone."

"I heard him cry. What's wrong?"

She wanted to say, "What *isn't*?" But she didn't. Nicholas would accuse her of being a pessimist, and though she'd argue that she was being honest, she couldn't win. Not with Nick. So she said, "Who knows? He may be hungry. Pam said he didn't eat much supper. Or he may be constipated. He doesn't have a fever, but his ear may be bothering him again. I wish he could tell me, but he can't."

"If you'd been back earlier, you'd have had a better chance of guessing."

"That's not true."

"You'd have been able to keep an eye on him."

"I have my eye on him now. Earlier wouldn't have made a difference."

"Well, it would have made a difference to me," Nicholas declared. "I've been leaving meetings to call you. It's annoying to find you're not there, especially when you knew I was due back."

"And I'm here, just when you said you'd be. But you're still in Chicago."

He ignored her logic as though it were irrelevant. "That was what I called to say. We've run into a last-minute glitch. I won't be back until tomorrow. If we wind things up by noon, I should be home by five-thirty—"

"But we're supposed to be at the Taylors' at six!" she cried. When an answering whimper came from Nicky, she realized that she'd stopped bobbing him. The muscles of her thighs were screaming for relief. Juggling the phone, she slid to her bottom, simultaneously maneuvering Nicky onto her lap. It was no mean feat; he was as helpful as a sack of flour.

"Half an hour is all I'll need to shave, shower and change," Nicholas went on.

"Oh, Nick," she sighed, then reasoned quietly, "We agreed that we'd take turns with Nicky when we're getting ready to go out. He wants to be held, and unless we want him to fuss the whole time—"

"You've spoiled him, Sabrina. He fusses, you pick him up. When you put him down, he fusses, so you pick him up again. At some point he's got to learn that he can't be held all the time."

"But he *doesn't* learn," she cried, as frustrated by her husband's tunnel vision as by the baby's shortcomings. "That's the problem!"

Nicholas didn't want to hear about it. "Mrs. Hoskins will just have to give you a hand."

"Mrs. Hoskins can't hold Nicky. She has a bad back."

"If she has a bad back, what good is she?"

"Beats me," Sabrina said dryly. She'd often argued that if they replaced Mrs. Hoskins with someone equipped to handle Nicky, Sabrina would benefit on two fronts. But since Nicholas refused to admit that Nicky's problems warranted special full-time help, Mrs. Hoskins had a staunch ally.

"I suppose she keeps things organized," he pointed out, just as Sabrina had known he would. "If you had to worry about making the beds and dusting and doing laundry and polishing silver on top of everything else, you'd be exhausted."

I am exhausted, Sabrina wanted to scream, but she knew it would do no good. Nicholas saw what he wanted to see. It had been that way from the first time they'd met, and it had been okay back then because they'd shared a vision of their lives and of the future. They shared few visions nowadays, though—which was why, when Nicholas pulled his blinder routine, Sabrina suffered.

"Would it be at all possible," she began, her body tense as she rocked Nicky back and forth, "for you to catch an earlier plane?"

"No."

"Just one hour earlier?"

"I'm not here on vacation, Sabrina. This is a business trip. And I'm not alone; there are a dozen people waiting in the other room. I should have been off the phone ten minutes ago."

Sabrina was annoyed enough to ignore that. "I'll call the Taylors and tell them we'll be late."

"Don't be selfish. You know they're on a tight schedule. They can't hold things up for us if they're going to get through a sit-down dinner and to the theater in time."

"Let them start dinner without us. We'll join them for the second course."

"That would be very rude, particularly when it isn't necessary. I told you I'd be home in time."

"But not in time to help me! My God, Nick, I can't do it all myself! As it is, Donna's doing us a favor by agreeing to sit"—Donna was the second of the therapists who worked with Nicky—"but she can't get here until six-thirty, which means that Mrs. Hoskins will have to do the best she can for half an hour—"

"I have to go, Sabrina."

"I didn't want to go to the Taylors' in the first place!"

"I'll see you tomorrow. Bye."

"But we haven't settled—Damn it, Nicholas Stone, don't hang up . . . Nick? . . . Oh, hell." She whispered the last in a plaintive tone, hating what she'd said, hating even more the shrewish sound of her voice. She'd been so easygoing and flexible . . . before Nicky.

With a sigh that carried a pained whimper, she tossed the phone aside, along with what little relaxation she'd found in the two days' break. Reality was back in full force—endless work, frustration and heartache. And responsibility. During those two days she was gone, she'd been free of responsibility. It had felt good, so good. But it was over. She was back. Nicky was her responsibility. Her shoulders sagged beneath the weight.

Nicholas was letting her down again. She should have guessed he would. Lately he'd been in his work world more and more. She could tell herself that he was legitimately busy, that the company was doing famously, that their financial status was better than ever, but somehow none of those arguments gave her comfort.

Dipping her head, she looked into Nicky's face. What would give her comfort would be his looking back at her, reaching up to grab her hair, maybe calling her mama. Hell, she wasn't fussy; he could call her anything his little heart desired, if only he would make the connection between his vocal cords and speech.

But he didn't make that connection. The sounds he made were involuntary, brought on by discomfort or displeasure or—on the rare occasion—delight. A helpless gurgle when his tummy was tickled. A reflexive gasp when he was tossed into the air. But he seemed to have no knowledge that he'd produced the sound himself, and he had no inclination to reproduce it at will.

Yet he was beautiful. Sabrina never failed to think it, and she knew that far more than maternal pride was at play. People stopped her on the street or in elevators or in stores to tell her. Nicky Stone was a beautiful child. No heat rashes for him, no excema, no chafed skin. His complexion was smooth, his cheeks soft. He had eyes that were large pools of mocha, fringed by unfairly long lashes. His hair was a cap of loose, pecan-colored curls that caught and reflected the nearest light. Sabrina dressed him in the most adorable clothes she could find—even now he was wearing a bright sweatshirt, pint-sized Guess jeans and tiny Reeboks—but she knew that with or without the duds, he'd catch the eye.

It was a cruel paradox. A beautiful shell housing a limited mind. A cruel, cruel paradox. She'd have traded looks for mental health in a minute. But it wasn't to be.

He was a slight child. Aside from the baby fat that gave his face a slightly rounded look, he carried no extra weight —no mystery, given the trauma of meals. Since he couldn't learn to swallow, his food had to be strained, and even then it was all Sabrina could do to massage half of it down his throat. He fought her. He could be famished— and she feared that half the time he was, which was why, on doctors' orders, he was fed six small meals a day—but he still objected to the intrusion of foreign matter in his mouth. He lacked all understanding. He couldn't make the connection between eating and survival, satiation or pleasure.

For all the times Sabrina had seen exasperated mothers trying to clean up chocolate-covered children, she'd give the world to see Nicky like that once, just once.

The phone rang, jarring her from wistfulness. Knowing that Mrs. Hoskins would answer it, she gathered Nicky into her arms and pushed herself to her feet. She supposed she was lucky that he was light for his age. The strain on her back from holding him for hours each day was bad enough; had he been heavier, she'd have been in serious trouble.

"How about a bath, bud?" she asked, nuzzling his temple. He was facing outward, sitting in the chair she'd fashioned out of her arms and her hip, and the extra bounce in her step was designed for play. "I'll add some bubbles and bring ducky in and you can stretch and kick and swim. Sound good?"

She was halfway to his room when Mrs. Hoskins caught up with her. "That was your husband again, Mrs. Stone. He didn't want to disturb you, but he forgot to ask you to pick up his new tuxedo. It's ready and waiting at the shop. He couldn't remember whether he'd ordered a dress shirt, but he said they had his size on file. Also, he's out of shave cream and deodorant. And he suggested picking up sweets of some sort for the Taylors."

Sabrina stopped in her tracks, dropped her chin to her chest and squeezed her eyes shut. Pick up his new tuxedo. Pick out a new dress shirt. Pick up shave cream, deodorant, sweets, a new cordless. Nicholas had a knack for tossing off little orders, totally oblivious of the effort required to carry them out. Errands that would have been simple three years ago weren't so simple now. She sighed against Nicky's head as she continued into his room.

A short time later, he was in the tub. Sabrina had a firm grip on him, which put her practically in the tub herself, but that was okay. She'd change into dry things later. For now it was enough that he was calm.

She ran a washcloth along his chest and around his neck, then positioned her hand under the cloth and pretended it was a dog—not that he knew what a dog was, despite the endless hours she'd spent pointing at picture books or ooohing and aaahing over the real thing in the park. But something about the yipping sounds she made and the gentle patter of the puppy's paws on his tummy made him gurgle. She repeated the patter again and again, laughing, praising, coaxing. The results were sporadic, a few gurgles, then silence, another gurgle, then a whimper or two. She continued to bathe him until the gurgles were absent and the whimpers increased to three or four; then, for her sake as much as for his, she took him out.

Dried and diapered and dressed in a fresh sleeper, he was precious. She sat in the rocking chair by his crib and held him close, loving his softness and his baby-sweet smell. She read him a story—*Green Eggs with Ham*—because the pictures were bright and might catch his eye and because she'd always found the cadence catchy. Nicky wasn't being caught by either the pictures or the words, but he was getting sleepy.

She helped him along by singing softly—humming, actually, with a few words stuck in. "Hush . . . mmm . . . baby . . . mmm-mmm . . . a word." The important thing was the movement of the rocker, the warmth of her body, the gentle vibration of the small sound she produced.

Carefully, she transferred him to the crib.

And then came the one time each day that Sabrina looked forward to. With only the dimmest dresser light on, she bent over the crib and smiled at her son. He looked back at her. He always did at night like this, when he was as relaxed as it was possible for him to be and was tired enough to tune out everything but that which was directly in front of him.

Sabrina was directly in front of him. She blocked out the bright red clown mobile that hung over the crib and the vivid yellow cars that raced across the nearby wall and the turquoise Care Bear that sat between a pair of Cabbage Patch twins at the foot of the crib.

"Sleepy, angel?" she crooned in little more than a whisper. She rubbed his cheek, then his neck. "Been a rough day, has it?" She ran her thumb back and forth just under his jaw. "Who's mommy's good boy?" she asked, but her voice cracked halfway through when he broke into a smile. "Ahhh, that's what I like. That's what I like, Nicky-ricky. How about another one? Another one for mommy? A nice big one? A nice big, toothy one? Mommy loves that kind. How about it, Nicky-ricky?"

But one smile a night was all she got, so when Nicky's eyes began to droop, she turned him onto his stomach and rubbed his back for a while. Then she stood with her elbows braced on the crib rail and smiled through her tears.

He looked so normal. At night like this when he was sleeping, when his limbs were loose and his diapered bottom was slightly raised and his hands lay—palms open and up—by his sides and his curls hugged his head, she could pretend that he was like any other three-year-old. She could pretend that he was dreaming sweet dreams, and that he'd be awake at dawn jumping up and down, clamoring to be free of his crib.

Was she lying to herself? Sure she was, and it had nothing to do with better judgment. It had to do with hopes and dreams and the fact that she was desperate. Ninety-nine percent of the time she was realistic; one percent of the time she allowed herself to dream. Only at night. Only when she was alone.

Derek McGill felt very much alone that night. Oh, he was alone very night, but that night it felt worse, and it was all *her* fault.

Up to then, he'd been in control. He'd learned to slow down his thoughts and narrow them. Prison was too confining for the free run of reason; a man could go mad if he didn't conform. So Derek had conformed. In those idle hours—so many idle hours—he focused his thoughts on the crime he'd committed, his trial, the work he'd been doing when he was arrested and the connection between the three. He read the papers each day—it was a compulsion, he decided.

He didn't think about driving to the North Woods of

Maine as he used to do each summer. He didn't think about fastening his shell to the roof of the Saab, driving north from Manhattan and sculling along the Mohawk as he'd done when he had just a single day free. He didn't think aboiut filet mignon, water beds or clothes washed in fabric softener. He didn't think warm or soft or gentle.

Sabrina made him think warm and soft and gentle.

His cell was dim. Stray shafts of light fell through the bars: not enough to keep him awake if he'd been inclined to sleep, but—since he was up—just enough to illumine his surroundings and remind him where he was. Not that he could have forgotten even if he'd been blind. The night was punctuated by muted snores and grunts, the occasional sleep-talker, the shuffling and rummaging of insomniacs, the punctual footfalls of the guards taking count. There'd been many a night before his imprisonment when he'd fallen asleep over the Kem machine at the office, or at home on his sofa with the television on, but no broadcast studio or late movie had ever sounded like this. The sounds and smells of prison were unique. It was mankind at its worst.

Derek wanted to know why she'd come. He'd asked her over and over again, and she'd hemmed and hawed, then finally blurted out something about wanting understanding and warmth. Understanding and warmth from *him*? It would be laughable if it weren't so sad.

He'd told her, and he'd meant it, that she was naive. It was particularly true if she believed that he had something to give. She had no idea of the hell that was his life. Boredom. Isolation. Wasted days, one after another. Frustration. Distrust. The constant battle against an inner fury that would easily eat him alive if he didn't appease it with carefully sculpted plans for revenge.

He wanted to know why she'd come, because he couldn't shake the picture she'd left in his mind. It brought a new and different kind of ache, and he resented that.

He'd never claimed to be a monk. At the age of thirteen, frighteningly soon after he reached puberty, he bluffed his way into the arms of the hottest seventeen-year-old number in the neighborhood, and he never looked back.

He'd been a sexual terror by twenty. By the time he reached thirty, he'd grown more discriminating; and by the time he reached thirty-five, he'd had several long-running affairs. The past few years had been dry by choice: sex for the sake of sex had grown empty, and he'd been too involved in his job to spare the emotional output that would have made the difference.

In that sense, and in that sense alone, his incarceration had been bearable. He hadn't left behind a special woman. It had been years since he'd seen his sex drive as a source of status. He hadn't had a hell of a lot to lose in the sexual sense by being imprisoned.

He wasn't a prig; he didn't begrudge the men whose muffled moans suggested self-gratification in the night. Nor did he begrudge those who found willing partners, though he'd had no trouble refusing the invitations he received himself. He had contempt, though, for the groups who cornered innocents in isolated spots and caused anguished cries of pain and degradation. Had it not been for razor-sharp reflexes, a mean left hook and the strength born of revulsion, he'd be one of those victims himself.

Strength born of revulsion? It had been born of fear, too, but even more of anger and frustration and impotence. That night little more than a year ago, in another town, another prison, he needed an outlet for his rage. There was nothing sexual about the way he battered his attackers. It earned him ten days in the hole, a scar he'd wear for life and a reputation that would stay with him for the duration of his imprisonment.

No, there'd been nothing sexual about his thoughts that night, or on any other night. Until now. Sabrina Stone touched him. She'd done it that first time they'd met, when he'd equated her with innocence and serenity, and she'd done it today. She touched him, heated him, made him ache.

Arms folded rigidly beneath his head, he stared at the shadowy cracks on the ceiling. Like a Rorschach test, they took shape, forming a slender body in a large sweater and long skirt with a chic belt and imported boots. And there was more. In the cracks he saw her hair. She wore it in a vague pageboy—vague because it was mussed by the wind, by the collar of her coat, perhaps even by her fingers. And she didn't seem to care, since not once did she attempt to neaten the blond riot. And there was more; he saw the slenderness of her neck, the gracefulness of her wrists, the gentle tilt of her breasts beneath a sweater that should have hidden everything but didn't. And jasmine perfume. No, not perfume. It had been too light, too delicate. Shampoo, perhaps. Or body cream.

He squeezed his eyes shut and took several deep, tortured breaths. He thought about the pathetic something that had masqueraded as hamburger at dinner, about the guard he'd seen kick an inmate whose sole reason for not rising from his cot that morning had been acute appendicitis, about Crazy Louie's latest—and dumbest—escape attempt. In time the swelling between his legs eased. Only then did he open his eyes. The cracks on the ceiling were back to being cracks on the ceiling. But, damn it, he could still smell her.

She was all style and class. Everything about her—clothes, jewelry, makeup—was understated and very obviously of fine quality. The difference between her and the other visitors in that room had been ludicrous.

She shouldn't have come. She didn't belong here. But God, she'd looked lovely. Tired, perhaps, and tense, but he'd seen all that before. She'd still been lovely. And he ached for her as he hadn't ached for a woman in months and months, which was absurd. This woman was as off-limits as any woman could get.

Item one, she had problems. She had a child who needed every last bit of her love and attention. And she had a husband—not just any husband, but one who had a fair amount of prestige and power. Derek wasn't sure where she found the strength to contribute to that particular relationship once she'd finished taking care of her son, but that wasn't his worry. The fact was, she was married and married well.

Item two, *he* had problems. He was a man standing at the crossroads of life, looking down one bleak path after another. He was in prison, stuck there for at least another nine months and beyond that at the whim of the parole board. He was a man with talent and no place to use it, if the grim predictions of his agent were to prove correct. And he was from the wrong side of the tracks.

Lord, how he'd fought that. He'd left home at eighteen, on the day of his high school graduation, and he'd been determined to put as much distance between himself and his past as possible. He'd enlisted in the Marines, done a stint in Vietnam and been thoroughly disillusioned. But he'd been in too much of a rush to take the time to protest the killing and maiming of innocent people. If gaining distance from his roots was his goal, he had too far to go to dally.

He enrolled in college, earned a degree in political science, then one in communications. Long before graduation, he was delivering on-the-hour middle-of-the-night news summaries at a local radio station. From there, he made a steady climb. He bounced from city to city, which was fine since he loved travel and adventure; but more important, each move meant a job that was one step up the ladder.

At the age of thirty-five he was named one of the three principal correspondents on *Outside Insight*. That had been four years ago. The sense of triumph he'd felt then had been incredible. He'd made it. He'd hit the big time in a big way. An honest way. A lawful, respected way.

That was one of the things that hurt most now—it had been a goddamned waste of time and effort. He'd worked his tail off all those years. He'd earned each and every promotion. He'd paid his taxes on time and in full. He'd been the yo-yo to return the extra ten dollars that the supermarket clerk had mistakenly given him in change.

Legally he'd gone by the book. And still he'd been screwed. He was right back where he started—no, worse, because now he wore the stigma firsthand.

Why in the hell would Sabrina Stone want to have anything to do with him? Warmth and understanding, she'd said. Apparently her husband didn't provide those, but Derek could have guessed that months before. After that day on her terrace, he'd studied each story, scrutinized each picture of Nicholas Stone. A few of those photos had included Sabrina, and in those Nicholas had always been a step ahead of her, with his face to the flash and his eyes on the world.

So Sabrina was in need. But she was beautiful and intelligent. She was wealthy. She was Society. If it was warmth she needed, she could surely find it in dozens of willing and suitable pairs of arms. She didn't need to go slumming.

Which brought him back to square one. *Why in the hell had she come?*

Someone had sent her to drive him mad. That was all there was to it. It was psychological torture, pure and simple.

Annoyed and frustrated, he rolled to his side. The cot creaked. He heard the distant sound of the guards' footsteps and automatically began to count. Five paces, stop, search. Five paces, stop, search. The footsteps grew nearer, louder. He was fully prepared when a beam of light searched his cell, then searched his face, then left.

He lay quietly, listening to the footsteps systematically recede. He inhaled, exhaled; he counted the beats of his heart. He closed his eyes and pictured nothingness. He concentrated on nothingness. He tried to make his mind mirror nothingness. It usually worked, but it didn't now.

She was still with him.

Abruptly he was up, sitting on the edge of the cot. He flexed his fingers, alternately extending them and curling them into fists. He wanted to touch—suede, leather, mohair, skin—woman's skin, Sabrina's skin. Since he couldn't, he thrust an impatient handful of fingers through his dark hair and swore under his breath. He hadn't thought prison could get worse, but it had today. He'd been aware of intellectual stagnation and emotional vegetation. But sensual deprivation had only hit him now.

Bolting upright, he began to pace. He padded to the bars, wrapped his fingers around them for a minute, turned, strode to the rear wall of the cell, turned, strode forward again.

Sabrina had been telling the truth about why she'd come.

He knew it in his gut, knew it with a confidence that increased with each oblong he paced. She wanted comfort. She really did.

That told him something. She'd felt it, too, the rapport on the day they'd met. She was reacting to it at some level, though how conscious the level was he just didn't know. He did know that every one of his reasons for steering clear of her was valid.

And still he wanted her.

Which was why he felt so alone.

And why he couldn't possibly let her come again.

Two weeks later, he came closer to death than he cared to come. Acting on impulse, he violated a basic rule of penitentiary self-preservation: He tried to break up a fight between two other inmates. The incident was in the shower room. There was no clothing to blunt the blow when a razor blade connected with his neck. Had it been in inch farther forward, it would have severed the jugular.

His skin was stitched and by evening he was back in his cell, but the throbbing kept him awake for much of the night. The next morning, he penned a brief note, sealed it in an envelope and dropped it in the prisoners' mail slot.

· *CHAPTER 3* ·

Sabrina felt like death warmed over. She'd had the flu for three days running, and it showed no sign of letting up. When she sat up, she got dizzy. She couldn't hold down food. And she was very hot. Or very cold.

She tried to take care of Nicky, but it was impossible. She'd make it to her feet long enough to change his diapers, then collapse back with him onto the bed. He'd cry. She'd gather her strength. Then she'd try again, this time to feed him, but she'd end up in the bathroom, retching. He'd cry. She'd have that much less strength left to gather.

Mrs. Hoskins kept to herself. She went about her business unobtrusively, as was her way. Sabrina had liked it that way when she first married Nick and inherited Mrs. Hoskins in the bargain. The housekeeper knew just what she was supposed to do around the house, and she did it. Unfortunately, she did nothing extra. Sabrina could appreciate Mrs. Hoskins' back problem, but there were times soon after the flu hit when she wondered how the woman could not offer to help, given the obvious way Sabrina was struggling.

And Sabrina couldn't ask. Nor could she command; it wasn't *her* way. And though her pride was tattered, she still had a bit; she wouldn't give Mrs. Hoskins the satisfaction of hearing her beg.

The only thing that enabled her to make it through the first day was the conviction that she'd be better by the next. But the next was just as bad. Even Nicholas agreed, albeit grudgingly, that she needed help. So they hired a day worker, and though the woman, Doreen, was slow, she was sweet.

That was more than Sabrina could say for her husband. Forget the sweet nothings he might have done to make her feel better—the flowers he might have brought her, the cup of tea, the back rub. She could live without those—God knew she had, for months and months anyway. But she firmly believed Nicholas could have taken a day off from work to care for his son. That hadn't occurred to him, or if it had, he thought himself above the task. Either that, or he'd been intimidated: Nicky's peculiarities were enough to try a saint, and Nicholas was no saint.

He was barely even human when he strode into the bedroom on the fourth night, sat down in a huff on the chintz-covered chaise to unlace his shoes and began to complain. "Dinner isn't ready. Can you believe that? I'm supposed to play handball in an hour, and dinner isn't ready! Mrs. Hoskins says that Doreen is monopolizing the kitchen."

"She's feeding Nicky," was Sabrina's muffled response. Her face was half-buried in the pillow. She didn't have the strength to move.

He tossed one shoe in the direction of the closet. "When you feed Nicky, I get dinner on time."

"I'm efficient."

"I don't see what the problem is. How can dinner for one three-year-old be such an effort?" The second shoe followed the first. He stood and unfastened his trousers.

Sabrina tugged the blankets more tightly to her stomach. The pressure felt good. "Everything has to be strained. He still hates it."

"So don't strain the food."

"He'll choke."

"If he's hungry enough, he'll eat."

She didn't bother to answer. That seemed to goad Nicholas on.

"If you weren't lying around in bed, this wouldn't happen. How long do you plan on being sick?"

She stared at him in disbelief.

"Other people have the flu," he said. "They're sick for a day, maybe two, then they're back to normal. Not you. It's been four days. Are you enjoying the vacation?"

She managed a weak, "You're nuts."

"Not me. Maybe you. Maybe your flu is psychosomatic, Sabrina. Have you stopped to consider that possibility?"

"Please, Nick."

"I'm serious," he said. He was standing in his underwear, with his hands cocked on his hips. "It's clear that Nicky is a problem for you. You've had trouble with him from the start. What better way to get time off than to be sick?"

Sabrina continued to stare. Somewhere in the back of her mind, she knew that Nicholas was an attractive man. He was of average height, nicely built. His features were blue-blooded, and rightly so—given the presence of two marquises and a duke several branches up and over in his family tree. His skin was lightly tanned and firm of tone; even with more gray than brown in his hair, he looked younger than his forty-three years. And he held himself well. Confidently. Arrogantly. Even in his underwear.

But all that was somewhere in the back of her mind. At the moment, and at more moments than she cared to count of late, Sabrina found him offensive.

"I can guarantee you, Nicholas, that I don't choose to be sick. I lie here feeling guilty for everything I should be doing but can't do. Doreen barges in with questions, and Nicky has been fussier than usual. It's not much of a vacation. And yes, you're right, Nicky's been a problem from the start. He is severely and multiply handicapped."

"Baloney."

"Where've you *been*, Nick? Haven't you heard a word the doctors said?"

"They've said that his development is delayed. He's just slow. That's all. He'll catch up in his own good time."

"That's not what the doctors say."

"They don't know what to say."

"And you do?"

"Yes. The child needs time and discipline. And he needs to be with other children. You isolate him, Sabrina. He should be in a play group. He needs to be with *normal* children his age. If he could see what they're doing—"

"My God, Nick!" Sabrina cried. A fine wire of frustration napped inside her. In a burst of angry energy, she sat up. "Nicky is three years old and he can barely hold up his head. He can't sit. He can't crawl. He can't hold things or feed himself or talk. What in the *devil* is he going to do in a play group?" She was shaking all over, but she couldn't stop the words. "What in the devil is a play group going to do with *him*? Children can be cruel, Nick. They don't mean to be, but they are. You won't be the one who suffers when they stand around, pointing and giggling at him. Maybe they'll use him as a beanball target. That'd be—"

"That's enough!"

"It's not! Face *facts*, Nick!"

"You're getting hysterical."

She was on her knees on the bed, swaying slightly but keeping her eyes on her husband. "Hysterical? *Me*? What cause would I have for hysterics? I've only spent three

years in nonstop hell trying to deal with a child who is
severely retarded—"

"Sabrina—"

"And I've had no help from you, Nick! You're too busy
to lend a hand in the everyday care. You object when I
want to see a new doctor or try a different training program. You fight me every step of the way. You deny that
there's a problem. Well, there *is* a problem. And I'll tell
you something else. Maybe the reason I can't shake this flu
is because I've gotten run down trying to cope with the
reality of Nicky and the reality of you and the reality of
me . . . if there is a me anymore. I sometimes wonder about
that. I was a writer when I married you. What am I now?"

"A mother!" Nicholas snapped. He was pulling on his
sweat suit as quickly as possible. "That was what you
wanted to be. Why are you complaining?"

"Because Nicky isn't just another child!"

"You can't custom-order kids, Sabrina. You can't check
off the traits you want them to have and expect that you'll
get your every wish. So Nicky is high-strung. So he's
fussy—"

"He's a godawful wretch most of the time! I love him to
pieces, but there are times when I can't stand him. He
needs help. *I* need help. It's getting worse and it'll continue
to get worse. He'll just get bigger. That's all, Nick. Just
bigger."

Nicholas was back on the chaise, this time tugging on
his sneakers. "My God, you're a bitch."

"I'm a realist. I can't handle this, Nick. I can't take the
constant tension and worry. I can't take the physical strain,
day in, day out. It's not what I want."

"I'm leaving," he said coolly, heading for the door. "I'll
be back by eleven."

"You can close your eyes to it, Nick, but it won't go
away. We have to do something. You may have your life,
but mine's falling apart. There's nothing left of our marriage. We barely see each other, and when we do, we
argue. I have no career, no social life. Every ounce of my
strength is committed to Nicky, and it does no good. I can
love him until I'm blue in the face, but he isn't ever going

to be normal. It's only a matter of time before we have to think about putting him in an institution—"

The bedroom door slammed, blotting out the loathsome word. Sabrina continued to kneel on the bed. Her breathing was shallow. Sweat beaded on her upper lip; her nightgown was damp. After a minute, she staggered from the bed and made it to the bathroom just in time to lose the tea and crackers she'd eaten so gingerly an hour beforer. Then, not caring whether it was the wisest thing to do, she turned on the shower. She wedged herself in a corner, slid down until she was sitting with her knees tucked to her chest and let the tepid spray course over her.

Once out of the shower, she couldn't make it back to bed fast enough. She pulled the blankets to her neck because, though her skin burned, she had the chills. Her limbs ached. Her insides were raw. She felt miserable—but the more she concentrated on her misery, the less she had to think about the argument with Nick. So she concentrated on her misery.

In time, other thoughts intruded, and when she'd stopped quaking quite so badly, she freed one arm from the covers and reached back for the book she'd left on the headboard shelf. She opened to the place where page 209 met page 210, removed the plain white envelope she'd tucked there, then set the book aside.

For a time she just lay, tucked beneath layers of blankets, looking at the envelope. The average eye would find nothing distinctive about it, but Sabrina's was not the average eye. She saw that the envelope had no return address, and assumed that was by design. It was metered, rather than stamped, which she assumed to be regulation, and the postmark, reading Parkersville, MA, was dated three weeks before, which was just about how long it had been since she'd received it.

For what had to be the hundredth time, she removed a single sheet of paper from the envelope, unfolded it and read its brief message.

"Thursdays are fine. D."

Closing her eyes, she pressed the letter and its envelope to her breast.

By the next day, she was feeling better. Doreen was staying on for another day, so she napped. She took a leisurely bath, then napped some more. She was feeling more composed than usual when, late that afternoon, her mother phoned.

Sabrina had never quite figured out whether her mother's otherworldliness had preceded her profession, or vice versa. Amanda Monroe was like a character from one of her books. Petite, almost waiflike, she was a sprite who'd reached her mid-fifties with few of the usual signs of life's wear and tear. Her skin was smooth and porcelain-like. Her hair was long and blond. There was a fluidity to her walk, a lyricism to her talk. And when she smiled, she sparkled.

She had an ethereal quality that made people stop, look once, then again, then approach her with caution lest they cause her harm. It was really quite ironic, because the woman was strong. She looked as if she could splinter apart and disperse with the breeze, but the fact was, she had an iron constitution and a will of steel. In her soft, shimmering way she was a controller. She choreographed those around her; they danced to her tune.

Every five years and ten books or so, she created a new galaxy to explore. Her fans loved it. Her family hated it. Her husband, who was nearly as eccentric as she and had an ego the size of Texas, to boot, had long ago decided that *no way* was the Old West going to shrivel in the shadow of the Vaspatian moons. He had gallantly deeded the spacious San Francisco townhouse to his wife, bought a ranch in Nevada and moved there lock, stock and barrel. He returned to the Coast periodically, the bounty hunter returning to his woman, but it was clear that he had no wish to wipe the range dust from his boots.

Sabrina had grown up shuttling back and forth between her parents' homes, and at the time she'd thought nothing of it. Amanda and Gebhart loved each other. When they were together, they were openly and honestly affectionate. They simply couldn't live with each other full-time—or so they explained to Sabrina when she began to wonder and ask—and she accepted that, too, for a time. In recent years, though, she'd had doubts. She'd come to see her

parents as lonely people, people caught between creative
needs and emotional ones. Each had achieved success, but
at a price.

For that reason, Sabrina no longer begrudged her parents
the odd upbringing she'd had. And for that reason, she
always tried to receive her mother's phone calls with an
audible smile.

"Hi, Mom. How're you doing?"

Amanda answered in the feathery tones that fit her well.
"The most wonderful thing just happened, sweetheart.
Glendine escaped from the last of the Wuftigs. She's on her
way to the Jennery Fields now, and assuming she doesn't
fall on any gluxide mines, she's home free. He's waiting
for her at Konrell, sweetheart. Zaaro's waiting at Konrell!"

"That's great, Mom. I take it Konrell wasn't destroyed
by the Jaspards?"

"A little damage," Amanda admitted airily, "but nothing
that the corps couldn't fix in an afternoon. Their technol-
ogy is incredible, sweetheart. A few molecular transfers
and things were perfect." She sighed. "If we only knew
half of what they do . . ."

Sabrina bit her lip. When she was sure she could sound
properly respectful, she asked, "Is that the end of the Dusalon series?"

"No, no. There are two more books left. I still haven't
settled the fates of Quist and Fravilon."

"Mm. Right. I'd forgotten."

"Quist's story is next. I'll be starting it at the end of the
week, and unless your father distracts me with a surprise
visit, I'll finish it before my birthday. I'd really like to do
that. J. B. is coming up with the girls. He hates it when I
talk Dusalon."

"But he always talks whatever it is that *he*'s writing."

"But that's different. His horror stories are his identity.
He hides behind them. If only he could find a woman
who'd bring him out. Jenny and he were ill-suited."

"She loved him for a time."

"I was never quite sure whether she loved him or his
royalties."

Sabrina snorted. "It would take mighty hefty royalties to keep a woman with J. B."

"He gets mighty hefty royalties. Sabrina, he's not that bad."

"No?"

Amanda was still for a minute before conceding, "Well, he's easy to look at. And speaking of easy to look at, how's gorgeous Nicky?"

"Gorgeous."

"How's he doing?"

"Lousy."

"I thought you were seeing Howard Frasier. As specialists go, he's the best. Wasn't he any help?"

"Not really."

"You sound down."

"I am. I'm tired, Mom."

"You haven't been sleeping?"

"Oh, I have. I mean, I've had the flu for the past few days, and that's taken something out of me, but there's more. I'm burning out."

"What do you mean?"

"Nicky is taking too much from me."

"He's your son."

"And I love him, love him so much, but it's not fair."

"Life isn't always fair. What's your alternative?"

"A private hospital," Sabrina said, deliberately avoiding the word "institution." She'd tried that once on her mother. It hadn't gone over well. "There's a place in Vermont that I've been—"

"Don't, Sabrina. He'll come along. Give him time."

"That's what Nick says, but it isn't working. Nicky has serious problems."

"He's a special child."

"He's handicapped."

"Yes, but is putting him away the solution?"

Sabrina curled into herself. "You make him sound like a dog. I'm not 'putting him away.' I'm simply looking for a place where the people are equipped to handle problems like his."

"You can handle them. You've been through training programs. You can go through more."

"But the emotional price—"

"Nicky is your son. He needs to be with you."

"I can't deal with it, Mom. If I knew things would improve by next year or the year after, I could hang on. But things aren't going to improve in five, ten or twenty years. We're talking full-time custodial care for the rest of his life."

"Is that what the doctors say?"

"Yes."

"Oh, sweetheart . . ."

"I know. There are times when I'm so embroiled in the everyday trauma that I don't see the larger tragedy. There are other times when the entire picture is crystal-clear, and it eats me alive."

"The tragedy," Amanda decided, "is that Nicky isn't on Dusalon. They'd be able to do something for him there. Actually, they wouldn't have to do anything for him, because they'd have caught and corrected the problem before he was born and you'd have a wonderfully healthy boy."

"He's not on Dusalon, and we don't know that the problem is genetic. It could be—"

"If the problem weren't genetic, they'd be able to fix that, too. Even the Wuftigs know about reconstructing cells and reversing brain damage. Why is it that doctors *here* can't do it?"

The sound of her pout brought a sad smile to Sabrina's face. "Because this is reality, Mom." Her smile listed wanly. "Maybe you could give the doctors a little hint . . . you know, a shove in the right direction?"

"I can't do that. My books are copyrighted."

It was the standard answer Amanda gave when Sabrina teased. The fact was, Amanda had imbued the Dusalonians with their extraordinary medical powers only after Nicky was born. If J. B. Monroe hid behind his horror stories, Amanda Monroe expressed her wishes through science fiction.

"And besides," Amanda went on, "Earth doctors are too full of themselves. They'd never listen to an alien. When I dared suggest to the young doctor who lives next door that he should have his wife drink my ambrosia each night, he looked at me like I was crazy. That, after asking me why I look forty when I'm about to turn fifty-six. You are coming out for my party, aren't you, Sabrina?"

"Uh, Mom, I don't know."

"Why not? It's not every day that I have a birthday. You didn't come for Thanksgiving or Christmas. I haven't see you since last summer, and only then when I flew into New York for my publisher's party."

How could Sabrina explain the pain she felt seeing her family, when she didn't wholly understand it herself? . . . No, not seeing her family. Having her family see Nicky. She wasn't ashamed of him, at least she didn't think she was. But she'd wanted to do motherhood right, and Nicky hadn't worked. She loved him. She loved her parents. She watched them watching him, and she felt odd—self-conscious and guilty, maybe disappointed.

And she had trouble being with J. B. He would stare at Nicky, then declare that the problem was a spirit that had entered through a hair follicle and had taken control of the child—or something else equally bizarre. And she had trouble seeing J. B.'s daughters, who were seven and ten, adorable, outgoing, and quick. They had all their marbles. Her son didn't, and it hurt.

It occurred to her to wonder whether she was competing with her brother, which puzzled her, because she didn't know why she should. But she had too many things to think about, so she simply said in response to her mother's question, "Traveling with Nicky is such a hassle."

"But we want to see him. We want to see *you*."

"Nick's been very busy. I doubt he could take the time."

"Fine," was Amanda's reaction. "Leave him home."

Sabrina gave a dry chuckle. "No love lost there."

"I've always found Nicholas to be a little stiff for my tastes. And that was even before Nicky was born. Is he still being difficult?"

"He's okay."

"Is he accepting Nicky any more than he did?"

"He still denies the problem, if that's what you mean."

"Does he spend time with him?"

"Once in a while. He tosses him in the air, roughhouses a little—anything to give a semblance of normalcy. I hold my breath when Nicky's head wobbles, but the worst of it is that Nicholas always manages to get a sound out of him. The sound may be Nicky's version of a terrified scream—we'll never know, but it is a sound."

"Is Nicholas at all supportive of you?"

Sabrina bowed her head and rubbed the frown lines between her eyes. Her mother wasn't in outer space now; she was right there, all there, summarizing the worst of the situation in a nutshell.

"Nicholas thinks I'm an alarmist."

"Regardless of what he thinks of you, he has to have some respect for the doctors, doesn't he?"

It had been months since Nicholas had gone with her to any of the appointments. "He hangs on to his dreams."

"Sounds like he needs a counselor himself."

Sabrina wanted to laugh. Nicholas saw himself as being in total control of his life. He wouldn't admit that Nicky had problems. He'd never admit that he had problems himself. She could just imagine his ridicule if she dared to suggest marital counseling.

She wanted marital counseling. She wanted *something*. She wanted to spill everything, to tell her mother about the wreck that was her marriage, but she couldn't, she just couldn't. She'd taken such care in choosing a husband, finding a man she thought to be stable and successful. Her parents had had reservations about Nicholas Stone from the first, and for reasons similar to that her mother had just named—they'd thought him to be Establishment to the core, which wasn't saying all that much, given Amanda and Gebhart's nonconformism. And it certainly wasn't a case of saying that they'd been right. Nick's conservatism hadn't destroyed the marriage. Life had done it. Fate had done it. When things had soured and the chips were down, Nicholas and she were no good together. Neither could offer what the other needed. They let each other down. They clashed.

"Nicholas will come around in time," Sabrina ventured.

"I hope so for your sake. What will you do if he doesn't?"

"I don't know." It was as close as she could come to admitting that the marriage might be doomed.

"Oh, sweetheart . . ."

"Mmm. Pretty depressing, isn't it?"

"You do need to get away. Why not come for my party and plan to stay a few weeks?"

"But the problem will be with me whether I'm here or there, and the advantage of being here is that there are a few trained people I can fall back on when I've had it up to my eyeballs."

"You do need to get away from Nicky for a few days. Just for a breather. If you were to do that every once in a while, you'd be able to manage just fine. You wouldn't have to think about putting the child in a hospital."

Later that night, then at odd times during the next few days, Sabrina took the plain white envelope from its spot between pages 209 and 210 of the book on the headboard shelf. She read and reread the message inside. She listed the pros and cons of her returning to Parkersville, reviewed them time and again in her mind. Inevitably, she refolded the paper, returned it neatly to its envelope, returned the envelope to that safe spot in her book and the book to its shelf.

Maura Coryelle was a bundle of energy. She was by profession a literary agent, but at any given time she had her fingers in a dozen other pies. She'd had grand successes and gross failures, but she was a survivor. She bounced back. Single, and generally on the make, she was alternatively an angel, a devil and a minx. She was wily. She was loyal. She made the society pages of *Town and Country* as often as Sabrina. She told jokes that were more than a little off color, and her conversation was peppered with swear words. She was just what Sabrina needed.

A week had gone by since Sabrina had talked with her mother. Six days had gone by since she'd resumed caring for Nicky. Her husband's face had been as scarce as ever during that time.

"Ah, Maura," Sabrina said with a voluminous sigh moments after the maitre d' seated them, "it's great to be out of the house. It's great to be in a restaurant. And it's great to be with you. Not in that order, of course."

"Of course," Maura said with an acknowledging nod. "But you can't fool me. And I know just what the attraction is. As we get older, we revert to our youth. I represent your youth."

Sabrina and Maura had been high school pals in San Francisco, and a more improbable friendship wasn't often to be found. They were different in looks, background, personality and aspirations, but they complemented each other and had continued to do so even through the college years when they'd come East—Sabrina to Columbia, Maura to NYU. Their relationship now had the benefit of history.

"You represent my *adulthood*," Sabrina corrected. "It's been so long since I've been out for lunch that I feel like I'm *playing* grown-up." With a regal air that she pulled off with grace, she settled her elbows on the velvet arms of her chair, looked up and around and caught the eye of the wine steward. He was at their table seconds later. "We'd like a dry Vouvray, please."

The steward nodded and left.

"Who's picking up the tab?" Maura asked.

"Me."

"Great." She relaxed and sat back. "Are we celebrating?"

"We're relaxing."

"Uh-oh, things are as bad as ever at home?"

Sabrina held up a hand. "Shh. Not today."

"What do you mean, not today?"

"I don't want to think about home. I'm tired of hearing myself whine all the time. I'm as bad as Nicky . . . unnnh, I don't want to talk about it."

"But this is *me*. *Maura*. If you can't pour out your heart to me, who *can* you pour it out to?"

Sabrina set her chin at a confident angle. "I'm not pouring today. So. How's work? By the way, you look terrific. I love your hair."

Maura shook the mass of long, Titian waves back from her face. "I thought I'd try life as a redhead."

"How is it?"

"Not bad. Hmmm, pretty good. Actually"—she gave a Cheshire cat grin, leaned forward and lowered her voice to a conspiratorial level—"it's fuckin' great! I met a guy last night who is not to be believed. I mean, tall and dark, good-looking as hell, silent, mysterious—and an absolute dream in bed."

"What's his name?"

"His name?" A moment's pregnant pause proceeded a mischievous shrug.

Sabrina stared. "You're kidding."

Maura shook her head.

"How could you not know his name?"

"That was part of it," she explained excitedly. "It was fantasy from the word *go*. Our eyes caught in the elevator of the Park Lane; we kept tabs on each other through three hours' worth of dinner with other people at the restaurant; he was at the door when I was leaving, escorted me around the block, in the back door of the hotel and up to a room on the eleventh floor. It was unbelievably romantic."

"It was insane. He could have been a mugger. Or a pervert. For that matter, he could have given you something. Have you stopped to consider that?"

"Why should I consider it with you here to do it for me? That's why our friendship works, Sabrina. You're rational. I'm impulsive."

Sabrina realized that she'd summed it up pretty well. Maura counted on her practicality; she counted on Maura's freshness. Not that picking up a guy in an elevator thrilled Sabrina. . . .

"You can relax," Maura went on. "He was okay, really he was. He's a lawyer form Houston."

"Married?"

Maura sucked in her lips and rounded her eyes. The expression said, "How should I know?" She said, "He said no."

"Did you give him your name?"

"Why in the hell would I want to do that?"

"So he could contact you again?"

"But giving him my name would have been too easy. I made a point to drop the names of a few of my more prominent clients. If he's interested in finding me, a phone call to any one of them will do the trick."

"Very clever."

"Maybe. But the fun was in the anonymity of it, the naughtiness, don't you see?"

Sabrina didn't see at all, but then, she was the nesting type. Maura was not. "I'll take your word for it," she said with a smile for the wine steward, who had returned to present the bottle he'd chosen. "That looks fine." After the bottle had been uncorked, a sample tasted and approved and their glasses filled, she raised hers. "To freedom."

"Freedom? Where did that come from?"

Sabrina was at that very instant asking herself the same question. Images flitted through her mind—of prisons, one on Fifth Avenue, the other in the Berkshires. She dislodged them with a tiny, almost imperceptible shake of her head. "I don't know. It just came. See what you do to me?"

"I wish I could do more to you," Maura said. She sipped her wine and carefully set the glass down. "I wish I could get you to write again."

"Work is slow?" Sabrina teased.

"Work is never slow!"

"Then you can't be missing me. What're you into now?"

"Besides books? A little music, a little art. And lots of cheesecake."

Sabrina covered her face with a hand and moaned. "I don't belive it, Maura. Cheesecake?"

"Not *that* kind of cheesecake. *Cheesecake* cheesecake— you know, the kind you eat? I met a girl who makes the most delicious cheesecake you've ever tasted . . . plain, chocolate, marble, raspberry, you name it, and in any shape and size. Baby Watson moooove over."

"That good?" Sabrina asked, amused now that her faith had been marginally restored. She still wasn't sure about the fellow at the Park Lane, but at least Maura's mind wasn't stuck in one track.

"That good. She's been running a small catering busi-

ness out of her house, but she'd like to do something bigger—I mean, *much* bigger, with factories and trucks and
nationwide distribution—only, she needs financial backing
and has no idea how to get it."

"Which is where you come in."

"Exactly. And why not? Christ, I haven't got much to
lose. If I put the deal together, I get a percentage, which
could turn out to be pretty damned sweet if the cheesecake
sells."

"But will it?" Sabrina asked gently, almost apologetically. "Cheesecake's been around for a while. You won't
be breaking any new ground, and you'll be competing with
well-established companies."

Maura leaned forward, looked to either side, then whispered, "How do . . . goose eggs . . . grab you?"

"Goose eggs?"

"Shhhhhh! What I'm telling you is confidential, Sabrina.
Yes, goose eggs . . . as in what the golden goose lays . . .
except made of cheesecake. Think of the marketing possibilities. The upwardly mobile American is watching TV at
night, gets a little hungry, goes to the freezer and reaches
for a treasure."

"Ah. I see. Mmmm, that's interesting."

Maura pulled a crestfallen face. "You don't like the
idea."

"I do; it's just that you took me by surprise. Somehow I
wasn't prepared for goose eggs."

"Don't you dare laugh, Sabrina Stone."

"I'm trying not to, Maura, really I am."

"Damn it, I wouldn't have to muck around with cheesecake if you'd give me another book to peddle."

"I'm not the only author you represent."

"But you're the best. Whenever I see Norman Aguire,
he asks about you. He's still selling your first." Sabrina
had written a biography of her paternal grandmother,
whose work with the Tennessee Valley Authority in the
1930's had been legendary. The book was historically exact
and presented a view of those times not often seen.
"Schools are snatching it up for textbook use, libraries
want it—but you know that. You're still seeing nice royal-

ties. Norm will pay top dollar for another. And don't tell me that the money isn't important," she said as Sabrina was about to say just that, "because it doesn't have to be the money. You could do it for the intellectual stimulation. You could do it because you were meant to be a writer. You could do it to show up J. B. Or you could do it for something as pure and simple as ego gratification. How about it?"

Sabrina took another sip of wine. "Do you think I'm competing with J. B.?"

"I didn't mean—"

"I know you didn't, but I'm curious, because I was wondering about that myself not long ago. I've never been aware of being in competition with him. It's always been a more general thing, not so much competing with my family as establishing a separate identity."

"That sounds about right. But you're evading my question. Why won't you write?"

"No time."

Maura made a face. "You make time for what you want."

"My circumstances are extenuating."

"Haven't you heard of hiring baby-sitters?"

"Doesn't work with Nicky."

"You look tired, Sabrina. You need a break."

Sabrina rolled her eyes.

"I'm serious," Maura went on. "Writing was always an outlet for you. Why not use it to help you now, when you need it most."

"I don't want to talk about this," Sabrina hummed in a soft, impromptu tune.

"But I want you to write!"

Sabrina looked at her friend and sighed. "Oh, Maura. It's not only a matter of time and space. It's a psychological thing. I feel emotionally shriveled. Bone dry. The creative juices aren't flowing. Right now, I'd be hard pressed to name a topic about which I'd have the slightest interest writing."

But there was one topic. It stayed at the edge of Sabrina's mind through the rest of her luncheon with Maura and came to the fore only later that day, when she was putting Nicky through the motions, repeatedly and with monotony, of reaching for an object he wanted.

She could write about Derek. His experience interested her. She felt an affinity for him. On the surface, their situations were as different as night from day. Beneath that surface, she wasn't so sure. There were similarities. She could explore them.

It was as valid an excuse as any for returning to see him again, she thought.

· CHAPTER 4 ·

When Sabrina arrived at Parkersville this time, there was no delay. The guards found her name in their book, and she was promptly searched and escorted to the visiting room.

Again she arrived before Derek. Again the room was uncomfortably warm. This time, rather than sitting, she waited by one of the windows. A thick lock held it shut. She wished she had the courage to ask one of the guards if she could release the lock and let in a little air, but she remembered what Derek had said about the heat. It promoted docility, a desirable quality as far as prison administrators were concerned.

Sabrina didn't feel at all docile, or sluggish. Adrenaline was pumping through her veins as it had been doing since she'd left New York. It was a percussive sensation, a rhythm that cried, *What're you doing what're you doing what're you doing?*

I'm not sure I'm not sure I'm not sure, was all she could answer. She shifted her voluminous twill topcoat from one arm to the other, ran a hand across the back of her neck, then raked her fingers upward through her hair, letting the thick flaxen strands fall as they would. She thought calm, cool and collected. She felt antsy and unsure. With a con- certed effort, she fixed a steady stare out the window.

She couldn't quite understand the necessity for bars. They made a statement, that was all. A prisoner who man- aged to elude the guards in the room and make it through the window would escape nowhere. He'd find himself on a narrow ledge thirty feet above the prison yard, or whatever it was that lay below.

She'd always thought of a prison yard as resembling an urban school playground—concrete underfoot, wire fences all around—but what she saw wasn't so much that as an open area of walks that spread weblike toward various out- lying buildings. Grass and shrubbery edged the walks, though most still had the drab, dried hue of winter. It was barely the first of April.

"Pretty place," came a sardonic observation from a point over her shoulder. Sabrina didn't have to look around to know that the voice was Derek's. She turned, wanting to see him. She'd pictured him many times in the last six weeks, more so in the last two. He looked as strong, as dark-haired and brooding as she'd remembered him. But good. Strangely good. The unsureness she felt began to recede.

"I was just thinking," she said, "that the greenery will come alive in another month. Do the inmates do the gar- dening?"

"There's a detail for lawnwork."

"The men must fight over it. Being outside has to be better than doing floors or bathrooms."

"It is, and they do. Not that there's much point in fight- ing. Work details are assigned by the front office. You can express a preference, but it's usually a case of being in the right place at the right time or, more often, taking what- ever's open. You either get a good assignment or you don't, and if you don't . . ."

He shrugged to finish the sentence, then lapsed into si- lence, but he'd said a lot in one breath. She took that to be an encouraging sign and asked, with a tiny head toss to- ward the window, "Where do all the paths lead?"

"To fences."

"Within the fences?"

"There are six houses."

"You don't call them cell blocks?"

"Not here."

"Does that mean they're less prisonlike?"

"Not necessarily."

"Is the living dormitory-style?"

"In some."

"In yours?"

He shook his head.

The encouraging sign Sabrina had seen was nothing but a memory. She tried to decide if she'd said something offensive. Her questions had been simple, spawned by sheer curiosity. She hadn't been critical.

She wondered if he had simply gotten out of the habit of talking, and that possibility seemed a crime in itself. He'd been a talker by profession—actually a question-asker, but he'd had plenty to say in the course of his interviews, and she was sure that in the planning of stories he'd said much more. He was a man to call the shots.

Standing beside him, she felt not so much the warmth of his body, since the warmth of the room overrode most else, but his sheer size and physical presence. He was an imposing figure. His hair was windblown, almost defiant in its tumble on his brow. That same wind had painted faintly ruddy patches on his cheeks. His jaw was firm-set and deeply shadowed, lending him an air of mystery. Pride squared his shoulders, drawing his shirt smoothly across the muscular swells of his chest, causing his name and prison number to glare boldly from the cloth. He wore his jeans low and beltless. His legs were endless.

Peripherally she noted that his scar had faded, but she was busy trying to decide whether his eyes held that little bit of warmth she craved. His voice gave nothing away; it was a guarded band of sound.

"The drive in was easier today," she said lightly. "No snow."

He nodded.

"I noticed that some of the trees out front were tapped."

"It's sugaring time."

"Does the prison make much syrup?"

"Enough for one morning's worth of pancakes."

She thought she saw a wry twitch at the corner of his mouth, but if so, it was quickly controlled. Sighing, she glanced toward the paved webwork outside. "I imagine that once spring comes the walks might actually look pleasant."

"They might, if you can overlook the chain-link fences, the barbed wire and the guard towers."

She shrugged and gave a tiny smile. "Can't have it all."

Derek, who had been feeling his way since he walked into the room, was mesmerized by that tiny smile. More than that, he was amazed to find her there. Even more than that, he was amazed that he still *wanted* to find her there.

It had been six weeks. After she'd visited last time, after he'd sent her the note, he'd waited for her to come. And waited. And waited. Rationally, he'd known that she couldn't possibly understand how slowly time passed behind bars, one minute dripping slowly into the next like cold, dark molasses. She couldn't know how much he needed her visit. Irrationally, he'd been furious that she'd kept him on tenterhooks for so long. He'd also been furious at the system that made him sit and wait until she chose to visit. He didn't like feeling helpless, and sixteen-and-a-half months' worth of practice hadn't helped.

When he'd been informed that she was here, he'd felt a renewed spurt of that fury. It had dissipated somewhat during the walk to the administration building. He still felt it, but it had competition now. For everything she'd been in the cracks on the nighttime ceiling of his cell, she was more in person.

"I got your note," she said. "Thank you. After last time, I wasn't sure what you were thinking."

Derek was thinking that he was allowed a beginning-of-the-visit embrace and that he'd be a fool not to take it, but he couldn't. Sabrina was untouchable. Pristine and pure. She was off limits. So why had he asked her back? "I wasn't sure myself."

"You seemed annoyed that I'd come."

"I was."

"Why?"

He knew the answer. The question was whether he wanted to pass it on. He pondered that for a minute, finally deciding that the humiliation wouldn't be quite so bad if he admitted to being humiliated, which he could do in a proud sort of way, or so his reasoning went.

"A man doesn't always like to be seen in surroundings like these."

"What made you change your mind?"

"I haven't. I'd still rather be anywhere else."

"But you changed your mind about my visiting."

"My Thursday afternoon work assignment is lousy. I don't have to do it if I have a guest."

"Mmmm. That's flattering."

He shrugged, but this time she was sure she saw a tiny kernel of warmth somewhere in the depths of those gray eyes of his. It was that tiny kernel of warmth that took the sting from his next words.

"It took you long enough to get here."

"My time isn't always my own."

"Did you leave a number for the sitter?"

"Not quite."

"Why not?"

"Because they don't need a number. If they can't function without me for a day, then they're not worth the money I'm paying, and I'm paying a whole lot. Besides, it's nobody's business but my own where I go and what I do during my free time. God only knows I have precious little of it."

He grinned, and if she hadn't been so surprised at her own outburst, she'd have caught her breath, it was so beautiful. It was lopsided, as though rusty, yet it lightened his face, took ten years off his looks, displayed fine, even teeth and a dimple in his cheek . . . actually, it was more a slash than a dimple, but it had the same heart-stopping effect.

He looked more mischievous than she wanted him to look.

"Hit a sore spot, did I?" he asked.

She would have indulged him anything just then; smugness was the least of it. "Guess so."

"You feel your life has been taken over?"

"Yeah."

"Imagine what I feel."

She sobered. "I can't."

Derek, too, grew serious. His eyes held Sabrina's, held them and wouldn't leave. He saw so much in her, so much goodness, too much goodness. She said the right things at the right times with just the right inflections, and there was nothing programmed about any of it. He'd have known if there were. Her eyes betrayed her thoughts.

"I shouldn't have asked you to come," he muttered.

"Why not?"

"You don't belong here. You're too clean."

She thought of all the things she'd done wrong in her life, things she was still doing wrong. "I don't think so."

"Why not?"

"I did something awful this morning," she heard herself say. "I was getting dressed to leave New York, and Nicky was fussing. I'd already worked with him and fed him and bathed him and held him, but I had to put him down so I could do things for me. And he kept fussing." She took a quick breath, but the words weren't to be stopped. "The therapist wasn't due for a while, but I wanted to be on my way out the door when she came in the door. I don't know why Nicky was so cranky—then again, I suppose he wasn't any crankier than usual, its' just that I had other things on my mind. I was anxious to be gone, so I guess I was tense. He fussed and fussed. I thought I'd go out of my mind listening to that awful whine over and over and over again. I tried to coo and cajole, but nothing worked, so I lost my temper."

The radiator hissed its disapproval, but Derek showed none. "What did you do?" he asked.

"I spanked him."

"Every kid needs a good spank every once in a while."

"But Nicky's not 'every kid.' He can't help what he does. And I yelled at him. I yelled. I yelled that he was a selfish little brat and that I hated him."

Derek had thought himself pretty hardened when it came to other people's problems. He was surprised, then, when he felt her dismay. "And that hurt."

"Yes." She had her arms crossed, her hand kneading her arm in the same way he'd seen her do weeks before. She took a shaky breath. "So," she said, "I have my faults."

"I wouldn't call that a fault."

"Bellowing at a child who can't help himself?"

"You were venting your frustration. I'm sure Nicky grasped that."

"Are you kidding? Nicky doesn't grasp a thing!"

"Then he didn't grasp the spanking, and he certainly didn't understand the words you said."

That gave Sabrina a moment's pause and Derek a moment's gratification. She was thinking that he had a point, though she still felt like a heel for what she'd done. He was thinking that he liked it when she got a little upset, because he could calm her down. It gave him a semblance of control, something he hadn't felt much of lately.

He decided to goad her a little more. "Does your husband know you've come?"

"No. That's another of my faults. I can get around it by saying that he's away."

"Is he?"

"Yes."

"He was away last time, too. Did you tell him you'd come then?"

"No."

"Why not?"

"He wouldn't understand. Besides, he was upset enough that I'd left Nicky for so long. I didn't see the point in compounding the error."

"Do you always have to wait until he's gone to sneak off?"

"He's gone more often than not, so it's not a question of sneaking."

"Business must be good."

"Either that, or he's got a hot mistress on the side." She shot the ceiling a helpless look. "I can't believe I said that.

It must be the warm air in here." She was feeling a little
light-headed. It had to be the air.

"Are you uncomfortable?"

"In the heat? A little."

"In this prison."

"A little."

"That's honest."

"I try," she said, but she was puzzled. She did feel that
she could be honest with Derek, which was why she was
blurting out the little things that she'd otherwise have kept
to herself. But she didn't understand it. For one thing,
she'd thought she was going to have to measure each word,
to sort out the acceptable from those that were offensive or
tactless, but she wasn't doing that. For another thing, there
were guards in the room, guards in the halls, bars and
fences and electronic surveillance, and still she felt free.

It had to have something to do with Derek, with the fact
that he was removed from the rest of society, that he had
pain just as she did, that on some very basic level she
trusted him.

As she stood there looking up at him, she thought of
trust. She also thought about how tall he was and how
broad his shoulders. She'd dumped the incident with Nicky
on those shoulders, and they'd held it well. Somehow
she'd known they would.

Derek, who'd spent the last sixteen-and-a-half months
fighting for his life, would very happily have drowned in
her eyes just then. He didn't get the chance, though, because the moment was shattered by the crack of the door as
it slammed on its hinges. His head shot around. One of the
guards had taken off after a prisoner who'd left in a fury.

"What was that about?" Sabrina whispered, shaken.

Derek, too, was shaken. He thought he was used to the
sudden spurts of violence, but he was wrong. "Who
knows," he muttered, then cleared his throat and forced a
look around. "Uh, want to sit down?"

She nodded.

He led the way to a pair of chairs, let her choose one and
sit before following suit. This time he sat closer, facing her
with his chair turned only enough to allow for leg room.

And Sabrina didn't mind. She wanted the closeness. Derek was her buffer from the prison's darkest sides.

"Are you okay?" he asked, searching her face for the kind of momentary panic that he knew from experience could hit when the prison air closed in.

"Uh-huh."

"You look tired."

"I'm always tired."

He gave her a very slow, very thorough once-over in an attempt to lighten the mood. "But you do look springlike."

The once-over had been nice—not lecherous or suggestive but cognizant of her femininity. It wasn't often nowadays that Sabrina felt feminine. A shrew wasn't feminine. Nor was a diaper changer or a strained-beef feeder or a mini-limb exerciser. She liked feeling feminine. It relaxed her. It brought a flush to her cheeks and made her feel a little less tired and, yes, even a little springlike.

She plucked at her sweater. It was a cotton knit, white with splashes of pale blue and peach, and it fell low over a long, peach skirt. "Last time my sweater was mohair, and I thought I'd melt. This one's cooler." She tucked in her chin and studied the sweater. "By March I'm sick of winter. I need a pick-me-up. A new sweater does the trick every time." She cleared her throat. "That's another of my faults."

"What is?"

"Buying."

"You like to spend?"

She raised her eyes to his and announced, "No, not spend. Buy."

"But buying requires spending."

"But the spending is incidental to the buying, which is the part I enjoy. When I get upset, I buy. It's not boredom, because God knows I have enough to do when I'm free without running over to Third Avenue. And it's not to spite Nicholas, because I support the habit myself. And it's not because I *need* anything . . ." She didn't have to finish. "I pamper myself, I guess. I keep looking for a deep psychological meaning, but I can't find one. When I get upset, I buy."

Derek was thinking that if Nicholas Stone pampered her, she wouldn't have to pamper herself. He was thinking that Nicholas Stone was a fool, but it wasn't a new thought. "What do you buy?"

"Sweaters."

He waited for her to go on, arched both brows, even opened a palm in invitation. When she said nothing more, he coaxed, "That's all? Just sweaters?"

"That's enough."

"Have quite a collection, do you?"

"I've been upset a lot, lately."

He studied the sweater from hem to collar, making careful note of the curves along the way. "Nice," he murmured, then quickly raised his eyes. "The sweater . . . it's perky. And you're right about March. Manhattan always was pretty dreary this time of year."

"It hasn't changed." She paused, took a breath. "Do you think about it much?"

"Not when I can help it."

"Last time, you mentioned reading the paper. . . . No," she corrected herself, "you said you'd seen recent pictures of my husband, so I assumed you read the paper."

"I do."

"Does that bother you?"

"Like rubbing salt on the wound?"

She nodded.

"It bothers me, but it serves a purpose. Prison life is totally regulated. It's monotonous and boring. It's marking time, going nowhere, doing nothing."

He stopped speaking. His eyes clouded. Sabrina could see him begin to turn off his thoughts and tune out the world. But she didn't want him to do that.

"Go on," she coaxed.

He held her with a blank stare for the space of several breaths, before chasing off the cloudiness and resuming. "There are days when I feel like I'm suspended in time, like my mind is on hold. Reading the paper helps. It's frustrating to see the rest of the world pass me by, but at least I won't be emerging from a total vacuum when I'm released."

"When will that be? Three to seven isn't really three to seven, is it?"

"I'll be up for parole after serving two-thirds of the minimum."

"That's two years. Do they credit you with the time you spent awaiting trial?"

"Damn right."

"Then you could be out in eight months."

"Seven and a half."

"You think about it a lot," she said unnecessarily.

"I think about it a lot."

She let her own mind wander seven and a half months ahead and couldn't imagine what her life would be like then. She couldn't go on as she was now; she knew that. There was Nicky and Nick and the matter of her own identity . . . loose pieces that didn't fit into the puzzle, and until they did, she could only plod on.

"What do you want to do when you get out?" she asked, then sat helplessly by while his features hardened. The hardening took nothing from his handsomeness, but it distanced him from her.

"What I want to do is very different from what I will do."

"Start with what you want."

"I want to go back to doing what I did before."

"*Outside Insight* was canceled."

Abruptly he grinned, that same heart-stopping, half-mischievous grin that brought a dimplelike slash to his cheek, and this time she felt it full force. "Isn't that great?" he asked.

It was a minute before she could rebound enough to gather her wits. She was a yo-yo and Derek held the string; he tossed her away, then brought her close, tossed her away, brought her close. He set her off balance, but she didn't mind as long as he flashed that grin from time to time.

"I'm, uh, is it . . . great? If it's been canceled, it isn't there for you to go back to."

His grin persisted. "But do you know why it was canceled?"

His self-satisfaction was a dead giveaway. She said, "Ahhhh," and gave a sage nod.

"The ratings plummeted," he went on, savoring the explanation, however superfluous. "Mind you, I didn't get gobs of supporting mail when I was on trial, but after I was gone, something must have been missing from the show." The grin faded. His voice dropped, and though his words were innocent enough, his tone had an edge. "They stole hot shots from other shows, but it made no difference. The mix wasn't right anymore. It was poetic justice."

"What do you mean?"

He shrugged. "I was working on a story for the show when the shit hit the fan. It's kind of nice to know I wasn't the only one soiled."

"Your personal revenge?"

He looked off, pushed out his lips in contemplative fashion, wanted to say, "Not yet, baby, not yet," but didn't. Particularly in its planning stages, revenge was private and very, *very* personal.

Sabrina saw the look in his eye and wanted to get away from the topic of revenge as quickly as possible. It was dangerous and ugly and frightening. "Then what you meant," she said, "was that you want to return to investigative reporting."

"That's right."

"And the discrepancy between want and will?"

"Marketability."

It took her a minute to follow, and when she did she was skeptical. "No one will hire you? I don't believe that. You have the talent. You have the name. You obviously have the following, if what happened to *Outside Insight* accounts for anything. Fame, notoriety—both work in the field of entertainment."

"I killed a man, Sabrina," he said tightly.

She didn't blink. "I know."

"It may not bother you, but it sure as hell may bother Ms. and Mr. Middle America out there."

"I was under the impression that your audience was a little more savvy than the average."

"Some, not all; and besides, before I get to the audience,

I have to pass through the producers and the network. If they think that potential sponsors will shy away from a murderer, I'm sunk."

"But you acted in self-defense."

"I was *convicted*." He could feel the agitation growing, as it always did, at the injustice of it. The day-to-day hell of prison life was controllable through carefully constructed defenses and mind-numbing techniques; the mental anguish wasn't. The agony he'd felt when the jury's verdict had been returned had long since become a visceral thing. Frustration spread through every muscle in his body like a noxious gas, making him wire-tight and clammy. If he'd been in his cell, he'd have dropped to the floor and done push-ups to oblivion. Now, though, all he could do was to tap his foot, clench his jaw and say, "I was found *guilty*."

"A jury doesn't have the final say. Not in this day and age."

"Sabrina, I'm *doing time*! How much *more final* a say—"

"McGill!" came a sharp bark from one of the nearby guards. Derek whipped his head around in time to see the guard arch a brow and aim a rigid thumb toward the door.

"It's cool," he said, holding up both hands. "I'm cool." With carefully measured movements that belied the pounding in his chest, he turned back to Sabrina.

She was staring at his neck.

Her fingers flexed, then left her lap.

Derek was caught in a cross fire. He wanted her touch. He wanted, no, needed, no, was *desperate* for something soft and warm and caring. But he was tainted. His skin was infused with prison air and prison grime, and if she touched him, she'd feel it and be repulsed.

Indecision held him immobile for seconds too long—or perhaps it wasn't indecision at all, but the reverse. He'd be touched. He'd see what she felt.

Feather-light, her fingers probed the ridged scar. "This is new," she said with unnatural calm. "What happened?"

Her fingers remained on his skin. Not repulsion. Oh God. In the space of a blink, he tuned out the guard and his threat, the jury and its verdict, the future and its haze. He concentrated on those small spots of heat where Sabrina's fingers gently touched his skin.

He didn't want to move, didn't want to rock the boat, scare her away, unintentionally dislodge her fingers, lose her touch for any reason. Breathing as shallowly as possible, he said, "I was cut."

She gave him a do-tell look, then whispered, "How?"

"A razor."

"If you're going to tell me you were shaving—"

"Actually," he murmured back, still barely moving, barely breathing, "one of the other guys was shaving. Two of them started to fight. I got in the middle."

The words echoed in his mind, reverberating in and around other words spoken years before and worlds away. He was ten. He was trying to worm his way out of a beating. His mother had him by the scruff of the neck and was shaking him . . .

But it wasn't his mother's hand on his neck. It was Sabrina's, and the only shaking going on was something akin to a tremor deep in his belly.

She moved her palm to cover the scar, letting her fingers curve gently around the back of his neck. His muscles were drawn tight, but his skin was warm. Her forefinger tangled readily with the hair that fell over his nape. "If it had been a little more to the front—"

"I know," he bit off.

"Why can't they protect you?"

"They can't be everywhere at once. They can't see everything. Anyway, it was my fault. If I'd kept to myself—"

"And this one?" she asked in the same whisper. She splayed her fingers so that her thumb grazed the scar by his eye.

He swallowed hard. "A small price for preserving my chastity."

"Oh God." Her eyes enlarged, filled with the same kind of horrible images he still saw too often himself.

He hadn't wanted to taint her, but he was doing it. Her

hands wouldn't show the stain, but it would linger in her mind like black ink spattered on fine white silk.

Forgetting everything but the need to undo the damage, he covered her hand, pressed it to his neck. "It's okay, Sabrina. It's okay. A scar isn't so bad."

"But you could have been——"

"I wasn't." He smiled crookedly. "Got into a humdinger of a fight, though. You should've seen the other guys when I was done."

"Guys plural?" She choked out another, "Oh God," more high-pitched this time.

"Hey, it's okay. I got all of them—a punch here, a kick there. Bam, wop, splat—I was a regular Batman and Robin rolled into one."

Her whisper jumped an octave. "How can you joke about it?"

"It's either that or go crazy." He lowered her hand, but he wasn't letting go. Instead, he propped his elbows on his thighs and held her hand between his knees. He liked the feel of her skin, which was smooth, and the feel of her bones, which were delicate, and the feel of her fingernails, which were neatly trimmed, wore a coat of clear polish and looked eminently feminine.

"When did it happen?" she asked.

"A long time ago."

She tightened her fingers around his. "When?"

"Three weeks after the trial."

"You were in another prison then."

He nodded. "Maximum security. Ironic, isn't it?"

"It's disgusting!" she said in an angry whisper, then forced herself to take a calming breath. "I don't understand why you were there in the first place."

"Classification. It's routine."

Her gaze fell to where their hands were joined. His fingers were as long and strong as the rest of him, and they retained a gentleness while his voice had grown harder. "What happens during classification?"

He slid his thumb up and down her forefinger and found a small, lightly scabbed nick. "Paper cut?"

"No, I misjudged a diaper pin. What does classification entail?"

The scab was a point of reference on her hand; he traced it again, then again. "Intelligence tests, psychological evaluation, medical workup, analysis of the record—crime, sentence, criminal history, aptitude for violence. They decide where to send you based on the results."

"So you were transferred after that. Was it very different there from here?"

"In some ways."

When he didn't go on, she squeezed his fingers. "What ways?"

"You don't want to hear."

"If you don't tell me, I'll imagine."

He stared stonily at the faint pencil pad on her middle finger. "You really don't want to hear."

"I'll imagine the worst."

"Why should you imagine anything?" he asked. "You have enough grief of your own. You don't need mine."

"I'm tired of my grief. Give me a diversion."

He grew very still. His eyes were focused on the meeting of their hands. His hair tumbled over his forehead. The wind kiss on his cheeks had long since faded, leaving the shadow of his beard darker than ever against his prison pallor.

Though he'd argued that she didn't want to hear, there was more. He didn't know if he wanted to tell her about what it had been like in maximum. Prison was little more than an animal cage, and he was one of the animals. It was degrading.

He ran his thumb over the ridge of her knuckles, then slowly dropped her hand, straightened and said the only thing he could think of to avoid the discussion she wanted. "I don't think I like being a diversion."

Sabrina's hand felt naked. She buried it in her lap, curling her fingers under the low ribbing of her sweater. "A few minutes ago, you told me that you asked me to come because my being here would get you out of work. Did I get offended?"

"No."

"Well, you have no right to get offended now."

"I take whatever rights I can get, because there aren't a helluva lot that come my way."

"I'll rephrase that, then. You *shouldn't* have been offended, because I didn't mean it derogatorily. A diversion can be good and positive. I meant it that way. You give me something else to think about."

Taken in its broadest sense, the statement was revealing. Derek's eyes reflected the revelation, but he said nothing.

Sabrina wondered if she'd overstepped her bounds. She knew that she was being a little foolish, a little shortsighted and more than a little unfair to Derek. To cover up her faults, she raced on with perhaps a little more spirit than she normally would have. "Lately, my whole world revolves around Nicky. I've become a very boring, one-dimensional character. You're not the only one who feels penned in, you know. Maybe it's a matter of misery liking company."

"Your pen has doors. You can walk out anytime you want."

"Spoken like a man who has never been a mother."

He had no proper retort for that and could only offer a begrudging, "True."

"And it's also true that you relax more when I talk about Nicky. I've seen it, Derek. Six weeks ago . . . today . . . you listen to my problems, and for a few minutes you forget about your own. Mine are a diversion for you. Why shouldn't yours be a diversion for me?"

"Maybe because I don't want to talk about them."

"Oh." It was her turn to sit straighter in the chair. "Okay." She looked at him, then looked away. The coldness was back, and she didn't want to see it. He was the felon again. The convict. The murderer. His features were granite-hard, his expression nearly as steely as the bars through which she'd passed to see him.

The silence between them lengthened. She thought about cold steel. Did convicts bring it in with them, or was it something they caught from the bars, inhaled like asbestos, poisoning the system?

Movement caught her eye, but it wasn't Derek's. He was

sitting in his chair, offering her a hard-carved profile as he glared at the window, looking for all the world as though Michelangelo had told him not to breathe. The movement was from one of the other visitors who was leaving. Sabrina wondered if she should do the same. If Derek didn't want to talk, if he was tired of her chatter, if he'd suddenly decided that his Thursday afternoon work detail was preferable to her company after all . . .

"The difference between maximum and medium security," he began coolly, "is one of degree. The bars are thicker, the locks louder, the body counts more frequent, the privileges more sparse. If this were a maximum security prison, we'd be separated right now by a wall of thick wire mesh."

Sabrina wasn't sure why he had changed his mind about talking, but she felt as though she'd been given a reprieve. She wasn't ready to leave yet. "The atmosphere must be much more oppressive, then."

He took his time answering, finally saying, "Yes and no."

She waited. When he didn't elaborate, she said, "Start with yes."

Derek worked the muscle in his cheek as he stared at her. He wanted to talk, but he didn't. He wanted to share, but he didn't. His toe tapped the floor, beating the rhythm of energy crying for release.

"There are the obvious reasons why maximum is more oppressive," he began tightly. "Less freedom. Less choice. Every hour is programmed. Body counts are more intrusive. Visiting is more restricted. Privileges are fewer and farther between."

He barely paused for a breath. Pandora's box had been opened; the evils were spilling out. Sabrina was convinced that the airing was healthy, still, she couldn't help but feel that there was something of a defiant *You wanted to hear, lady—well, hear*! in his presentation.

"In maximum, the nature of the beast is different. Inmates there have been in the system longer. Often they've committed more serious crimes. More violent ones. The average sentence is longer. Hopelessness, despair—

they're greater, if that's possible." His eyes grew distant. Whether he'd planned it or not, he was slipping away, down the black tunnel that had shaped his experiences for the past months. "There's no trust. Terror moves freely, back and forth between the bars. The inmates fear each other; the guards fear the inmates. It's something you can almost smell and taste and feel. Like hatred." His Adam's apple moved. "Like bigotry. Or suppressed violence."

Sabrina could see it all on his face. His eyes were dark as pitch beneath low-lying brows. A fine sheen of sweat covered his skin, like an ill that had emerged from inside him with the spilling of his words. Tension rode the bridge of his nose. His nostrils flared with each breath. His lips curled in disgust.

He was there. He was in it. He lived the fear and the hatred, the bigotry and the violence, suppressed or otherwise, because he had no choice. He was in a terrifying world, and because he had to go along to survive, he was one of them. A stranger.

Sabrina didn't want that. She knew the Derek he'd been before, the one who was calm, creative, capable of compassion. She believed that he still existed, even if he was momentarily overshadowed. So she pushed on. "And no?"

He blinked. His shoulder twitched. He drew himself back, clearly confused.

"The second half of the yes and no," she explained gently. "In what ways is the atmosphere here as bad?"

He gnawed on the inside of his cheek until he'd found himself. "Psychologically. The sense of helplessness and dependency and emasculation. It's there wherever you turn. Maximum . . . medium . . . doesn't matter."

"I'd think," she said, "that those things might be worse for you than for some other men."

His dark eyes asked, "How so?"

"The contrast, one life to another. I don't picture you as ever having been helpless. To suddenly be that way—"

"Is infuriating. But is my fury any less than that of the man who has always been helpless and is now even more so? Take the guy who's in for armed robbery. It's his third conviction. Why does he keep robbing banks? He's out of a job, out of cash, he feels helpless, so he dreams. He robs banks to make those dreams come true. He robs banks with a *gun* in his hand for the sense of power it gives him. Then he ends up in here, where he's even more helpless than he was before. He turns on the TV in the rec room or picks up a paper and sees how the rich and famous live. And you think that he doesn't feel fury?

"Or the kid who steals cars. Again and again he steals cars. Why? So he can tool down the road totally free, on his own, independent, the big man and his powerful machine. He's picked up by the police for running a Stop sign. Twenty-two years old and it's his fourth conviction, so he winds up here. Bye-bye freedom. Bye-bye independence. Bye-bye macho man."

He'd been working himself into a pious rage, but the air suddenly left his balloon. He slumped back in his seat, crossed his arms over his chest and scowled at the floor. Then he touched Sabrina with his scowl en route to anchoring it on the window.

She gave him a minute. When he didn't budge, she asked, "No more talking?"

He shook his head.

"You have a lot to say. If you could write it down—"

He shook his head.

"Why not?"

"I can't write squat."

She pursed her lips and nodded. "Uh-huh. Sure. The illiterate investigative reporter."

"Not illiterate. I can read."

"But not write. Uh-huh."

"It's true. I had the ideas. I did the interviews. I could stand in front of a camera and talk for an hour, but I couldn't write it down."

"Are you dyslexic?"

He let out an impatient breath. "No, I am not dyslexic."

"Do you have some other kind of learning disability?"

"No, Sabrina."

"Then why can't you write? It doesn't make sense. If you have the ideas, all you have to do is pick up a paper and pencil, or sit down at a typewriter and go to it."

He drew his scowl from the hapless window and bestowed it on her directly. "Life isn't laid out in blacks and whites. It isn't tied up in neat little packages with the contents listed on the front. How in the hell do I know why I can't write? Do you know what's wrong with your son?"

It was a cheap shot. He regretted it the instant it left his mouth, when he saw her crumble. Swearing softly, he came forward, bracing his elbows on his thighs and his forehead on the heels of his hands. Head bowed like that, he could be very close without meeting her eyes. "I'm sorry, Sabrina. But you push me. I'm a little tense."

She wanted to touch him, wanted to stroke his hair and tell him that it was all right, that he could be tense with her and that she wouldn't mind as long as he didn't go all dark and brooding and angry. But she was afraid to touch. Touching him was dangerous. Last time she hadn't wanted to let go.

"I suppose," he said, still without looking at her, "that I don't have the patience to write. I could never sit still long enough when I was a kid, and I get a bad taste in my mouth when I remember the measures taken to make me do it. I have patience for most other things. Just not writing. So I talked my thoughts to my assistants, who wrote them down and polished them up." He darted her a quick glance around his hand. "I can't write about this place."

"Can I do it?"

He dropped his hand from his head and steepled his fingers between his knees. "If you want to write about bank robbers and car thieves, be my guest."

She came forward to meet him. "I want to write about you."

He shook his head.

"Why not?"

"Because I say not."

"But why?" she asked, then argued softly, "The same people who watched you week after week would read your story in a minute. They identified with you. They'd want to read about the things you've seen and experienced."

"That's sick."

"Come on, Derek. If you were back on *Outside Insight*

and someone else were here in your place, you'd do a story on him."

"That's different."

"How so?"

"This is me."

"Do as I say, don't do as I do?"

"Something like that."

"It'd make a great book."

"Sorry."

"It'd be an outlet. You could tell your side of the story. It's done all the time. Colson did it, Dean did it—"

"I'm not Colson or Dean," Derek snarled under his breath. "They knew exactly what they were doing when they did it, and they deserved what they got. The crime was compounded when they cashed in. Books, the lecture circuit—they squeezed by before the Son of Sam law took effect. I don't want or need the money—"

"Neither do I. But think of the satisfaction you'd get—"

"No."

"It'd give you something to help pass the time."

"I don't need anything to help pass the time. I still have a whole wall of holes to count."

"Holes?"

"Where the guy before me threw his dart. One wall has six hundred and eighty-seven holes, the other has eight hundred and ninety-eight. Just think of the wrist action involved."

"I'm riveted," she said with a dry twist of her lips, but in the next breath the twist was gone and her tone grew urgent. "I could do it, Derek. I could write your story and do it tastefully. Biography is my field."

"You don't have the time to write."

"I know."

"Then why did you suggest it?"

"Because it feels right."

"But if you don't have the time—"

"I'll find it!"

Their heads were close, shoulders almost touching. He inhaled the faint jasmine scent that wisped around her. She

had a wide-eyed look that held more than a hint of desperation. It was one of those times when he felt in control.

He took her hand, then spoke in a voice that was quiet,
even gentle. "When I talked with you at your place that
time, you said that you don't write because you don't have
the psychic energy left after dealing with Nicky all day.
Has that changed?"

"No. But it has to soon."

He studied her face. "You're going to Vermont from
here?"

She nodded.

"Is it the place for Nicky?"

"I think so. I'm meeting the director for dinner. I'll talk
with more of the other personnel tomorrow."

"Shouldn't your husband be there?"

She gave a short, high, sad laugh. "Yes."

"But he won't go. He can't face it."

"No."

"He's a schmuck."

She tipped her head and shrugged, but she wasn't feeling
at all nonchalant about the facts. Suddenly she felt very
close to tears. "I have to go," she whispered.

"I know," he whispered back.

"I wish I could stay longer—"

He put a finger to her lips. "Shhhh." The finger moved,
so lightly that at first she thought she'd imagined it. Upper
lip . . . gentle arch . . . tiny dip . . . lower lip . . . a slow circle, setting sparks along the way. Again it went round. Her
lips softened, parted on a short breath, and she wasn't
imagining any of it. The sparks turned inward, spiraling in
similar slow circles through her chest. This time the breath
she took shuddered.

"I want to kiss you so bad I can taste it," he whispered.
His eyes were coal-black, but the coal smouldered, spread-
ing faintly glowing embers to his cheeks.

"Don't," she gasped. She curled her fingers around his
wrist but didn't pull his hand away. She just held on, held
on.

"I want to."

"But I'm married."

He brought his other hand to her face and watched his fingertips trace her eyebrows, then her cheekbones. "Married people kiss people other than their mates."

"Not the way you'd kiss me," she whispered half-dazed, then rushed on in the same breath. "I have to leave."

"You'll come again."

"I don't know."

He held her face. "Soon."

"I don't know."

His thumbs inched over her cheeks, callused pads whispering. "You have to."

"It's not smart."

"Do it anyway."

"Derek, I can't think."

"Then listen," he commanded in a deep murmur that was hoarse and intimate enough to send tremors down her spine. He kept her face imprisoned, and his hands were the least of the chains. "We're going to stand up. I'm going to put my arms around you and give you a hug."

"No—"

"I need to feel you against me, even if it's just for a minute."

"Derek—"

But he was already rising, and her body went to his as though it had learned the way years before. His arms encircled her, then tightened when he felt her palms sliding up his back. He held her close, savoring her feel from head to toe.

A warm body. A heartbeat. For all his deficiencies, Nicky Stone did know a thing or two.

Derek heard the shallow intake of Sabrina's breath, the whimper that was muffled against his throat. He absorbed the rapid tattoo of her heart and the fine tremors that arced between them. He whispered her name, but it was lost in the thickness of her hair.

"Derek?"

"Don't talk."

"I'm frightened."

"Shhhhh."

"My life is such a mess."

"So's mine. Can I kiss you?"

"No."

"I need your mouth, Sabrina."

She tucked her head lower, but that mouth he needed was parted, warm lips burrowing into the dark tufts of hair at his open collar. He felt hard, tasted hard, smelled of man—and she was beguiled.

"Will you come back next week?"

As she shook her head, her lips brushed over that V of flesh.

"The week after?"

"I don't know," came her muffled reply.

"I'll think about letting you write your book."

She went still, then raised her head. "You will?"

"I'll *think* about it. I won't make any promises."

Her heart was pounding. She was aware of every long inch of him, of the power that lay in wait beneath muscle, of the heat that could consume in a minute. She was a married woman. She had a sick child on her hands. She should turn and run and never look back.

"Three weeks from today," she whispered. "I'll try." Then she freed herself from his arms and beat a hasty retreat.

· CHAPTER 5 ·

Three weeks from that day was the twentieth of April, and Sabrina spent the twentieth of April at the hospital. Nicky had gone into convulsions the night before. Once the doctors had set to work, he quickly stabilized, but finding the cause of the seizure was slow.

Sabrina wasn't able to reach Nick, who was in Dallas. She tried repeatedly through the course of the night, but if he was at his hotel, he was neither answering the phone nor receiving the urgent messages she left.

She was furious. It wasn't that he could be doing anything more than she'd already done if he were in New York: Nicky was at the best of hospitals with the best of doctors. But sharing the worry would have helped. She could have used some emotional support through the long hours of waiting. Nick had let her down again.

Dawn found her curled in a chair in Nicky's room. The child was sedated. Wires radiated outward from various points on his tiny body, offering a steady readout of his condition. Sabrina felt as though she were monitoring it herself. She was exhausted, but her eyes wouldn't close. They clung heavily to the shape of her son, leaving him only periodically to glance at one or another of the machines.

Her mind churned. She thought frightening thoughts, frustrated thoughts, discouraging thoughts, dismaying thoughts. Her emotions ran the gamut, leaving her stretched to the limit.

Just when she thought she would snap, memory of Derek came from the corner of her mind where she'd stashed it, and her tension eased a bit. He'd held her with such strength. She wanted that strength now, oh Lord, she did. She wanted a hand to hold or an arm around her shoulder. She wanted someone to lean on, to talk to, someone to see her pain and understand it, someone to assure her that no matter how hopeless things seemed, they'd get better.

Wrapping her own arms around her middle wasn't the same, but it was better than nothing. She shifted her weight from one hip to the other, tucked her stockinged feet beneath her and let her head loll against the winged back of the chair. She focused on Nicky's small chest as it rose and fell, rose and fell with the typically quickened cadence of a child and with such regularity that she wanted to scream. That everything should look so right but be so wrong was cruel!

From time to time she glanced at her watch, shifted position, glanced at her watch again. Shortly after nine, when the clatter of the breakfast trays that had never been brought to her intravenously fed son were a memory, she left the room. Wedging herself into a corner of the phone booth down the hall, she called Parkersville. She fully expected that she wouldn't be allowed to talk with Derek, and that was the case, but she conveyed her message and was told that he would receive it.

"Please. It's critical. He's expecting me to be there this afternoon and I can't make it."

"He'll get the message," said the male voice at the other end of the line, but it sounded terribly uninterested to Sabrina.

"Soon? Will he get it soon?" She could envision one of the guards sauntering toward Derek in a day or two or three with a crumpled piece of paper in his hand. It bothered her to imagine him thinking, for even a minute, that she'd lost courage or given up on him or just plain forgotten.

"He'll get it."

"It's *very* important—"

"Ma'am, he'll get it."

Hearing annoyance in that voice, she decided not to push her luck. Very quickly, she repeated her message, then hung up the phone and returned to Nicky's room.

Nurses came and went. Doctors stopped by, new ones with the new day to ask the same old questions. When had the seizure occurred? Had Nicky ever had one before? What had she done with him that day, where had she taken him, what had she given him to eat? With each repetition of the story, her guilt grew. She fought the feeling, but her defenses were down. Nicky's seizure was somehow her fault; she'd done something wrong; she'd failed him again.

By late afternoon, she was beginning to feel as though she should be the one hooked up to wires on the bed, not Nicky. When the image of J. B. Monroe materialized before her, she wondered if she'd truly lost it.

J. B. was the last person she expected to see. He might have been the last person she would have *wanted* to see if the circumstances had been different; but when he walked through the door of Nicky's room shortly before six, she wasn't about to argue. She needed someone, and if her brother was the only one there, he'd have to do.

At thirty-eight, J. B. looked like the California dreamer who'd never grown up. His hair was long and blond, his skin tanned. The round, metal-rimmed glasses that sat on his nose gave him the air of an aesthete, which his distracted expressions did nothing to deny. He wore his clothes as loosely as possible, as though anything beyond shorts—in this case a shapeless blazer, baggy shirt and pants and canvas shoes—were offensive to the flesh. He could pull it off and look chic largely because of his lanky frame and his height, which was well over six feet and had been inherited from his father. From his mother he'd inherited the aquiline features that made him a frightfully handsome cad.

There was no mystery as to how he'd come by his writing skill. His oddness was another matter. Amanda and Gebhart were alternately thought to be unusual, unconventional and eccentric. No one had ever called them odd. Everyone called J. B. odd. He had the personality of a toad.

Hands tucked in his pockets, he came to a halt beside Nicky's bed. His gaze rode above it to the corner of the room in which Sabrina sat, and he chucked his chin her way.

She would have run to him had he been the type, but for all his laid-back beauty, J. B. wasn't a toucher. Sabrina knew that he'd kissed his wife on their wedding day because she'd seen it with her own eyes. She couldn't recall, though, ever seeing a repetition of it or a hug for either Jenny *or* his daughters. Likewise, as a brother he had never been physically demonstrative.

So she sighed his name, then asked, "How did you know?"

"The maid." He turned his attention to his sleeping nephew and stared emotionlessly for what seemed forever. He was still staring at the child when he said, "I flew in with a manuscript. Thought we'd celebrate."

"Oh J. B."

"My timing sucks."

"Yeah."

He crinkled up his nose, but only in an attempt to boost his glasses higher. No sooner had his features settled back into place when he tuned out. His expression went blank. He didn't move. He studied Nicky in a deep and profound silence.

Eventually he returned to the world with a quick breath and said, "He looks like Mom."

"And you."

He thought about that for a long minute that ran into three, finally nodding. After another minute he said, "Convulsions? The kid's a walking disaster."

"He doesn't walk."

J. B.'s shrug said, "Same difference." After a time, his voice added, "So, what is it now?"

The invitation was all Sabrina needed. She'd had no one to talk with during the long hours, and she desperately needed to share the grief. "They suspect he has a mild form of epilepsy. Can you believe it, J. B.?" She hugged her knees to her chest, letting the covering of her long skirt compensate for the propriety the pose lacked. "Since last night I've been praying that they'd find something concrete—maybe a brain tumor. I know that sounds awful, but at least it would be something solid and treatable and maybe it would explain Nicky's slowness." She took in a breath that was audibly shaky. "Epilepsy . . . epilepsy takes us nowhere but downhill."

J. B.'s attention had shifted to the machine closest to him. Most people would have looked at the dials and buttons and digital display. Not J. B. Hands still in his pockets, he was leaning this way and that, studying the sides and undersides of the machine. "Epilepsy?"

"They've ruled out most everything else."

He straightened and looked at her again, this time in the same way he'd been studying Nicky, with a vacancy that was somehow intense. The look was frightening; it gave most people the willies. But Sabrina was used to it. She knew enough to let him stare to his heart's content, while she looked wherever she felt like looking, which at the moment was at her son.

Nicky did resemble his uncle. The child's hair was more brown, but the nose and mouth were the same. And the unfocused eyes. J. B.'s eyes were often unfocused. For a while Sabrina had wondered if her son's dazed looks and reluctance to speak were nothing more than a baby version of J. B. Monroe's oddness. The thought hadn't thrilled her, but the alternative was worse, and she'd been grasping for straws.

J. B.'s voice cut into her thoughts. "Where's Nick?"

She batted the air in disgust.

"He's an asshole," was J. B.'s verdict.

"He's doing business."

"He should be here."

"Try telling him that, if you can reach him. I can't."

"Then he doesn't even know Nicky's hospitalized?"

"Nope." She dared meet J. B.'s gaze, wondering what she'd see, but there was only that same concentrated void. For the first time in her life, she found it an odd comfort. She wasn't in the mood to be judged.

Without fully emerging from the void, he said, "I want coffee," and invited her along with the toss of his head toward the door.

"Uh, I don't know . . . maybe I should stay."

"Sabrina, the kid's out of it."

"He may wake up."

"If he does, one look at you will scare the shit out of him."

She shot him a dry glance. "Thanks."

He repeated the gestured invitation.

A short time later they sat facing each other at a small table in the hospital cafeteria. To Sabrina's surprise, J. B., who normally carried plastic instead of cash, not only had cash—which was all the cafeteria accepted—but had insisted on buying her dinner. Actually, he'd bullied her into it by telling her that she looked like death warmed over, and he'd put the corned-beef-and-cabbage plate on her tray before she could escape.

"I hate corned beef," she said with utter calm. "You know that, J. B. I've hated it since I was five."

He transferred the corned beef to his own tray and helped her to some meat loaf.

"J. B. . . ." she warned. Meat loaf came second only to corned beef on her list of dislikes, and J. B. knew that, too. He was being perverse. When he exchanged the meat loaf for the stuffed chicken breast she might have otherwise enjoyed, she didn't bother to tell him that she wasn't terribly hungry. She didn't have the strength.

Now, though, he was perversely urging her to eat. She cut a piece of chicken and pushed it around her plate, but she was far more interested in the coffee, which was all she'd really wanted. Her stomach was upset. She just needed something to keep her awake.

J. B. ate with his typically absent attention, concentrating on his food as though it were anything but food and he were anywhere but there. Sabrina did manage to eat a little, but she was on her second cup of coffee before her brother returned from wherever his mind had been.

"Tell me about Nick," he said.

Nick was the last person she wanted to discuss, but since J. B. had sprung for dinner, she felt she owed him one. Setting down her cup, she tipped up her chin and said, "What would you like to know?"

"Why did you marry him?"

Her chin dropped right back down. She'd expected something neutral, something to do with business. "What kind of question is that?"

He was staring at her again, distractedly dissecting her through the lenses of his glasses. "Did you love him?"

A tiny frown crossed her brow. "Yes."

"Do you still?"

She opened her mouth, then closed it without saying a word.

"He's never here. Are you separated?"

"Come on, J. B.—"

"Are you?"

"Of course not."

"But the marriage stinks."

"Who said that?"

"No one had to. I've been there."

"J. B., your marriage was different from mine from day one."

"Maybe. But still I can see it. You're angry, and it's not the kind of anger that'll go away. Nick isn't here when he should be, and you're angry."

She shook her head. "I'm too tired to be angry."

"You're still angry. And you have a right. You had certain expectations when you married him. He was your Prince Charming. He wooed you in high style. He did all the traditional little things that Mom and Dad called corny. He was steady and dependable and devoted. I thought it would last, Sabrina. I really did. I thought you'd *make* it last. You managed for eight years—"

"Not eight," she said, abandoning all pretense of denial. Her brother had seen through it anyway, and there was something about the way he was speaking—the insightful, rational, personal way he was speaking—that was uncharacteristic enough to demand a straightforward and honest return. "Not eight. Five."

J. B. lapsed into a prolonged and pensive silence. He separated the saltshaker from the pepper and sugar, turned it one way and then the other, studied its contents, scrutinized the tiny holes on top. Then he crinkled his nose to hike up his glasses and said, "It's not Nicky's fault."

"What isn't?"

"Your marital problems."

"I know."

"When alien spirits intrude—"

"Oh no." Sabrina bowed her head. She knew it; he'd been too eloquent when he'd been talking of Nick. J. B. was only eloquent when he was weaving a tale, or about to. "Please, J. B."

"Please, what?"

"Don't start. We've been through this so many times before. I can't take it now."

"But my theory hasn't been disproved."

"Just because the doctors can't put their finger on the specific cause of Nicky's brain damage doesn't mean that he's been taken over by foreign spirits."

"But the possibility is intriguing, Sabrina. What if—"

"Not now," she pleaded.

J. B. had pale green eyes like hers. Unlike hers, his had an iridescent quality that was visible only at certain times and was nearly as eerie as the stories he wrote. Sabrina saw the iridescent quality just then and knew that, short of getting up and walking away, she was in for an earful. She chose the earful because, faults and all, J. B. was her brother and she needed to be with someone close. And, anyway, she was too tired to move.

"What if," J. B. began, using his lean fingers to frame the scenario, "we go on the theory that Nicky was taken over at birth by a spirit that entered his body through the incubator hose. Just suppose that this spirit is of superior intelligence. It's been grooming Nicky for the past three years and will probably keep it up awhile longer, until the indoctrination is complete."

"No spirit of superior intelligence is going to adopt a kid whose body doesn't work. Try again."

"Why do you think Nicky's body doesn't work?" he asked smugly. "The spirit is concentrating on his mind while his body lies lax. His body *has* to lie lax for the spirit to do its thing. For all we know, Nicky is incredibly brilliant already. The development of his brain may be far beyond anything we can comprehend. He may be lying there looking at us, seeing so much more than we could ever see. He may be feeling sorry for us because of our limitations."

"It's a lovely thought," Sabrina said. "I'd have no objections to having a genius for a son. But what's the punch line? What happens when his body suddenly comes to life? Will he start killing off all of us inferior souls?"

J. B. shook his head. "This spirit is peaceful. Its purpose is colonization."

"Is it an alien spirit, as in coming from outer space?"

Another headshake. "The only thing alien is its form and level of intelligence."

"But where did it come from?"

"The center of the earth."

Sabrina rolled her eyes. "Come on, J. B. You can do

better than that. Hasn't the center of the earth been done before?"

"Not like this. We're talking germs that have existed since the planet was first formed, germs that have incubated in the heat of the earth's core all this time and only now are ready to emerge. Nicky isn't the only one whose body has been taken over; there are others like him. We think them to be retarded or autistic or comatose, but one day they'll band together and form an incredibly advanced society."

"How will they know each other?"

He eyed her impatiently. "Their brain waves will mesh. They're *brilliant*, Sabrina. Mental telepathy is just one of their talents."

"I see," she said, then asked, "Is there a happy ending to Nicky's story, at least?"

"I don't know," J. B. answered, sounding not at all upset. Every one of his books involved some sort of violent or near-violent conflict. He clearly loved the fray. "At some point, the human race as we know it will begin to feel threatened and try to control the core force. If it comes down to an out-and-out conflict, we won't stand much of a chance."

"I guess I'd better try to stay on Nicky's good side, then."

"I would."

For a long time they regarded each other in silence. Sabrina was thinking that, iridescent eyes and all, there was something sad about her brother. As well-known as he was, he had no close circle of friends. With his habit of tuning in and out and his proclivity for silence, he was hard to get to know. His fascination with the macabre made him hard to like. He had women, but there was no pattern to his tastes. Socially, he was pretty much on the outside looking in.

"There are times," Sabrina said—as she'd wanted to say for years but hadn't had the nerve, "when I don't know how seriously to take you, J. B."

"You're not the only one."

"Do you take your*self* seriously?"

"Not usually," he said, but he was as serious as she'd ever seen him.

"J. B.?"

He answered her with a somber stare.

"I don't know what to do about Nick."

"Divorce him."

A small involuntary sound came from her throat.

"You don't need him, Sabrina."

"I can't divorce him."

"Why not?"

"So many reasons. . . . I can't begin to explain. . . . I feel very confused."

"You deserve better."

Through the muddle of her mind, Sabrina registered the compliment. It was the first she could remember ever receiving from her brother. Ironically, it made her more vulnerable, thereby adding to her confusion.

"There's Nicky. I can't handle him on my own."

"You've been doing it all along."

"But there are decisions to be made. If he has to be put in an institution—"

J. B. interrupted her with an oath that effectively expressed his disapproval. She jumped to her own defense.

"I have to. He's not getting better. And now he's prone to seizures. I don't think I can do it all much longer."

"Get day help."

"I can't. At least, not enough."

"Then settle for less."

"I *can't.*"

"Don't do it, Sabrina. He's your son. Don't lock him up with a bunch of head-bangers and droolers."

Tears sprang to her eyes. "Don't say that."

"Don't do it."

"But he's one of them, J. B. Why can't you all see that?"

J. B. drifted off. His expression grew vague. Eyes on Sabrina, he dug at the Formica tabletop with his spoon. At length he set the spoon down and said, "Maybe because it's too painful. You're the realist. You try to see things as they are. I'd rather believe that he's in the hands of a spirit emerging from the earth's core and that he's on his way to bigger and better things."

Sabrina was momentarily without a retort. She'd never heard J. B. talk of himself that way. She'd never thought he understood himself that way. She'd been shortsighted.

It took a minute to compose herself. "Anyway," she said, "that's just one of the decisions to be made." She reached for her purse. "Excuse me a sec. I've got to try Nick again."

When she emerged from the phone booth a few minutes later, J. B. was leaning against a nearby wall. "Get him?"

She shook her head.

"You've been leaving messages for twenty-four hours and he hasn't answered a one?"

She sent him a pained look.

"Divorce him, Sabrina."

"I can't."

"Why not?"

"I need him."

"You don't."

"Nicky needs him."

J. B. didn't even bother to answer that one.

In frustration, she blurted out, "I'd be alone, J. B."

"So what?"

"That scares me. I went from home to college to marriage. I've never been alone in my life."

"No?" He asked, and lapsed into another one of his staring trances. Sabrina was about to scream when he did something that she didn't expect. He touched her. He closed his hand around her arm and started her walking down the hall beside him.

Nicholas called her that night after J. B. had brought her home. He made no apologies for his inaccessibility, simply asked her about Nicky, said he'd be home late the next day, then hung up.

Sabrina didn't take him to task as she might have. For one thing, she was too tired; she wanted to get off the phone and go to bed.

For another, she was unable to talk to Nick without

thinking about her talk with J. B., and when she did that, her mind clogged. She didn't know what to do. Her marriage was hanging by a thread. She had problems with Nick's behavior, his attitude, his style. But he was her husband.

And still . . . and still the one she really wanted to think about was Derek. He represented another life, another world; and in that sense, thinking of him was a relief. He was an escape—ironic, but true. Sick as it sounded, she found his problems refreshing. The thought that he might let her write his story after all excited her, and she was badly in need of a little excitement.

Nicky was awake the next day. The doctors wanted to keep him under observation for a non-sedated twenty-four-hour period before they sent him home. There was always the chance they'd see something they hadn't seen before— some tiny symptom, or the breath of a clue that could lead to an explanation for all the rest of his problems. An explanation could lead to treatment, treatment to a cure. Sabrina's battered hopes rose.

But in vain. Staff pediatricians, residents, interns, specialists, nurses—no one saw a thing. Nicky made up in crankiness what Sabrina had been spared the day before. She was more than a little cranky herself when she finally saw the child to sleep, took a taxi home and found Nick in the den with his feet on the coffee table and a neat whiskey in his hand.

"Welcome home," she said from the door.

Silent, he studied the ice in his glass.

"When did you get in?"

"Several hours ago."

Several hours ago? "I've been at the hospital. You might have joined me there."

"I had a lot to do here."

She stood very straight. She didn't speak. She clutched the strap of her bag hard and waited for him to explain himself. All he did was raise his glass and take a drink.

"The hospital, Nick. I've been at the hospital." Her

voice began to simmer with tension. "Your son is still at the hospital. Aren't you curious to know how he is?"

"I'm sure he's fine."

"He's not fine! He's epileptic!"

Without looking at her, Nick asked, "When will he be home?"

"Tomorrow."

"That's good."

"How so? Have you missed taking care of him? Or is it the hospital bill that bothers you?"

"Don't be flip."

Lips compressed, she sucked in a ragged breath. It hadn't taken much to snap what meager control she'd had. "Do you know what I've just been through, Nicholas?"

"You? I thought our son was the one—"

"Do you have any idea what it's like to walk into the bedroom at night and find your baby convulsing? Or to spend hour after hour watching him breathe along with the bleeps and hums of a dozen machines? Or to wait endlessly for the doctors to give you the results of their tests and then find that they have nothing good to say? No, you don't know. If you did, you'd allow me to be flip or anything *else* I chose to be!"

He took his eyes from his glass long enough to send her a look of disdain. "You're getting worked up."

"I think I have that right. Where were you, Nick? For twenty-four hours you were totally out of reach. I called the hotel. I called the office, your secretary, your vice-president. I called the hotel again. And again. I felt like a perfect fool. Where were you?"

A flick of his wrist sent the ice shimmering round in his glass. He was following the circles. "My clients unexpectedly asked me to their house."

"For twenty-four hours? And you never gave anyone else a thought during all that time? Didn't it occur to you to check in? You have a son whose health is iffy; what if something *really* critical had happened?"

"Nicky's fine."

"Okay, forget Nicky. Think about your dad. He's seventy-nine and has a heart condition. He has no wife, no siblings, no other children but you. What if something had happened to him? Or to *me*? What if I'd had a cerebral hemorrhage, or been hit by a taxi or something?"

Nick thought for a minute before speaking, and then his voice was measured. "If a message to that effect had been left, I'd have answered it."

She caught her breath. "Your son being sick wasn't enough?" She rubbed two fingers to her forehead and murmured more to herself than to him, "I don't believe it. You deliberately chose not to call me back."

"I knew you'd be on top of things. You thrive on dealing with doctors." His sarcasm was blatant.

"What does that mean?"

"You love it, Sabrina. You love running from one doctor, one specialist to the next." He must have found satisfaction in the drop of her jaw, because he went on in the same vein. "You drag Nicky to a new doctor at the slightest excuse."

"I don't—it's not—"

"And even if that weren't so, I knew you'd do fine. You're *used* to dealing with doctors."

"I'm used to dealing with them because someone had to and you're never around!"

He set down his glass and looked at her. "I'm never around because this place is depressing. If Nicky isn't fussing, you are. I'm tired of it, Sabrina. I've had about as much as I can take. I want out."

His words hung in the air, echoing, echoing. But it wasn't only his words. It was his look, his tone, his manner.

"E-excuse me?" she asked.

"You heard." He dropped his feet to the floor. "I want out. I came back here early and did as much packing as I could. I can get the rest another time."

Sabrina commanded herself to be calm, but she was shaken by the thunderous pounding of her heart. Knowing that she needed to sit down, she moved as smoothly as possible to the nearby armchair.

Nick was staring at her, but it was a totally different stare from J. B.'s. J. B.'s was harmless. Nick's was angry.

It was the antithesis of the loving husband's look and was hardened by the defensiveness that came only with guilt.

"It's over, Sabrina. There's nothing left. You said it yourself, only you didn't have the guts to say *fini*. Well, I'm doing it. I'm leaving."

"Just like that?"

"Just like that."

She tried to gather her thoughts, but she was shocked. Sure, she'd thought of divorce. Deep in her heart, she'd known that was where she and Nick were headed. But she'd expected a little more time to prepare. She'd expected that in the end she'd be the one to leave him, rather than vice-versa.

"Your timing is off," she said quietly.

"I should have done this months ago."

"I hadn't realized that living with me was that bad."

"It didn't used to be. We had some good times together. But those days ended when Nicky became your personal crusade. And it's living with what you've become that's so bad. I can't take the constant whining."

"Are you talking about Nicky or about me?"

"Both."

"You might have helped. If I'd had a little support—"

"Support *how*? I can't stay home from work to change diapers, and even if I could, I don't want to. If you'd had any brains yourself, you'd have gone back to writing after Nicky was born. Then you wouldn't have sat around analyzing every little thing he did or didn't do. You wouldn't have taken Dr. Spock as the be-all and end-all. You wouldn't have constantly compared Nicky to other kids."

"Wait a minute, Nick," she said shakily. "I was perfectly happy right after Nicky was born. If I recall correctly, we both agreed that I wouldn't do any work for the first six months so that I could devote myself solely to him. You wanted that as much as I did. And I didn't look for things to be wrong, as you suggest. But by the time Nicky was three months old, it was obvious that something *was* wrong and it got worse from there. Now, after three years, can you honestly, *honestly* look me in the eye and tell me that Nicky is normal?"

Nick looked her in the eye. "No."

"You admit it!"

He regarded her with disgust. "You should see yourself, Sabrina. Gloating over something like that!"

"Gloating? No, Nick. But if nothing else comes out of this horrid mess, your admission is something. Now that you admit Nicky has a problem, maybe you'll see about getting him—and us—the help we need."

"If you're thinking of counseling, it's too late. There's too much anger. And there's Nicky. He's alive. He's here. He's not going to go away."

"There are places for children like him—"

"I won't make that decision."

"For three years, I've tried," she raced on without hearing him. "I've tried everything—physical therapy, hydrotherapy, electrotherapy, reward-and-punishment, patterning—the list goes on and on. Nothing's worked. Nothing's going to work. And that's not my judgment; it's the judgment of many of the people who work with him. Nicky marks time, while I go backwards. There are good private places, Nick. I've been visiting one in Vermont that would give him the best possible care. The idea of putting him in an institution makes my stomach churn, but it's the only thing that makes sense."

Nick didn't even respond to her mention of visits to Vermont, which said something about his lack of emotional involvement with her daily life. "Maybe. Still, I won't make that decision."

She heard him this time and went very still. "What do you mean?"

"Nicky's yours. I'm leaving him with you. You'll be the one to make the decisions regarding his care."

She swallowed hard. "But he's your son."

"You'll have sole custody."

"That's not fair, Nick," she whispered, slowly shaking her head. "It's not fair to push that burden on me." When he simply shrugged and took another drink, she said, "You're a coward."

But he wasn't about to discuss it. "Money won't be an

issue. I'll give you what you need and I'll be generous. The divorce will be amicable."

Again, she was struck by the abruptness of it all. "Then, you want to go straight for the divorce? No trial separation?"

"What's the point?"

She wasn't sure, but the fragments of something deep inside made her say, "If Nicky was out of the house . . . if he was somewhere, and it was just the two of us, as it used to be . . ."

Nick was the one to shake his head this time. "Nicky could be on Mars, and it wouldn't matter. He'd still be here, don't you see? Every time I'd look at you, I'd see him and remember what he was and that we'd made him." He thrust a hand through his hair in agitation, as though he'd only then realized what he'd said. Bolting to his feet, he glared at her and said, "Goddamn it, I don't want to have to look at you, Sabrina! I don't want to be reminded day after day, week after week, year after year!"

His voice exploded into a silence that was profound and was broken only by the hand he slapped against the mahogany doorjamb as he stormed from the room.

The next morning, Sabrina brought Nicky home. She added another medicine bottle to the collection on the bathroom shelf. She penciled in another point at the bottom of the long list of "what-to-do-in-case-of's" that she had tacked on the bulletin board in his room. She put him through his paces at a very gentle speed and spent most of the time after that simply holding him to her, rocking him, humming softly when her voice didn't crack. She took her time bathing him, spent extra time rubbing lotion and patting powder on his small body. She talked to him, telling him of all the wonderful things the world had to offer, then she held him again, held him tight and cried.

"I only want to love you," she sobbed. "Let Mommy do that . . . please . . ."

· CHAPTER 6 ·

Sabrina was largely paralyzed during the first week after Nick's departure. Caring for Nicky was one of the few things she could do with any semblance of order. She felt, oddly, as though she were waiting to see if Nick would change his mind. A tiny part of her—the pridefully feminine part—wanted that, if for no other reason than that it would give her the chance to tell him, herself, that it was over. And that was what the larger part of her knew. What had happened was for the best. There was no chance of reconciliation; neither of them thought it, mentioned it, wanted it. Whatever had brought them together eight years before was gone. In its wake was an amalgam of resentment, disillusionment and disappointment. Nick had said it first, but Sabrina felt it too; when they looked at each other, they relived the anguish of the past three years. Better to be free of that ugly yoke.

She did feel regret when Nick returned to pick up the rest of his things, but it was a mourning not for the loss of the man but for the institution that had failed.

During the second week, she was able to think. Nick had said that he'd see she remained financially secure—which had been a chauvinistic touch on his part, since she was financially secure on her own. But she retained a lawyer to represent not so much her interests, but Nicky's, in the negotiation of a settlement. Yes, she was financially independent, but the Greenhouse was expensive. Should she decide to place Nicky there—or in a comparable institution—she wanted to be assured of Nick's long-range cooperation. Having opted out of all emotional responsibility, he owed her that much.

By the end of two weeks, she couldn't wait any longer. She needed to see Derek. She knew that it was crazy that she should feel better with him than with just about anyone else, but she did. On the outside he was tough, the son of a felon and a felon himself. But that toughness was born of things like anger and humiliation, and in spite of it all a soft streak showed through.

She identified with him. She felt as though they shared very different kinds of pain that were somehow the same.

With his dark side and his moods, he challenged her.

And the story of his experience was just waiting to be written. She wanted the professional focus it would give her life.

This time, rather than being led to the visiting room in which she'd seen him both times before, she was escorted to an open yard at one side of the prison complex. There were trees and benches, half a dozen picnic tables and lots of grass. In spite of the presence of the guards and the multiple rows of very high, very thick, very probably electrified wire fencing that encircled the prison, the overall atmosphere of the yard was more relaxed.

Sabrina chose a bench beneath a large maple. Sun shimmered through its newly budding leaves to dapple the bench's worn green paint. She sat down and crossed her legs, trying to look nonchalant when she felt excited and more than a little apprehensive. She was never quite sure how she'd be received.

Then he came. She caught sight of him at the far end of the yard, a dark figure in denim; she watched him approach in what she'd come to think of as the inmate shuffle, though it was truly more a saunter than a shuffle. They all did it; Derek was no different. It was a slow, indolent gait that alternately said, "I don't have anything better to do," and, more defiantly, "I don't give a damn what you say, I'll get there when I get there." She didn't know which he was feeling—indifference or defiance—but by the time he was within twenty feet, she saw something in his eyes that made the point moot.

That something grew stronger with each step he took. By the time he stopped, she'd risen from the bench, and in the next instant she was in his arms, being hugged up into his tall, lean frame. She was aware of feeling an incredible relief, as though she'd been hanging in midair for the past five weeks and only now felt safe. But there was more than that. Her senses were suddenly full in ways they hadn't been since then—full with the solidity of Derek's body, his warmth, his scent.

Implausible as it seemed with her life as messed up as his, she felt happy. At that moment she actually felt happy.

She let herself feast on that pleasure for a minute before raising her head. "You got my note, didn't you?" She'd followed up her call with a note to better explain why she hadn't been able to come.

Nodding, he took in her features one by one.

"And the phone message before that?" she asked, feeling warm all over and liking it.

"A little late."

"But I told them it was *urgent*."

He raised one shoulder in a negligent shrug. "It's okay now. At the time I was mad as hell." And crushed. He couldn't tell her how he'd been counting each day of those three weeks, how devastated he'd been when he'd waited and waited and she hadn't shown, how empty he'd felt—and how foolish.

"I'm sorry," she whispered. Her hands were clasped loosely around his neck, while his moved slowly over her back. She felt the heat of his body through her sweater and skirt, thawing parts of her that she hadn't known were frozen. "It all happened so suddenly, just the night before..." She was lost in the depths of his eyes, which were a richer gray than she'd ever seen them.

"It's okay."

"If it had been anything but that, I'd have come."

"I know."

"It was scary, Derek."

He loved the way she said his name. Even more than that, he loved the way she was looking at him. He saw hunger in her eyes, though whether her hunger was for compassion, companionship or sex, he didn't know. But she wasn't making any attempt to break from his embrace, even though she had to feel what she was doing to him. His insides were quivering, and he was growing hard in a place he hadn't been minutes before.

"Hey, McGill!"

Ice water couldn't have been more effective at dampening Derek's passion. His body stiffened. He tightened his hold of Sabrina and whipped his head around. A guard stood a dozen feet away, gesturing for them to separate. He muttered a crude oath as he held Sabrina tightly for a defiant minute longer. The guard had to call his name again, this time more sharply, before he gradually loosened his grip, slid his hands from her back to her arms, then finally released her completely.

He made a gesture of his own, indicating to Sabrina that she should sit. Taking deep, measured breaths, he bowed his head and ran a hand through his hair. With his weight set on one hip and a finger hooked through the beltless loop of his jeans, he glared at the ground.

Sabrina saw his fury and shared his frustration. She wanted to turn and shriek at the guard who had been responsible for destroying a rare and lovely moment. But it was a foolish impulse, quickly controlled. She waited silently for Derek to gather himself and join her.

"Why did he do that?" she asked softly.

He sat forward with his elbows on spread thighs and his fingers tightly laced. The muscle in his jaw worked. His nostrils flared around each angry breath. "Because I'm me."

She leaned closer, unconsciously seeking the warmth she'd had moments before. "What do you mean?"

His hardened gaze roamed the yard. "Reverse discrimination. I was a somebody in the free world, so I have to work twice as hard in here."

"But what was the problem if we were touching?"

"Not touching. Em-bra-cing."

"That isn't allowed?"

"Once at the beginning, once at the end."

"But this *is* the beginning."

"Fat Frank decided the beginning was over."

"That's not fair."

He sliced her a look that started with a sarcastic twist of the lips, then softened into a crooked smile when he saw her wounded expression. "Not fair, huh?"

"I've seen other couples hold each other much longer and no one says a word—even when their hands are all over the place. Look over there," she said, tossing a glance toward one of the other benches. "She's on his lap, and he isn't treating her for a scraped knee. If that isn't an embra-ce"—she drawled the word as he had—"I don't know what is."

"It's an embrace," Derek said, but he wasn't looking at the couple on the other bench. There was too much to see on Sabrina's face, like the brightness of her pale green eyes and the flush on her cheeks. And the faint smudges beneath her eyes and the worry lines between her brows. "How's Nicky?"

Her gaze flew to his. She took a deep breath. "Nicky's okay now."

"Has he had any other seizures?"

She shook her head. "I have medication in case he does, but there's been nothing since that first one. I wish I could say, 'thank God', but I'm not sure what's worse—the seizure itself or waiting for it to happen."

"That's because it's all still new. You expect a seizure any minute. Once time passes and nothing happens, you'll relax more."

That was what the hospital social worker had said. Coming from Derek it sounded less patronizing, more believable. "I hope so."

Derek wanted to know more. He'd often wondered about Nicky. Since Sabrina had refused to be interviewed for his story, he'd never learned the history of the child's illness. And he wanted something, needed something to overshadow his darker thoughts.

"What was he like, when he was born?"

"He was a complacent baby for the first couple of months. Actually, he was complacent even before he was born."

Derek tried to imagine her pregnant, tried to imagine her stomach puffed and round. He succeeded too well. The image was lovely. It was also sexy as hell, and his body responded quickly. He was glad he was sitting as he was.

"He didn't move around much inside you?"

"No."

"Did you have morning sickness?"

"No. He was a terrific little kid. Another cruel irony. I was so happy, so excited about having a baby," she said, and her eyes, those telling eyes of hers, reflected just that until they turned bewildered. "I wish I knew where it all went wrong."

"When did you first notice that Nicky was different?"

"On the day he was born," she said dryly. "I was like every other mother who looks at her child and worries. From the very beginning I thought Nicky was too still. I didn't think he was focusing the way he should. Even the little fussing he did seemed strange, somehow distant, ill-timed, inappropriate, distracted. But everyone said he was fine and healthy and beautiful, and I wanted to believe that. So I pushed my worries aside. If you're asking when I began to take them seriously, it was when I took him to have his picture taken. He was fourteen weeks old. It was a spur-of-the-moment thing—I'd been walking through Macy's; the photographer was there; I thought it would be fun."

"It wasn't?"

She shook her head. "I stood in line watching the other children go before us. They smiled and laughed. A couple of them were really homely, but still they were sweet, and the photographer was good with the ones who cried. She had a way with kids." Sabrina paused, sniffed in a long breath and arched a brow toward Derek. "Not with Nicky. He fussed the whole time. She shook a rattle. She waggled a furry rabbit. She put on a hand puppet. Nothing worked. She never got him past the fussing stage—forget trying to make him smile. But that wasn't all."

Any humor she'd exhibited in the telling of the story faded then, and the line between her brows grew more pronounced. "He couldn't hold himself like the others. I knew he wasn't doing well with his head, and I'd already asked my doctor about it and been given little exercises to do, but it wasn't only his neck. It was his hands and his arms, his legs, his whole body. He just . . . drooped . . . and looking at him in comparison to those other kids, some of whom were barely half his age, I knew. I *knew*."

Needing to give comfort, Derek smoothed a strand of blond hair back from her cheek. It was soft to the touch. He watched it settle over the greater mass of blond, then dance a little when the breeze picked up. "Did the doctors confirm it then?"

She dipped her head slightly in the direction from which that comfort had come, but the hand was already gone. "It should only have been that easy," she murmured. "When Nicky was five months old, my own pediatrician was still saying he'd be fine. I started seeing specialists then, and they all said, yes, he was slow, but there wasn't much that could be done until he was a little older. It wasn't until he'd hit a year that I finally had a doctor look at me and say, 'Your son is retarded.'"

Remembering that moment, she wrapped her arms around herself and dropped her gaze to her feet. She was wearing low heels that matched the khaki green of her long sweater and skirt. The way the color clashed with the grass was appropriate. "I never thought I'd face something like this. It's something that's supposed to happen to other people—to poor people who can't afford prenatal care, or cruel people who knock their kids around, or irresponsible people who leave their kids alone with plastic Baggies, or . . . or just *dumb* people." She raised her eyes to Derek's. "Pretty bigoted, huh?"

"Naive, that's all."

"Well," she said with a sigh that was part philosophical, part discouraged, "I'm paying for my sins twenty-four hours a day, seven days a week, fifty-two weeks a year— and you can add self-pity to the list. I know I'm indulging in it, and I don't care. I really don't care."

"Self-pity feels good sometimes."

"You do it, too?"

"Sure." And a lot more often lately, when he'd been rock-hard with no source of relief. But he didn't want to go into that. "I'm surprised you were able to get away. Who's with Nicky now? Another of the therapists?"

"As a matter of fact," she said, feeling a tiny burst of strength, "I hired someone new. Do you remember the maid who let you in when she shouldn't have?" He nodded, so she went on. "I let her go last week and hired a live-in nurse who could give me more of a hand with Nicky."

"The maid wasn't good with him?"

"She had a bad back. Or said she had a bad back. I think she hated kids."

"Then why did you hire her in the first place?"

"I didn't."

It took Derek just a minute to interpret the look in her eye. So her husband had hired the maid. "Then I'm glad you let her go," he said. His double meaning was clear and he felt not the slightest remorse. "Maybe things will ease up for you now."

"I hope so," she said quietly. *Tell him, Sabrina. Tell him Nick's gone.* "Things can't get much worse than they've been. Assuming there aren't any more emergency trips to the hospital . . ." Her voice trailed off. Suddenly she wasn't thinking of Nick, nor of Derek's right to know about the separation. She was thinking of that last emergency trip to the hospital and of the feelings she'd had. She needed to tell someone. She had held those thoughts in and held them in, but she needed to tell someone now, and Derek was there.

"It was difficult being with Nicky in the hospital like that." Her voice was small, which was how she felt. "In some ways it was no different from all the other times I've brought him in for examinations and tests. I sit and wait and pray that they'll find something, that they'll be able to give me a specific cause for his problems and then give him a little pill that will suddenly wake him up and make him like other children his age. Little pill, big pill, operation, something, anything. Lately . . ." She rubbed her arm. "Lately it's been even harder, because there are times when I almost pray that they diagnose him as having something terminal."

She dared a quick glance at Derek. "There are times when all I want in life is to hold him, rock him, sing to him, love him—and other times when I wake up in the morning bone-tired and trembling, and I go into his room half hoping that something will have happened to him during the night." Her voice had shrunk to a whisper. "That's what I've become."

At that moment, Derek felt even more compassion for her than he'd felt the first day he'd seen her on her terrace in New York. If he'd had any doubts about his capacity for feeling—beyond just sexual feeling—they were gone. "Don't say it that way," he chided. He wrapped his hand around the point above her elbow, gently removing the hand that was kneading the spot compulsively. "You're human. Anyone in your position would feel the same at times."

"But isn't it *awful*?" she cried. "A mother wishing her child dead?"

He slid his hand up to her neck, fingers finding their way under her hair to work at her tension. "You don't wish him dead, Sabrina. You wish him perfectly healthy and normal. But he isn't. So there are times—despairing times that always pass—when you wonder if being dead wouldn't be better than being severely and irreversibly brain-damaged."

"It's just that I had such dreams," she said, and her eyes were filled with them. "Dreams of him laughing, climbing trees in the park, playing baseball. He was going to be a swimmer, too, and an A student. He was going on to a top college. He was going to be well liked and happy. He was going to be a leader." Tears had replaced the dreams. "It's such a waste."

"I know," he whispered, then leaned closer and, still whispering, said, "I'm going to put my arm around you for just a minute. If Fat Frank yells, don't move." He slid along the bench, curved a long, sinewy arm around her back and drew her in. She wasn't aware of deliberately moving, but somehow she ended up with her face against his throat and her hand on his chest.

Fat Frank didn't yell, and still she didn't move.

Derek tightened his hold. He had his face in her hair and was inhaling the jasmine scent that was so faint and alluring. He'd built more erotic dreams around that scent in the last few weeks than he cared to count.

Sabrina did the counting—his heartbeats as they echoed against her palm—then wondered whether the heartbeats were his or hers. She knew that her pulse was racing and didn't pause to decide whether it was because of the naturally musky scent of his neck, the chest hair that curled beneath her thumb, or the threat of Fat Frank.

Fat Frank didn't yell, and still she didn't move.

Derek pressed her infinitesimally closer. He liked the way her breasts felt against him, not obtrusive, just enticing. He liked the slenderness of her thigh beside his. And the gentle sough of her breath by his throat was raising his temperature by multiple degrees. He knew he was playing with fire, but he didn't care.

Sabrina floated. If there had been tears in her eyes, they'd dried, and she could barely remember their cause. Derek had taken the weight from her shoulders and was supporting her with ease. She wanted to thank him, but to use her voice at that moment would have been unthinkable.

Fat Frank didn't yell, and still she didn't move.

Derek lowered his head and was about to press a gentle kiss on her forehead when Fat Frank yelled.

"McGill!"

Derek moaned. He held her tighter, arms trembling slightly before slowly, slowly setting her back. "Goddamned pig," he whispered, glowering at the guard.

Sabrina's returning whisper was far more vulnerable and immediately brought his attention back to her. "Derek?"

"Mmm?"

"I haven't ever told anyone what I just told you."

He'd pretty much guessed that by the desperate way she'd pushed the words out, as though if they didn't get an airing and quickly, she'd have suffocated. He wanted to know why she hadn't ever told her husband, but he didn't want to ask. He didn't want to acknowledge that a husband existed. He wanted to pretend that if it hadn't been for Fat Frank Ferrucci, he'd still have Sabrina in his arms.

"You can tell me your secrets anytime," he said thickly. "And I'll understand. I know all about broken dreams."

"Yours aren't broken, just deferred."

"That's a debatable point."

"Tell me about them, Derek. What do you dream of?"

"Now? Mrs. Fields' white-chunk macadamia-nut cookies."

In spite of herself, Sabrina smiled. As humor went, it was a little dry, but still it was humor. Derek had never joked with her before. She remembered how stern-faced and angry he'd been during her first visit. He'd come far.

"No, I mean more generally."

He was thinking that her smile had to be the most beautiful sight in the world. He wished he were a funny man, if only to see it again, but he wasn't; and unfortunately most of his dreams weren't amusing. "I dream of my release."

"And then?"

"Revenge."

She saw the little look that came and went from his eyes and couldn't resist a tiny shudder. "That's scary."

He shrugged, and wasn't about to add anything until he realized that she really was frightened. "Nothing to worry about," he said, but his voice was shadowed. "It's part of the mentality in here. Drawing up plans for revenge gives you a feeling of power, and power's the name of the game."

"Like Fat Frank's yells?"

"Like that. I intimidate him and the other guards too, because of who I am and where I've been. So they go out of their way to put me down. It gives them a semblance of control." He heard his own words, thought about them for a second, then grunted. "Who am I kidding? They *have* the control. It just gives them double satisfaction to rub it in in my case."

"Good thing you never did an exposé on correctional officers," she said dryly.

"Oh, I did. It was actually a story of the inmate bureaucracy in the state prison system in Indiana, but it did a job on the guards."

A grimacing Sabrina lowered her voice to a conspiratorial whisper. "Do you think they know about it?"

"I know they know about it. On the day I arrived here, the warden told me in no uncertain terms that he knew. Other guards have made comments since then. I assume the warden got a copy of either the tape or the transcript and passed it around."

"That wasn't particularly ethical."

"No, but then, it makes my point. Prisons aren't particularly ethical places."

"Is there an underworld here, too?"

"Yes."

"What does it do?"

"Provides goods and services inmates want and can't otherwise get."

"Like drugs?"

"Among other things."

"What other things?"

"Sabrina, you don't want to know." He narrowed his eyes. "It seems like I've said that to you before. Why do you ask so many questions? If I didn't know better, I'd think you had an obsession with prison life."

Ignoring that, she looked him over. "I don't see any new scars. Are you managing to stay out of fights, at least?"

"I wasn't in a fight," he said, scowling. "I was trying to break one up."

"Are there fights often?"

The scowl faded but didn't completely go away. "Yes."

"That's disgraceful."

"It's inevitable. Prisons are filled with angry men. Beneath the anger is violence just waiting to erupt."

"And when it does, what does the administration do?"

Derek stretched out, extending his legs, bracing his elbows on the back of the bench. His hands were balled. He was looking straight ahead. "In some cases, disciplinary measures are taken against the men involved. In other cases, the administration looks the other way."

"How can they do that?"

"They reason it's the practical thing to do. If the guy who starts a fight is a powerful figure in the inmate bureaucracy, punishing him could open the door to greater violence. No warden wants a riot on his hands."

Sabrina was sitting sideways on the bench, studying the hard lines of his profile. "Where do you fit into that bureaucracy?"

"I don't."

"You're not involved at all?"

He pushed out his lips and slowly shook his head.

"You're bucking the internal system?"

He nodded.

"Can that be safely done?"

"There's a price."

"What's that?"

"Isolation. You make it through each day on your own, and when the days begin to pile up one on top of another, that can be tough. Some guys can't take it. They give in."

Sabrina knew that he wasn't talking about physical isolation, but emotional. "It must be difficult."

"It's what I choose. I keep to myself. I do my time. I get out. That's it."

She thought of stories she'd read of celebrated inmates who had turned around and devoted themselves to improving the lot of the others. "I'd have thought you'd be in demand. You're intelligent, well-educated, literate. I'm surprised they haven't got you teaching a course or something."

"I wouldn't have done that even if they'd asked."

"Why not?"

"Because," he murmured angrily, "I'm not a do-gooder. The way I see it, I shouldn't be in prison at all. I'm here against my will. I'm being robbed of good, constructive time, months and months of my life lost forever, and for that my grudge is against the system of justice. But the correctional department, with its deliberate knee-buckling, is nearly as bad, and I'll be damned if I'll give it one iota of my expertise. In the first place, it would do no good. What in the hell could I teach the guys here that they'd be able to use on the outside? And in the second place," he said, losing a little of his fire, "it'd only set me up for abuse from those who think I'm lording something over them. The lowest possible profile is the only one I want."

Sabrina understood both what he was saying and the bitterness behind it. In an attempt to lighten his mood, she picked up his hand, turned it this way and that. "What *do* they have you doing?" His fingers were long, lean and blunt-tipped. They were masculine without being worn. "No dirt. No calluses. What's your work detail?"

"Laundry."

She was appalled. Okay, she could understand why he didn't teach, but she'd have thought they'd put him in an office doing typing or filing, something vaguely intelligent. But laundry? Her lip curled up at the thought of his handling the dirty laundry of the men she'd seen. They couldn't have given him a more humbling work assignment. Then again, maybe they could have. What did she know of the options?

Derek read her silence with ease. "I get clean clothes out of the deal."

"How many hours a day do you work?"

"Four."

"That leaves a few," she said, reluctantly returning his hand to him. "What else do you do?"

He flexed his jaw. "Mark time."

"Besides that."

"Count the holes on the wall in my cell."

She ignored his tone, and pressed on. "What's it like, your cell?"

He shot her an annoyed look. "It's like a cell. Come on, Sabrina, what do you want me to do—tell you that the rug is Persian, the drapes are Roman and the bed is an authentic reproduction of something Henry the Eighth ordered for his sixth mistress? We're talking a cot, a shelf, a locker, a desk and a toilet. If there were labels on any of them, they've long since been scraped off."

"Put up with me, Derek. I'm just curious."

His brows lowered harshly over eyes that were sharp. "I don't ask you about your bedroom."

Tell him, Sabrina. Tell him . . .

"You could ask. It's not very exciting. I'm not much of a

decorator myself, so it was done professionally. There are labels on everything. I wish I could *get* someone to scrape them off."

Derek wished he hadn't mentioned her bedroom. The thought of her there with her husband was doing nothing good for his mood, which had plummeted when she'd touched him. No, that was wrong. He hadn't minded it when she'd touched him, just when she'd let him go. And that was only a preview. Pretty soon she'd be leaving, going back through the gates, out the door to her car, down the road, onto the highway. He wouldn't see her for the next . . . however many weeks until she chose to come again. For all his macho talk about liking isolation, he could feel desolation waiting in the wings.

"Why are you so goddamned curious about me?" he snapped.

"Because you're interesting."

He snorted. "That's a good one. At this point in my life, I am probably one of the least interesting people you could have the misfortune to run across."

She ignored him. "I want to be able to picture where you are and what you're doing.'

"But *why*? What *is* it with you, Sabrina? You have a husband and a child and a luxurious apartment back in New York. You don't need this."

"You'd be surprised," she said with such quiet force that Derek did a double take. He was sure he'd caught a flare of desperation in her eyes.

"What do you mean?" he asked more calmly.

Sabrina couldn't think of a thing to say. She couldn't tell him that seeing his torment lessened her own, because it sounded cruel. She couldn't tell him that she trusted him with her deepest darkest secrets because it didn't make sense even to her. She couldn't tell him that she needed his shoulder to cry on, because then she'd have to explain why his was the only shoulder she had. She couldn't tell him that he excited her, that the thought of him was as much of a pick-me-up as any new sweater she'd bought, that she felt like a different person when she was with him. And somehow she couldn't get herself to tell him about Nick.

"It's the book, isn't it?" Derek asked. "You're still thinking about writing that book."

She could have kissed him for coming to her rescue. She could have kissed him anyway. "You, uh, said you'd think about it."

"Why is it so important to you? If you're looking for good subject matter, I can think of any number of others that'd be more intriguing."

"This one hits me right," she said, making a concerted effort not to stare at his mouth. That lower lip was sensual, even when it was drawn straight, as it was now. "With the nurse I've hired, I thought I might put aside four or five hours a day to work."

"Then you've decided against residential placement?"

"For a little while." She couldn't explain that one, either. She'd been so sure that institutionalizing Nicky was the only way for her to survive. Then Nick had left, and suddenly she wanted to wait. She wasn't ready to give up her baby. She needed to know that she could hold him and touch him whenever she wanted. In so many respects she was alone; the thought of an empty crib was too much. "I'm going to try handling Nicky with extra help. It might work."

"Why the change of heart? Are you still getting guff about placing him in a residential center?"

Was she getting guff? "Oh, yes."

"From whom?"

"You name it. My mother thinks Nicky would do best if he were with me, which is pretty consistent with the way we were raised. Aside from the time we spent with Dad, she prided herself on being there for us. Of course, her definition of 'being there' was a purely physical thing. To this day, Mom's mind is more often than not somewhere else."

"What does your dad say about Nicky?"

"He thinks we fuss too much. He thinks Nicky would do best if we'd all just leave him alone." Her mouth twitched at the corner. "It's the old keep-the-hay-in-the-barn-and-the-dogie-will-find-his-own-way-home approach."

The subtle amusement in her voice had its way. Derek could feel himself relaxing. "And your brother?"

"Oh, J. B. has a super theory. Are you ready?" she asked. When he nodded, she briefly outlined J. B.'s plot.

"Interesting," Derek said, rubbing his jaw thoughtfully. "Taken over by a spirit from the earth's core. Not bad."

"Mmmm. It's more than the doctors have come up with."

"And this spirit would want you to keep Nicky at home?"

"I'm not sure. It seemed to me the spirit could do its thing just about anywhere. But J. B. votes for home." She didn't repeat what J. B. had said about head bangers and droolers. It still hurt.

"Is anyone besides you in favor of institutionalization?"

"You," she said with a lopsided smile, then took a quick breath. "And Maura."

"Who's Maura?"

"Agent and friend. She wants me to write."

"How about other friends?"

"I've only discussed it with a few. They think I'm awful to even consider it. They say they don't see a problem, which is very loyal of them . . . and very dishonest. Then again, Nicky still does look wonderfully normal on occasion. But they don't live with him. They don't have the responsibility for his daily care. They don't have to look to the future as I do."

Derek mulled that over, then plunged in and asked the question that had been pulling at his tongue. "What does your husband say about it?"

Tell him, Sabrina. It's a perfect opening. Tell him now. "He's leaving the decision up to me," she said, averting her eyes.

"Sabrina?"

"Mmmm?"

"Look at me."

He'd spoken quietly, but there was command in his voice. She raised her eyes. Derek had shifted to face her, and his gaze probed.

"Does Nick know you're here?"

"No," she said softly.

"It's a dangerous game you're playing."

She agreed with that, though her reasons had nothing to do with Nick. Sitting here with Derek, looking at him, being looked at by him, she could no longer deny the attraction. Every one of the other reasons she'd given for coming to see him were valid, but there was another.

Derek turned her on. He lit a spark in her body. He made her feel feminine, desired and desiring.

"Do you love your husband?" he asked.

"Nick and I have been married for eight years," she said, but her voice was shaky.

"That wasn't what I asked."

"We have a son. I suppose it's a natural bond."

"Do you love him?"

"Nicky? I love him—"

"Nick. The father. Your husband. Do you love him?"

"I don't understand why you're asking—"

"Come on, Sabrina," he ground out. "I feel it. You feel it. There's something between us that has no business being there if you're in love with Nicholas Stone."

"I've never been unfaithful to Nick."

"There's unfaithful, and there's unfaithful. You may never have made it with another guy since you married Nick, but you may have wanted to; and if that's the case, something's missing. He's not giving you what you need."

Tell him, Sabrina. He's all but inviting you to. Tell him!

She needed space. Pushing herself from the bench, she began to walk along the edge of the visiting area.

Derek was quickly by her side. For an instant he'd feared she was leaving then and there, and his heart had sunk to his toes. Now it was back in his chest but still not beating quite right. "The book, Sabrina. Why is it so important to you?"

"I need to do something. I need to prove myself."

"To whom?"

She kicked at the grass as she walked. "Me. My family. The world."

"Isn't taking care of Nicky enough?"

"No. At the end of a day or a week or a month, I have nothing to show for it. Absolutely nothing."

"Why does there have to be something? Why can't there be the simple satisfaction of knowing what you've done for Nicky?"

She gave wide berth to a picnic table that was occupied by two very large, very mean looking men, and waited until they were well behind before speaking. "Because I'm getting nowhere with him. I'm marking time, just like you. You can look forward to freedom, revenge, justice or whatever. I need something to look forward to, too. I need to *achieve* something."

"Why a book?"

"Because it's what I know. It's what I was raised on. It's what I do best."

"Is your family pressuring you to write?"

"No."

"Do they think less of you because you aren't writing now?"

"No!"

"If you're trying to prove something—"

Her head came up. The eyes that caught his glittered with anger, but she kept on walking. "Yes, I'm trying to prove something. Everyone in the *world* is trying to prove something. In my case it happens that I need to prove my basic worth. Writing is my best shot at that. God only knows I haven't been able to do it any other way!"

"Wh-oa," Derek said, grabbing her arm and pulling her to a halt. "You think you're a failure?"

"That's exactly what I think."

"That's the dumbest thing I've ever heard! My Lord, woman, you had a full-length book published before you were twenty-three. Plus articles—how many were there— twenty? Twenty-one? And we're not talking fly-by-night magazines here. We're talking *The Atlantic, Esquire, Rolling Stone*."

She eyed him warily. "I didn't tell you about those."

"Yeah, because you're modest. I had to ferret out all the juicy little facts after I left you that day in New York. I went out, bought your book and read it cover to cover. Same with most of the articles."

Her heart skipped a beat, then sped. "But why? There was no need after I'd refused to be interviewed."

"*I* had a need," he bit out with the anger she'd abandoned. "I had to know because you intrigued me. You pricked my conscience. You made me think about things I hadn't thought about in years—like weighing and balancing the overall good of a story with its effects on its subjects. More personally, you made me ask myself where I was going in life and what I wanted."

"Did you find any answers?"

"I was thinking about it real hard when I got a call from a guy who said he had some vital information for me, and the next thing I knew the guy was dead and the cops were taking a smoking gun from my hand. No, I didn't find any answers, and now the issues are more clouded than ever. You want to write a book about *me*? How can you know me when I don't know myself?"

"Maybe we can both learn something from the writing. It's been known to happen. I ask questions a certain way, you look at something differently than you have . . . it could work."

"No."

"You're being stubborn."

"Damn right."

She started walking again, this time in the general direction of the gate. "Then I guess there isn't any point in my coming again."

"And that," Derek said angrily, "is even dumber than what you said before." Grabbing her wrist, he had her behind a nearby tree before she could anticipate the move. He backed her to the wide trunk, pinning her hands to the bark at her shoulders. His lower body pressed hotly. "You want to see me. I want to see you."

"Derek, I—"

"Shhh." He shifted against her, seeking to enhance the feeling of her curves against him. His voice was gritty and low. "We fit, Sabrina. I don't know how or why, but we fit.

It shouldn't be. The whole thing's wrong. We're night and day, good and bad, but we fit."

Her eyes were large, begging his for release. "Please—"

"Think about it before you come again."

"I can't—"

"You'll come again. You will." He lowered his head until he was nuzzling her cheek. "I want to touch you, touch and kiss you." He moved again. She felt the shift in her breasts, felt the tingle that the intimate brush of his chest had caused, and lower, felt the curling heat brought by the press of his hips. And she felt afraid.

"Derek, I can't think," she gasped.

"You have to. You have to decide—".

"Hey, McGill!" came a shout from the side.

Ignoring it, Derek leaned in even closer. His mouth was less than an inch from hers. "Work it out, Sabrina. Work it out in your mind, because when you come back here, I'm going to kiss you." He released her hands, which remained against the bark as though they'd been nailed, and slid his own upward from her waist. "There are ways to make love that can be done right here, right here in the yard. I'm hungry, Sabrina. You've stirred it up. I don't give a damn about your husband or anyone else who says it's wrong. It's not wrong. Maybe crazy, maybe hopeless, but not wrong."

"That's it, McGill," called the guard who was closing in on them. He wasn't fat like Frank, but he was big and burly and every bit as unfriendly.

"Hold on," Derek snarled, then lowered his voice again. "Do you hear me, Sabrina?"

She hurried the words out on a shaky breath. "You shouldn't be saying these things, Derek, shouldn't be *thinking* them."

"Why not, if it's what I feel?"

"Because I don't know if I—"

"Okay, McGill," the guard said. He was practically on top of them. "Time to get back."

Derek raised his head a bit and, without taking his eyes from Sabrina, told the guard, "I'm saying good-bye."

"From the looks of it, you've already said good-bye. Sorry, miss, but it's time to leave."

She couldn't move. Derek wasn't budging. "Derek, please," she whispered.

"Think about it, Sabrina. Think about all of it."

"McGill, you're asking for trouble."

"I've committed murder, Sabrina. I'm perfectly capable of making love to another man's wife."

She darted glances at the guard as she pushed urgently at Derek's chest. "Go, Derek," she pleaded, "please?"

With his hands flat on the tree at either side of her head, he levered himself several inches back. "Next Thursday. Same time, same place."

"I don't know . . ."

"Be here," he commanded, then gave a rough shrug to dislodge the hand that the guard had clamped on his arm. Holding his shoulders straight, he deliberately stepped back, then watched as Sabrina turned and half walked, half ran to the gate.

· *CHAPTER 7* ·

Two days later, Derek met with his lawyer. David Cottrell was in his mid-forties, with a wife, two children, an office in Manhattan, a house in Westchester and a reputation for being a quiet-spoken advocate with a firm grasp of the law, a keen courtroom instinct and a way with jurors. The two men had met when Derek had sought out a criminal-law expert for one of his early *Outside Insight* stories, and they'd quickly become friends.

David had taken Derek's conviction personally. "I'm not political enough," he told Derek in frustration during one of those first post-sentencing visits. "I don't swing the weight, damn it."

"You did everything you could have done."

"I should have played dirty."

"You can't. That's why I hired you. You have a sterling reputation."

"Sterling? No, friend, you've got it wrong. I'm the tarnish on the sterling. I'm a black lawyer in a white system, which is just fine when my clients are black and already have that strike against them, but it sure didn't do you no good." He ended with the ethnic drawl that he could put on or take off—and indeed, it came off in the next breath. "This case stinks. One too many things just haven't made sense. We'll get them on appeal, Derek. So help me, we'll do it."

But they didn't. One appeal after another, filed in one court after another—all denied. It was the latest denial that had brought David to Parkersville.

"The sentence stands," he said, dropping his briefcase on the table in the small, private room reserved for lawyer-client visits. "I was hoping to get it reduced, but the bastards weren't buying. I'm sorry."

Derek was leaning against the wall. He hadn't had to hear the words: one look at his friend's face had told him they'd lost. He wasn't surprised. "Don't sweat it, Dave. We figured as much." He pushed off from the wall, smirking cynically as he knelt down and peered under the table. "When you set out to screw someone, you don't stop in the middle, do you?" Spotting the telltale wire, he nodded toward David, who was already in the process of removing a minirecorder from his case. "Anyway, I'm on the home stretch—or I will be, assuming nothing happens between now and November."

David turned on the recorder, which, thanks to his fourteen-year-old son, spewed out a raucous heavy-metal sound. Setting it on the seat of the chair no more than twelve inches from the bug, he moved to join Derek against the wall.

"What's the feel here?" he asked in a low voice. "Any hint of trouble?"

Derek gave a noncommittal shrug. "The guards are breathing down my neck. They watch every move I make. But I don't think they'll be the problem. I keep to myself. I don't give them trouble. In their own warped way they respect that. It's the other guys who scare me."

"Like the two in the shower?" David asked, glancing briefly at the fading scar on Derek's neck.

"It was no accident. They were set up to involve me in their fight."

"Were they aiming to kill?"

"Does rain fall?"

"Were they disciplined?"

"Each did a day in the hole, but word has it that they got pizza for lunch, and when you get anything other than shit in there, it means you've got an in." His voice dropped even more. "I really thought Greer had chalked me off. At this point, anything else he tries to do to me has to be a risk to him. The more people he involves, the riskier it gets. Somewhere, sometime, someone is going to slip up and squeal."

David was more cautious. "He's a powerful man, Derek. He gets things done. And he keeps his own fingers out of the till. No direct contact. No fingerprints. My guess is that if you ever did manage to get a squealer, the squealer wouldn't know who in the hell Noel Greer was."

"Which is why I have to get the files," Derek muttered.

"Hmm?"

"He really is eyeing the Senate, isn't he?"

"Looks that way."

"I keep reading it in the papers, but, God, I find it hard to believe."

"Why so? The man's a natural. He's a media expert. He's suave, good-looking. At sixty, he's not too old, not too young. He's built himself an empire from the ground floor up, and all that began even before he took over the network. He's the consummate executive, the embodiment of the American Dream, and if you think New Yorkers won't eat him up, think again."

"Then he can make it?"

"You bet. The election's still a year and a half off, but

—barring a catastrophe—he can make it. He has the money, the power and the organization. It'd be a damn shame if he wins."

Derek had no intention of letting that happen. The Ballantine files were out there, and somehow or other they had to implicate Noel Greer. It was the only thing Derek had been able to come up with after months and months of racking his brain. The Ballantine files had to be the key.

"A lot can happen in a year and a half," he murmured. His mind skipped ahead, picturing some of the possibilities, and suddenly he wasn't thinking of Noel Greer. "David, have you ever heard of a man named Nicholas Stone?"

"I'm not deaf, dumb and blind. Of course I've heard of Nicholas Stone. There's another natural for you. He's got the golden touch. Has the smarts and the style. Tax laws change and investors panic. Not Stone. He's cool."

"I know his wife," Derek tossed out quietly. He wasn't quite sure why he did it. Maybe saying it aloud would make it more real. More likely, he wanted David's reaction; he trusted and respected the man as he did few others.

"Too bad about that, isn't it?" David tossed back, taking Derek by surprise. He'd been under the impression that the child's problems had been kept under wraps.

"It's hard on her. I don't know about him, though. From what I understand, he distances himself from the whole thing."

"Maybe that's why it happened."

"Nah. The boy isn't emotionally disturbed. He's brain-damaged."

David frowned. "Say what?"

"Nicky is brain-damaged."

"Who is Nicky?"

Derek frowned too. "Sabrina's son. *Nick's* son."

"I didn't know they had a son."

"Then what's 'too bad'?"

"The divorce. They're getting divorced."

Derek heard the words, but it was a minute before they sank in, and then he went very still. "How do you know that?"

"Read it in the paper. It's the kind of gossip society columnists love, and since I've always wanted to make the society page"—his eyes danced—"I study it faithfully for hints. I might've made it defending you if the trial had been in the city, but—"

"Getting divorced?" Derek echoed dumbly. There was a buzzing in his head that had nothing to do with the Motley Crue cacophony that shielded his conversation with David. "When did you read it?"

"A week, week and a half ago."

Well before Sabrina's last visit, Derek realized. "What did the article say?"

"It was more a little blurb than an article."

"Little blurb, then. What did it say?"

"That they're getting divorced."

"Was that it? Just that the Nicholas Stones have filed for divorce?"

"Hey, man, I was just kidding about studying—"

"I need to know, Dave," Derek said, his tone softening for the sake of his friend but losing none of its urgency. "Try to remember?"

David moved his shoulder against the wall and frowned. "It wasn't that big a thing—something to the effect that Stone has become the man-about-town now that his marriage is off. How do you know his wife?"

The man-about-town. Derek didn't know whom to be angry at, Sabrina or Nick. "We met a while ago," he said, speaking distractedly, his voice aimed at the floor. "She's been here a couple of times."

"Here? To *Parkersville*?"

Derek looked up. "Is that so strange?"

"Yeah, man. She's la crème de la crème. What's she doing *here*?"

"Visiting *me*," Derek answered indignantly. He was annoyed that David had so quickly and correctly summed up the situation. But he should have expected it. David was sharp. And honest. Which was why Derek had raised the issue in the first place.

"How well do you know her?" David asked.

"Apparently not so well as I thought."

"Do you think she knows Greer?"

Derek felt the hair rise on the back of his neck. "No!"

"You sure?"

"Damn it, yes!"

"But if you don't know her as well as you thought—"

"I know her well enough for that," Derek insisted. "The idea that Greer sent her is absurd!"

"He's capable of doing it, Derek. He's tried to kill you more than once. Failing that, he might settle for sending a spy to learn your plans."

"If he did that, it wouldn't be Sabrina."

"Why not? You know how the man works. He finds a person's weakness, then preys on it. Sabrina's marriage is on the rocks. You say she has a brain-damaged child. There's a lot going on in her life that a man like Greer could use . . ."

"She's a strong woman," Derek interrupted. His eyes were dark, his voice low but vehement. "Nothing she's done could be used for blackmail. Forget it, Dave. No way. And besides, the spy business is a little farfetched. Even the attempted-murder business is a little farfetched. Maybe I've imagined the whole thing. Paranoia is rampant in here."

"Maybe, but let me tell you, I didn't imagine what went on with that trial. The deck was stacked. We didn't have a chance. It was tight and skillful, what they did. Greer pulled some very solid strings."

Derek couldn't argue with that. "What I don't understand is why Greer doesn't just give up on me and go after the files."

"*If* the files are the problem, and it's a big if."

"There's nothing else," Derek said with a quick shake of his head. "I've been over the last four years of my life with a fine-tooth comb, and there's nothing else. Greer and I had our differences from the start, but he went berserk when he learned I was onto Ballantine. He felt threatened, threatened in a big way. It has to be the files. I know it does."

"My friend," David drawled sadly, "you don't even

know for sure that those files exist. I'd hate to see you put too much store in them."

"They exist."

"Then the pertinent question is the one you just posed. Why hasn't Greer gone after them himself?"

Derek inhaled deeply and shook his head.

"He has the resources," David pointed out.

"I know."

"All he'd have to do is find them and have them destroyed, and he'd be safe."

"I know."

"It doesn't make sense."

"Tell me about it," Derek said dryly, at which point David straightened and slapped his friend on the arm.

"Well, you've got till November to figure it out."

For a minute, Derek didn't respond. He pictured the calendar on the wall of his cell, pictured the X's he marked through each day of his sentence that had passed, pictured those days left to be marked. Those remaining days could be fewer . . . or greater.

"I hope that's all I've got," he said, and felt the familiar pressure begin to gather. Prickles starting deep inside, working their way outward. An itching beneath the skin. Nervous energy building from a whine to a cry to a silent scream. Panic in its rawest form. "What if I'm denied parole?" he asked.

"There's no reason why that would happen."

"There's no reason why *any* of this has happened." He gritted his teeth and repeated the question. "Dave, what if I'm denied parole?"

"You won't be."

"I'm not sure I could make it if that happened. I think I'd explode inside, burst a blood vessel or something." He wasn't kidding.

David closed a firm hand on his shoulder. "I try not to make the same mistake twice. I played it straight during the trial. I did everything by the book. And I'm not doing anything illegal now, but two can play the game." His eyes held Derek's, mirroring the confidence that was in his voice. "I'm speaking to people, Derek. I'm setting the scene to make a lot of noise if that parole doesn't come through when it should. Do you remember Jilly DeVries— the little girl who worked for me a couple of summers ago?"

Derek remembered her. She'd been in her third year of law school when she worked for David, and she wasn't that little a girl that Derek hadn't taken her out. She was cute and bright, a little wild, very aggressive.

"She's working as counsel for the Department of Corrections," David went on, "and she has access to figures— figures in New York, Pennsylvania, California, you name it. She gave me the figures for Massachusetts, and I'm letting certain people know I've got them. It's a matter of precedent—how this particular parole board has acted over the past five years. Given your crime, your sentence, your record here at Parkersville, your lack of a record elsewhere, your profession—I could go on and on—there's no reason for the board to deny your parole. And if they do, there'll be hell to pay." He paused for a breath. "The media is multifaceted. Greer's network isn't the only one in town. Okay?"

Derek wasn't counting on anything; he'd learned not to do that; but David's confidence had a calming effect. He held up both hands, yielding.

David nodded. "Good." He glanced at his watch. "Gotta run." Returning to the table, he snapped off the cassette. "Ahhh," he whispered, "peace." He put the recorder in his case. "Anything you need?"

It was the timeworn question. Derek didn't even want to consider it. "Nah—" Then he caught himself. "On second thought, got a pencil?"

David drew one from his briefcase and handed it over along with a yellow legal pad. On it, Derek wrote the names of Gebhart, Amanda and J. B. Monroe, then tossed the pad and pencil back into the case and said quietly, "I want the latest books by each. Any bookstore should have them."

David stared at the names on the pad, then stared at Derek. "Her family?"

Chewing on the inside of his cheek, Derek nodded.

"I take it this is important."

Derek repeated the nod.

"Do you know what you're doing, friend?"

"Why do you ask?"

"I don't want you hurt," David said. "You've got a lot on your mind. You'll have more on your mind when you get out of here. It doesn't matter who you are, why you're here, what's waiting for you when you get out. It's gonna be hard at first. Added complications you don't need."

"Now, why didn't I think of that?"

David studied Derek for a final minute before closing his briefcase. "Okay, so you've thought of it. But don't say I didn't warn you."

"Just send the books, okay?"

"Sure thing, friend." He took Derek's hand in a firm grip. "Watch yourself, y'hear?"

Unfortunately, it wasn't himself Derek had to watch, but everyone else. Second among the unwritten prison rules—after Don't Get Involved—was Guard Your Back. To do so meant being forever cautious, which required concentration, which was fine as long as one's concentration wasn't elsewhere.

Unfortunately, over the next few days Derek's concentration was elsewhere. He was trying to figure out why Sabrina hadn't told him she was getting a divorce. He'd always thought he could fathom the female mind with some degree of success, but he couldn't do it now. He supposed he was out of practice. More probably, he realized, he was afraid of what the fathoming would turn up.

Disillusionment was something with which he'd had to contend at an early age. As a boy, promises had been made to him, then broken. He'd idolized a father who had let him down at every turn. His mother had been a creature of high standards and lofty dreams—a lethal combination for a boy who wanted to see results. Derek had learned, therefore, to take promises lightly. He had learned to fully trust no one but himself. He had become an expert in self-reliance, which had proved its worth many times over during his climb to the top in a cutthroat field.

It was a little disturbing for him to realize that he'd come to rely on Sabrina's straightforwardness. It was more than a little disturbing for him to wonder if he wasn't in for a fall.

His mood went from bad to worse, from confusion to irritation to anger, which subsequently clouded his judgment.

That was why he wasn't prepared when he was jumped and dragged into the shadows on his way back to his cell after dinner Monday night. The attack wasn't life-threatening; it didn't involve a knife or other makeshift weapon; nor did it have anything to do with Noel Greer. Derek had brought it on himself by absently sitting at the wrong table in the dining hall, then not at all absently compounding the error by taking too long to move.

The beating was administered by the two bodyguards of the inmate whose turf he'd violated. Derek's first instinct was to fight back, and he had more than enough anger in him to do it with style. But he also had some sense. If he yelled or returned punches or did anything else to attract the attention of the guards, he'd be disciplined; and if that happened, the parole board would hear. His previous stint in solitary was the sole blemish on his record. He didn't want another.

So he didn't make a sound other than the occasional involuntary moan. He didn't take a single swing at his opponents, even when their taunts took the form of slurs against his profession, his dead mother and the color of his lawyer's skin. He did little more than try to protect those parts of himself that were more vulnerable than others.

Whether he succeeded was questionable. By the time he was left alone, his entire body was screaming in pain. Calling on the last of his battered reserves, he hauled himself up and stumbled to his cell. No one looked at him twice. No one noticed that he was clutching his middle, that blood stained his face, that he was half doubled over and limping.

He fell on his cot and, for more than an hour, didn't move. Then, wincing with each breath, he made his painful way down the row of cells, past the common room where a group was watching the baseball game on television, and into the shower room. No one looked, no one saw, no one cared.

Clothes and all he stood, shaking badly, under the spray until the pain began to localize. He knew that his left eye and bottom lip were swollen, but his nose had stopped bleeding and didn't seem to be broken. There was pain in the area of his ribs. He assumed he'd bruised, if not broken, a few, but he could handle that. What bothered him more was his stomach. He prayed that the pain he felt was caused by muscle bruising, rather than internal bleeding, because he had no intention of reporting to the dispensary.

He remembered hearing of an inmate who, after a fight, had lain for days on his cot holding together a gash that should have been stitched. He supposed he could do that, too—if there was a gash to be held. But when he'd completed the excruciating ordeal of peeling off his clothes, he found nothing but badly discoloring flesh.

Not knowing whether to be relieved, and feeling distinctly sick to his stomach, he made it back to his cell in time to throw up in the toilet. Then he collapsed on the cot and waited for death.

Death didn't come that night or the following morning. And that afternoon, shortly after three, it wasn't death that came, but Sabrina.

Derek would have been better prepared for death.

Sabrina's appearance took him totally off guard. It was Tuesday, for one thing, not Thursday, and after the way she'd run off the week before, he hadn't expected her to show at all. For another thing, he didn't know if he *wanted* to see her. He was still furious that she'd been less than forthright with him, and he blamed that fury on the distraction that had caused his lapse in the dining room, which in turn had caused the beating that was responsible for his present agony. Which led him to the last point—that he wasn't sure he wanted her to see *him*. He looked awful.

"Well?" demanded the house guard who'd notified him of her arrival. "She's waiting in the yard. Are you going or not?"

Derek hadn't moved a muscle, partly because he didn't know if he should and partly because he didn't know if he could. Sheer grit had enabled him to struggle through his work assignment, but the effort had drained him. He hadn't made it to any meals since dinner the night before. The thought of moving was nearly as painful as the deed itself.

"What'll it be, McGill?"

Carefully, Derek maneuvered his legs over the side of the cot and sat up. He took several shallow breaths, then pushed himself to his feet. Straightening his shoulders, he set off.

Pure determination kept him walking. He had a thing or two to tell Sabrina Stone, and the sooner he said them the better off he'd be. He wasn't a plaything. He wasn't a spectacle or a novelty. And he wasn't a man to be lied to. If she couldn't come clean and accept that, she could just stay the hell away.

In fact, staying the hell away wasn't such a bad idea, he decided. He didn't need her. David was right: she was an unnecessary complication. What in the hell good was she doing him—besides stirring him up and then walking away?

Past the row of cells, down a flight of stairs, out the door, along a lengthy path—he plodded on. His anger helped: it kept his spine stiff and his pace remarkably steady. Something happened, though, when he reached the visiting yard and caught sight of Sabrina standing by a tree with her back to him.

Anger fled. His heart started pounding. He struggled to swallow. He felt—though he didn't understand it, because he couldn't remember the last time he'd done it—as though he were going to cry.

Then she turned and he knew he couldn't cry. On top of everything else, the humiliation would have been too much. So he steadied himself, sucked a stream of air into his lungs, held it there and sauntered forward.

Sabrina stared. Her eyes widened with each step he took, and by the time he was standing an arm's length away, she had lost what little color she'd had. "My God!" she cried hoarsely. "What *happened*?"

All he wanted to do was take her in his arms, hold her and weep, and he couldn't do any of it. "I walked into a wall," he said in the somewhat weak and grainy voice that had been his since the beating.

"You didn't walk into a wall." She looked over his face again and whispered another horrified, "My God"; then she raised a hand to touch the scabbing cut on his lower lip, thought twice, pressed the hand to her own lips.

"I didn't expect you today," he said stiffly.

Sabrina had been so upset by his appearance that it took her a minute to recall why she'd come. She dropped her hand from her mouth and closed it around the soft leather of the purse that was clutched under her arm. "I had to see you," she said, but distractedly. Having given up on the cut lip, she was studying his eye. He had a whopper of a purple shiner, which was in turn rimmed by skin that was scraped and red. She couldn't help but wince. "Have you seen a doctor?"

"No."

"You're not walking right."

"I thought I did pretty well, all things considered," he quipped, then wished he'd saved the cockiness for a more appropriate time. "I've got to sit down," he mumbled and moved as fast as he could to the nearest seat, which happened to be a picnic table that was unoccupied. Gingerly he eased himself down, facing outward on the bench. He leaned back until the table touched his spine, further braced himself with his elbows, and with a small moan, extended his legs and closed his eyes.

Sabrina sat down beside him. "You've hurt your ribs, haven't you?"

"Yup."

"Are any broken?"

"Your guess is as good as mine."

"And you haven't bothered with a doctor? Derek, even your voice sounds strange. What if you've broken a rib and it's punctured a lung?"

"I'd be coughing up blood and I'm not."

She reached out and lightly touched his middle. "You've wrapped it?"

He nodded. "Tore up an old shirt." Then he opened his

eyes and smirked as much as his crusted lip would allow. "One advantage of working in the laundry."

Her hand stayed where it was, resting lightly, very lightly on the worn blue fabric of his shirt. "What *happened*?"

"I fell down a flight of stairs."

"You were in another fight."

"I didn't fight."

"Then you were beaten."

"I decided not to fight, so, yes, I was beaten. For Christ's sake, Sabrina, stop staring at me like that. I know I look awful, but you're making it worse. Say something nice. Lie a little." He was about to say that it wouldn't be the first time she'd lied to him, when she started to speak.

"Nick and I split. It happened almost three weeks ago. I should have told you when I came last week, and I don't know why I didn't, but I've been having trouble knowing what to do lately. I'm sorry."

The words had come in a soft-spoken rush, and if the urgency of her tone hadn't taken the wind from Derek's sails, the apology in her eyes would have. And then he felt even more contrite when she said, "I wrote three separate letters to you, but none of them said what I wanted to say. The problem was that I didn't *know* what I wanted to say. So I figured I'd come instead. I decided that this morning, and it seemed foolish to wait until Thursday, but I wasn't able to get Nicky set as quickly as I'd hoped, so I'm a little late."

Looking at her as she sat beside him, Derek was reminded of the first time he'd ever seen her. Then, as now, she was the picture of innocence. She was even wearing similar clothes—a long, softly pleated skirt and a full overblouse that gave her a delicate look. Mint green was the color this time, and it added a dimension to her eyes that refreshed him like cool spring water.

He felt the pinching in his body ease a little. "Do you know what you want to say now?"

"No." She swallowed. "Maybe you could ask questions."

He didn't want to ask questions. His jaw hurt when he

spoke. But he remembered how angry he'd been, and that kind of pain was worse than anything with his jaw, so he asked, "Why didn't you tell me about you and Nick last week?"

"Not that question. I don't think I have the answer yet."

"How about what went wrong with the marriage?"

She lowered her eyes and drew her hand back to the shelter of the folds of her skirt. "It's a temptation to say that Nicky went wrong with the marriage, but that wouldn't be fair." Her voice was muted by shame. "Or accurate. If Nick and I had been right for each other, we'd have been able to handle Nicky's problems. Some couples come through hard times closer than ever."

"Why didn't it work?" When she simply frowned at her skirt, he prodded. "You must have thought it would when you married him."

"I did," she said, meeting his gaze for a minute before looking off down the yard. "Nick struck me as being very strong, very organized, very dedicated, very normal."

"Normal?"

"He wasn't weird like my family."

"Don't you like your family?"

"I *love* my family, but they're weird. They are their books, and that'd be fine if they wrote something that related to reality, but they don't. Mom is spacey, Dad is an anachronism, and J. B. is his own little shop of horrors. And it isn't only what they write, it's how they do it. Twenty hours at a stretch—honest, twenty hours—and when they finally stop you never know what mood they'll be in. They could walk out of the room and take your head off if the writing went poorly. Or they could spring for dinner at the Top of the Mark and throw in a carriage ride through the hills for good measure. Then again, they could come off their writing to find that the others were *on*, so there was no one to go to dinner *with*, and then there was trouble."

"All three work that way?"

She nodded. "It's one of the reasons Mom and Dad don't live together; one of the reasons J. B. is divorced. That kind of life doesn't make for easy companionship."

"And you thought you'd have that with Nick?"

"You look skeptical."

"I've never met the man myself, but from all I've heard, Nicholas Stone isn't the companionable type."

"He was at first."

"But it ended with the 'I do's'?"

"No. It went on a little longer, until business really got hot. Then he was putting in sixteen-hour work days, and when he came home he didn't have time to relax with me."

Strange, Derek thought, but if he'd ever married, his wife would probably have said the same about him. Some men were driven. He'd always assumed that it was inherent to a particular personality. He was a natural competitor. He wanted success and he wanted it badly. Now, though, he wondered if being driven was simply a way of compensating for what one's life lacked. He couldn't imagine not wanting to spend time with Sabrina if she were his.

"It wasn't the long work days that bothered me, though," she continued. "I had my own writing. I could easily fill my time while Nick was working. But I wanted time with him. He seemed to think that was frivolous. He said that he had to make the most of his free time, since he had so little of it, and making the most meant exercising— playing handball or tennis or golf—or attending to social obligations."

She fell silent, thinking about what she'd said, wondering if she sounded like a spoiled brat who wanted attention, wondering if she *was* one. But no, it wasn't attention she wanted so much as love. There was a difference.

She looked up to find Derek studying her, and she was struck again by his bruises. "You really look awful," she whispered, knowing that if he wasn't normally so handsome she'd never have been as blunt. "Do you feel as bad as you look?"

He would have shrugged but didn't dare. "It comes and goes."

"You're very pale."

"That's prison pallor." The good corner of his mouth curved. "You've got it, too."

She returned a small smile. "As wardens go, Nicky is

tough. He doesn't allow me much yard time." The smile waned. "You're *very* pale. Are you sure you're okay.?"

"I'm not going to be sick, if that's what you're asking. I haven't eaten a thing since last night."

She was about to tell him that that was why he was so pale, that he needed food if he wanted strength. But she'd done enough hovering. She wasn't his mother. She didn't want to be. So instead of browbeating him, she opened her purse and took out a small bag.

He looked from her face to the bag and back. "What's in it?"

"Open it and see."

He looked at the bag again. "I can't. It takes too much effort. You do it."

Carefully unfolding the top of the bag, she removed a thick cookie, one of several inside, and handed it over. He took it with a minimum of movement, just the slight swivel of his forearm on his elbow. "Oh God," he said hoarsely, "Mrs.   Fields' . . . white-chunk . . . macadamia   nut . . ." Squeezing his eyes shut, he looked in more pain than ever.

"Derek? Are you okay?"

"Oh, yeah," he croaked, but she didn't know what to think, so she began to babble.

"You said you dreamed of them. I thought you'd like a few. I didn't know if they'd let me bring them in, but I couldn't not try. You don't have to eat any if you don't want. I'll take them back home if—"

With a suddenness of movement that surprised them both, he shot out a hand and grabbed the bag. "No way," he gasped, eyes wide open. "I'll keep them, thank you." He raised the cookie and took a small bite. It all but melted in his mouth. This time when he closed his eyes and effected the look of pain, she understood that the agony was ecstasy.

"They're not *that* good."

"Fine for you to say. You haven't had to go without them for eighteen months." He took another bite, let it linger on his tongue until it slid down his throat. And he realized that, prison or no prison, no one had ever brought him little goodies before. He'd never been the little-goodie type. He was always on the go, never sick, usually the one in charge, the one to order the tickets, send the bouquet, pick up the tab. Oh, women had given him things—coffee-table books, silk dressing gowns, cologne—and Sabrina could have afforded the best of any of those—but she'd chosen to bring him the one thing he'd mentioned wanting.

His throat tightened up, and again he had the unsettling urge to cry. He sat forward with deliberate force, knowing that the pain would stem that urge. It did.

"Derek?"

"Just stretching," he managed to grunt, then settled carefully back again. Aware that Sabrina was watching him, he finished the cookie as nonchalantly as he could, then said, "Tell me more about your marriage."

"Ask another question."

Another question. Another question. Derek took a breath that was a little too deep. He flinched at the sharp pain in his ribs, then tightened his jaw in compensation. "Do you love him?"

He'd asked the question more than once when she'd visited him last. She'd been evasive then. Now she felt she owed him more. "No. I don't love him. I did once, or I think I did, but I may have just been in love with what he represented, I don't know."

Derek felt immeasurable relief. He didn't know why, because there were still a million obstacles standing in the way of any relationship he and Sabrina might have. But one less was one less. So he enjoyed the relief for a minute, which was just about all he had. Sitting up was doing him no good. He hurt. In an attempt to ease the pain, he shifted gingerly, but the new position was even less comfortable, so he returned to the old.

"You're feeling worse, aren't you?"

"Just a little stiff."

"I have aspirin. Will you take some?" She was already digging in her purse for the small, commercially labeled container.

Derek wasn't a masochist. He opened a hand to receive the two tablets and was about to slap them toward his throat when a guard came from nowhere and clamped an iron hand on his wrist.

"Hold it right there."

"It's aspirin, damn it," Derek grunted. "Look for yourself. The name's right on the pill." The way the guard was leaning put pressure on his shoulder, which in turn compressed his ribs and hurt him all the more.

"Here's the tin," Sabrina said in a frightened voice. She held it out to the guard, but her eyes were on Derek's ashen face. "They checked it when I came in."

That made no difference. Taking his time, the guard examined each of the pills in Derek's hand, then took the tiny tin from Sabrina and studied the remaining six tablets. When he'd satisfied himself that nothing but aspirin was being exchanged, he straightened and walked off without the slightest apology.

Derek tossed the pills back, swallowed them dry, then muttered, "I gotta lie down."

For a split second, Sabrina feared that he meant to end the visit and return to his cell. Her heart dropped, then lifted when he pushed himself from the picnic table and limpéd toward a nearby tree. Moments later, he was lying on the thick bed of shaded grass, but her heart had dropped again, because she'd seen the pain he'd endured to get himself there.

Without a qualm, she lowered herself to the grass with her back against the tree. "Lift up a little," she whispered, and very gently eased his head onto her lap. "Better?"

He closed his eyes and sighed. "Mmm."

She began lightly to massage his temples. It seemed the most natural thing to do. She couldn't imagine letting her hands lie idle when they could so easily offer a little relief.

"You seem exhausted," she said. "Is it from the pain?"

"I didn't sleep much last night."

"This happened yesterday?"

"Mmm." Her fingers were warm, smooth, gentle, and they worked magic. "Sabrina?"

"Yes?"

"If Nick were to be waiting for you when you returned to New York, would you take him back?"

"No."

"Not even if he begged?"

"Not even then, but he wouldn't beg. I think he's as relieved to be free of me as I am of him."

"Are you really?"

"Relieved?" She thought for a minute. "Yes, and I don't think I'm saying that out of pride or defensiveness or anything emotional like that. When Nick walks into a room, he brings with him a certain tension. He's on all the time, wants things done yesterday and wants them done well. Even before Nicky was born, I used to scurry around trying to please him. Then, after Nicky, when things got so heavy, there was no pleasing Nick.

"It was a strain knowing that everything I did was open for attack." Her voice was soft, a little distant. Her fingers whispered, stroked, occasionally combed through Derek's hair. "I've spent the past three years living with fear and tension and worry. Nick wouldn't accept what had happened to Nicky. He couldn't understand what it was doing to me. I was awful at times. I admit it. I was short-tempered and demanding." She paused. "Maybe, subconsciously, I was pushing him toward making a move."

Derek registered the words and was vaguely aware of their insightfulness, but he couldn't focus deeply when one part of him was floating. The best he could do was to ask, "Have things been better since he moved out?"

"Things have been different."

Understandably, Derek was more concerned about her present and future. Opening his eyes, he looked up into her face. "Where do you go from here, Sabrina? Are you staying put in New York?"

Her thumb had come to rest, ever so lightly, by the cut at his lip. She made no attempt to move it. "For the time being. At least until I know more of what's what with Nicky."

"Do you think he knows what's happened?"

"No."

"Do you think he misses Nick?"

"For a while he seemed to recognize him. He'd start breathing a little faster, like he was excited, when Nick started talking to him. Lately—the last six or eight months—there's been nothing. Maybe it's just as well. I'd probably be more torn over the divorce if I felt Nicky would be affected."

Derek bent up one knee, tipping his body slightly toward hers. He'd been lulled so well that he was taken by surprise when the faint movement made him wince.

"Is the aspirin helping at all?" she asked worriedly.

"I think so," he answered. But her touch was more powerful a balm than aspirin. Closing his eyes, he gave himself up to those wonderfully fluid, ever serene fingers. "Feels like heaven," he murmured. The fingers were on his scalp, seducing his skull. "You're good at this. Is it the Nicky treatment?"

She chuckled softly. "No. He doesn't appreciate the finer points of massage."

"I do."

"I'm glad."

Derek repeated those last lines to himself. They could have been suggestive or sexy, but they weren't. Sex was the last thing he wanted; given the pain he felt when he moved, he doubted he could perform if he tried. But Sabrina wasn't demanding performance. She wasn't demanding anything. She didn't ask if she could touch him here or there—and there, now, was the crook of his neck, which she was kneading with soft, easy strokes—but she touched him with the gossamer sureness of a woman whose instincts were his.

He gave a soft moan of pleasure and rubbed his cheek against her thigh. "Sabrina?"

"Mmm?"

"How do you feel when you come here?"

"I feel . . . glad to see you."

"I mean about the place. Does it depress you?"

"What's to depress? We're nestled in the foothills of the Berkshires, in a yard with trees and grass and benches. The air is fresh. The sun is shining. The birds are singing."

"And the guards in the watchtowers shoot real bullets."

"Shh. Don't spoil it. As a matter of fact," she resumed brightly, "if you squint, the fences disappear."

"You're not squinting. You're wearing rose-colored glasses."

"Maybe so, but I'm tired of being down all the time." She gave a light snort. "All this is easy for me to say. I'm not the one in prison blues."

Derek was, so he found little solace in the fresh air, the shining sun, the singing birds; and when he squinted, his eyes hurt. But that didn't mean that he couldn't dream. "If you could choose to be anywhere else right now, where would it be?"

"Anywhere else? Hmmm . . . let's see . . . I think maybe Ireland."

"Ever been there?"

"Once, when I was very young. I remember everything being lush and green, cool and moist and clear. It would be nice to be there, sitting just like this." She wondered if she'd been too revealing, but then she didn't care. She'd already told him that she was glad to see him, and that was modestly enough put. When she was with him, the prison faded away. She could *easily* imagine they were in Ireland. "Why do you ask?"

"It's a game I play sometimes. Not often; but once in a while at night, when I'm really down, when I think that I'm going mad lying in that damned cell, and nothing else works to take my mind off it, not even the anger, I close my eyes and picture myself in some exotic place."

"Like?"

"Tahiti. I've never been there. I'd like to go. Or the rain forest of Brazil. Or New Guinea."

"Mmmmm." She wore a small, dreamy smile as she continued to stroke him. *Tahiti.* The pad of her thumb moved slowly along his jaw, back and forth, up over his beard-roughened cheek to his sideburns, then, slowly, all the way down to his chin. *Peaceful, unspoiled, idyllic.* She traced his ear, rubbed its small lobe. From there she followed a tendon down his neck, drew her fingers across his throat, slid them under the tabs of his shirt and began gently, rhythmically to massage his chest.

She could easily go to Tahiti. She didn't know if she'd have the nerve to play bare-breasted in the surf, but Derek could do that. His bare skin was a joy. Stretched over well-defined muscle, it was warm, firm, softened by fine swirls of dark, curling hair. As her fingertips played in those swirls, her eye roamed his body. There was the bulk under his shirt that she knew to be the wrapping around his ribs, but his waist and hips were as narrow as ever, his legs exceedingly long. His jeans weren't tight, but the force of gravity settled the denim against his flesh, outlining lean calves, well sinewed thighs and . . . and sex that was heavy and full, even at rest.

Her hands went still and she looked away, embarrassed by what she'd thought. But within the space of several short breaths, she was looking back. Derek's body fascinated her. She couldn't remember ever feeling quite the same fascination with a man's body, though whether that was because Derek's body was so beautifully made or not, she didn't know. Nick was good-looking, but she'd never felt this kind of excitement.

Just then Derek's cheek touched her arm. Her eyes flew to his face, shadowed now by the folds of her skirt, and she turned crimson with guilt at having been caught with lascivious thoughts. But there was no need. His eyes were closed, more relaxed than they'd been before. In fact, his entire face—what she could see of it—was more relaxed, and it was only a minute before she realized that his breathing was slow and even.

A well of emotion surged within her. Tenderness, caring, pleasure—all peaceful, removed from time and place —deeply gratifying and renewing. With one hand cradling his head and the other on his chest, she rested against the tree and watched him while he slept.

· *CHAPTER 8* ·

Derek slept for forty minutes and would surely have gone on far longer had Sabrina not awakened him. She called his name softly, lightly shook his shoulder, then held him steady when he came to with a start.

"You fell asleep," she whispered, leaning over him. "Visiting hours are over. They're kicking me out."

Disoriented, he stared up at her, then forced his eyes wider and looked around. "I don't believe it," he said hoarsely.

"You were worn out."

"God, I'm sorry."

"Don't be. I didn't mind. How do you feel?"

"Better, I think." He hadn't slept long, but he'd slept soundly, and he had Sabrina to thank for that. For the first time in eighteen months, he'd felt safe. Struggling to a sitting position, he asked, "It's four?"

"Uh-huh."

He looked around. The visiting yard had emptied. The prison had swallowed its own, except for him. Knowing that shortly he too would be swallowed and that there was nothing he could do about it, he put on his bravest front. "Where to from here? Are you going on to Vermont?"

"Not this time."

That meant she'd driven the distance solely to see him —and he'd fallen asleep on her. He felt like a heel. "Are you staying overnight somewhere nearby?"

She shook her head.

That meant she was doing the round trip in a day. It was a lot of driving, too much, he thought, and she was alone. "Sabrina..."

"Driving relaxes me. It lets me unwind, lets me think. I hadn't realized how much I missed doing it until I started coming up here." She dropped her gaze to his shirtfront. Barely moving her lips, she whispered, "I put the tin of aspirin in your pocket. I don't think they saw me do it."

He found her attempt at subterfuge adorable. Sabrina was that, along with everything else. He hadn't seen it at the start because it only came out when she was relaxed. It pleased him to think that she was relaxed with him. It astonished him that she could relax at all in a place like this, but that said something about her versatility.

"I hate to tell you this, sunshine," he drawled, "but they'll find it in a minute. As soon as I walk through that door, I'll be searched."

"Is that routine?"

As he nodded, he felt sadness stalking. As soon as he walked through that door, she'd be gone. She'd be gone. The thought of it was like a tear in the fabric of his heart, and that gave him something else to consider.

"They'll let me keep the aspirin," he said in a more subdued tone.

"How about Ace bandages? If I pick up a couple in town and drop them at the administration building, will you get them?"

"Not necessarily."

"Should I try anyway?"

"Nah."

"Let's go, folks," said a guard sauntering by. "Time's up."

Sabrina scrambled to her feet. It took Derek a minute longer. Tiny beads of sweat had broken out on his forehead when he turned to her, closed a hand around her arm and asked, "Why didn't you tell me about Nick and you last week?"

She saw the urgency in his eyes and knew that she couldn't postpone the answering. She'd been too honest about other things. It was time.

"I was frightened," she said in a whisper-soft voice that trembled. Her eyes begged for understanding. "I was using Nick as a buffer because I was frightened. I'm still frightened. You keep asking me what I'm doing here, and I can tell you that I want a friend, someone to talk to, that I want to write a book, but there's more. You said it. You feel it. I feel it too. And it frightens me, Derek. It's so"—she caught her breath—"strong."

Unable to help himself, Derek took her face in his hands. It didn't matter that his lip was bruised and swollen, or that his eye was a sight, or that the way his heart was pounding threatened imminent damage to his already damaged ribs. He brushed a light kiss on her forehead, then the bridge of her nose, then her cheek.

She closed her fingers around bunches of his shirt. "I'm frightened, Derek."

"Me too."

"So much is happening. I don't know who I am or where I'm going."

His mouth touched hers once, then again in feather-soft touches that sent airy crinkles to the tips of her toes. "Later. Think later," he whispered and kissed her a third time. Then he tipped his head and tried a new angle.

It worked magnificently. How something as light could be as powerful was beyond her. She could almost imagine a magnetic pull, a pull that rendered the slightest touch evocative, deep and clinging. "Derek?"

"I know. It's happening." He drew her against him with a low, guttural sound.

"I'm hurting you!"

"No, no. Shhh. It's okay." He wrapped his arms around her and pressed her body to his, imprinting the feel of it on his mind. He wanted to be able to call it back during the lonely hours, when angry eyes surrounded him and there was little to do but count the holes in the wall. At those times he would remember her shape, her smell, her gentleness. She was his escape. She was a ray of sun in a world that was hostile and gray.

With a wrenching groan, he set her back. He took her hands from his neck, closed them in his and brought them to his lips. He wanted to know when he'd see her again, but he hated to have to ask. He hated being helpless. He hated being the one visited. He hated having to sit still and wait for her return. So, instead, he said gruffly, "I'd call you sometime, but the phone's bugged."

"I could give letter writing another shot."

He received mail. There were typewritten letters from David, from his agent, from one of his ex-producers and a few loyal members of his crew, as well as from a handful of friends who didn't quite have the courage to visit but wanted to keep in touch.

But all that was different. He imagined receiving a hand-written letter on jasmine scented paper, imagined himself lying in his cell at night reading and rereading it, deriving untold pleasures from the words. Then he imagined the guards reading it before him, soiling it with their beefy fingers and their petty minds. Or worse, reporting on its contents to the warden. Or *worse*, to a faceless agent of Noel Greer.

Derek knew that Sabrina could never work for Greer. What he didn't know was whether Greer could somehow, sometime, someplace use Sabrina to get at him. The thought was chilling. He had to see that she was protected.

"They read my mail," he said.

"Then I'll have to make sure I don't write anything incriminating."

"No, Sabrina. Don't write. I think it might be better that way."

"Are you sure?"

He nodded.

She would have argued, except that he was looking pale again. She searched his face, making no effort to hide her concern. "If you don't feel well, if you start to feel worse, will you tell someone?"

"I'll be fine."

"Derek . . ." Her voice trailed off. She was lost in his eyes. They were every bit as magnetic as his mouth. "I have to leave now," she whispered dumbly. Gray . . . silver . . . varying in hue with his emotion . . . gunmetal now in frustration. "I may not be able to get back for a couple of weeks. The doctor suggested we try Nicky on a new program."

"Sabrina . . ."

She put her hand up to his face, stopping his words. She bit her lip, studied him for a lingering moment through troubled eyes, reached up and put a light kiss on his cheek, then broke away and headed for the gate.

June passed for Sabrina with the speed of a snail and the sword of Damocles hanging over her head. Not until the start of July did she see her way clear to meeting Maura for lunch.

"You're a damn busy lady," Maura drawled, holding her back after the requisite hug. "Mornings at the museum, afternoons at the polo grounds, evenings in the royal box at the ballet."

Sabrina sputtered out a weak laugh. "Sure. Right."

"Well," her friend went on with a magnanimous sigh, "I must say that such frivolity is taking its toll. Your eye is twitching."

Not knowing whether to laugh or cry, Sabrina bit hard on her lower lip. She didn't let up until she and Maura were seated in a plant-infested corner of the trendy restaurant. She took a long drink of ice water, then spread the thick linen napkin on her lap.

"Sorry I had to cancel on you last week. The doctor forbid me to get out of bed."

"What happened?"

"I passed out wheeling Nicky through the park."

"Christ!"

"It's been one of those months."

"But what was wrong?"

Sabrina shrugged. "I'm a little anemic and a lot exhausted. I'm taking vitamins. They should help."

"And sleep? Are you getting it?"

"Some. Soon."

Maura studied her friend's face. It was tired but calm, a calm that was disturbed only by troubled eyes. "Sabrina?"

"I'm doing it, Maura. I'm placing Nicky at the Greenhouse. I've agonized and agonized over it, and if you say that I'm being selfish, I'll get right up from this table and walk out—"

"You know I won't do that."

Sabrina paused, slowly nodded, then resumed quietly.

"It just hasn't worked. I've given him everything I have, but it isn't enough. He's unhappy. *I*'m unhappy. The program we had him on last month did nothing. Even the doctors agreed."

How well she remembered that conversation—every word, every gesture, every feeling. She had gone for a consultation with Howard Frasier, the specialist who had directed her on the new program, and they'd been joined by his associate. Both men had looked grim, but in a different way from that to which she was accustomed. Even before she'd heard the solemnity in Frasier's voice, she sensed that a bridge had been crossed.

"Frankly, Mrs. Stone," he said, "I'm surprised you kept at it as long as you did. I assumed you'd stop when we agreed the program wasn't working."

"I had to be sure," she explained. "I kept thinking, 'Today's the day he'll respond.' And when he didn't, I said, 'Tomorrow's the day he'll respond.' Even now I'm worried that I've given up one day too soon."

"You haven't," Frasier said. His expression had gentled, and there was a stoic regret in his voice. "I don't believe you'll ever see results."

Sabrina had been taken off-guard. In her months, years of dealing with medical and social service personnel, none had ever been as blunt. A bit wide-eyed, she switched her gaze to Frasier's companion, who shook his head and said quietly, "If your son had been stuck in a corner and ignored since birth, I'd have said that maybe this intensive program was too much too fast. But you've been stimulating him since birth. You've been talking to him, exercising him, working him on various other programs before this one. Theoretically, he'd have been ripe to respond. But he didn't. If as rigorous a program as this hasn't produced any results . . ." He gave a subtle shrug as his voice trailed off.

At that moment, Sabrina had felt both devastated and relieved. The best she'd been able to do was to look from one doctor to the other and let her eyes ask what her tongue wouldn't.

But Howard Frasier had only shaken his head and smiled sadly. "I can't tell you that. I can't recommend that you institutionalize your son, if by doing so you'll be miserable."

"Would I be wrong to do it?" she asked cautiously.

"I can only answer from a medical standpoint—and even then, what I say is nothing more than my opinion. No, you wouldn't be wrong to do it." He raised querying brows toward his colleague, who tossed a hand at the file folder that lay on the desk. It was bulging with papers.

"You son has undergone every imaginable test. Researchers are always studying brain damage, and it is possible that in five or ten years a new test will be devised to better identify the source and scope of the problem, but as far as medical science has evolved today, there's nothing more we can do for Nicky."

"Do *you* recommend institutionalization?" Sabrina had asked, seeking direction.

"I'd have to agree with Howard. You wouldn't be wrong to do it, but the decision has to be yours."

Sabrina had sat quietly, weighing—again, still—the pros and cons of the move. Finally she confessed, "I think what worries me most is the prospect of placing Nicky and then, when he's in a different environment, seeing an improvement."

Frasier had held up a cautionary hand. "That might happen. We have no guarantee that it won't, but you have to understand that if it happens, and that's a big if, it will be a small improvement and most likely temporary. Nicky simply doesn't have the wherewithal—" he tapped his head, "—to think." He let out a breath. "And that's what you have to accept. Finally."

It was at once the easiest and the hardest thing to do, and on some level Sabrina was still grappling with it as she talked with Maura. "I left that office and went home determined to prove them wrong. But two more days was all it took. I couldn't keep up the pace. I don't have what it takes."

"Maybe not to be a full-time caretaker, but very few people can be that."

But he's my son. If I love him, I should be able to rise to the occasion. I'm his mother. I carried him for nine months. I brought him into the world with a defect. He's my responsibility. He has no one else. Can I really be so cruel as to send him away . . . send him away . . . send him away?

The arguments echoed in her mind as they'd been doing for months, and lest she forget one, she'd been reminded of them often in the past few weeks. Family . . . friends . . . all with opinions about the fastest route to martyrdom.

"Anyway," Sabrina said, "I brought him to the Greenhouse for an evaluation." She smiled crookedly, doing her best to mask the emptiness she felt each time she thought of it. "They fell in love with him. Who wouldn't? He's an adorable little bugger."

"Can they help him?"

"No one can help him. But they'll take him." She thought back to her most recent visit there and the warm reception Nicky had been given. "I suppose I could do a lot worse. As institutions go, the Greenhouse is un-institutional."

"Well, it's a cute name."

"It is, literally, the Greens' house. They're a middle-aged couple—professionals, he was a teacher, she a social worker—who went through hell trying to find a placement for their own son. They finally decided that if they wanted a place that was progressive and upbeat and clean, they were going to have to make it themselves. So they bought a huge house on dozens of acres in Vermont, renovated it, added a series of smaller outbuildings, got licensed, hired help and went into business." She sighed but said nothing more.

"Are the Greens nice?"

She nodded.

"And theirg staff?"

"Efficient and dedicated."

"I take it the facilities are good. How about the other inmates?"

"Not inmates. Residents. There are only about twenty-five. They're from all over the country, range in age from three to eighteen, come from families that can swing the stiff cost, which means that they're well dressed. They have varying types and degrees of handicaps, but they're all mentally deficient."

"Sounds ideal," Maura said dryly.

"As ideal as any institution for the retarded can be." The void yawned in the area of her heart. Ideal or not, she'd be leaving her baby there. Her baby. She'd give her right arm for a better solution, but there was none. "The thing is, I don't want to be a caretaker or a martyr. I want to lead a normal life."

Maura sent her a sympathetic look. "You always did." Then she scowled. "Old Nick was supposed to do it for you, but he blew it."

Sabrina snorted. "Old Nick. Old Nick may be smarter than me. Know what he did last week?"

"What did he do?"

"Flew off to Haiti and got a divorce." She tossed it off with nonchalance, but there was hurt beneath her bravado.

"What was the friggin' rush?"

"It seems that he's fallen in love. He married her last weekend."

"The rat!"

"Our relationship was over. We reached an amicable settlement. It was all very legal."

"But to turn around and run to someone new before the ink had even dried—he must be very insecure."

Sabrina found Maura's analysis disconcerting. More than once she'd wondered if that was what she was doing with Derek—running to him out of insecurity. She didn't think so, though he was good for her ego on many scores. But if her insecurity was man-related, it didn't make sense that she'd run to *him*. He was in prison. He couldn't squire her around town. She couldn't preen on his arm the way some women did their latest conquests. Or brag about his sexual prowess.

Not that she'd ever do that.

No, she didn't think it was insecurity. And, in any case, the theory that Nick had been insecure enough to marry the first woman he found wasn't apt.

"The fact is," Sabrina said, "that Nick's been seeing Carol for over a year."

"Shhhit."

"Mmm."

Maura said nothing for a minute, then asked in a low, slow voice, "How did you find out?"

"Cybil Timmerman. Nick and Carol held their reception at the club. Cybil is the club maven. She couldn't resist calling me to get my reaction to the wedding. I suspect she rather enjoyed worming that little tidbit into the conversation."

Maura offered a murmured evaluation of Cybil Timmerman that would have shocked a truck driver, but there was something about the annoyance on her face that gave Sabrina pause.

"Maura . . . did you have any idea?"

"Any idea of what?"

"Nick and Carol."

"Me?"

"Yes, you," Sabrina came back with dawning light. "You knew, didn't you? You knew he'd been seeing her before he and I split."

"I didn't *know* it," Maura protested, then began to waffle. "I may have *suspected* it, but you know me. I have a filthy mind. I can't trust half of what I think."

Sabrina was distressed and more than a little disappointed. Maura was her good friend, and a good friend was to be counted on for the truth, regardless of how filthy it was. Closing her eyes, she took a deep breath. It came out in an airy, "Oh, Maura, why couldn't you have told me?"

"Because I didn't know for sure, and anyway, you don't just go up to a man's wife and pop news like that."

"There is such a thing as a subtle delivery."

"Not my specialty, hon."

"You could have written me an anonymous note."

"You're the writer."

"And you're my friend. If I can't rely on my friend to tell me something like that, who *can* I rely on? You could have saved me a little humiliation."

"Oh? Now how could I have done that? The facts haven't changed. Infidelity is infidelity, and it's always a bitch for the one who is two-timed. Would it have been any less humiliating if you'd learned *while* you were married that he was screwing around?"

"Yes. Then I could have had the upper hand. I could have had the satisfaction of kicking him out on his ear."

Maura shifted in her seat, ordered a double scotch to Sabrina's wine spritzer, then finally met Sabrina's gaze. "Okay. I was wrong. I'm sorry."

But Sabrina, too, had given it more thought. "Don't be," she muttered. "You did what you thought was right, and anyway, I should have seen it. I should have known . . . all the business trips . . . not being able to reach him on the phone. I should have guessed it, but I didn't. Maybe I didn't want to. Subconsciously, I may have been fighting the idea of divorce. Maybe things had to happen the way they did for me to accept it. The marriage was over. It wasn't Nicky. It wasn't Carol, or any other woman. It was us."

"That's philosophical of you."

Sabrina gave a low chuckle. "You've caught me in a mellow moment. By the way, your hair looks great. More auburn than Titian this time?"

"Mmmm. I think it looks more mature. At least, that's what Franco says."

"Franco?"

"My stylist. He loves Titian hair, and he lo-ves mature women."

"Franco?" Sabrina echoed dubiously.

Maura flicked several fingers into the air. "For a little while. But he's only a means to an end. Mature is very definitely in my future. Want to hear about my latest project?"

"Goose eggs are *mature*?"

"Not goose eggs. You were right. Cheesecake is overdone. No, no, this is more exciting." She paused and held her breath, eyes glowing.

Sabrina waited expectantly, then, when Maura simply beamed, opened a hand and said, "Well?"

"Urban spas."

"Urban spas?"

"Urban spas. You know, health spas. There are loads of

them outside the city, but practically none in. And why not? Why shouldn't a woman—or a man—be able to walk uptown, check into a spa for the weekend, come out massaged, sauna-ed, exercised and five pounds lighter? Most people gain their weight on the weekend. My plan would prevent that. It would be a first-class pampering operation, but so close to home that it would be just as easy to go in the middle of a blizzard as during the dog days of August."

"But going to a spa is an escape. Part of the joy is the change of scenery."

"With the proper décor and ambience, an urban health spa can provide that. And if you're going to say that people from the city want the country, I answer that the country can be simulated right here."

Sabrina was skeptical. "I don't know. Most of the services you mention are already offered in health clubs, of which there are dozens and dozens in the city."

"It's the whole package, Sabrina. The idea of checking in, severing oneself from the rest of the world for two days, or three or four." She held up both hands, palms out. "Just think. I'd start small, with a flagship spa in one of the better hotels. I could then franchise out into other hotels, other cities. The possibilities are vast." She ended with her brows raised expectantly. They lowered seconds later. "If I can get the backing. It's the old Catch-22. Y'need money to make money."

"Got any leads?"

"A few," Maura said in a voice that implied that she hadn't contacted any of them yet. She seemed to realize that she'd betrayed herself, because she rushed on. "I can do it, Sabrina. This time I'm serious. I think it's a solid idea. I have confidence it'll work."

"Urban spas?"

"Yup."

"In five-star hotels?"

"You bet."

"Well," Sabrina said thoughtfully, "it's a better idea than some you've had."

"It's a five-star idea," Maura returned, proud of the joke.

"I think," Sabrina said offhandedly, "that I'll have to

write a book. It may be the only way I know of to save you from yourself."

Maura sucked in an audible breath and held it for a minute before asking, "Are you serious?"

Sabrina nodded. She'd been waiting for the opening. She was suddenly very serious. "Pretty soon I'll have the time. I have a feeling I'm going to be desperate for ways of busying myself once I bring Nicky"—her voice wobbled, then steadied—"once I bring him to Vermont."

"Damn right you will. Any ideas?"

"Uh-huh. Derek McGill."

"Derek McGill?" Maura repeated blankly, then her eyes went wide and her voice jumped. "Derek McGill? Of *Outside Insight*? But he's in prison." She stared at Sabrina for a minute, then broke into a slow, calculating smile. "It would have all the ingredients—good-looking stud who makes it big then loses it all, and his name is more recognizable than your grandmother's. Not bad. Not bad at all. In fact, I love it. From media master to murderer. What a *terrific* idea!"

"From media master to murderer is *your* idea. I had something a little more . . . dignified in mind."

"Dignified doesn't make best-seller lists."

"I don't care. It's either dignified or nothing."

Given that particular choice, Maura yielded. "What, exactly, did you have in mind?"

"A biography of the man, with the emphasis on his experiences since the shooting. He was a visible and well-respected reporter before it happened. Suddenly he's seeing the justice system from the inside. I think that he'd have a lot of light to shed on the strengths and weaknesses of that system."

"An exposé on the prison system in America?" Maura sighed. "That does sound like something you'd want to write."

"Not an exposé of the prison system. The study of a man intimately involved in that system. I want to get into his feelings about the crime, the conviction, the sentence, and so on. If you're worried that it'll be dry, don't. Derek argued that he shot Joey Padilla in self-defense. He still maintains that."

Maura eyed her cautiously. "You sound like you've already started researching. Do you know Derek McGill?"

"We met a while back. I've visited him several times in prison."

"You're kidding."

"No. The prison is in western Massachusetts. I pass fairly close to it on my way to Vermont. It's easy enough to stop." She purposely didn't mention those times when she'd made the trip solely to see Derek. She was still trying to understand her personal feelings for him. She certainly wasn't ready to share them with Maura.

"He's agreed to the project, then?"

"Uh . . . well, not exactly."

"What do you mean?"

"I mean that we haven't worked out the details." Which was bluffing in a big way. It had been several visits since Sabrina had mentioned writing the book. When she'd been with Derek lately, there had been other things on her mind. Mostly *her* problems, she realized, but Derek hadn't objected. The few times she'd tried to turn the tables and talk of what was happening to him, his eyes had darkened and he'd grown distant. Not wanting that, she hadn't pushed.

The week before, when she'd spent several hours at Parkersville while Nicky was being evaluated in Vermont, she'd needed every bit of Derek's support. She hadn't wanted darkness or distance. She'd wanted understanding. She'd gotten it, along with comfort and encouragement. And stimulation.

She'd been aware of his body. It was incredible, because she'd been so upset about Nicky, but it was true. It was hard not to be aware of a chest that was snugly fitted with a scooped-out piece of thin white knit, and Derek's chest wasn't run-of-the-mill. It was well developed. It was skin rolling tightly over sinewed shoulders, a shy display of dark chest hair, virile contours lovingly outlined.

The skimpy undershirt made him look rugged, a little dangerous, a lot carnal. It also made him look sexy.

"Jesus!" Maura exclaimed in a whisper. She twisted in

her seat to scan the diners who sat behind her. "Your eyes are positively smouldering. Who are you *looking* at?"

Sabrina went bright red. "No one. It must have been a trick of the light."

Maura turned front again, clearly disappointed at not having seen anyone even remotely interesting. "Well, then, I'll repeat what I just said. If I read between the lines, I come up with the uncomfortable notion that Derek McGill doesn't want you to write the book."

"He has some reservations," Sabrina conceded. "He doesn't like the idea of being spectacularized. He's a very private person."

"Do you think you can get him to change his mind?"

"I think so."

"Any sex?"

Sabrina's eyes widened.

"In the book," Maura specified. "Any sex in the book?"

It was a minute before Sabrina got her pulse under control. "No. No sex." She folded her hands in her lap. "So. Do you think it'll sell?"

"Oh yeah, it'll sell."

"Then why the glum face?"

"Because it has the makings of a blockbuster, but you're cutting off its balls."

"Maura. Listen. Sex or no sex, this is a celebrity book, and there is a loyal market for celebrity books. In addition, I was under the impression that my last book won me some clout in literary circles. Any book I write, celebrity or otherwise, will be capably done. I would think it fair to assume that we both stand to make a little money here. Correct?"

"Correct."

"Then smile." She leaned forward and said, *sotto voce*, "There's a good-looking guy who just took a table on your right. He is alone. He has cast several lengthy glances your way. I may be mistaken, but that looks like a diamond tie tack."

Maura smiled.

· *CHAPTER 9* ·

J. B. Monroe didn't smile when Sabrina mentioned that she was thinking of writing Derek's story.

"It's a dumb idea."

"Why's that?" she asked, giving a little push with her foot to keep the glider moving. The terrace was shaded from the morning sun, leaving the air pleasantly warm, rather than hot. Lying in her arms, Nicky was content as long as the motion went on.

"For one thing, you're a woman."

"What does that have to do with anything?"

"You can't sashay into an all-male prison to interview the guy."

"I've been sashaying in there for the past five months."

J. B. didn't respond to what should have been a minor bombshell. He was too busy staring at Nicky. He was sitting in a chair opposite the swing, wearing nothing but a pair of Jams. Even faded, they clashed with the floral-colored cushions.

Like the time he'd shown up at the hospital. J. B.'s appearance the night before had surprised Sabrina. She'd seen him twice now in three months, which was a record of sorts. The official story was that he was in New York to discuss the choice of a screenwriter for the adaptation of one of his books into a movie, but Sabrina assumed much of that could have been done on the phone, particularly since J. B. hated New York.

She wondered whether he had another reason for coming. She didn't think he'd come just to see Nicky and her. He'd never been attentive.

Resting her chin on Nicky's head, she continued rocking. J. B. stared on. She wondered what he saw when he looked at Nicky that way, but she wasn't about to ask. If her brother started in on brilliant little spirits from the center of the earth, she'd have to get up and leave.

She didn't want to have to do that. She was comfortable. It felt good to sit and swing.

"You've been to Parkersville?" J. B. asked.

She nodded.

"What's it like?"

"Restrictive."

"What's McGill like?"

She thought for a minute, trying to choose words to describe Derek that wouldn't be too revealing. She didn't want J. B. to ask questions she wasn't ready to answer. "He's very bright. And interesting. He doesn't belong there."

"Is that what he tells you?"

"No."

"Then how do you know?"

"I just . . . know."

"How much longer does he have?"

"A few months."

"And then?"

She shrugged. "I don't know if he's made any immediate plans."

"When would you write this book?"

"I'd try to do all my interviewing before he gets out. He has the time now. He may not then."

J. B. thrust a hand through his hair, then forgetfully left the hand on his head. His expression was blank as he continued to look at Nicky.

Closing her eyes, Sabrina rocked. She breathed in Nicky's fresh-bathed scent, pressed one kiss on his head, then another, began to hum a little song. It was a happy song, one she'd deliberately chosen for its cheer, because when she sat here with her baby, knowing that before long he'd be hundreds of miles away, she felt cheerless.

"You shouldn't send him there," J. B. said, reading her mind.

"J. B.—"

"Don't do it. What so awful about this—beautiful terrace, beautiful day, beautiful child?"

"Nothing. You're right. It's all very beautiful. But life is more than a single beautiful moment. This is a rare breather for me. In a few minutes I'll have to get Nicky back to work."

"I thought you said you stopped the drills."

"Intensively, yes. But he still needs to be regularly exercised for muscle tone and flexibility." As she talked, she looked down at the small arms and legs that wouldn't work by themselves. They were bare now; Nicky was wearing a diaper, bright red terrycloth shorts and nothing else. His skin was smooth. Since he didn't play, he had none of the scrapes and scabs that other three-year-olds had. And his hands and feet were perfect.

"Mom isn't thrilled."

"I know. Neither is Dad. He called the other day just to make sure I knew. But they don't know what it's like, J. B. They don't know what it's like to wake up to a nightmare and find that it's real. They don't know the heartache . . . the frustration . . . the exhaustion." She held her hand straight. It had a faint tremor. "That's nervous tension."

J. B. looked at her hand, then at the arm of his chair. The wrought iron had fancy scrollwork that would normally have occupied him for a while. Surprisingly, though, he looked back at her after little more than a minute. "Why didn't you tell them about the divorce?"

"I did."

"Not until a month later, and only after Mom heard it through the grapevine."

Sabrina sank into a silence of her own. She figured that if J. B. could tune out, she could too.

"You thought you were different," he said.

The glider moved back and forth, its tick-tick not quite in tune with the sounds of the city below.

"You thought," he went on, "that your 'conventional marriage' would be the exception to the rule in our family."

Sabrina brushed her lips back and forth over Nicky's soft pecan curls.

"You're embarrassed," he stated, shoving his glasses up

with the tip of his finger. "You're embarrassed to have to admit that you're not superior after all."

That brought her from her silence. "Superior? I never said I was superior. I never *thought* I was superior. Just different." She met her brother's gaze and found surprising clarity there. "You're right. I am embarrassed. None of you liked Nick, but I chose him. I chose him because I thought he'd make the perfect husband, and I was wrong. I failed. I seem to be doing that a lot lately. I've failed as a wife, failed as a mother, failed as a writer."

As though to make one of those points, Nicky wailed. Sabrina had stopped pushing the glider. Quickly she resumed.

"As a writer?"

"I haven't written. I haven't been *able* to write. I always loved writing, and I was good at it. To some extent, I define my self in terms of it, and I suppose that's inevitable, coming from a family like ours. But I've done nothing for three years. Do you have any idea what it's like to feel stunted that way?"

"No."

"What's your secret, J. B.? How do you manage to keep on writing, regardless of what else is happening in your life?"

"Nothing else is," J. B. answered. "I write. Period. Mom and Dad write. Period. Is that the kind of life you want?"

Sabrina didn't have to give it much thought. "No. That's where I'm different. I want it all. I thought I had it all: husband, child, career—a cornucopia."

"But it fell apart. Y'know, Sabrina, you're not any different from us. We wanted all that too, but we weren't willing to work for it. One makes choices in life. I only hope you're making the right ones."

J. B. stayed with Sabrina for two days, which was a first. Always before he'd had hotel reservations. He hadn't cared for Nick, and Nick hadn't cared for him. But with Nick gone, he felt perfectly comfortable imposing on Sabrina.

Strangely, though, she didn't find it an imposition. Her

brother had definitely mellowed. He was more focused than he'd been. He still had his tuned-out moments, his moments of absent concentration, but he wasn't so contrary as he might have been—and as though sensing Sabrina would kick him out if he hatched a horror plot in her living room, he behaved. He didn't go so far as to work out with Nicky, but neither did he make any comments about the Greenhouse. He even offered to stick around the city and drive her there on the day Nicky was to be enrolled.

But she refused. That was something she had to do alone. And besides, she would be visiting Derek.

She was clinging to his neck. Her arms trembled. Her whole body trembled. He tightened his hold, trying to absorb the tremors and impart strength in return, but she continued to shake. So he held her and felt inadequate, wanting to do something to help, not knowing what she needed.

"What is it, Sabrina?" he whispered, dipping his mouth to her ear.

She gave a quick, almost convulsive head shake.

Leaning back, he tried to get a look at her face, but she wasn't having that either. She overlapped her arms at his nape and made a sound of protest against his throat, but the sound was followed by another, and though she seemed to regain control from there, he realized she was crying.

"Oh baby," he moaned. He didn't know the exact cause of her tears, but it didn't matter. He grief became his. "Shhhh," he whispered, rocking her gently. "Shhhh."

Minutes went by. At one point a nearby guard caught Derek's eye and must have seen something powerful there —vulnerability, pleading, pain—for he turned his back on the embrace that had gone on too long and walked away.

Gradually, Sabrina quieted. She sandwiched a hand between Derek's throat and her face and tried to blot her tears.

"Is there a tissue in your purse?" he asked softly. When she nodded, he tugged at the purse strap, one-handedly opened the purse, found the tissue and pressed it to her.

Head bowed, she stepped back from him and dabbed at her eyes and cheeks. Still without raising her head, she folded the damp tissue and slid it into the pocket of her dress. Then she reached for his hand and held it.

Derek had had little experience with weeping women. He'd had little patience with them, so he'd always walked away. Cynically, he'd believed that women used tears as a tool, and he supposed that was true in some cases. Only now he wondered about the others. It occurred to him that he'd copped out. It was far easier to see tears as a tool than to try to understand and deal with the underlying problem. He'd been a coward. By disgustedly stalking from the room—or the office or the apartment—he'd taken the easy way out. He'd never had the time or desire to offer comfort.

Now he had both.

Sabrina hadn't planned to cry. She wouldn't look at him. She was clearly embarrassed by her tears. Putting her at ease was a challenge he intended to meet.

Without a word, he led her to a bench and eased her down. Then he settled himself so that he faced her. His thumb lightly caressed the back of her hand.

"How was it?" he asked softly. He knew that she'd come from Vermont. She'd told him in her last visit that she'd made her decision.

It was a minute before she could speak, and then only after she'd taken a shaky breath. "Let me put it this way. When you drive twenty miles down a lonesome country road and you can't see the road for the tears in your eyes and you don't crash into a tree or a fence or a cow, you know that Someone's watching over you." Her voice fell to a breath above a whisper. "It's reassuring. There are times when I've wondered if He exists."

Derek knew the feeling all too well. He'd never been overly religious, but he must have assumed there was a God, because he'd been upset by the thought—and it had come to him more than once in the past twenty months—that He wasn't there. "I guess the proper attitude is that things happen for a reason."

"Mmm. That is the 'proper' attitude. The only problem I have with it is figuring out the reason. Why was Nicky born brain-damaged? To punish him? Or me, or Nick? To give the Greens another boarder? And why are you here?"

"That one's obvious. If I weren't here, you'd be making that trip to and from Vermont without a break."

Sabrina was astonished by his tongue-in-cheek humor. If she'd asked why he was at Parkersville when she'd first started visiting him, his eyes would have darkened, his jaw would have clenched, he'd have glared off into the distance. She knéw that he hadn't come to terms with his incarceration, which meant that his good humor was for her benefit. That knowledge was both warming and humbling.

"I hope you know," she said quietly, "that given a choice of having you here or free, I'd have gladly made the trip without a break."

Derek had to swallow down the hardness in his throat. She did it to him every time—looked at him a certain way, spoke in a certain tone, said certain words that touched the raw and sensitive spot no woman had touched before. He was never quite expecting it, and wondered if he ever would. He felt so unworthy at times.

He kissed her cheek, then her forehead. Drawing her arm through his, he started to walk.

They walked the length of the yard, then sat beneath a tree and quietly discussed Sabrina's feelings about leaving Nicky at the Greenhouse. She told him about the Greens' enthusiasm and understanding, and about the concern she felt nonetheless. She told him about simultaneous feelings of letdown and relief, and about a sense of floundering. Tears came to her eyes when she mentioned the pocket of emptiness that was a dull ache in her chest. And the guilt. She told him about the guilt.

Derek was a good listener. As an interviewer, he'd had to be. But his patience now came not from that training, but from the heart. He wanted to help Sabrina. Offering a sounding board was one of the few things that circumstance would allow him to do. Moreover, he thought her decision was the right one. When she was finished, he told her so.

"Trust yourself, Sabrina. You've done the right thing."

She shot the sky a beseechful glance. "Lord, I hope so." But her gaze quickly returned to Derek. He was looking at her as though he wanted to wrap her in silk and love her.

At that moment she wanted it, too. When, with the slightest tilt of his head, he beckoned her into his arms, she went willingly, then sighed in sheer pleasure. There was something of a homecoming in the embrace, something comfortable and right. The hardness of Derek's body was a perfect foil for her softness, her vulnerability. In his arms, she felt shielded from the woes of the world.

For several minutes, holding each other was enough. Then, just when she was beginning to feel the need for something more, Derek took her face in his hands and tipped it up. Starting at the spot near the bridge of her nose and working slowly, symmetrically and with the slightest of tremors, his thumbs traced her eyebrows, arced back to skim the beginnings of her ears, swung down along her jaw and met at her chin. With a smile in his eyes, he lowered his head and found her lips, close to the center of the heart he'd drawn.

Sabrina was startled. She'd known not to expect the feather-light kisses of earlier visits, and had truly been prepared for the hunger of a man who'd been without for too long. She'd seen that hunger, had heard it in his voice and felt it in his body on other days. And the hunger was there now, but it was different. It was everything he'd been all afternoon—gentle, understanding, compelling, intelligent, stimulating in the most subtle of ways.

His lips were warm, firm yet mobile. They caressed hers, slid and shaped and enveloped her with such incredibly tender force that she had to fight for breath.

The shock registered through the fingers she dug into the hard flesh of his shoulders. Quickly releasing her mouth, he gave her a minute's breath while he stroked her back and gentled her with whispered words. Then, unable to deny himself, he captured her mouth again.

He was bolder this time, because the shock of gentleness had hit him too, zeroing in on his loins. His mouth grew more daring, coaxing hers wider, and when the only resistance she offered was a tiny gasp, he touched his tongue to hers.

The jolt was physical, frightening in its intensity. Sabrina pulled back, and the fear she felt must have filled her eyes, because rather than forcing her, Derek cupped her face and held it tenderly. His eyes touched each pale feature. A tiny smile touched his mouth. "You're beautiful, do you know that?"

She was about to say that she didn't feel it, that she rarely had in the last few years. But at that moment she did. Derek's caring acted on her like a master's brush, painting beauty where there had been none. He made her feel feminine and confident. She wanted the first and needed the last. Very badly.

"I think you'd better leave," he whispered, dropping a soft kiss on the tip of her nose. "If not, I'm apt to get rough. I can feel it coming, and you're not helping."

Sabrina could feel it coming, too. His arousal was very real, not complete but getting there. "Oh dear," she murmured.

"'Oh dear' is right."

"Shall I step back . . . or wait?"

Derek took a good look around the prison yard. He saw an inmate named Foss, a specialist in armed robbery, and Webber, who had earned hard time by selling crack to a group of high-schoolers, one of whom had later died. He saw Hamhock, whose real name was as much a mystery as his crime and whose reputation was based on his way with his fists. Then there were the guards. Derek looked from one to another of them, and by the time he looked back at Sabrina, his ardor had cooled.

"I'm okay," he said somberly and stepped back. "Drive carefully."

She nodded but didn't move.

"Go, Sabrina."

With her eyes focused on his face, she took a single step backward.

"Sabrina . . ." he warned with just enough frustration to sound like anger, and that brought her to her senses.

"I'm going," she said quickly and started to walk. After several paces, though, she paused, turning back for a final look. Derek stood watching her. His shoulders were straight, his feet planted firmly on the ground. He looked grim and determined as he hitched his chin toward the gate.

Not wanting to make things worse, she left.

Sabrina slept for nearly three days straight when she got back to New York. She didn't get dressed. She didn't make the bed, since she wasn't up long enough to bother. She took an occasional bath, made an occasional meal. Then she went back to sleep.

Though she knew that she was making up for three years' worth of fatigue, she also knew that there was an element of escape in her rest. When she slept, she didn't have to think. And more than anything, that was what she wanted—and needed. She'd done too much thinking lately. The decision to place Nicky in a residential center was the hardest she'd ever made. She'd earned the rest.

At the end of those three days, she got out of bed, bathed, dressed and went for a walk. She walked very slowly. It struck her as she walked that she was the only one doing it. In spite of the heat, people were passing her, rushing off to wherever it was they were headed. Hundreds of people, hundreds of different destinations. Facial expressions ranging from preoccupied to bored to hassled. There was something disconnected about it all that she found depressing.

But then, New York was that way. When she'd been at Columbia, she'd been insulated; the college and her friends had offered a haven from the anonymity of the city. When she'd married, her husband had taken over that role. He'd been joined in time by friends, then her son. Now Nick was gone. Nicky was gone. Other than Maura, there were no friends she cared to call. She was an anonymous face in an anonymous world. She was alone.

Two weeks later, on a Sunday, Sabrina went to see Nicky. The Greens had suggested that she plan on monthly visits, but this first time she needed to see him sooner. She needed to know that even without forewarning, she'd find her son clean and well cared for.

"And was he?" Derek asked several hours later. He and Sabrina were walking the perimeter of the yard.

She nodded, but didn't speak. Seeing Nicky had been a heart-wrenching experience. Seeing Derek helped, but she was still feeling a little bruised.

He caught one of her hands and threaded his fingers through hers. "Want to talk about it?"

She looked up at him, smiled sadly and shook her head. "I'd only be repeating things I've said before. I'd bore you."

"Nah."

But she really didn't want to talk about Nicky today. She had already talked too much about Nicky, about Nick, about herself. So she remained quiet, holding Derek's hand, walking.

"More crowded today," she commented.

"It's a Sunday. You've never been here on a Sunday."

"No." She nodded at one of the other visitors, a woman she'd come to recognize over the course of five months. A bit later she smiled at another. They no longer seemed as coarse or downtrodden to her, but had taken on the identities that Derek had helped flesh out. Each was an individual. A sad individual.

"New York is weird," she said.

"Weird?"

"Lonely."

"You feel that way because Nicky's in Vermont."

"No. It's New York. I'm not sure I want to stay."

"Where would you go?"

"I don't know. Some place peaceful . . . friendly."

As they walked on, Derek pictured a place like that. Two years before, he'd have equated peaceful and friendly with boring and nonproductive. Now peaceful and friendly sounded nice.

At length, they stopped beneath a tree and slid down against its trunk. The prison was behind them; before them were the woods. A bluejay alighted on the top of one of the fences. A bee buzzed nearby. The smell of newly mown grass surrounded them.

"Deceptive," Derek said, and she knew just what he meant.

"How does the jay know which fence to land on?"

"He doesn't."

"Aren't some of them electrified?"

"One of the three. Don't know which one."

She shuddered. "The birds must take a beating."

"Actually, most know not to come anywhere near us. The jay is a little perverse, that's all. And cocky. He likes to stand at the top of the heap, so he takes his chances. Once in a while he gets burned."

Derek's somber tone drew her eyes away from the bird. She studied him, saw that his gray eyes had gone cloudy, knew what he was thinking. And she was thinking about it, too. She'd been thinking about it a lot as she'd wandered through New York.

She was tired of talking about herself. It was time to turn the tables.

"Tell me about it, Derek. Tell me about what happened that night."

He tipped his head back against the tree and closed his eyes. A pair of geese flew overhead. Bested, the jay left its perch and returned to the woods.

"I told the court what happened."

"You told them the bare facts. But there's more. You have a theory. I know you do. Tell me."

His jaw tensed. "There's no point in hashing and rehashing."

"You do it."

"I don't have any other choice. There isn't a hell of a lot else to think about around here."

"Maybe if you could share it . . ."

He shook his head.

"Don't you trust me?"

"Of course I do," he muttered, opening his eyes to scowl at her. "But, God, Sabrina, it's so damned frustrating! I've been over the facts hundreds and hundreds of times, and I can't see it any other way. Sometimes I wonder if I'm going mad."

"Do it one more time, Derek. For me. I'll let you know if you're off the wall."

He didn't know why he decided to tell her. Maybe it was because he needed to talk to someone, needed a fresh opinion. Maybe it wasn't just anyone he needed to talk to, but Sabrina.

He chewed on the inside of his cheek for a minute, then slowly released it and began to speak. "I was working on a story for the show. It was on the accuracy of eyewitness testimony. I was spotlighting three cases where men had been convicted of crimes and then subsequently released when eyewitnesses recanted their testimony." He fell silent, staring off into the depth of the woods.

"Go on," she prompted softly.

"I wanted a *pièce de résistance* to make the story special. So I started looking into the case of a Massachusetts man who had been convicted of armed robbery and given a pretty stiff sentence. He was an unlikely armed robber—black, but an engineer, distinctly white-collar. There was no motive to speak of. His conviction was based largely on the testimony of three eyewitnesses. During the trial, the defense tried to cast doubt on their testimony. Not only was it dark on the night of the robbery, but it was a while—several months—before the eyewitnesses had come forward. On top of that, two of those eyewitnesses had criminal records, while the third was on bail awaiting trial."

Sabrina was intrigued. If what Derek was telling her had come out during his trial, it never made the papers. She'd never heard this part of the story. "Were they being blackmailed into testifying?"

"It was beginning to look that way. The man awaiting trial got away with probation on a larceny charge that should heave earned him hard time. And more than one person I interviewed said that the other two got away with hell after testifying."

Sabrina shifted to lean against one of Derek's bent knees

and face him. "Who could have been behind it? The police?"

"More likely an ambitious D.A. who wanted a conviction for at least one of a series of armed robberies that had the people of the county riled up."

"And the phone call you got? Where does that fit in?"

"This particular robbery had taken place in a small town in the southwestern part of the state. I'd been fairly visible talking with people there, so I wasn't surprised when I got a call from a man who said he could personally place those two other witnesses on Cape Cod at the time of the robbery. He said he had proof—signed IOU's from a poker game, motel receipts—but he said that if I wanted them, I'd have to come quickly, because his wife was very nervous about his sticking his neck out and she'd already threatened to destroy the papers."

Derek looked at Sabrina. "He sounded legitimate, so I went." His lips twisted in self-disgust. "Dumb of me. Shortsighted to have gone alone, but it was late at night. I decided that—based on what he'd said about his wife—the man would never permit himself to be filmed, so I didn't bother with a camera crew. And it seemed crazy to wake the producer from a sound sleep when I could do the work myself." His voice grew tighter. "If only I had. If only I'd called someone—anyone—to go with me. Then I'd have had a witness of my own. If only I'd called someone and that person had refused for an invalid reason, I'd have been able to point a finger."

Sabrina ran her hand around his neck and kneaded the taut muscles she found. He rolled his head in appreciation, then sighed.

"Anyway, I went alone. I drove up from New York—it was an easy enough drive at that hour—and I was familiar enough with the town so that I had no trouble finding the spot he'd named. It was a parking lot behind a block of stores. Pitch-black, let me tell you, and deserted except for one other car, a Cutlass, just as he'd said. I remember thinking to myself, 'What harm can there be? He's a poor henpecked schnook.' So I parked, got out of the car and waited. The door to the other car opened and a man got out. We must have been about thirty feet apart. I called his name—he's said it was Walsh. He called mine for confirmation. Then we started walking toward each other."

Sabrina's eyes were wide. Her hand had come to rest on his collarbone. "When did you see the gun?"

"I didn't. It was too dark. But when he was about ten feet away I noticed that there was something odd about his shape, odd about the way he was holding his arm." Derek didn't move, but his body had tensed to a state of coiled readiness. He was back in that parking lot, reliving the moment of awareness. "I never saw the gun with my eyes, only with my mind in a flash of recognition. The way he was holding his arm, at just that angle, supporting just that much weight. It was an instinctive thing. A split-second image. A gut conviction." He sent Sabrina a pleading look. "Does that make any sense?"

"I can imagine it happening."

The pleading look remained for a minute more, then faded. "Well, the prosecutor couldn't. He made a big thing about why I didn't just assume the guy was holding the papers he'd promised."

"But why would that have mattered?"

"I claimed I'd come to that meeting totally innocent of a setup. The prosecutor claimed that I knew there would be trouble. If I'd been truly innocent, the prosecutor went on to say, I wouldn't have been on the lookout for a gun."

"He must be equating innocent with dumb," Sabrina commented a bit dryly. "It was dark. You were alone and unarmed. Only a fool would have been blind to the possibility of foul play."

"The thing is, Sabrina, that I wasn't considering the possibilities at that point. It all happened so quickly." He took a shuddering breath. "My mind told me he had a gun. I dove and tackled him. We struggled, the gun went off, he fell back."

His pulse had picked up speed. She could feel it beneath her hand, beneath the heat of his skin. Beneath his hair, his forehead was misted with sweat. And in his eyes she saw something she's never seen before. Sheer terror.

For the very first time, Sabrina realized that on top of

everything else, Derek McGill had to deal with the knowledge that he'd ended a human life.

Whispering his name, she went forward and wrapped her arms around his neck. It was a minute before she felt his arms complete the circle, but their strength more than made up for the delay. "I'm sorry I asked," she whispered. "I didn't mean to put you through it again."

"I do it nearly every night," came his hoarse reply. "What's one more time?"

"It helps me understand when I hear."

"As long as you don't write it."

She drew back her head. "I want to. You know that."

The terror was gone from his eyes, replaced by determination. "And you know that I don't want you to."

"It would be so *good* to have your side of the story put into print."

"You haven't heard half of my side of the story."

"I'm ready whenever you are."

"I'm not now."

"Then when?"

"Maybe never."

"But maybe before never? Come on, Derek. Let me give it a shot."

But he was shaking his head in slow, firm shakes. "I can't let you do it. Not yet. It could spoil everything. No one can give me back the twenty months of my life that I've lost, but someone's going to be very sorry for having made me lose—"

Her fingers covered his mouth, cutting off his threat. She gave a quick head shake to deny both the words and the vengeful look in his eye. But the look didn't go away, and when she released his mouth, he immediately said, "I mean it, Sabrina. Someone's going to pay."

"Don't say it. Don't even think it."

"Why not?" he asked coolly.

"Because it's dangerous."

"Someone should have thought of that when he set me up first to be murdered, then to take the fall for murdering my would-be murderer."

"Who was it, Derek?"

His angry mouth stayed closed.

"Do you know?" she asked.

"I have a pretty good idea."

"And you're going to pay him back," she said, nodding as she slid from his lap. "That's brilliant. You could well end up right back here and for a much longer stretch next time."

He stiffened his spine. "Come on, Sabrina. I'm not that dumb. I'm not planning murder. Believe it or not, I'm not a violent man."

"I do believe it—except for the times when you get that look of revenge in your eye. If it isn't violent, nothing is."

"That's anger you see, and yes, it's violent. It seethes inside and is as violent as anything I've ever felt. I am my father's son in that sense. But man evolves. Each generation is a little more advanced than the one before. I have more smarts than the old man did. Before my anger escapes, it passes through the filter of my mind. I'm a calculating man. No, I don't have anything like murder in mind. Murder would be too easy."

"A very trite expression."

"Sometimes things are trite because they express very simple truths."

"And what is the truth here? Is it mental torture you have in mind?"

He clenched his jaw. "You could say that."

"Do it through a book, Derek. Do it through *my book*. Wouldn't that be vengeance enough—to lay it all out in black and white for the world to see?"

"No."

She drew her knees up and fastened them in with her arms. "I see. Simple vengeance isn't enough. You want"—she dropped her voice and droned—"re-ven-ge. Y'know, you should speak with my brother. J. B. has all sorts of meaty ideas for inflicting mental torture."

Derek's eyes were dark, as was his mood. "Make fun of it if you want, but you haven't been the one rotting here for twenty months. You haven't been the one sitting and stewing, watching the world go by without you. You haven't been the one to look back on your past and see years of effort go down the tubes. You can make fun of it, Sabrina, but that just goes to prove where you're coming from, and where you're coming from isn't where I'm coming from."

"You're wrong, Derek."

"Oh? What do you know of me? What do you really know of me, of my life?"

"Not much. You've guarded the facts like gold bars at Fort Knox."

"And you want to know why? Because I was protecting *you*. You're clean, you're good. You're like the fairy princess I might have read about when I was a kid, except that I didn't have much time to read because I was too busy defending my name on the street."

"I'm not a weakling, Derek. I can handle just about anything you give me."

"As you handled the beating I got? I'll never forget the look of disgust on your face when you took a good, close look at mine."

All too clearly she remembered that day, remembered Derek walking toward her, trying to look normal even though his body listed and his face was a mass of bruises. "That wasn't disgust," she said quietly. "It was horror— which you'd have realized if you'd been in less pain. Would you rather I'd looked at you and laughed?"

"I'd rather," he said in a low, tempered voice, "you mind your own business when it comes to something that doesn't concern you. Whether or not I exact revenge is no concern of yours."

Sabrina was stung. She had honestly thought that Derek and she had come beyond that. She thought they were friends—no, more than friends. Friends didn't kiss the way they did, or ache to touch each other as they did. She'd simply assumed that they'd see each other when Derek was released. And now he was telling her that his future was no concern of hers?

"You are a self-pitying bastard," she heard herself say as she scrambled to her feet.

"Where—Sabrina, wait!" Derek was up, loping after her, catching her by the arm and halting her flight.

Blond hair flying in a shimmering arc, she rounded on

him with a fury that was born of very deep, private, very
new feelings. "You think you have a monopoly on pain,
but you don't, Derek, you don't." She shook off his hand.
"The last three years of my life have been a living hell. If
you want to talk anger or frustration or waste, I know all
about it. I've been in a cage just as binding as the one
you're in, and the worst of it is that now I'm out, there's
nothing I can do. There's no one to blame for what happened to Nicky. I couldn't take revenge if I tried. But you"
—she gasped for a breath—"you have choices. A wrong
was done you. You can trace that wrong, document it in
detail, do something with the information. You want to be
your father's son . . . Okay, track down the man who set
you up, then follow him, follow him wherever he goes, let
him know you're following him, let him know that when
you get tired of following him you'll pick up a rifle with an
infrared long-range sight and shoot him. Let him shake a
little. How does that sound?"

Shaking, herself, she rushed on before Derek could
speak. "Of course, you'll be wasting that many more years
of your life if you do that. You won't be moving ahead.
You'll be giving that creep the satisfaction of knowing that
he's taken not two, but three or four or five years of your
life. Think of the sense of power he'll have. And you? You
won't be an investigative reporter anymore. You won't be
any kind of reporter, because you won't have the time.
And even if you did, you'd be branded obsessed. No one
would want to work with you. And that goes for me. You
want me to mind my own business when it comes to things
that don't concern me? Fine. You're right. I deserve
more."

She turned, knowing that if she didn't make good her
escape, she'd dissolve into tears. This time, though, Derek
didn't only grab her arm. He had her pressed to his body
before she had time for a breath.

"Jesus," he whispered against her hair, then inhaled
sharply. "Don't leave." He backed up to a tree. "Not like
this. Don't leave yet."

"If you don't want me involved—"

"I do. You're the only thing that's held any meaning in

my life for the past five months." Bracing his legs apart, he drew her into the cradle of his hips. "I need you, Sabrina."

"But—"

"I don't want you involved because I don't want you hurt."

"I'll be hurt if I'm *not* involved." She raised her head, and in that instant she identified the very deep, very private, very new feeling she had. She touched his cheek with a trembling hand. Her fingers whispered over his cheekbones, soothed the scar by his eye, erased the last of the scowl lines from his brow, sank deep into his thick, dark hair. "Please?" she mouthed.

Derek had never seen love in a woman's eyes. He'd seen affection and desire—even adoration in the eyes of the occasional fan—but never love. The difference was in depth. When he looked into Sabrina's eyes, he was looking into a fathomless well of warmth, of caring and giving and need. It had to be the most wonderful, most humbling sight he'd ever seen.

"Oh baby," he murmured and lowered his mouth. He didn't kiss her, but paused just shy of the act, retreated, sought her eyes again to make sure he hadn't imagined what he'd seen.

It was there. All of it. Everything he felt, himself, and more.

This time he did touch her lips, but very, very gently, as though too much pressure might shatter something so new. He covered her mouth, lightly sucked it in, slowly released it, drew back, then dipped his head and kissed her again in the same, slow, sipping way. He discovered that the taste of love was that much more rich, that much more sweet than anything he'd ever tasted. It was also more lasting, causing each successive kiss—and one followed the other in lingering progression—to be even more rich, even more sweet. And addictive. And arousing.

"Sabrina . . ." he whispered against her mouth as the heat rose in his body.

She opened her eyes. Her hands held his head, fingers lost in his hair. She was vaguely aware of standing on tiptoe, but she hadn't knowingly made the effort. Derek's arms had done it for her, closing around her, lifting, supporting.

Her gaze went from his eyes to his mouth and lingered there. His lips were moist, parted. She wanted them again. But more than that, she wanted *him*. She didn't yet know in what capacity, but she knew that she wanted to make love with him, wanted to sleep with him, wanted to wake up in his arms and lie with him in the sun.

Needing to tell him how she felt, she initiated the kiss this time. But initiation was all she got, because Derek met her, matched her, and the kiss became one of mutual dawning. Everything was new. Sabrina was far from a virgin, yet the small sounds that came from her throat when he filled her mouth with his tongue, the helpless gasps when he slid his hands up by the sides of her breasts spoke of a near-virginal surprise. Likewise, Derek's blood was running hotter than it had run since he'd been twelve.

"We have to stop," he gasped.

"Oh no."

He put his forehead to hers and squeezed his eyes shut. His breathing was rough. "Do you know . . . there are some weekends when they have games and family picnics . . . nine months later some of the wives give birth."

"How?" she whispered. She had both hands flat on his chest and was moving them up and down over the thin, white knit of his tank top.

"In the bathroom. I want you so bad that I'd almost think of dragging you there, but it'd be so dirty, and you're so clean."

"I'm not—"

"You weren't made for quick and shabby. You were made for slow and rich, silk sheets, soft sounds."

"I'm not a—"

"I couldn't take you there," he said more harshly. "I couldn't take you anywhere in this place. I'd lose it, I know I would. Psychologically, I couldn't do it. I'd think of all these guys screwing bimbos against the wall . . ."

"Don't, please don't." She knew that he was working himself up, taking sexual frustration and letting it mushroom into a more general anger. "It doesn't matter, Derek. We'll have time."

"God, I hate this place!"

"You won't be here forever."

"But will you want me when I'm out?"

She looked at him in surprise and saw the vulnerability that he either hadn't bothered or been able to hide. "Of course I'll want you when you're out," she answered, puzzled. "How could you think I wouldn't?"

"I'll be an ex-convict."

"Is that supposed to be worse than a convict?"

"I don't know. Maybe this place . . . it's convenient for you when you see Nicky."

"Derek, I haven't been stopping here just because it's convenient."

"Maybe it's that little bit of danger here that turns you on."

She took his hand from the back of her waist, held it in both of hers, kissed his knuckles, then pressed it to her heart. Her eyes held his. "It's not that."

"Sabrina . . ."

She was very carefully separating his fingers, shaping his hand to her breast. Wanting to concentrate on the sensation, she closed her eyes.

Derek swallowed hard. He knew he should tug his hand away, knew that feeling her would only make things worse, but he couldn't deny himself. There had been so few pleasures in his life in the last twenty months. Most had revolved around Sabrina. Just as he'd needed to kiss her before, he needed to touch her now.

Her breast filled his palm. She wasn't large, but she was well formed and firm. Heat shimmered through layers of fabric—chic, stylishly wrinkled cotton and beneath that a bra—and those layers kept him from feeling her nipple, even when he stroked her lightly. But he heard when she sucked in her breath, and he knew from the way she arched her back that she enjoyed his touch.

"Come here," he whispered hoarsely, turning so that she was beneath him against the tree. He'd been to his share of orgies, but making love with an audience had never turned

him on. He was very turned on now. He couldn't help
himself. At least he could shield Sabrina some.

Thrusting a leg between hers, he leaned into her. He
ducked his head and traced her lips with his tongue while
he carefully released a button of her blouse and slid his
hand inside. Sucking in a breath, Sabrina opened her eyes
to his.

"I have to touch," he whispered. The urgency of it was
written all over his face. He found her breast, circled it,
covered it, then began to knead. "Have to touch . . . Is it
good?"

Eyes glued to his, she nodded. She was biting her lower
lip to keep from crying out. Her hands clung to his sides,
fingers digging into the hard skin just above his jeans.

Derek was panting softly when he put his lips to her
temple. He moved his hips against her thigh, but she was
the one to put the need into words.

"I want you," she whispered. Heat was gathering in her
body, pooling between her legs, and just above that the
ache was intense. She'd never in her life felt the kind of
driving desire she felt at Derek's hands. To say that she
loved him only went partway in explaining that desire.
Once upon a time, she'd loved Nick, yet she'd never felt
what she did now.

Nick had wanted her. Derek needed her. She supposed
that was the most immediate of the differences.

A small cry slipped from her throat. Long, lean fingers
had stolen beneath the lace of her bra and were setting fire
to her bare breast. She cried out again when a fingertip
grazed her nipple, which was already taut and straining.

"Oh God," she cried in a high whisper. "Oh God . . ."

"Not Him," Derek returned on a hoarse but regretful
note, "just me." Taking back his hand, he drew her from
the tree and crushed her to his length. His body trembled in
longing. "I can't give you what you need just now. I wish I
could, but I can't."

It wasn't a question of impotence: he was stone-hard
against her. Reassured, she said, "I can't give you what
you need, either." Her voice was muffled against his chest.

The scent of his body was cushioning her descent from desire's high.

"If we were somewhere else, somewhere private—"

"Yes. In a minute."

He moaned. "I don't deserve you, Sabrina."

"I refuse to argue about that. Not any more today."

"When will I see you again?"

"I don't know." She rubbed her cheek against the fine, curling hairs that his shirt didn't cover. "Another two weeks?" The sound she made, a swallowed groan, mirrored his own feelings about a two-week separation. Pushing off from his chest, she raised urgent eyes. "Give me something to do, Derek. Please. Give me something constructive."

He knew that she wanted to write. He also knew that he had no intention of letting her publish his story before he had done what he was set to do.

But there was another need he had. When she came to see him, he knew that he was her focus. He was selfish enough to want that even when she was back in New York. Besides, what he'd be asking was right down her alley.

"You can help me," he said very quietly. The process of thought and its direction had effectively cooled his heat. He sniffed in a breath and straightened, lifting his weight from her. "Does the name Lloyd Ballantine ring a bell?"

It was a minute before she realized what he was saying, a minute before she'd recovered enough from his touch—and its sudden loss—to do that. "Lloyd Ballantine was . . . a justice of the Supreme Court. He died in an automobile accident several years ago." She wondered why Derek had asked.

He didn't let her wonder long. "I want to know anything and everything you can learn about the man."

She nodded, but she was wondering again. It was only natural.

"Don't ask," he said, and there was something in his quiet tone that underscored the request. Cupping her shoulders, he looked down at her. "I shouldn't be involving you at all this way, but you wanted to help—"

"I do!"

He gnawed on the inside of his cheek and contemplated the eagerness in her eyes. Then he gave a single, resigned nod. "Lloyd Ballantine. Anything and everything. As discreetly as possible."

It wasn't until later, in the car heading back to New York, that Sabrina wondered about the rest of Derek's story. She hadn't heard his theory about what had happened. She hadn't been able to offer an opinion.

But she would see him again. There would be other visits, other talks. She was deeply and emotionally committed.

And able. She didn't know why learning about Lloyd Ballantine was important to Derek, but one thing she did know was that when it came to doing research, few people were more thorough than she.

· *CHAPTER 10* ·

Learning about Lloyd Ballantine was a far greater undertaking than Sabrina had imagined, both because there was an abundance of sources to plumb and because the initial sampling she made of those offered little. Newspaper and magazine profiles drew identical pictures of a hard worker, a scholar, a family man who had been a moderate force on the bench.

She waded through a biography that had been written shortly after his death, but it was a long-winded and saccharine affair. What surprised her was that it had been penned by a well-known author, a man whose past work had led her to expect something more than Pablum.

She spent several mornings at the public library working with microfiche and took out an armload of magazines to pore through at home. But she made less headway than she'd hoped, because she had decided to put the Fifth Avenue apartment on the market, and there was immediate activity.

On a Saturday in early August, after nearly two weeks in New York, she drove north again. This time she stopped at Parkersville first.

The guards at the front desk had come to know her. She stood apart physically from many of the other regular visitors—and beyond that, she was friendly. Once she had begun to recognize the faces behind the glass, she'd offered smiles in greeting. In time the smiles were returned.

There were no smiles on this day, though. "He's not here, Mrs. Stone."

Sabrina was sure she'd heard wrong. "Excuse me?"

"He's not here."

She frowned, then swallowed. "Not here?" Possibilities started popping into her head, the first of which was that there had been another fight and Derek had been hurt seriously enough to warrant transfer to another facility. Her heart began to pound. "Where is he?"

"I can't tell you that."

"Was he hurt?"

"Not as far as I know."

"Then he's all right?"

"I presume so."

She tried to keep calm and consider the other possibilities. She knew that he wasn't due to appear before the parole board for another two months, but perhaps that process had been hastened. "Has he been released?" she asked, afraid to hope.

It was just as well she hadn't, because the answer she received was a firm, "No. No release."

"Is he in *solitary*?"

It might have been the loss of color on her face, or the worry in her eyes, or the goodwill her smiles had built up over the past months. But the guard seemed to soften. "I'd tell you if he was. I'm sorry, Mrs. Stone, he just isn't here. I know he's been transferred, but that's it."

She believed that the man really did know nothing, but

that was small solace. "Why would he have been transferred?"

The guard shrugged.

"Was there trouble here?"

Another shrug.

"Did he—was there any message left for me? He would have known I'd be coming."

The guard arched back from the speaker and said something to his colleagues, who rummaged through several small piles of papers. Their search turned up nothing.

Taking a deep, steadying breath, Sabrina tried to understand her options. "How," she began quietly, "would I go about learning where Derek *is*?"

"I'm not sure, Mrs. Stone. If it was public knowledge, we'd know ourselves."

"The guards in his house—they'd know, wouldn't they?"

"No."

"Then the warden. I'd like to see the warden."

"He's away for the weekend."

"He must have left someone in charge. An assistant warden?"

"That's right, but you can't see him. Not today. You'll need an appointment, and you can't get that till Monday."

"I don't believe this," she whispered in dismay, then moved on to her next option. "Since it's Saturday, I'll probably run into a dead end with the Department of Corrections, too. Do you have an inside number I can try?"

The guard cast a glance behind her at the line that was beginning to form. He leaned closer to the speaker. "Try the phone book. The commissioner's Lou DeGenio. He lives in Watertown."

Her eyes went wide. "The commissioner? *He* was personally involved in Derek's transfer?"

"Not necessarily. But McGill isn't our average customer. If DeGenio doesn't know about the case, he'll tell you who does."

Sensing that she would get no more, Sabrina thanked him with a final sad smile and left. Stopping at a pay phone in town, she found that the phone book had been stolen.

Not that it would have solved the problem. According to Directory Assistance, there were four Louis DeGenios in Watertown.

Sabrina was just bold enough, just desperate enough to call each of the four and ask if she'd reached the commissioner of Corrections. She was holding her breath when she reached the last, then let it out in a groan when she was told that, no, this wasn't the commissioner and that the commissioner had an unlisted number.

Feeling an incredible emptiness, she drove on into Vermont, to the small inn where she'd planned to spend the night. There, in a room that might well have hosted George Washington in his day, she phoned New York. After trying each of the city boroughs, the operator finally found a Westchester number for the name Sabrina had given. Sabrina prepared herself for the probability that the man wasn't home as she dialed it.

A deep, gravelly voice answered. "Yeo."

"Mr. Cottrell?"

"Mmm?"

She let out a grateful sigh and followed it with a rush of words. "My name is Sabrina Stone. I'm a friend of Derek McGill's, and I wouldn't be disturbing you at home on a Saturday if I didn't feel the situation was urgent. I went to Parkersville today and Derek wasn't there. He hadn't said anything to me about the possibility that he might be transferred, even though he knew I'd be back to visit, and he didn't leave a message. None of the guards could tell me where he was. I'll need an appointment to meet with any of the prison officials, the Department of Corrections is closed, and the commissioner's phone is unlisted." She was close to tears. "Do you know where he is?"

There was a brief silence on the other end of the line, and for a split second Sabrina wondered if she'd gotten the wrong man after all. She clearly remembered the name David Cottrell from newspaper reports of Derek's trial, but she couldn't rule out the possibility that in her upset she'd remembered wrong. Fears were crowding her mind, confusing her.

Then David's voice came across, still sandy but alert and cautious. "Are you all right, Mrs. Stone?"

She breathed again. "I'm fine, but is Derek? I saw him the last time he was beaten. He should have been taken to a hospital then. Now I'm imagining all kinds of awful things. Do you have *any* idea what's happened?"

"Derek is fine."

"Are you sure?"

"I'm sure."

"How do you know?"

"I spoke with him this morning. I've been trying to reach you ever since. If you were on your way to Parkersville, that would explain why I couldn't get through."

Sabrina sank down on the the the bed. David Cottrell had spoken with Derek, and he was all right. "Where is he?" she asked weakly.

"He's been transferred."

"They told me that much, but to where?"

There was a pause. "I'm afraid I can't say."

"Do you know?"

There was another pause. "I shouldn't say that either, but, yes, I know."

"Why can't you tell me where he is?"

"I'm told that information is classified."

"But I'm his . . . I'm . . . I've been visiting him regularly."

"I know that, Mrs. Stone," David said in his deep voice, "and I'll tell you what I can. Derek was transferred because of rumor of trouble. Nothing has happened," he assured her, as Derek had instructed him to do. "Nothing *will* happen. But the authorities want to keep him under wraps until his release."

"What does that mean?" she asked very quietly. She'd have been prepared to climb the Rockies if Derek was stashed in a hut on the top, but she had the disturbing notion that she wouldn't be allowed even that.

"It means," David confirmed, "that no one will know where he is until he hits the street."

"You do."

"I'm his lawyer. I was instrumental in getting him transferred. Two months, three at the outside—that's all he has left. To let something go wrong at this late date would be insane."

Sabrina heard his determination. He was on Derek's side. Instinctively she knew that she could trust the man.

"But I want to see him," she said. Two months, maybe three going without? The thought was painful.

"I'm sorry. And so is he," David added wryly. "He's not at all pleased with the Department of Corrections or with me right about now, but, believe me, this is the best way."

Sabrina didn't want to believe that, so she tried a new tack. "I can be trusted. If I was allowed to see him, I wouldn't tell a soul where he is. You could even blindfold me," she pleaded, "drive me around for hours, change cars in the middle."

David had to laugh at that. "The Department would never buy it." He hesitated for an instant. "On the other hand, the Department never said you couldn't write letters." It was Derek who'd said that. He'd been afraid her letters would be read. "If you were to send them to my office, I'd be glad to forward them in a packet of legal papers. That way you'd be insured privacy."

"Could Derek write back the same way?"

"Sure."

"Do you think he would?"

"I don't know. He hates writing."

"I know."

"On the other hand . . ." He was remembering Derek's voice when he'd asked him to call Sabrina. The man was in love. There was no mistaking it. Nor was there any mistaking that Sabrina returned the feeling. "On the other hand, I think it would be good for him. He's been calmer since you've been seeing him, more frustrated in some ways but calmer overall. I think it'd be great if you could write." He paused, then asked cautiously, "What say you to that?"

"I say that it's not as good as seeing him."

"True, but it's better than nothing."

"I'm not sure I like the kinds of choices you give, Mr. Cottrell," Sabrina said, her voice stern yet without rancor.

"Neither do I. But trust me. That's all I ask. I think the world of Derek. He doesn't deserve what he's gotten in the past two years, and he certainly doesn't deserve what's happened now. All we can do is try to make things a little easier for him." He hesitated. "Will you write?"

"Of course I'll write."

David gave her the address of both his home and his office, then said, "Thank you, Mrs. Stone. Maybe when all this is over, we'll have a chance to meet."

"I'd like that," she said sincerely, then went on with greater urgency, "You have my number. I should be back in New York by the middle of next week. If anything comes up, if there's any change, if there's any *possibility* that I can see Derek, will you call?"

"Sure thing, ma'am."

She had to settle for that.

"Dear Derek," Sabrina wrote on stationery that had the tiny emblem of Cedar Ledge embossed on its upper left-hand corner, "What a horrible day! I couldn't *believe* it when I arrived at Parkersville to find that you weren't there. No one could tell me where you'd gone, or if they could they wouldn't, and all avenues I might have taken to find out were closed for the weekend—"

She crumpled the paper and tossed it in the wastebasket. She couldn't write to Derek and complain!

Taking another sheet of paper from the rolltop desk, she picked up the pen and tried again. "Dear Derek, I'm not sure I'd want to relive today. I popped in at Parkersville and promptly panicked when they told me—"

Again she crumpled the paper and tossed it in the basket. If Derek learned she'd made a wasted stop at Parkersville, he'd feel bad. Besides, *panicked* was the wrong word. It made her sound like the alarmist Nick had thought her. In truth, she felt that she'd had cause to panic, but that wasn't the issue. The word was revealing on several different levels.

Taking a third sheet of paper from the desk, she gave it another shot. "Dear Derek, I'm writing you from a charming inn, old New England at its best. The furniture is of polished mahogany, Colonial-style and weathered. The artwork is classic Americana, the rugs handwoven, and the canopy on the bed—"

With a clipped growl, she crushed the sheet in her hand and sent it after the others. Derek didn't want a decorator's manual or a travelogue. He didn't need to hear about all the charm he was missing. And if she went on about the canopy on the bed, he'd think she had a one-track mind.

There were times when, where Derek was concerned, she too thought that. But this wasn't such a time.

Before she took another piece of stationery from its narrow shelf, she composed her thoughts. Only when she was sure she was ready did she start. The pre-planning paid off.

"Dear Derek. You are very fortunate to be working with David Cottrell. Not only is he loyal and devoted, but he is a whiz at dealing with people. He explained—patiently, with understanding and encouragement—that you've been transferred for security reasons, and I agree that keeping you safe for the next few months is a small price to pay for my not being able to visit. I can be selfish at times, I guess. I'll have to work on that.

"Exciting news: I've sold the apartment and taken a studio. It's a loft, actually, and it's huge. It's in an old warehouse that's being redone. One entire wall is of glass and looks out on the Hudson, and there are four skylights.

"You're probably wondering whether I know what I'm doing, making momentous decisions like this at the drop of a hat. I didn't plan to do it. I called my broker idly to ask what the chances were of selling my place, and it happened that she had a buyer right there. We signed the preliminary papers last Monday. On Tuesday I took the studio.

"The thing is, I've always taken my time with decisions. But it has occurred to me that, for all my care, some of my decisions have been duds. So I made this one on impulse." She recalled another decision she'd made on impulse, the one that had taken her to Parkersville that first day. She hadn't regretted it yet.

"You're probably asking yourself what happened to leaving the city and finding someplace peaceful and friendly. Well, that's why I'm here." She drew an arrow from *here* to the inn's emblem. I'll be seeing Nicky tomorrow, but after that I'm going house-hunting. I've never lived in the country. I thought I'd give it a try."

Having reached the bottom of the page, she took another sheet from the desk.

"I know what you're thinking. You're thinking that I'm hanging on to Nicky, and you're right. I miss him. When I'm in New York, I feel too distant. Maybe this will help. Ideally, I'd like to be an hour away from the Greenhouse. That way I'll know I can reach Nicky in an emergency, but I won't be able to stop in too often—which wouldn't be any better for Nicky than it would be for me.

"I was thinking of looking for something near Bennington. I'm told that there are writers scattered around. It might be fun—uh, forget I just said that." She'd written too much to crush the whole sheet. "I'm not doing this for social reasons. Most immediately, I'm doing it because I need a change. New York holds memories for me that aren't all fantastic. For professional reasons, I want to keep a place there, but I'll be spending most of my time in Vermont. I want land and trees and fresh air. I want to be able to drive into the nearest town and greet the grocer by name, and I want him to return the greeting. I want to walk down the streets and see people smile. But then I want to be able to return to my own place and just breathe."

She paused, settling against the ladder back of the chair for a bit. She could almost hear Derek asking Why. He probed her feelings that way. It surprised her that in such a short time she'd come to expect it, rely on it. And now she'd miss it.

Perhaps, though, it was for the best.

Tugging her feelings from the corner of her mind where they were trying to hide, she struggled to put them to paper. "I need to be alone, I think. No, *alone* is the wrong word. I need to be *on my own*. I've never really been that. I think it's about time I was. When Nick left—" she wrote, then raised her pen from the paper. Derek didn't want to hear about Nick. What man wanted to hear about a woman's husband—or ex-husband?

Then again, Derek was different. He had already lived

through much of her personal turmoil. He would appreciate her thoughts.

So she lowered the pen and went on. ". . . I was terrified. There was no real reason why I should have been, but I was. Was? At times I still am. Before, even when things were unhappy, I could define myself in terms of wife and mother. Now I can't. I can't rely on anyone to give me definition.

"Being by myself is something I have to do. Maybe it's part of the growing-up process. Then again"—she set aside the second completed page and started a third—"maybe it's an early mid-life crisis. For the first time in my life, I'll be answerable to no one but myself. It should be interesting."

She gnawed on the end of the pen for a moment, then wrote, "I haven't forgotten what you asked me to do the last time we were together. I've already begun. Would you like me to send you information as I go along, or would you rather a single comprehensive report? I'm not sure how much you want there." She shivered, then wrote, "I'm not sure how much you *have* there. I'm hoping that the conditions are better than those at Parkersville—more room, more privacy, more sun—something, anything to compensate for the restrictions."

Dropping the pen, she steepled her hands at her mouth. She could see him so clearly, a tall, tapering figure with dark hair and dark eyes, ropy arms and long, lean legs. She could see him coming toward her in that tight-hipped, sexy gait, and she wanted to touch him.

Pressing her hands tighter together, she waited until the wave of yearning passed; then, with a slightly unsteady sigh, she picked up the pen.

"David is a sweetheart to be forwarding this on to you. I think I would feel totally stifled if I couldn't communicate at all—unless—would you rather I not write? Once before you said I shouldn't, and if you still feel that way, I'll understand. The same goes for your writing back. If you decide to do it, David will know where I am."

"In the meantime, I'll be thinking of you. I'll be thinking of you often."

She held the pen in midair and contemplated the next wording. *Sincerely*? Too formal. The same for *Yours Truly* and *Best Wishes*. *All My Best* wasn't too bad, but it still wasn't right.

There was only one thing that was right, and it seemed pointless not to use it. Lowering the pen, she wrote, "Love, Sabrina."

Derek read and reread Sabrina's letter. Sitting on the floor of his cell with his back to the cinder-block wall, he closed his eyes, thought about it, then opened his eyes and read it again. Would he rather she not write? Would he rather not *breathe*?

Sure, he'd told David she shouldn't write, but that was because when he'd spoken to David it had been just after dawn and he'd been furious. He'd been shoved awake in the middle of the night and, without a word of explanation, smuggled out of Parkersville in a windowless van, driven the three-plus hours to Boston and shuttled by police boat to Pine Island. Only then had he been told about the threat to his life.

It wasn't a new threat. Derek knew who'd made it, knew that it had resulted from a petty argument he'd had with one of the other inmates months before and that the only reason it had reached the warden's ear was a need on the part of a third inmate to earn brownie points.

The threat had no substance, but David Cottrell's threats had apparently reached the warden's ear as well, and the warden had been more intimidated by those. He wasn't taking a chance on dirtying his record. Far easier to wash his hands of Derek.

David, who had pushed for the transfer as a tactical measure and had even chosen the spot, hadn't been Derek's favorite person at that moment shortly after dawn. Only later, when Derek had calmed down, had he understood that the condition of secrecy hadn't been David's to impose. It had been imposed by the commissioner, who, frankly—he told David—wanted Derek the hell out of his system as soon as possible. But the law was the law, and Pine Island would be as safe a place as any, so said the commissioner, and David had agreed.

Pine Island stood in the waters outlying Boston Harbor. The island's only structure was a large stone fort that had once served as a military station. It had been intensively renovated two years before, when the overcrowding of prisons had reached such a critical level that the choice had been between preparing a new facility or releasing inmates from old ones. Now the refurbished fort housed three hundred men.

Pushing himself up from the floor, Derek slipped into the desk chair. He read Sabrina's letter again, then placed it on the desk and mopped his face with the towel that hung around his neck.

He hated writing, hated it with a passion. But he'd do it, if only to make sure Sabrina would write back.

Dragging a yellow legal pad from one side of the desk, he picked up his pen and scrawled, "Dear Sabrina. Thank you very much for the letter. I enjoyed receiving—"

He tore off the sheet of paper, compacted it in one hand and lobbed it into the wastebasket. Too stiff and formal. Sabrina would think he had a textbook in his lap.

Drawing the pad closer, he tried again. "Dear Sabrina. Thanks for the letter. I'm glad to hear someone's doing exciting things—"

He tore off the sheet of paper, crushed it, dunked it. Sabrina didn't deserve sarcasm.

He hated writing letters. Hated it.

Taking a deep breath, he gave it another shot. "Dear Sabrina. Guess where I am?" *Brilliant, McGill. Just brilliant.* He crumpled the paper in disgust.

Then he closed his eyes and pictured Sabrina sitting by his side holding his hand. He imagined the softness of her eyes and the non-judgmental way she looked at him, the sweet curve of her mouth as it gave him encouragement, and her ever-present, ever-pleasant jasmine scent.

Opening his eyes, he wrote as he might have talked. "Dear Sabrina. I hate writing. I've already told you that, I know, but I do hate it. When I was a kid it was the discipline that killed me. Now, it's not so much the discipline as the solitariness of the activity. I'm writing because I can't see you, and that hurts.

"I miss you."

He looked at those three words, considered underlining them or writing them a second time for emphasis, then decided that he didn't want to sound like a sissy. Perish the day.

"Derek McGill is alive and well and living in—they won't let me tell you where, but it's not so far away that I can't look at the stars and imagine your looking at the same ones at the same time."

This time when he looked at the words he'd written, he was a bit astonished. Had he actually written something poetic? On occasion he'd thought things poetic or said things poetic, but he'd never written them. Was it that he'd never had the time to do it? Or the patience?

Standing half-apart from himself, he picked up the pen and wondered curiously what he'd write next.

"Aside from the fact that we can't visit, this place is an improvement over Parkersville. I'm in a wing reserved for special guests"—he smirked at that—"and though my cell is no bigger than the one I had before, it has a sink, the bed and desk are newer, the toilet flushes without spattering"— he couldn't believe he'd written that, but he couldn't erase the ink—"and the holes in the wall are natural, rather than man-made.

"The best thing, though, is that there is a special contingent of guards in this wing and one of them runs. The higher-ups have agreed to let me go with him. I used to run at Parkersville, but only around the prison yard and then listening to the jeering of the prison toughs. The path here is longer and more isolated." He wanted to tell her that it circled the island and that the pulse of the tide swallowed up the sounds of the prison, but that would be giving hints that he'd be better not giving. So he went on to write, "The exercise feels good. It always does. Being outside beats push-ups in my cell any day."

Dropping the pen, he tore off the sheet, then flexed his fingers and scanned the page. His sixth-grade teacher had been right. He wrote like a doctor. At the time he'd been flattered, only later realizing what a slur it had been. Sabrina would be lucky to decipher his words.

Determined to write more clearly, he picked up the pen and started at the top of the second sheet. "The loft in New York sounds perfect. I think you were right in taking it, and I wouldn't worry about the time factor. If you'd waited, you might have lost your buyer. When will you be moving?"

"I also like the idea of a place in Vermont—but part of that's because I'm a country boy from way back. I grew up in the city and I still have a place in the city, but the country is the first place I run when I need soothing. It sounds pretty good right about now."

He stopped writing to think about Sabrina and the country. He could see it; the image fit. It brought back the vision he'd had of her so long ago when they'd first met, when he'd thought of her as a flower child. Remembering it, he felt more peaceful than he had moments before.

Then he sighed and resumed his letter. "Hold onto the notes you've taken regarding that other matter. You're right; I don't want them here. There are no safe-deposit boxes in the manager's office. I have no guarantee that someday when I'm out my things won't be rifled. That's happened—not here, but in Parkersville. The sense of violation is infuriating. I tell you this so that you'll guard what you write. Sending things through David offers privacy, but only to a point." He paused, jiggled his jaw to relax it. "Keep taking notes, though. I know you won't have much time, with moving and all, but anything you can do would be a help. I have only preliminary information on the matter. It will be wonderful to have something more to use as a stepping-off point when I get out.

"How's Nicky? I think of him often. I think of you often. You have me bewitched, y'know. Please write again."

He picked up Sabrina's letter, read it again to make sure that he'd answered every question she'd asked, then focused on the closing. "Love, Sabrina." A common closing. "Love, Sabrina." Could be just a figure of speech.

But he'd seen her eyes and felt her touch and he'd

known. So it wasn't just him. He had nothing to lose by being honest.

Picking up his pen, he wrote, "I love you, too. Derek."

"Dear Derek." Sabrina wrote back on the very same day she received his letter. "You have no idea how much it meant to me to hear from you. I've been worried. David had assured me you were fine, but I wasn't quite sure until I got your letter. You're probably thinking that 'fine' is relative, and I know it is, but I'm thinking that 'fine' means healthy, and I'm relieved that you are. I had visions of black eyes and broken ribs and broken arms and legs. If they can keep you safe there, I'm glad.

She paused, pen poised above her monogrammed stationery. Her heart was beating faster than normal. She'd been smiling since she'd read his letter. Hearing from him had meant more to her than simply the matter of his health. There was the fact that he'd decided to write at all, and of course, there were those four special words.

Shaking her head a little, she forced herself back to her letter. "In the two weeks since I wrote last, lots has happened. I found the most wonderful place in Vermont"—she went back to underline *wonderful* because she felt it was warranted—"a turn-of-the-century farmhouse that is in such a state of disrepair that you'd probably choose your cell over it—except, and I repeat, except that it comes with ten of the most beautiful acres you've ever seen. There are woods and meadows and streams. The house itself is located on a rise and looks down over grass and trees to the Quandahoosic River, which flows into the Connecticut, which means that it's nowhere near Bennington. It's on the other side of the state, about thirty miles north of Brattleboro.

"I've hired a contractor to start work on the farmhouse —new roof, new electrical and plumbing systems, extra insulation, that sort of thing—but I'm thinking of doing some of the inside work myself. I've never painted walls or stripped wood moldings. I'm hoping the work will be for me a little like what your running is for you. I need the outlet. I hadn't realized how hard it would be to learn to

relax. I suppose I'm not making things easier for myself—
I'll be moving out of the apartment and into the loft within
two weeks—but once I've done that I'll be able to concentrate on the farmhouse."

She thought for a minute, then couldn't resist putting the
thought to paper. "Interesting how we find things to divert
our minds—moving from one place to the other, renovat-
ing a third. I want to get back to writing, but no sooner do
I clear my mind for that purpose when it is filled with
thoughts either of you or of Nicky, and the emotions are
too strong to concentrate on much else. I suppose time will
solve that problem, too.

"They tell me at the Greenhouse that I'll come to accept
Nicky's living there. I hope they're right. It's still hard. As
of a week ago Sunday, Nicky was fine, which, in his case,
means the same. He recognizes me when I come—gurgles
a little and smiles—and I end up laughing and crying,
holding him and not wanting to let go."

The pen wavered. She hesitated, frowned, wrote on.
"But I do let go. One part of me is really *glad* to let go. I
feel guilty about that, but it's the truth. I love seeing Nicky,
and the mother part of me dies a little each time I have to
leave, but when I think about taking care of him again, I
get a knot in my stomach and I start to shake. I'm not
knocking the staff at the Greenhouse, but they can afford to
be wonderful; they only work eight-hour shifts, five days a
week at most, and when they leave, they can go back to
their nice, quiet, normal lives. The emotional involvement
is different. A mother takes personally what her child does
or doesn't do. She can't turn off those feelings after an
eight-hour shift. She can't just hand over her baby to someone else when he starts to fuss. A grandparent can, I suppose, but I'll never be one, will I?"

Putting down her pen, Sabrina turned away. She hadn't
had that thought before, and she found that it was as sad as
any. Having children, then grandchildren, had always been
part of the dream. Now what?

She didn't have an answer. Her life was still too much in
a state of flux. Perhaps when things quieted down, perhaps

when she got back to writing, perhaps with the simple passage of time she'd see the future more clearly.

Turning back to her letter, she wrote, "I'm sorry, Derek. I didn't mean to go off on a tangent like that. I think you've spoiled me. I've never talked to anyone the way I talk to you. I miss you, miss the questions you ask and your support. I'd gladly go back to Parkersville—or to any other prison—if it meant I could see you.

"Three months, maybe less. Have you heard anything more about that? Will the transfer make a difference either way?"

More than once, she'd allowed herself to imagine that Derek would get an early release, that she'd open her front door and find him there. She wasn't optimistic; from what he'd said, he wasn't getting any favors. The law was the law, she supposed, and if the law said that he had to serve at least two-thirds of his minimum sentence, an early release was a pipe dream.

Three months, maybe less depending on when the parole board heard his case. But three months at the outside. That was all.

It was too long.

Feeling down, she picked up the pen and closed the letter by writing, "Please know that I think of you often. My love, Sabrina."

At the end of August, Derek wrote back to say that the farmhouse in Vermont sounded perfect. He meant it. Woods, meadows, streams—and a river. He was familiar with the Quandahoosic. It was narrow at spots, where rocks taxed even the most experienced of paddlers, but at other spots it opened into a breathtaking corridor of fresh water lined with willows.

He wasn't surprised that Sabrina had bought into the fixing-up of a broken-down farmhouse. She had time for the work, and she had the energy. He agreed that it would be a good outlet. And not once did he doubt that she'd do that work herself. She wasn't a snob. She wasn't one to sit back and watch others work. Ironically, if she'd been that way, she'd have had an easier time with Nicky. She'd simply have hired more help.

Repairing the farmhouse would appeal to her nurturing instinct. She would steam tired old paper from the walls and replace it with new with the same care that she'd shown when he'd been beaten up that time and she'd stroked him to sleep.

He only wished he were there to help.

At the beginning of September, Sabrina wrote that she had finished decorating the loft and was in the process of moving the rest of her things to Vermont. Work on the farmhouse was progressing faster than she'd dared to hope. The new roof was on, as were new windows and doors, loose fieldstone had been repacked and broken clapboards replaced—which meant that she could live there without fear of the elements. At first she'd planned to stay in New York until the electrical and plumbing work was done, but her need to be out of the city, closer to Nicky and involved in the renovation on a daily basis overrode any qualms she had. She could rough it for a while.

Her last few days in the city were busy with the arrangements for the move north, yet she managed to squeeze in a fair amount of time at the library. More than ever, she wanted to talk with Derek. She wanted to know why he was interested in Lloyd Ballantine, who, as far as she could see, was one of the least notable of the Supreme Court justices to occupy the bench in years. She learned that he had, by and large, voted with the majority, and that the opinions he'd written were thought to be competent, though far from inspired. Off the bench he was just as bland.

Derek had written that her notes would be a stepping-off point for him when he got out—but a stepping-off point for what?

Since Sabrina couldn't put the question to him, she simply gathered what new details she could find on Ballantine, then filed them with the rest of her notes for transfer to Vermont. She intended to install a computer once the farmhouse was functional, and a modem would give her access to a broad range of resources. Between that and use of the library at Dartmouth—which was less than forty-five minutes away—she hoped that by the time Derek was released, she'd have a full dossier to present to him.

By the middle of September, Derek was discouraged. It had been nearly two months since he'd seen Sabrina, and there were times when he wondered if she was real. Sure, he had her letters. He read them so many times that he could replay them in their entirety in his mind's eye. But it wasn't the same. She wrote that she'd moved into the farmhouse, but he'd never seen the farmhouse, so he couldn't picture her there. She wrote that she was literally camping out on the bedroom floor, that she was still without lights and a stove, that she'd picked up poison ivy in the woods—and he couldn't imagine any of it because he'd never seen her wearing anything but a skirt!

Letters couldn't take the place of flesh and blood, and that was what he craved—flesh and blood, warmth, smiles, the kind of sunshine that could light him up inside, the kind only Sabrina produced.

His everyday life had fallen back into the same tedious existence he'd known before she first came to Parkersville. There were no visits to look forward to. One day dragged into the next. There was no one to bring him from a sour mood, no one to diffuse his anger or offset his frustration.

His running helped some, as did the sight of his calendar with more and more X's and fewer and fewer blank spaces. But without Sabrina's letters—real or not—he'd surely have gone mad, because she signed each with her love, and he needed that.

At the beginning of October, Sabrina wrote that her family had descended on the farmhouse. "All three of them, all the way from the Coast, totally without warning! I was sitting on the floor of the front porch, filthy and exhausted after a day sanding woodwork, when a honking car barreled in. It seems that they'd conspired at the last minute to see for themselves where I was 'hiding away' (their term, not mine). It's actually a miracle they made it in one piece. My dad is a terror behind the wheel (horses are more his style), but he'd insisted on driving the rental from Boston. My mother was furious with him by the time they got here, and J. B. was as pale as a ghost (poetic justice there).

"I had honestly thought I'd reached the point of not feeling in a state of crisis. Then they showed up. They do something to me, Derek—stir me up, put me right on the defensive, make me feel inadequate. If it wasn't Mom telling me that I couldn't possibly live so far from civilization, it was Dad telling me that the plasterer was using the wrong mix on the ceilings. Thank God, J. B. didn't say much. He just kind of stared at everything, then went out back to the barn and stared at that."

She didn't write that—later that night, when they'd been having dinner at an inn in nearby Grafton, where Amanda had insisted they all spend the night—J. B. had made a point of asking about Derek. Sabrina hadn't previously mentioned him to either of her parents, but her brother gladly filled them in on what they'd missed.

Amanda and Gebhart both felt that Derek's story, when fictionalized, could be a hit. But Sabrina had no intention of fictionalizing anything. And in that spirit, she took them to the Greenhouse the following day to visit Nicky. She did write to Derek about that.

"It was a mistake, Derek, an awful mistake. I never should have taken them there. They said that they wanted to see their grandson, and since I'd spoken of the Greenhouse only in glowing terms, I had no choice. But no amount of glowing terms can disguise a home for the handicapped. My mother grew very pale and very quiet. Worse, my father, who has a macho thing about control, seemed to crumble inside. J. B. was surprisingly good—probably because Mom and Dad were both so clearly upset. He carried Nicky while we took a tour of the grounds, then played with him a little. Nicky was himself. He is as beautiful as ever, but the bigger he gets, the more noticeable the discrepancy between his physical age and his mental age. It was very hard for my parents to see. And for me."

Derek's heart went out to her when he read that. He'd always felt a soft spot when it came to Nicky, perhaps from the time so long ago when he'd held the child. He'd always felt Sabrina's pain. More than anything he'd have wanted to be with her then.

Then again, he wasn't sure he wanted to be with her family. When he thought of them, he felt out of place. He came from a very different sort than they were. His life experiences had been altogether different. He wouldn't fit in.

Especially now.

He was a convict, and the countdown had begun. Word had spread that the parole board would be hearing cases at Pine Island on the ninth and tenth of November. With little more than a month until then, tension was up throughout the prison.

Derek felt it as keenly as he ever had, because this time his own future was on the line. During daytime lockup, he would sit against the cinder-block wall of his cell and wonder where he'd be five weeks from then.

At night he would lie on his cot, stare at the ceiling and know that he wanted to be with Sabrina.

David was sure that his release was a safe bet. Derek had learned not to bet on a thing.

By the middle of October, Sabrina was able to write that the farmhouse was nearly livable. "I haven't begun on the decorating, but the dusty work is almost done, and once that's finished, I'm home free. My kitchen is already functional. One more bathtub has to go in, but other than that the plumbing's done. I can't wait till you see it!"

She agonized over that last sentence. Not once, either during her visits to Parkersville or in the letters they'd exchanged since, had Derek committed himself to any post-release plans. She knew that he feared the release wouldn't come, and she feared it too, but she needed to be hopeful and, therefore, she dreamed.

She wanted to believe that he loved her. She did believe it when she thought back to the way he'd been during their last few visits—and he wrote the words in every letter—but it wasn't the same as having him there with her, being taken in his arms and hearing the words whispered with the force of their meaning.

The problem was that other than his love, she didn't know what she wanted from him. She knew she loved him, and that meant she wanted to be with him, but where and on what kind of basis was unclear. She had needs of her own. *He* had needs of his own. Whether the two could mesh was anyone's guess.

"Nicky is having seizures more frequently," she wrote. "The Greens aren't alarmed, but they suggested that I may want to take him back to his regular doctor for an evaluation at some point. I think they're right, though I don't look forward to the trip.

"On a lighter note, my friend Maura was up to visit this week. She said that she wouldn't believe I was living on a farm until she saw it. I tried to explain that I'm not living on a farm, per se, just living in a farmhouse, but she took one look at the barn and decided that I should raise sheep, then spin their wool into gold."

Maura had actually said that in disgust, when Sabrina had been evasive about Derek. Maura made no secret about wanting her to write, and, in fact, Sabrina had several ideas for articles she was toying with, but Maura had her mind set. She wanted Derek's book. Since Sabrina had no intention of mentioning the book to Derek when he had so much else on his mind, she put Maura off as best she could.

By the end of October, letter writing was growing harder. Sabrina could tell Derek that she'd just finished papering the bathrooms, that the autumn foilage was breathtaking from her front porch or that that she'd met an interesting pair of transplants from New York who had opened a nearby inn, but she knew that his thoughts were on far more consequential things. As were hers.

She enjoyed the work she did. It exhausted her in a satisfied way, giving her something to show for her time. And the exhaustion helped at night, when pangs of loneliness could be swept under the carpet of sleep.

The mornings were tougher. Dawn. Shortly after dawn —when she awakened with the sun, feeling refreshed, wanting him. For someone who had never defined herself in sexual terms, it was an awakening in more ways than one.

Derek, on the other hand, hadn't needed any kind of awakening. He'd been wanting Sabrina for months. On more nights than he cared to count, he had suffered the pain of arousal, but that pain told only half the story. His longing encompassed everything she was, and became so strong as November approached that there were times when he bolted up from a doze in a cold sweat to find that fear and longing, even in his semiconscious mind, had combined to produce panic.

He couldn't write Sabrina about that. True, he'd told her many times that he loved her, but he didn't want to sound totally obsessed. He didn't want even to think that himself, because he'd never been a man of obsession. Determination, perhaps, and ambition, but never obsession. He knew that he loved Sabrina, knew that it was strong, but he wondered whether his feelings were magnified by the situation.

He couldn't write that to Sabrina, either.

What could he tell her? That he was scared? That he was strung as tight as he'd been at any point during his incarceration? That he walked the corridors of the prison with an eye for every shadow, constantly on guard lest someone make a last attempt to trip him up?

He couldn't tell her that he rarely slept at night, that too many thoughts plagued his mind—thoughts and fears and dreams that were as intricately connected and as fragile as a house of cards.

And so he who had hated writing from the start but had come so far wasn't able to scrawl much more than the briefest of responses to Sabrina's letters. He bottled everything in, and grew more tense. His daily run did little for the cramping muscles in his shoulder or the clenching muscles at his jaw. Nothing could help, he feared, but release.

Eventually, in the name of emotional survival, he tuned out all else but the thought of his parole. He didn't think about what he'd do when he was released. He didn't think about Noel Greer and revenge. And he didn't think about Sabrina.

The only thing that mattered was getting out. Just getting out.

On November ninth, the parole board interviewed twenty-two men whose parole eligibility was forthcoming. Seven were granted parole, fifteen were denied it, and word spread through Pine Island that things were tough.

As fate would have it, Derek wasn't called before the board until November tenth. Of the sixteen inmates interviewed that day, nine were approved and seven deferred. Derek was one of the nine.

· *CHAPTER 11* ·

On the fifteenth of November at seven in the morning, Derek left Pine Island and returned to the mainland a free man. As they'd arranged, he was met by David, who had driven Derek's Saab from New York the night before. The two men talked over breakfast.

"How do you feel?"

"Tired," Derek said because it was the first thing that came to mind. He hadn't slept in two days, hadn't *really* slept in far longer than that. "A little numb," he added, casting a glance around the modest coffee shop where at his own request they'd stopped. "A little incredulous. A little skeptical."

David felt a little sad, because Derek's response illustrated the toll the past two years had taken. Derek had always been a positive man, but his faith in the positive had been badly shaken.

"How about excited?" David asked, giving him a push in the right direction.

Derek smiled. "That'll come once the numbness wears

off." The smile faded as he stole another darting glance around the shop. Then he looked down at his half-eaten Belgian waffle, then, in more surreptitious glances, at the jeans and shirt he wore. The jeans were faded Calvins, the shirt a plaid number with a similar label. They were his, taken from his closet and forwarded on by David in anticipation of his release. They didn't fit as well as they once had.

"Do I look funny?"

"Of course not."

"I feel it. I feel like those people can tell right off just where I've been. I should have told you not to send jeans."

David arched a brow. "My friend, there wasn't a hell of a lot of a casual nature in your closet *but* jeans. I didn't think you'd want to travel in a blazer and slacks, or a suit or a tux."

Derek was silent. Lifting his fork and knife, he carefully cut off another piece of the waffle. After he'd swallowed it, he said, "I'll have to shop when I get back to New York."

"Where are you headed now?"

Putting down the fork and knife, Derek dropped his hands, pressed his palms to his thighs. "To the airport to drop you off so you can catch a shuttle home. I really appreciate this, David. The thought of being confined in an airplane didn't appeal to me." He paused. "The thought of being confined *anywhere* didn't appeal to me. Doesn't. This way I can take my time, stop and get out when I want, roll down the windows and breathe fresh air." He jumped a little when the waitress suddenly appeared at his elbow with refills of coffee. When she left, he asked, "Are you sure you won't drive back with me?"

"I don't drive in no forty-degree weather with the windows down," David drawled, then added, "And besides, I have to be back for a hearing at eleven." He scratched his cheek. "To tell you the truth, I thought you'd be heading to Vermont."

Derek raised his coffee cup, took a careful sip, set the cup down. He wiped his upper lip with his lower one. His eyes went to those of his lawyer and friend. "Did you call her?"

"Right after you called me." Which had been on the tenth, several hours after Derek had learned that he'd been granted parole.

"What did she say?"

"Nothing at first. It took me a while to figure out she was crying."

Derek squeezed his eyes shut and sucked in a shaky breath. "She did that to me once, too." It was a minute before he opened his eyes. "She's a special lady."

"Yeah. So why aren't you driving up to see her?"

Derek had been asking himself the same question for the last four days. "I need distance. I need distance between me and"—he tossed his head in the vague direction of the harbor—"that place before I go to her. I need to feel a little more human. I need a good night's sleep. I need to know I can get one without jerking up in a panicky sweat." He took another shaky breath. "It's been a fucking lousy few weeks."

"It's been a fucking lousy few years."

Having no argument with that, Derek cut off another piece of waffle and nudged it idly around his plate. "What's the latest on Greer?"

"He's running. He'll probably announce it right after the first of the year."

"Do you think he'll be watching what I do?"

"You bet. I don't think he'll try any more funny stuff, though. It was one thing when you were in the can with dozens of violent men. A murder there can easily be made to look like something else. But he knows you were transferred from Parkersville, and he knows why, and he knows *I* know why. He won't risk murder again, particularly not after he declares his candidacy."

Derek wasn't sure whether the logic was correct, but his mind had already moved on down the road. "If he's running, I've got a year. One year to link him to Lloyd Ballantine."

David shifted in his seat. He was always uncomfortable when Derek started in on the business with Ballantine. Not that there was any doubt that Derek had been set up for murder, nor that powerful fingers had pulled strings during the trial. David just wasn't so sure of the Ballantine connection. He'd hate to see Derek waste valuable time chasing a wild goose.

"Don't go at it yet. Take some time off. You need it, Derek. You said so yourself, you need to breathe a little. Relax. Have some fun. Decide what you want to do about work, and when you've got yourself together, *then* you go after the Ballantine files."

Derek thought about David's words a lot in the week to come, especially the part about relaxing and having fun. He didn't do much of either. It wasn't that he didn't want to, just that it didn't work out—which wasn't to say that he didn't enjoy his freedom. He valued all the little things he'd taken for granted for years. He went where he wanted when he wanted, did what he wanted when he wanted—and if that meant taking a hot shower at two in the morning, going out for a Big Mac at nine o'clock at night or wandering around the city for hours at a stretch, so much the better. The problem was, he couldn't forget where he'd been.

He was self-conscious. He felt as though anyone who looked at him *knew*. Unfortunately, many people did. He'd been seen regularly on prime-time television for four years before his arrest, and the publicity that had accompanied the trial had, if anything, raised his familiarity quotient. People with familiar faces did double takes, then stared, cracking wary smiles only in response to Derek's quiet-spoken hello. Even his agent, Craig Jacobs, seemed not quite sure what to do with him when he met him for lunch the day after he got back. For the first five minutes they were together, he went on and on about how surprised—and pleased!—he'd been to receive Derek's call and how wonderful Derek looked. Derek knew that he looked tired, pale and thin, so Craig had already blown his credibility by the time he reached the part about things not being the same since Derek had left.

But Derek was polite. He nodded and thanked Craig for

the thought, then suffered through the gossip session that accompanied a lunch so "nouvelle" that he would have found it bizarre even if he'd spent the last two years in Paris, rather than prison.

He was experiencing culture shock. After his prolonged period of confinement, New York was overwhelming. When he left his apartment on even the simplest of errands, his pulse raced. He was familiar with it all—the traffic, the people, the buildings—yet he wasn't. Any sudden noise made him jump, and the city streets were full of sudden noises: the honk of a horn, the blare of a siren, the squeal of brakes. And sudden movement. That set him off, too. For two years of his life, sudden noise or movement had spelled trouble. The deconditioning, he realized, would take some time. In many respects, he was still a prisoner.

And a murderer. That fact hit him now that he was free in ways it hadn't hit him when he was in prison. He could understand why, he supposed. In prison, he'd been but one of many, and most of those had been such clearly violent types that he hadn't identified with them. Here, he stood out. It occurred to him more than once when he bumped into someone he knew that what he interpreted as awkwardness was, in fact, fear. He was a murderer. He'd done hard time with hard men. He could be dangerous.

What bothered him most, though, was not what people thought. It was what *he* thought. For two years, he'd refused to dwell on it. He'd relived the crime, but mainly in terms of what had happened where and when and why. He had preoccupied himself with a sort of mental police report, and when his mind had dared stray to the moral implications of the crime, he pushed them aside by focusing on the farce that had been his trial and the horrors of prison.

He couldn't do that now. He was a free man. And Joey Padilla? He was dead. Derek had *made* him dead—unintentionally, perhaps, but it had been his hand that directed the gun to Padilla's stomach.

Derek thought about that. He thought about it a lot, and

it dragged him into a blue funk. Because two other thoughts came on the heels of that one.

The first was that he was his old man's son.

The second was that Sabrina deserved better.

Sabrina. As the week went on, he thought about her more and more. Each thought tugged at his heart a little, stirred his insides a little, did something vaguely debilitating around the backs of his knees. He might have called or written, but he didn't, and he knew that she was very probably worried and hurt. More than once he told himself that it was for the best, that if she was worried and hurt, she'd realize sooner that she was buying grief she didn't need.

The problem was, he didn't want her to realize that. He wanted to be with her. And the bitch of *that* was that the ball was in his corner now. She'd had it before. She'd been the one to go to Parkersville, then return month after month. She'd been the first to write after his transfer to Pine Island. But now she was in her farmhouse in Vermont and she wasn't making a move. She knew that he'd been released. She could have gotten his phone number and called. But she hadn't. Because it was his turn.

Even in the bluest of moments, when Derek felt like the scum on the pond in Central Park as he ran by it each day, it never occurred to him not to go. The only question was when.

After six days in the city, when he'd reached the point where Sabrina dominated his thoughts, he knew the time had come.

Packing a duffle with clothes to last him anywhere from two days to a month, he drove north. He had her address packed away in his mind, committed to memory since the instant it had appeared on the left-hand corner of the envelope that came in David's packet. With each rest stop he passed, he wondered if he should call. But he should have called a week before. Since he hadn't done that, and since she might be upset with him, and since her love might even have fizzled and died in that time, he didn't dare.

So he never did stop to call. He did stop, though, once to fill the car with gas, once to get some coffee, once to use the men's room, once to stretch his legs and contemplate the blanket of clouds overhead. He was stalling, he knew, stalling like a yellow-bellied coward, and it gave him one more reason to hate himself.

Then, midway through the drive, two things happened. The first was outside. The clouds began to lighten, then thin, then slowly but surely allow for the spotty appearance of blue.

The second was inside, inside himself. He felt a pull. It came from the north, and it caused his foot to press a bit more heavily on the gas, caused his heart to beat just a little faster. He supposed that it might have been there all along; that it might have been responsible for the restlessness he'd felt those last few days in New York; that he might have sensed it earlier but for the doubts and fears that had worked against it. It was the magnetic force he'd felt before, and it grew stronger with each passing mile.

With strength came greater clarity and need. Just as he had seen Sabrina's face in the cracks on the ceiling of his cell, now he saw it on his windshield. He could see her, see her smile, feel the warmth of her sun. His fingers felt, not the hard leather of the steering wheel around which they were wrapped, but the softness of her skin. The scent of jasmine wafted through his mind, overpowering the diesel fumes that drifted through as he passed a truck.

By the time he turned off the highway and started along the back road that led to her farmhouse, his heart was thudding.

He had no trouble finding her driveway, since her mailbox was new and prominently marked with the number he knew. He paused for a minute, forced himself to breathe slowly and deeply, unclenched his hand from the wheel, shifted and drove on.

Thick, shady trees lined the route, crowding the road so tightly at times that branches slapped the sides of his car. And then it came again, an omen that was too trite to be believed. The farmhouse lay at the end of the drive, bathed in sunlight. The light at the end of the tunnel.

Swallowing his trepidation, Derek drove the last few yards and drew the Saab to a halt beside a small, sporty green Mercedes that wasn't at all new but looked well kept. He'd often wondered what kind of car Sabrina drove. This one was classy and suited her well.

For that matter, he mused, shifting his gaze, the house suited her, too. It was of modest design, done in the finest of materials. In typical Cape style, only the first floor was visible from the front, but the size and slope of the roof suggested a bounty of second-floor space. The roof was of fresh cedar shingles, the facade of fieldstone, the sides of clapboard newly painted a light Nantucket gray.

He climbed from his car and started toward the front door, his stomach knotting in anticipation. At least she was home, he reflected. He'd have hated to arrive like this and find her out. Then again, he didn't know she was here. She could be out with a friend. He should have called.

The antique brass knocker made a resounding thud against the door. Derek focused on its barnboard planks. He waited, listened for footsteps. Hearing nothing he lifted his hand and swung the knocker again. Though the sound jolted his own body, it had no apparent effect on any occupant of the house.

She was out. He should have called.

He looked around. The day had turned into a beauty— sunny and just warm enough for him to leave his jacket in the car. Maybe she'd taken advantage of the November treat, too. She'd written of woods and meadows and streams. He glanced to the side of the house, where deciduous trees stood mostly bare before more dense stands of pines and firs. Maybe she was out there. Somewhere.

Discouraged, he stuck his hands in his pockets and started walking idly around the house to the stretch of lawn that opened onto the river. Sabrina hadn't exaggerated the beauty of the setting. The grass was still green, though strewn with drying leaves in an assortment of late fall shades. The river curved around the edge of the lawn, not much more than twenty-five feet wide. The slate-blue water was lightened in spots by rocks beneath the surface. Several boulders broke the surface. A bird landed on an overhanging willow branch, but if it chirped, the sound was swallowed by the gentle rush of the water.

Derek stood still, drinking in the serenity of the scene.

Or did the serenity come from Sabrina? He always thought it, though what he'd felt during the drive from New York had not been exactly serene.

Remembrance of those feelings brought the moment to an end. Turning away from the river, he spotted the barn. He'd always been intrigued by barns. They represented everything he'd never had as a kid—a loft to play in, a pet to care for, a way of life that was slower, wholesome, more gentle. There was something peaceful about barns, and though this one wasn't anything special to look at, it beckoned.

He completed the walk around the back of the house until he stood before it. As barns went, it was modest in size. A worn path leading from its front toward a break in the woods suggested that at one point it had housed some form of livestock. It showed its age. Random strips of weatherboarding had come unnailed, the hay door hung askew, and the red paint was tired and worn.

Unable to resist the invitation of the half-open great door, Derek moved forward. His deck shoes made no sound on the apron. He slipped through, then stopped and caught his breath.

Inside, the barn was a cavern of shadows. From a single high dormer, a beam of sunlight cut a conical swathe through the dark. In that small pool of sunlight was Sabrina.

She was sitting on her heels beside an old captain's table. A piece of sandpaper lay on the wood; the ultrafine grains of sawdust floating in the light attested to the work she'd been doing. She wasn't working now, though. She was grasping the edge of the table with one hand, while the sun glittered off her bowed blond head. And as Derek stood hidden in the shadows, he saw her brush tears from her cheeks.

Something inside him twisted and turned. She was everything he'd ever dreamed, kneeling there in a pair of dusty white jeans and an oversized blue shirt. Her hair was a wild tangle. Her feet were bare. And she was hurting.

"Sabrina?"

Her head came up fast, a look of alarm on her face as

she peered into the dark. He went forward—two steps, then a third. He stopped. Her eyes had widened. She was staring, just staring, and for a minute fear pounded through him so strongly that he couldn't move. But only for a minute, because he had a need to hold her that wouldn't be denied.

When he started forward again, he saw her blink, then saw her eyes fill with fresh tears. He hastened his step when she rose from the floor, and by the time he had reached the small circle of light she was throwing herself into his arms. He caught her to him, swinging her off her feet and around.

She couldn't talk at first. Her throat was filled with soft, slow sobs that shook her entire body. Derek held her tighter, his long arms crisscrossing her body while he brushed his face back and forth in the wild waves of her hair.

"I thought—" she cried in a high tremolo that spoke of something akin to panic. "I thought you weren't coming!"

He moaned and crushed her even closer.

The tremolo came again. "I thought you'd changed your mind—that you didn't—want me now that you're free!"

Letting her feet touch the floor, he took her face in his hands and tipped it to his. "I could never change my mind," he said raggedly. "I love you too much."

Before she had a chance to respond, his mouth took hers in a kiss that was wild and hungry. They were both breathing harder by the time he was done, and then, between those rapid breaths, he pressed moist kisses to her nose, her eyes, her forehead. He returned to her mouth with one that was deep enough to touch her soul, and when he raised his head, his gray eyes were smouldering. "I need you," he whispered hoarsely. "I need you badly."

The need was electric. It was the culmination of months of desire, of foreplay that had been enacted in their minds, where no guards could stop it. It was spontaneous and inevitable and hot.

As he bent his head to her again, she met him halfway, her lips as anxious as his. Their hands moved over each other, trying to touch everything, to know everything at once. But it was impossible, and the touching they did wasn't enough.

"I need you," he whispered again, this time easing his tongue into her mouth while his impatient fingers worked on the buttons of her blouse. In no time the blouse was opened and he was touching her bare flesh.

Clenching handfuls of his hair, Sabrina let her head fall back. She was panting softly, trying to release the heat that was building too quickly. But the more he touched her— and he was a master with his palms, the heels of his hands, his fingertips—the hotter she grew. When he ducked his head and sucked her breast into his mouth, she began to shake.

"Derek . . . ahhh . . . please . . ." She slid her hands over his waist, then his belly, and touched him where he was hard with desire. Singed, he jerked back, but in the next shallow breath he was straining forward, needing more, then more still.

But it was still not enough. He needed to be embedded inside her. Tugging at the snap of her jeans, he lowered the zipper and pushed the fabric down. His own shirt got in his way; since it had no buttons, Sabrina had pushed it up and was trying to work it over his head. He paused long enough to whip it off, while she pulled at the drawstring that held up his pants. He took care of that, too, shoving the pants and his briefs down and off while his heated eyes held hers. Then he reached for her again with the urgency of one too long denied.

Leaving her shirt as it was, he lowered her to the floor of the barn, rushed off her jeans and panties, and in that single ray of November sun, took his place between her thighs and surged forward.

His possession was full and deep and brought him a pleasure so agonizing that he barely heard Sabrina's own cry. Even when he realized what the sound was, he couldn't possibly have stopped. His face was a mask of sweet torment, his body glistened with sweat, and the need that pulsed through him was a relentless force centered in his loins.

Sabrina did not stay him. She wound her legs around his

waist and lifted herself to meet his thrusts. He wanted to take his time and savor the fine nuances of her sheathing, but the urgency of his body wouldn't allow for that. Nor would hers. She was tightening around him, milking him with love. He stroked her forcefully. With each incursion, he felt himself going deeper into that love, until he thought he would lose himself entirely to it. He loved her more with each thrust.

Long arms trembling, he fastened his mouth to hers and drank in her impassioned cries until he felt her arch up, catch in her breath, then burst into flames. The ripple of those spasms inside her sent him reeling, back arching, muscles quivering, sweat beading. With a mighty moan, he followed her into a prolonged and powerful climax.

For a time, the sounds of panting were the only ones in the barn. Then, incredibly, Sabrina began to cry again. Still buried in her warmth, Derek rolled to his side and gathered her in.

"I hurt you," he cried, calling himself a million names for having taken her like an animal. He should have known. He should have given himself more time, perhaps slaked his sexual needs on other women before coming to her. He'd been caged too long.

His hand shook as he stroked her hair, "God, I'm sorry, Sabrina. I just needed you like I've never needed anyone or anything before. I kept thinking that if I didn't hurry something was going to happen to stop it, and I had to be inside you—"

Her arms were tight around him. Her face was buried against his throat. She continued to cry, but very, very softly.

Derek died a little with each sob. "Don't baby, please don't."

"I'm h-happy."

His hand stilled on her hair. "You don't sound happy.'

"But I am."

"Do you always cry when you're happy?"

"I don't know. I h-haven't been happy very much lately."

He gave a low moan, closed his eyes and rolled to bring

her on top of him. Then he lifted her face with his hands. "We'll have to work on that." He took his time examining each of her features. His thumbs followed his eyes, tenderly wiping tears from her cheeks. Then he smiled and whispered, "I love you."

Watery-eyed, she smiled back and whispered, "Me too." She repeated the words in a kiss.

By the time it was over, his smile was gone. "Did I hurt you?"

She shook her head.

"You cried out when I—"

"It was so strong. I was frightened."

"Are you now?"

She hesitated, then nodded. "What just happened—I've never felt anything like it."

"Never climaxed?"

"Never like that."

"Like what?" he asked, needing to know. Where Sabrina was concerned, he had a barrelful of insecurities.

Her eyes held his. "Deeply. Endlessly. Almost... violently."

"Not violently. I didn't want violently."

"But it was so good." Her voice dropped to a whisper. "I can still feel it."

He sucked in a loud breath, said, "I know," and rolled over again. This time, as soon as she was beneath him, he slid his hands under her and scooped her up, then reared back to sit on his heels. She was straddling his lap. He was still inside her.

"I love you," she whispered, winding her arms around his neck. She kissed him lightly once, then again, and hugged him tightly.

A familiar knot rose in his throat. He hugged her back, unable to get enough of her softness. When he could speak again, he said, "I worried about that. The closer my release got, the more I worried."

"I love you."

Tipping her face up, he took his turn kissing her once, then again. Neither kiss was as light as hers had been, but if the purring in the back of her throat was any indication, she didn't mind. Then he combed her hair back from her face. "Comfortable?"

She nodded. "A little sandy." They'd done enough rolling around that not even the shirt she still wore had been able to protect her from the wood dust.

"Me too. Nice table, though."

"It will be." She touched his cheek, the tiny mole at his temple, the faded scar by his eye. She wove her fingertips into his hair. "You had it cut," she observed. It looked perfect, even mussed from their loving. "I like it."

He nuzzled the shell curve of her ear. "I like your barn."

"Musty."

"Nice musty."

"I like your clothes, too." She knew that she would never, never forget that moment when she'd looked up and seen him. She'd been thinking about Nicky, thinking about Derek, feeling very low and very alone, and then he'd called her name. "I wasn't sure it was you, at first. I've been picturing you in blue denim."

"Never again. I cleaned out my closet and gave every pair of blue jeans I owned to the Salvation Army." He kissed her right eye and said in a deeper voice, "I like your body."

She blushed.

"Your breasts are perfect."

She lowered her forehead to his chest. "They're too small."

"They are not." He ran his hands over her hips and down her legs. "Do you know that I've never seen you in anything but a skirt?"

"Mmm."

"I like your legs." His hands were making the return trip, palms creating a sensual friction upward from her thighs and over her hips. She sighed when they came to rest under her arms, thumbs lightly rubbing the outer swell of her breasts.

Sabrina felt herself tingling inside. She wondered if it was a lingering after-effect of their lovemaking, but when she shifted her hips ever so slightly, the feeling grew.

Something else grew, too. She raised questioning eyes to Derek's.

"It was only a matter of time," he answered with a mischievous grin that created a slash in his cheek that stirred her even more. Cupping her bottom with both hands, he urged her more snugly over his heat. "Once would never do it." He captured her mouth and gave her a long, thorough kiss. By the time he was done, the tingling inside her had become a slow burn.

Arms around his neck, she strained closer to his body. But Derek wanted to touch her, wanted to touch her breasts and her belly and that place between her legs that was so moist and hot against him. So he held her back a little and gave his hands the freedom they craved.

Sabrina didn't protest. He brought her too much pleasure. Too soon, though, she was flaming, and when she tried to tell him to slow down, he smothered the words with his mouth, and then it was too late for them both, because, again, her climax sparked his.

When it was over this time, Derek lay on the floor of the barn and tucked her to his side. He wanted to shut his eyes and rest, but he was afraid that if he did, she'd disappear. So he settled for looking at the comfortable way she'd draped her body against his. And after a bit, when she tipped her head to look at him, he said, "I couldn't come here before, Sabrina. I wanted to, but I couldn't. I felt too dirty."

"You were never—"

He put a finger to her lips. "I felt it. I took three showers a day." His finger came to rest on her chin. "But it wasn't only physical. I felt that I had to air out my mind, as if it reeked of hatred and resentment and violence. Prison is a poison. It gets in your system. I wanted to get it out."

"Did you?" she asked, but she knew the answer. She saw the shadow on his face.

"Some of it, I guess." He lay his head back and looked up at the rafters. After a time he said, "It was just as well I went to New York. There were things I had to do."

"Like . . . ?"

"Sleep. I hadn't done it in a while."

"It must have felt good."

"The first two nights were a little rocky, but after that it was okay."

"Bad dreams?"

"Yeah. I kept dreaming I was back inside. I'd wake up disoriented and shaking."

"Oh, Derek."

"It's okay. Once I started sleeping, I made up for lost time."

Her lips curved against his chest. "So you slept most of the week away?"

"I should've. The rest of what I did wasn't worth much."

"Like . . . ?"

"Lunch with my agent."

Sabrina knew that would have to do with work. "Was he any help?" she asked, not sure whether she wanted him to work or not. She liked the idea of Derek's staying with her, which she doubted he'd be able to do once he found work. Vermont wasn't exactly in the mainstream for investigative reporters.

"Oh yeah," Derek said. "Cliff was a help. He was sure every talk show in the country would jump at the chance to have me on. He envisioned a national tour—until I set him straight."

"You won't do talk shows?"

"Not as a guest. I want to be the one asking questions, not the other way around."

"But if it was good publicity—if the producer of a program could see you and realize that you were back in circulation and say to himself, 'Hey, that guy's the one I need,' wouldn't it be worth it?"

Derek's voice was chilly. "I don't need a job that bad. In fact, I don't need a job at all. I never had time to spend the money I earned before, so I invested it all. The interest alone can keep me in style."

"But you want to work."

"And I will. Somehow or other, I will."

Sabrina had other questions on the subject but was reluctant to ask them. She could feel Derek's tension and wanted it gone. To that end, she slid her open hand over his chest, soothing him with a gentle massage. "I'm glad you're here," she said softly.

He closed his eyes and concentrated on the feel of her hand moving over his skin. Her touch was the balm he needed. His muscles gradually relaxed. "So am I," he said and stroked her hip. Then he raised his head. "Cold?"

"No."

"You have goose bumps."

"I'm okay."

He hadn't noticed until then that the spray of sunlight on the floor of the barn had shifted. "I think we'd better get up."

But when he made to rise, she held him tighter and protested, "No. Stay."

"I'm not leaving," he said very gently.

"Don't move. I don't want anything to change."

He eyed her in amusement. "We can't stay here forever."

"I know, but just a little longer?"

"You're getting chilled."

"I'm fine."

"I'm getting sore."

"Oh."

"And besides," he said, bringing her up with him this time, "I want a tour of the place." Standing, he grasped the lapels of her shirt and drew her body flush to his. "And maybe something to eat."

Her eyes widened. "I have to get food. I don't have any food. I wasn't expecting anyone, and since I don't eat all that much myself, I—"

He silenced her with a kiss, then said, "Is there a market nearby?"

"In the village."

"We'll go together."

"Will you stay?"

"For a meal?"

"For more than one?"

"Am I being invited?"

"Yes."

"I'll stay."

"Good."

That settled, they grinned at each other. She put a finger to his dimple. "I like this."

"And I like this," he countered, running both thumbs very lightly under her eyes.

"What?"

"No smudges. The smudges are gone." So was the tic. "You're getting lots of rest."

"There's plenty of time for that up here. Want a bath?"

"Real men don't take baths."

"It's a Jacuzzi."

"It is?"

"But it just went in. I haven't tried it out yet."

"You haven't?"

She shook her head.

"Sabrina," he chided, "how can you have a Jacuzzi and not try it out?"

"I was waiting for you."

"And if I hadn't come?"

"I guess the Jacuzzi would have gone to waste."

"It's a big one?"

She nodded.

"Where?"

"The master suite."

"*Suite*? I have to see this."

At that moment, with her arms looped loosely around Derek's neck, her naked body pressed to his and her gaze held by one that was warm as toast, Sabrina felt happier than she'd felt in years. "I'm ready whenever you are."

· *CHAPTER 12* ·

They helped each other dress—not in any teasing prelude to further lovemaking, but simply because they wanted to touch. They needed the reassurance that the other was there, that the other was free, that the other loved.

Sabrina's hands brushed Derek's lean hips as she tied the drawstring of his cotton pants. The backs of his fingers skimmed her soft flesh when he rebuttoned her blouse. She held his shoulders for balance when he helped her into her jeans. And together, with Sabrina warming his side first, they maneuvered his shirt over his head.

"This is all pretty unnecessary," he said, grinning as he took her hand. She had his deck shoes tucked under an arm. "We're going right in to take a bath."

"But we have to cross here to there, and it's cool out."

He sent her a doubting glance.

"Then look at it this way," she returned indulgently. "You can never tell what form of beast is spying from the woods."

Derek didn't want to look at it that way. It had occurred to him more than once that if Greer was still after him, the last thing he should have done was come to Sabrina. But he'd been selfish. He'd needed her. He hadn't been aware of being followed in New York, and he knew he hadn't been followed when he drove north. As he saw it, he had a choice: he could either spend every waking hour looking over his shoulder, or he could relax and simply keep his eyes and ears open.

Right now, though, his eyes and ears and all his other senses were calling for Sabrina. Bringing her close to his side, he guided her from the barn. The air was indeed cooler than it had been when he'd come, and though it was only mid-afternoon, the sun was leaning toward the horizon.

She squeezed his waist and tipped her head up to him. "I'm so glad you're here."

Twenty minutes later, she repeated the words. Derek was leaning over the Jacuzzi, adjusting the water temperature. She'd slipped her hands under his shirt and was stroking his back.

Satisfied with the heat, he turned, sat on the broad ledge of the tub and tugged off the shirt. Then he brought Sabrina to stand between his legs. His hands stole under the tails of her shirt but went no farther than her waist because he was suddenly distracted. The look in her eyes was something to behold.

She was focusing on his chest, looking as though she'd never seen anything so beautiful. She ran her hands lightly around the broad curve of his shoulders, brought them skimming over the muscles that defined his upper chest, slid them over warm, hard flesh to where his pants rode low on his hips, then dragged them back up the narrow line of soft, dark hair that bisected his front. Where the line flared, her fingers followed until each palm covered a small, hard nipple.

Then Sabrina was the one to be distracted, because the slightest pressure of Derek's hands had arched her toward him and his mouth was opening over her breast. The barrier of her shirt enhanced the feeling as his tongue dabbed her nipple to hardness. Propping her forearms on his shoulders, she closed her eyes in pleasure.

He continued for several minutes. But when both nipples were taut and her breath was coming less steadily, he set her back and said hoarsely, "Water's ready."

It took her a minute of lingering delight to realize what he was saying. She opened her eyes to send him a look of pleading, which he answered with a gentle kiss. To make up for what he'd done, he helped her undress.

Moments later, she was settled in the crook of his shoulder in the warm, swirling water. She gave a soft sight of contentment, but other than that neither of them spoke. They simply surrendered to the warmth and let the water massage their entwined limbs.

"Sabrina?" Derek asked after a while.

"Mmm?"

"How's Nicky?"

At first she didn't respond. Then, with a sad sigh this time, she gave a one-shouldered shrug.

"Any change?"

She shook her head.

"Don't want to talk about it?"

"Not now. It hurts. I don't want to hurt right now."

"You made the right decision."

"But it hurts anyway."

He drew her in a little closer, offering whatever silent comfort he could. Several minutes later, he said, "I think you've done a great job with this place."

She twitched her nose against his chest. "You're just saying that to make me feel better."

"Would I do that?"

"I don't know. Would you?"

"No. I really like it."

"Really?" she asked cautiously.

"Uh-huh." And he meant it. The inside of the farmhouse was simply done, clean with newly stuccoed walls and polished wood floors, warm with area rugs and native artwork.

"I don't have much furniture."

"You have what you need—sofa and chairs in the living room, bed in the bedroom, a few dressers and desks." He paused, then tried to sound casual when he said, "And a completed guest room. Why is the guest room the most finished in the house?"

She heard something behind his attempt at casualness that made her bite back a smile. "Are you worried?"

He considered denying it, but only for an instant. "Yeah," he said gruffly. "I haven't waited all this time for you, only to sleep in a guest bedroom."

She cupped the water and sent it rippling higher on his chest. "Not to worry. It's for my guests."

"Aren't I a guest?"

"No."

"What am I?"

Her smile was soft, shy, innocent. "Loved one. Lover."

He liked her answer as much as he liked her softness, her shyness, her innocence. Sliding an arm beneath her knees, he shifted her until she lay across his lap. With his upper arm bracing her head, he kissed her, then asked, "So why is the guest room all done up?"

"Because my brother has taken to visiting."

"How come?"

"Beats me," she said. "It's like he's looking for family after all these years."

"But he has your parents. He lives a lot closer to them than to you."

"It's not the same. There's something here. I'm not sure I can explain, but he likes this place. He doesn't do a lot, just kind of sits and thinks and asks me questions about what I was thinking and feeling when we were growing up."

"What do you tell him?"

"That I was wishing our family was like other families. That I wanted everyone to be attentive and warm and close."

"You still want that."

She hesitated for an instant before acknowledging it with a nod.

"Do you tell him that?"

"I have."

"What does he say?"

"That I'm no different from him, or my mother or my father. But they're so lonely, Derek. Each one in his way."

"So are you," Derek said very softly.

She held his gaze for a minute, then closed her eyes and turned into his body. She didn't feel lonely. When Derek was with her she felt that she could dream again. She knew that it was an illusion, that he had designs on his life and that some of them frightened her, but she felt she'd earned an illusion or two.

"I love you," he whispered.

"I want that," she whispered back.

Tipping her chin up, he kissed her in a way that left little doubt as to his sincerity, and by the time he was done, his hands were on her body, working with the gentle pulse of the water to give her pleasure. But the pleasure wasn't only hers. It was Derek's, too. The way she sighed when he caressed her breasts, the tiny moan she let out when he traced the outline of her bottom, the small feline sounds she made when he found the special heat between her legs —all heightened his own arousal to such an extent that while she was still throbbing in climax he lifted her over him and arched deeply into his own release.

Some time later, when their bodies had calmed, they climbed from the tub, wrapped themselves in large terry bath sheets and stumbled to Sabrina's bed, where they shed the towels, climbed under the covers and fell asleep in each other's arms.

By the time they awoke, it was dark and too late to go to the market. Not that either of them was sorry. They didn't feel like getting dressed, and it turned out that Sabrina had food in the house after all.

"That is awful," she decided as she opened an envelope of dried soup.

Derek had already put the prescribed amounts of milk and water in a pan. "Not so awful," he argued, taking the envelope from her and adding its contents to the liquids. "I like cream of broccoli soup. And besides, if you bought it, you must have been planning on eating it yourself, so why is it so terrible if I have some?"

"Because you deserve better. And because I should have been prepared."

He set the pan on the stove, lit the gas under it, then turned and took her by the shoulders. "If anyone's at fault here, it's me. I didn't say when I was coming. I didn't say *if* I was coming, so there was no reason for you to stock up."

"It occurred to me to buy food, it really did. But first the kitchen wasn't ready, and then I was afraid."

"Afraid?"

"Like if I gave a party and no one came."

He rotated his thumbs. Not even the thick terry of her robe could hide the delicacy of her bones. That delicacy was only part of what inspired his gentleness when he asked, "Is that why you don't have a room set up for Nicky?"

She swallowed hard, but she didn't avoid his eyes. "No. I wanted you to come, so I was superstitious about making preparations. With Nicky, it's different. I'm not sure I want . . ." She couldn't finish. The thought was too cruel.

But Derek saw it differently. "You're not sure you want all that work again. It's understandable, Sabrina. Nothing to be ashamed of."

"But he's my son. I love him. There are times when I'm torn to bits, when the anguish of not having him is as bad as the anguish of having him. I thought about decorating a room for him. I even pictured how I'd do it. Then I thought about seeing that room day in, day out, and I didn't think I could take it. I try—" She swallowed again, and her eyes were growing moist. "I try not to think about Nicky too much. When I do, I go nowhere. I have to move on in my life."

Derek took her under his arm and held her close while he stirred the soup. "Would you want to have another child?"

"I couldn't."

"Physically?"

"Emotionally. I couldn't go through another pregnancy knowing what happened."

He hesitated for just a minute before saying, "I didn't use anything, Sabrina."

"It's okay. I have an IUD."

He gave the soup another stir, then another. Then he said, "If you were to have a second child, it could be totally different."

"Or it could be the same."

"Did the doctors say that?" When she didn't answer, he prodded. "Did they give you odds against it happening again?"

"Yes."

"What are they?"

"Very slim," she said in a small voice, then rushed on, "But that's irrelevant. Even if the odds were a million to one, I couldn't risk it."

Derek felt saddened. Not only did he believe that Sabrina was made to be a mother, but he had images from time to time of her mothering a child of his. They were fleeting images. He hadn't given much thought in the past to having children, and his future was too murky for him to dwell on it now. But those fleeting images brought him a strange, unexpected sense of peace.

Riding on the tails of that peace, he gave the soup a last stir, gave her shoulders a squeeze and turned toward the refrigerator.

The master suite was on the ground floor at the back of the house. It actually consisted of three smaller rooms that had been added on after the original farmhouse had been built, but Sabrina had had the walls broken down and the cathedral ceiling exposed. The room looked out over the woods and was lit by two large skylights through which, on a clear night, moonlight poured.

Moonlight was pouring in this night, but that wasn't what kept Sabrina and Derek awake. It was each other and the fact that they were together. The slightest movement of one caused the other to stir. There was surprise, occasional alarm then reassurance. A kiss led to a touch, which led to a caress, which often led to something far hotter.

Then again, there were times when they simply lay in each other's arms and talked. "Do you enjoy living up here?" he asked in a tone compatible with the quiet of the night.

"Uh-huh. I try to get back to New York once a month, but I feel better here."

"Better in what way?"

"Less pressured. New York is such a *doing* city. When I'm there, I feel inadequate."

"That's bullshit, y'know. You have no reason to feel inadequate."

"But I do. I'm leading an unproductive life."

"I wouldn't call what you've spent the last two months doing to this farmhouse unproductive."

"You know what I mean. And anyway, life is calmer here than in New York. I like it this way."

"You don't mind the isolation?"

"I don't feel isolated. At least, no more so than I did in New York. I keep in touch with a few friends by phone, and Maura pops in sometimes."

He took a playful bite of her chin. "Another guest for the guest room?"

"Mmm. She wants me to write your story. I keep telling her that I'm working on you, but I don't think I'm doing a very good job of that, either." She took a quick breath. "Derek, why do you want to know about Lloyd Ballantine?"

"Shhhh," he whispered against her earlobe. "Not now."

"Then when?"

"Later."

The next morning—late, late morning—Derek opened up a bit. "I always wanted to be able to do this. When I was a kid, breakfast in bed seemed the ultimate luxury."

Tucking the sheet across her breasts, Sabrina reached for a cracker. "I'll bet you dreamed of something better than Saltines and jam."

"Hey, we have a cheese omelet here."

"Mmm. One egg and two slices of cheese, and most of that is stuck to the plate."

"Still, this is a luxury. Where I came from, you didn't risk getting crumbs on the sheets. Crumbs brought ants, so my mom said, and since we already had plenty of cockroaches—"

"We had cockroaches on Fifth Avenue," Sabrina said as she handed him a cracker neatly spread with jam. "Where did you have them?"

"Not on Fifth Avenue, not even in New York." He downed the cracker in a single bite. "We lived in a little town about forty minutes out of Philadelphia. I can't say we lived on the wrong side of the tracks, because there weren't any tracks. The whole town was pretty depressed.

We had a tiny little two-bedroom place that wasn't worth the money it would have taken to make it livable, but it was the nicest house in the neighborhood. My mother did what she could, but my father usually bet away what money he earned before he got home."

"What did he do for a living?"

Leaning against the bed's brass headboard with the sheet draped loosely over his hips, Derek had a sudden panicky urge to change the subject. Getting into his father's job was getting into the really dirty stuff, and he didn't want to do that. He felt at home in Sabrina's farmhouse. He felt at home with Sabrina. She made him feel that he was worthy of what she offered.

But he owed her the truth.

"My father was the brains behind one of the biggest loan sharks in Phillie. He set up deals, saw them enforced. He would have been a wealthy man, himself, if he hadn't had a compulsion to gamble." He frowned at the folds of the sheet. "My mother suffered. She was a principled woman to the point of being obsessed, while my father was loose as a goose and twice as dirty. God only knows what they saw in each other."

"Opposites attract?"

"The thing was, they didn't attract."

"They must have at some point. They made you."

He snorted. "I've often wondered if it was rape. The only sounds I heard coming from my parents' room at night were unpleasant ones. They argued a lot."

"Did he beat her?"

"No. I'm not sure he could have. She was nearly as tall as he was, and she was physically strong. I know," he said in such a way that Sabrina understood that he'd felt the brunt of his mother's physical strength more than once. "But my father wasn't like that, anyway. He wasn't one to get his hands dirty. When it came to delivering messages that loan payments weren't being made on time, he had other people do the ugly stuff."

"Then why—" She closed her mouth on the question, but Derek could easily follow the direction of her thoughts.

"Why was he killed? He was killed because he got too

smart for his britches. Or maybe too greedy. Or too desperate. He'd done time for being an accessory to murder. He
was feeling pretty low, and he didn't like that. He decided
his life would be improved if he took a bigger cut in the
loan payments, and he thought he could do it without his
boss knowing." He paused, and when he spoke again, his
voice was strained. "Joey Padilla used to run the money
with him. He was a punk kid, a bodyguard. At some point
he figured that he stood to gain more by snitching on my
dad than by sticking by him, and he was probably right.
Money is power, and my dad couldn't hold money any
longer than it took to reach the nearest racetrack."

"But why did they have to kill him?"

"To set an example."

"How old were you?"

"Fifteen."

"Did you know all this then?"

"Oh, yeah. In a neighborhood like ours, you didn't miss
much, and what you missed, someone else made sure to
fill you in on." His eyes reflected that remembered pain. "I
was no model child. People took pleasure in telling me
why."

"Derek?"

"Mmm?"

"You think about Joey Padilla a lot, don't you?"

Derek scuffed up a bunch of wet leaves. He and Sabrina
were walking through the afternoon woods. Tall evergreens
sheltered them from the fine rain that fell. "Yeah. I think
about him."

"How much older than you was he?"

"About eight years."

"Did he have a family?"

"They told me he had a wife and two kids."

"Did he have a job?"

"Officially, he was a mechanic. Unofficially, he was
moving drugs. And he drank a lot."

"What was he doing in the parking lot that night? Why
was he the one to call you? Was it an honest coincidence?"

Derek nudged her hips with his own, an easy thing to do

since they were sharing a poncho. "You're full of questions."

"Once before, at Parkersville, you were going to tell me what happened that night. You didn't get beyond the bare facts."

"Those bare facts are the only 'facts' there are. The rest is conjecture."

"I'm game for conjecture."

For several minutes, the only sound was the patter of rain as it dripped from the tips of the pine needles and the squish of the wet leaves underfoot. She looked up at Derek's face. His hair lay in damp spikes on his forehead. His features were tense, his eyes distant.

"Things didn't make sense," he said out of the blue. "For months after the trial, I sat in my cell and went over and over what happened that night. I looked at things one way, then another. I looked from every angle, and only one thing was clear. The phone call was obviously a setup, because Padilla had planned to kill me. He came from his car holding a loaded gun. If he'd been on the level, there'd have been no need for a gun. I wasn't any threat to him. I didn't know who he was."

"Did he know that?"

"He had to have known it. He gave me a phony name, and it was too dark that night for me to see a thing. So I asked myself why he wanted to kill me. I couldn't believe that it had anything to do with what happened between my father and him more than twenty-five years before. He was the one who did the snitching; if anyone had wanted revenge, it would have been me. But I didn't want revenge. The thought never occurred to me. And it wasn't like I'd followed him around or threatened him. In all those years I'd never made the slightest move toward him."

They reached the remains of a stone wall and sat down side by side. Sabrina had an arm wound through his, a hand in the pocket of his slacks.

"At first I thought it had to do with the eyewitness story I was doing. That was the most obvious thing. But I couldn't find the Padilla link. And then there were the other things."

"What other things?"

"Things related to the trial. They denied me bail. David had a hard time preparing the case. Witnesses appeared out of nowhere. I am sure, *sure* that Padilla and I were alone in the parking lot that night. But suddenly the prosecution produced two witnesses, two kids who were supposedly screwing in their car when we drove up."

"David must have checked them out."

"Sure he did, and he found that their records were clean as a whistle. We put a private investigator on the case, and he learned that the kids had been involved in an automobile accident that had maimed a traveling salesman, but the witness who let it slip to our investigator that they'd been stoned at the time of the accident refused to testify."

"Couldn't you force him to?"

"He'd only lie on the stand. Someone had gotten to him. It looked like the kids were given a clean slate in exchange for perjury, only we couldn't prove a thing. In fact, that was the story in a nutshell. We couldn't prove a thing. We couldn't prove that the judge who denied me bail had been bought, or that the one who denied David's pretrial motions had been bought, or that the one who presided at the trial and subtly favored the prosecution had been bought. We couldn't prove a thing.

"That was when I began to realize that we were dealing with someone very powerful, and there had been no one of *that* caliber even remotely involved in my eyewitness story. So I started looking at the rest of the things I'd been working on at the time. I figured someone was threatened. Someone was threatened enough by what I was doing that he needed me out of the picture, and that someone had to have been powerful enough to carry it off without getting caught."

He felt silent, thinking, brooding.

"Who, Derek?" Sabrina asked very softly.

It was a minute before Derek answered, and then it wasn't in response to her question. He was moving chronologically, reliving each bit of frustration. "I had to dredge everything up in my mind because the studio had sealed all my files. A few people helped. A few others said they wanted to help, then suddenly lost interest. I went over every story—not only those I'd been working on at the time, but ones I'd done three months, six months, a year before. Lots of those stories had stirred up flak, but it was the kind of flak that was good, that we wanted; and none of the people involved had the kind of power—or the balls, for that matter—to do much more than make noise. Then, though, there was the business about Lloyd Ballantine."

"What business?" Sabrina returned in a faintly despairing tone. "Lloyd Ballantine was the kind of boring man that you figured had to have been leading a double life to keep from falling asleep on himself. . . . That's it, isn't it, Derek? He had a whole other side."

The sudden excitement he saw on her face raised his spirits. "That was my theory," he admitted. "The accident that killed him was too pat. There was no reason for it. He wasn't speeding. He wasn't drinking. He wasn't taking drugs or any kind of legitimate medication. Nor was he driving in his sleep. He got up in the middle of the night from the bed he shared with his wife, climbed into his car and drove over a cliff."

"Are you thinking it was murder?"

"No. The police were pretty thorough, given who he was. They found no evidence for that."

"Then suicide. I saw the word mentioned in passing in several of the articles I read, but it was always ruled out as a theory that lacked substance. Ballantine hadn't left a note. No one having to do with him would admit that he'd been depressed, and he hadn't sought psychiatric help." She hesitated. "Do you think it was suicide?"

"I do," Derek said as he drew her up and headed back toward the house.

Later, stretched on his side by the living room fire, he went on. "About two years after Ballantine's death, I received an anonymous letter. It suggested that if I wanted the story to beat all stories, I should look into Lloyd Ballantine's life. Normally I didn't pay much heed to anonymous letters like that; people often wrote with suggestions for stories, and often they involved personal vendettas that the police wouldn't touch. But there was something different about this letter. Maybe the sheer simplicity of it. It gave no details, named no names but Ballantine's. Then again, Ballantine had been a Supreme Court justice, and I knew that if I could find something startling in his life—or death—I *would* have the story to beat all stories."

Using his legs as a backrest, Sabrina draped an arm over his hip. "Were there any hints at all about who could have sent it?"

"It was postmarked New York and was handwritten, but the script looked as though it was purposely distorted— you know, like a right-handed person writing with his left hand?" At Sabrina's nod of understanding, he went on. "I showed it to a handwriting expert, but the only thing he was able to suggest was that it had been written by a woman. Not much to go on. I really didn't have the time then to research Ballantine, and I couldn't justify putting any of my people to work on something so vague. So I filed the letter for a rainy day." He stretched to reach the poker and give the burning logs a shove.

"Then, about eight months after that, a second letter came. It was nearly identical to the first—same postmark, same handwriting, same message. Only, soon after I got it, I happened to be in a Washington bar with a well-known Washington lawyer. He'd had a little too much to drink and was making some pretty imprudent statements about a case he'd just finished trying, and just for the hell of it I tossed out Ballantine's name. I got an earful."

"Ballantine did have a hidden life?"

"We didn't get around to what he did when he was off the bench, but according to this lawyer, Ballantine wasn't as much of a Boy Scout as he wanted people to believe. Allegedly, he was well paid for casting the deciding vote in several critical rulings. This guy specifically referred to Ballantine's having committed suicide, and he went so far as to say that Ballantine left files detailing the corruption."

"Why would he do that?"

"To incriminate whoever else was involved."

"But he could have gotten himself in lots of trouble if the files were found before his death."

"Maybe he made sure they wouldn't be found. Or maybe

the risk was worth it. They were an insurance policy. A surefire shot at revenge. There are all sorts of possibilities about what was going on, including blackmail."

"Has anyone ever seen the files?"

Derek shook his head. "Not that I'd take a half-sloshed lawyer's word for gospel, but in light of the letters I'd received, I had something to consider."

"Incredible," Sabrina breathed. "And what's most incredible is that it never came out. Not one of the three books I've read even suggested that he was corrupt."

"He may not have been. But from the point of view of an investigative reporter, the thought was intriguing."

"Wouldn't something like that be the business of the Justice Department?"

"Sure. I went to a friend there and asked. I figured maybe the Department had already investigated and found nothing. But there had been no investigation. My friend admitted—only by accident when I tripped him up with questions—that there'd been some rumors about Ballantine, but he claimed that's all they were."

"Had he heard about the existence of any files?"

"No."

"Wasn't he curious after you mentioned them?"

"Are you kidding? You have to understand something about government employees, Sabrina. As a rule, they don't go looking for trouble. Oh, there are exceptions. But when it comes to political corruption—or judical, in this case—they get real nervous. To point the finger at a man —even if that man is guilty as hell—could mean the end of the pointer's career."

"And the career of an investigative reporter?" Sabrina asked.

Derek gave a bitter half-laugh before returning to his story. "I went to see Noel Greer. My boss. Founder and chairman of the board of the network."

"I've heard of him."

"Right. Well, I *knew* the man, and let me tell you, it was no pleasure. We had trouble with each other from the start. He didn't like me and I didn't like him."

"But he hired you."

"Yeah. The token rebel. I'd established a reputation for tackling touchy stories and asking hard questions while I was at it." His nostrils flared when he inhaled. "Greer is ultraconservative. But he's shrewd, and he's a master of appearances. He knew that his network had a reputation for leaning to the right in newscasts, and he wasn't about to change that. He liked it. He designed it. His team reported the news in a light that was consistent with his own ideology—which was what he wanted the American people to hear. But he knew that it was about time for an added shot of credibility, and the simplest way to get it was to hire someone like me. And I took the job. I took it knowing exactly why I was hired, but I figured that a token rebel was better than no rebel at all."

After listening to himself, he snorted. "Hell, who am I kidding? I took the job for me. I knew that I'd have better resources at my fingertips, better funding, better exposure. I told myself that it was the creative opportunity I wanted, but it was really the position. I'd have more power and respect—not within the network, but outside it—and I wanted those."

The fire crackled softly. The shadows it made danced on the hearth, and were made macabre only by the thoughts of the two people watching.

"I can understand why those two things would be important to you," Sabrina said—and she could, given what he'd said about his childhood. "But wasn't it also true that you *would* have more creative freedom in a position like that? Or did Greer set the limits?"

"He wasn't too bad at first. He made it clear that he wanted all my plans approved by the network before a penny was spent, but that approval was usually forthcoming. I had more trouble—and increasingly so—with the stories themselves. I don't know if Greer thought I'd pick provocative subjects and then treat them like milquetoast, but we had some pretty heated arguments over what should or should not survive the cutting room."

"You worked directly with Greer?"

"Not officially, but when it became obvious that the people under him did little without his say-so, I got sick of wasting time, so I went straight to the top."

"You went to him on the Ballantine case?"

Though the corners of Derek's mouth turned down, it was clear that his answer was yes. "All I had were two letters and the hearsay of a sound D.C. lawyer, but I wanted to put a researcher on it just to see what he'd find."

"What did Greer say?"

"He hit the roof. He was furious that I'd even *thought* to question the integrity of a justice of the Supreme Court of the United States of America. His reaction wasn't surprising given his political stance, but what was surprising was the strength of it. In the past, I'd come close to stepping on some political toes and he'd warned me off, but not like that. He overreacted. And that made me all the more curious. I assumed he knew something that he either didn't want me to know or didn't want the world to know, and I had just enough of the rebel in me to go after it. Unfortunately, I didn't get very far. I had barely started researching—on my own time, because I wasn't about to commit a breach of contract, not at that point, at least—when I was arrested for murder. Since bail was denied, my research stopped cold."

He grew very still as he lay there, propped on his elbow, staring at the flames. His profile was Sabrina's to study, which she did with growing discomfort. The angry set of his features reminded her of the earliest visits she'd made to Parkersville, when she'd wondered if the anger had left any warmth. She knew now that it had, that it did, and she knew that the warmth was precious to her, which made his anger all the more painful to see.

"Is there a link between Greer and Ballantine?" she asked, deciding that the sooner it was out, the sooner his anger would ease.

"I don't know."

"But you think there is."

"Yes."

She waited, but he didn't elaborate. "What kind of link?" she asked gently.

"Those swing votes he cast. One or more have to be tied to Greer."

"Then Greer paid him off?"

"Somehow. Not necessarily in greenbacks, but somehow." He sniffed in a long, loud breath, then released it along with the worst of his tension. His determination remained. "I'm going to find out, Sabrina. If it's the last thing I do, I am."

Sabrina asked no more questions, because the answers were making her uneasy. That evening, though, he offered answers. They were sharing wine, sitting cross-legged opposite each other on the floor of the glass-enclosed room that, when painted and furnished, would be a second-floor solarium, when he caught in a sudden breath and picked up as though there had been no break at all.

"You're probably thinking that I'm nuts, that I have no proof of any connection between Ballantine and Greer, but, believe me, Sabrina, I know. There was something about Greer's expression when I mentioned Ballantine's name. It's common knowledge that Greer had a pretty big interest in some antitrust cases that made it to the Supreme Court a while back. And Noel Greer is one of the few men who wields the kind of power that could have put me behind bars so quickly and firmly. His arm is long and has incredible strength. He could have done it."

Sabrina dropped her eyes to her wineglass. Its rim reflected the flicker of the candle that burned in its holder between them.

"*Do* you think I'm nuts?" Derek asked.

She wanted to tell him no, to be supportive at all costs, but he'd come to expect honesty from her, and her honest opinion was that the scenario he'd outlined left room for doubt. "I don't know Greer, but I find it incredible that any one man could have that much power—not that he could have it, per se, but that he could abuse it like that."

"Greer is an old hand at the abuse of power. He wrote the book on wheeling and dealing. The network is basically a dictatorship. Greer wants things his way. He wants to be the one in control."

"But . . ." She struggled to find the words to express her

skepticism without offending Derek. "But how can he get away with it? You're suggesting that he was involved in an extensive cover-up—not only of his relationship with Ballantine but of your commission of murder."

"Oh, I committed the murder, all right," Derek said in disgust.

"You did it in self-defense and probably would have been acquitted of all charges had it not been for the witnesses who testified that you had Padilla down and could have tossed the gun away but instead chose to shoot him. How could Greer buy off those witnesses, buy off judges along the way, even, for all we know, buy off prison officials to give you a hard time—and have no one tell what he'd done?"

Derek brought the wineglass to his mouth and downed its contents in a single swallow. Sabrina had a right to her skepticism, he supposed, and it was no more than he could expect from the rest of the world unless he produced those files. "Greer has a method. It isn't unique, but it works. He goes on the theory that every man has his weakness, and that all he has to do is to find that weakness, and the man is his."

"Are you saying that Greer had something on a nobody like Joey Padilla?"

"That's exactly what I'm saying. The nobodies of the world have just as much to lose as the somebodies, Sabrina. Don't fool yourself into thinking otherwise. You did it once before, when you suggested that I had more to lose in terms of independence and pride than some of the other guys in prison, and I told you then you were wrong—just like I'm telling you now."

"That's not—"

"Joey Padilla might have been shit to us, but at some level his life had meaning, and if someone or something threatened that meaning, he may well have bargained to preserve it."

Sabrina felt chastised. "I'm sorry. I didn't mean to say—"

"His wife and kids—maybe they were his weakness. Maybe the wife was sick. Or one of the children. You never had a worry about money in caring for Nicky, but not everyone is as lucky as you."

"No," Sabrina said in a small voice, "but no amount of money paid for even the most sympathetic cause can justify murder. Joey Padilla was hired to kill you, Derek."

Derek stared at her for several long, silent moments before slumping a little. "I know."

Setting down her glass, she slid around the bottle of wine and the candle and put an arm around his neck. "You value life. Where you find sympathy for a man who would have killed you himself if he'd been a little stronger or quicker is beyond me. I admire you for it."

"Don't admire me. I killed him."

"In self-defense."

"He's just as dead."

She put her lips to his ear and kissed him there, slid her other arm around him and held him tight. She wished she could do more, but just then, hugging him and letting him know that she was on his side was all she could do to help him fight his demons.

· *CHAPTER 13* ·

"I spent hours piecing together the parts," Derek told Sabrina the next day as he sanded one of the captain's table legs. "Hours and hours. Prison is great for that. Nothing to do but work yourself into a fury over things you can't touch. I used to lie there drawing outlines in my head, turning little events this way and that, trying to make it all work. I kept telling myself that if I had a day, one day, to ask questions, make phone calls, study files and records, I'd have answers, because I was an investigator, as good as any damn cop. But I didn't have a day. I was a carpenter without tools. And then I'd lie there picturing Greer grinning smugly behind his big glass desk, in front of his big glass windows that looked down on all of New York, and I knew that if he'd been in front of me that minute I'd have strangled him." Lips compressed, he looked away. Then, with a small head shake, a silent personal order, he determinedly distanced himself from the anger.

It was a cloudy afternoon. He and Sabrina had slept late, treated themselves to brunch in town, then returned. They were in the barn—this time wearing sweaters to ward off the nip in the air—but still they were barefoot, seated side by side on the floor.

"Anyway, as I see it, Greer got scared when I approached him about Ballantine. He knew how I worked—that I went after stories with a vengeance—and he guessed that I might keep at this one even though he'd told me not to. He must have panicked when he found out I was doing that."

"But how could he have found out? You said you were doing it on your own time."

"One of the show's associate producers was a nice girl, a little insecure but eager to get ahead. We'd worked together a lot. I could bounce ideas off her because she was bright. She was also a second cousin to Gerald Carruthers, the man who filled Ballantine's spot on the bench. If there had been dirt floating around, Carruthers would have known it. Dori was going to see him at another cousin's wedding, and I thought it would be great if she felt him out, maybe set up a meeting for me. Greer must have known that she and I had a close working relationship. He must have gotten to her."

"Did you ever ask her about it?"

"David did. She denied it, but soon after she got a promotion. She's been producing stories herself since then. And when I saw her last week—"

"You saw her?"

"At the studio. I stopped in to see what was happening, and she was one of the ones who wouldn't look me in the eye."

"There were others?"

"Oh yeah."

"What was their problem?"

"I don't know for certain, but it sure looked like guilt." He applied the sandpaper with greater force to the molded pine. That visit had been discouraging. A few of his former staff had greeted him with genuine smiles, others with less genuine smiles, still others with averted eyes and sudden errands to run. He'd felt like a pariah. "I got the distinct impression that I wasn't welcome there. Some of it had to do with where I'd been, but it went beyond that. Even those people who talked with me seemed edgy, like they wanted to talk but didn't dare. I'm assuming someone let it be known that I was *persona non grata* at the studio."

Sabrina, who was doing more listening than sanding, wasn't sure what to say. She could only look at the line of disgust that thinned Derek's mouth.

The line moved. "Anyway, that's probably how Greer found out I was still after Ballantine—and if it wasn't through Dori, it could have been through a handful of others who had access to my files. None of the people I worked with was perfect. We all had places to go, things to do, and all it might have taken was a little boost from Greer to help one or another of them on his way.

"So," he said, taking a breath, "Greer knew that I wasn't letting the Ballantine matter go, and at that point he must have analyzed his options. He could have fired me, but I wouldn't have taken that sitting down, and he would have ended up in a worse position, because I'd only have taken my story to another network and done it up with no restraints. He could have kept me on but tried to intimidate me—but he knew I wouldn't stand for that, either. After all, I was his rebel. I was outspoken. Given the history of our relationship, I'd have jumped at the chance to accuse him of blackmail."

"So he decided to kill you," Sabrina said in a very quiet voice.

Derek frowned at the wood, brushed the dust aside. "It probably looked like the only way to silence me. Greer hated me enough to do it. He felt threatened enough to do it. And he was just arrogant enough to believe that he could pull it off."

That said, he sanded in silence for a time. Working by his side, Sabrina didn't hurry him on. There was no rush, no prison guard to make her leave. Sometimes she forgot and felt the little knot in the pit of her stomach that had come at the end of each visit to Parkersville, and then she'd shake herself and look at Derek and know he was staying and smile. If her smile was inappropriate, given what he was telling her, he never said so. He was involved in his storytelling. It was a catharsis for him.

"Somehow Greer found Padilla—a link to my past— and theoretically it would have worked well. Greer knew I was doing the eyewitness case; he could have had one of his lackeys contact Padilla and tell him just what to say on the phone to lure me to that parking lot. I don't know what he offered Padilla. David's investigator couldn't find evidence that money was exchanged, but money can take different forms. Or it could have been promise of protection from something or someone. For all I knew, Padilla was told that I was after him because of what he'd done to my father and that he'd better kill me before I killed him."

The sound of his voice faded beneath the scratch of sandpaper. Sabrina found the subject matter nearly as abrasive.

"The most incredible part of all this," she complained, "is that Greer wasn't caught. How could he know he'd get away with it? Even if he offered Padilla something he wanted, how could he know that Padilla wouldn't go to the police and turn State's evidence? Did he actually trust Padilla not to breathe a word of what he'd done to anyone?"

"I doubt it. He probably planned on a double murder— and that's where Padilla's connection with my father was so neat. A double murder. Clean. No witnesses. The police would assume that to avenge my father's death I'd gone after Padilla, who had then managed to shoot me before he died."

Sabrina's shudder had nothing to do with the chill outside. "What if someone had gone with you that night?"

Derek's hand stilled, long fingers curling tightly around

the wood. "I don't know. I've asked myself that question dozens and dozens of times, and I don't know the answer. Most likely, if I'm right in what I've assumed, he'd have had both of us killed." He resumed sanding with a fury. "Probably made a calculated guess that I'd go alone, though. That was more my style."

Sabrina tucked her feet beneath her for warmth. "If you're right in what you've assumed, Greer must have had his own man there in the parking lot that night to make sure the job was done. Wouldn't it have been a lot easier for that man to just kill you himself, without involving Padilla?"

"But then there'd have been no explanation for my death, and Greer wouldn't have wanted that. He likes things neatly tied up. He wouldn't have risked some detective's looking a little too deeply into the case. And since Padilla was a perfect pawn . . ."

"Then things went wrong. You killed Padilla. Why didn't Greer's man just come forward and kill you?"

"Because," Derek said with a quick release of breath, "the cops came. The goddamned cops came while I was still standing there in shock holding the gun. At first I thought that was part of the plan. I thought that they'd been given a tip. I mean, their timing was like something out of a script. And I was furious. It wasn't that I'd have left Padilla's body and run. I'd've called the cops myself. But they denied me that show of integrity."

Sabrina ran her hand along the curved lip of the table, now down to its last layer of aged varnish. "And Greer's man? What did he do then?"

"I'm assuming he hightailed it out of there, got to a phone booth a safe distance away and called Greer, who began pulling strings to make sure that I was locked away and that no one looked too hard for the keys."

"But what about the kids in the parking lot? Wouldn't the police have seen that they were there—or that they weren't?"

Derek stared at the sandpaper for a second, then tossed it aside. "We're talking local cops here. You have to remember that. We're not talking big-city cops or FBI or private investigators. We're talking guys who don't have a hell of a lot of experience dealing with murder. I don't doubt that for some of them it was the first dead body they'd seen."

He gnawed on the inside of his mouth. He drew one knee up, set his forearm on it, let his hand dangle. Only it didn't dangle loosely. Tension prevented that.

"So they didn't look around a hell of a lot," he went on. "They had a body. They had a guy with a gun—a guy who admitted to the shooting. What more did they need? When David questioned them on the stand about whether they'd seen that third car, they said they hadn't looked. Maybe someone got to them, too, but I doubt it. Greer was concentrating on the guys higher up, the ones who would see I went to prison."

Sabrina touched the scar by his eye. "Was Greer responsible for this?"

"Probably."

Her fingers moved to his neck. "And this?"

"Most likely."

"Then he was hoping you wouldn't leave prison alive."

Closing his fingers around hers, Derek brought them to the warm spot at his throat where his pulse throbbed. "Guess I fooled'm, didn't I?"

With a groan, Sabrina leaned closer. She pressed her face to his neck and breathed deeply of the honest male scent that was his and his alone. She slid an arm around his body and, when he kissed her, she told him how glad she was that he'd been so clever. She slid a second arm around him when he eased her back to the floor; and, arching to his, her body repeated the message.

Sabrina was forever amazed by the passion Derek roused in her. She'd lost track of the number of times they'd made love—not that the number counted, but the hunger behind it was very new to her. Needing to be with him, near him, touching him was an awakening. And she wasn't alone in her need. Derek felt it, too. He told her that he was a plant and she his sun, and that without her he'd die, and they laughed at the imagery; but when they were in each other's arms that laughter was soft and gentle, maybe a little husky.

As it was this day. They kissed slowly, languorously. They touched each other in those special places they'd learned were the most sensitive. As they rolled over on the floor, taking turns bearing each other's weight, Derek suggested that they had a thing for barns. They both chuckled about that, then kissed with their tongues; and when she'd taken her own back into her mouth, Sabrina said that it had something to do with animal behavior, over which prospect they chuckled again. The more he thought about it, between feels and kisses, Derek decided that animal behavior had its pluses. By the time he'd shared the insight with Sabrina, he was removing her pants, and by the time he'd opened his own, she was waiting to take him in.

The next morning, they sat in the kitchen with their legs entwined on the meeting-house bench that Sabrina had bought for the front porch but that had been reappropriated until the captain's table and chairs were refinished. Sabrina was wearing her long terry robe, Derek a pair of sweatpants that matched the light gray of his eyes. The dishes that had earlier held eggs and toast now lay stacked on the floor nearby.

Chin on her palm, Sabrina was deep in thought. The thought she entertained wasn't a new one. It had come to her more than once since the afternoon before, and she'd tried to avoid it. But it had followed her like a mosquito, buzzing, annoying. She needed to share the worry with Derek.

"Does that mean he'll be after you now?"

Derek looked up from the morning paper. "Hmm?"

"Greer. Will he be after you now that you're out of prison?"

"I hope not." He returned to the paper.

"He's tried to kill you three times. Why would he suddenly give up?"

"Maybe he's bored."

"Derek."

The paper rustled as he lowered it. "I don't think he'll come after me because, A, he knows I suspect him; B, he knows other people know I suspect him; and, C, he's reached the stage where he has too much to lose. He's running for the U.S. Senate."

"I know."

"It'd be another feather in his cap. He wants it bad. The slightest hint of a scandal could ruin it all. I doubt he'd risk that."

Sabrina studied Derek's face. It was fully composed, but his eyes were darker now, his features set in stone. "You're not going to let him win, are you?"

With deliberate slowness, Derek shook his head.

She hugged her knees to her chest and rocked slowly back and forth. "You're going after the files."

With deliberate slowness, Derek nodded.

"Don't do it," she whispered. "Let it be."

"I can't. The man took two years of my life, not to mention that many more in mental anguish."

"But it's over. You're out. You can start again."

"Easier said than done, and, damn it, I shouldn't have to start again. I worked too hard to build what I had. Noel Greer knocked it down with a deliberate sweep of his hand, and he's going to pay for that."

"It'll only bring more trouble."

"Not the way I've planned it."

"You could end up dead."

"We all end up dead, Sabrina."

Her eyes continued to plead while she held up a hand. "Let me write it. Just write it. You can tell your story to the world."

"What story?"

"The one you've been telling me."

"That's no story. It's my supposition, and it isn't worth shit without proof. I can't go public with accusations about a man like Noel Greer without evidence to back them up. No one would publish a book like that. I would be a sure target for a libel suit."

As a writer, Sabrina could easily see his point. As the woman who loved him, she was less easily swayed. "What, exactly, do you plan to do?" she asked quietly.

"Find those files."

"Where?"

"Wherever they are, and don't ask me where that is, because I don't know. They were Lloyd Ballantine's files, and there has to be a clue to them somewhere in his life. I'll use your research as a starting point and go on from there. If Ballantine was corruptible, it had to be because he had a weakness. Greer found it and used it. I have to learn what it is if I want to locate those files."

"And when you do?"

Derek held her gaze with one that was formidable. "Then you write, but not a book. That would take too long, and if my hunch is correct, what we find will be hot news. Noel Greer can go ahead and campaign for the Senate, but when my find hits the newsstands, his campaign will be shot. And that's what I want, Sabrina." His tone was low and vengeful. "I want him ruined."

His words seemed to echo in the air, tapering gradually to a thundering silence. Sabrina didn't move, other than to swallow hard once.

"Are you okay?" he asked cautiously.

She nodded.

When he talked about Greer, Derek lost himself to his anger, but Sabrina's pale face and worried eyes led him back. He needed to know where he stood. "Do you think I'm wrong?"

"No."

"You don't sound sure."

"I am."

"I hear skepticism."

"No. Maybe sadness."

Derek's brows lowered. He tugged at a rip in the knee of his sweatpants. "Sadness for me? Or for you?"

"For us."

"Why?"

"I was hoping . . . wishing . . . we could be happy for a while."

"We can be."

"But there's that shadow. There's where you've been—"

His eyes shot to hers, suddenly hard and probing. "I thought you didn't mind that. I thought you accepted the fact that I've done time."

"I do. But everything that's happened to you is so real that it's almost *un*real, and that frightens me. I listen to you and watch you and I'm frightened. I can forget that you've been in prison, but you can't."

"Damn right I can't," he said with a vehemence that made her point.

She tried to see it from his side, but it was hard when she loved him so much. She wanted him safe. She wanted them together and happy. "This isn't fair. It should be over."

"What isn't fair is that it happened in the first place."

"You won't be happy until you get your revenge."

"Correction. I won't be *satisfied* until I get my revenge. I can be very happy in the meantime." He was facing her on the bench; his position hadn't changed; but there was an alertness to his body, a caution to his expression that hadn't been there earlier. "What do you think, Sabrina? Can you handle it? Can you handle being with me, knowing what I've got to do?"

"I don't have a choice."

"You do. I'm giving you one. If it's going to be too rough, I can leave. I can go back to New York. You don't deserve this. I've known it since the first time you came to Parkersville, and it's still true. You've had enough to live with in the last three and a half years. You're just beginning to emerge from that other nightmare. Maybe my being here is the last thing you need."

"Or the first."

He barely heard her soft rejoinder, so intent was he on baring his concern. "You wrote that you wanted to be alone. That you *needed* to be alone. You wanted to find out who you were and where you were going. I haven't given you much time for that."

"One of the first things I learned when I moved up here was that I didn't want to be alone."

"You were just lonesome. The shock of leaving the city."

"It was more than that. Once the novelty of having the ultimate freedom to do what I wanted when I wanted wore off, I realized that I missed having someone to be with."

"I thought you'd met people up here."

"I have. They're really nice. But it's not the same."

"The same as what?"

"Belonging."

Derek felt a familiar tightness gather in his throat because he knew exactly what she meant, only he hadn't realized it until then. She had put the word to a feeling he'd been blindly reaching for since the very first time they'd met.

Unsure of his silence, Sabrina hurried on in her own defense. "It's a strength. Two months ago I didn't know that. I thought that if you weren't able to live alone there was something wrong with you, some deficiency." She took a quick breath. "But I am able to live alone. I guess I did prove that to myself. I got everything settled in New York and moved up here, and functionally I was doing just fine. But then it became a matter of choice. Personal preference. I like sharing. I like doing for other people. I like having other people do for me once in a while. In a nutshell, I'm able to live alone, but I don't choose it."

Derek studied the earnestness of her expression. There was something so serious about her that he couldn't resist teasing. "Then anyone would do?"

"Anyone?"

"For a roommate."

For several minutes she stared at him. Then the corner of her mouth twitched in the beginnings of a chiding smile. "No, anyone would not do. I'm very fussy about roommates." Reaching forward, she drove a handful of fingers into his hair. "I want someone with dark hair, for instance. I like dark hair."

"I like blond hair."

"Then there's no problem. And shoulders." Her hand fell to glide over the skin in question. It was firm, buttressed by muscle. "I like strong shoulders. I noticed that about you from the first. Your shoulders hold a lot." Her gaze slid lower. "And your chest. A roommate of mine has to have a chest like this." Her free hand had joined its fellow in touching him. She was really getting into the game. "Warm skin, just enough hair, needs a little filling out around here"—she patted his ribs—"but I'm working on that."

"*You*'re working on it?"

"Feeding you."

"Seems like I'm doing my share of the cooking."

"Ah," she said in a magnanimous sigh. "Another requirement in a roommate of mine. Just and fair division of labor."

"You could have hired a dark-haired maid and paid her to do it all."

But Sabrina was shaking her head. "A woman wouldn't have the right equipment." Her palms were flat on his abdomen, fingers dipping under the waistband of his sweatpants. Her fingertips brushed the more curly hair that she couldn't quite see.

Derek was beginning to labor at breathing. "Already filling out there," he managed, but hoarsely.

Her hands slid lower. "So you are," she observed in a siren-soft voice.

He pressed his fists to the wooden bench on either side of his hips. While one part of him ached to grab Sabrina and drag her over him, the other part didn't want anything to disturb what she was doing. She knew just how to touch him. She knew the movement, the pressure, the little tricks that set him on fire. He'd taught her some of it himself; the rest she'd learned through adventure and instinct.

Muscles quivering at the restraint he imposed on himself, he gave a quiet moan, then murmured thickly, "You do it to me every time, Sabrina. I haven't been this miserable since I was a kid. It's like being born again."

She chuckled, a throaty, sensual chuckle that turned him on even more. "Not quite the way the Jesus freaks would put it."

"Screw the Jesus freaks."

"No," she whispered, looking up at him with eyes that were green and hungry, "don't waste it on them. I want it."

He sucked in a harsh breath and covered her hands with his own to still their movement. Then, sliding his arms under her, he scooped her up and strode from the kitchen through the hall and the living room into the master suite.

The bed was a tangle of sheets, but that was irrelevant. What mattered to Derek was laying Sabrina down, opening her robe and devouring her nakedness with his eyes while he divested himself of his sweatpants. He was fully aroused when he lowered himself to her heat.

She framed his face with her hands and made him look at her in those last lucid moments. "This is why just any roommate wouldn't do. You set me on fire, Derek. I've only had one other lover, and he never turned me on this way."

"Then you'll let me stay?" Derek whispered.

Her smile grew silky as he slowly entered her. "I'll let you stay."

"It's not just sex, is it?" he asked. He was standing in the bathroom later that day watching Sabrina dry her hair. Her body was bound in a large terry towel that matched the one swathing his hips.

"Of course it's sex." Her teasing gaze slid over his chest and belly to the faint bulge below. "You are very well endowed."

"Sabrina."

"I'm serious." She pressed her lips together for a minute, then ventured with a glint in her eye, "Well-hung— isn't that the expression?"

"Sabrina!"

"Hmm?"

For the space of several breaths he said nothing. Then he tipped his head just the slightest bit and asked with just the slightest unsureness, "Do you really think so . . . uh, like it . . . notice things like that?"

"Sure I do," she said, then added more quietly, "but it's not just sex and you know it." She flipped on the dryer and resumed work on her hair.

"I want to stay."

"Hmm?"

He raised his voice to make himself heard over the dryer's hum. "I do want to stay. I like it here."

Sabrina kept at her hair because it was the most casual thing to do. She felt far from casual inside. Each of

Derek's words counted toward a dream. "It's not too quiet for you?"

"Quiet? After what I've lived through for two years?"

"I was thinking of your life before that. You were used to things happening. Not much happens up here on a day-to-day basis."

"That's a matter of opinion. Since I've been here I've seen sun, clouds, rain and snow." The last was falling outside the window just then, but it was a wet snow that promised to revert to rain before long. "And as for my life before, it was a rat race—a blur of airline flights and interviews and screenings and red tape. I'm not sure I could handle that right now even if I wanted to. I need this, Sabrina. I need to be here with you."

She did turn off the dryer then. "Will you tell me when you get tired of it?"

"When, or if?"

"Either. Both."

"And if I never do?"

"Then I'll know it, because you'll be content. That's what I want, Derek. I want you to be content. If you are, I am."

He lowered his head and arched a brow her way. "That's a heavy load. Your happiness shouldn't be dependent on mine."

"Maybe not. But if you stay here, it will be. That's what love is about."

Leaning forward, he caught her lips in a soft kiss that lingered. In time, though, he drew back. His eyes held their familiar shadow. "Can you accept that I have to go after those files?"

"I'm working on it."

"Will you help me?"

"Only if I can't convince you to change your mind."

"You can't."

She dropped her gaze to the dryer—which at that moment resembled the nozzle of a gun—and thought about the possible danger. Then she looked back at Derek and thought about the alternative. Frustration and helplessness could eat a person alive. She knew. When it came to

Nicky, there had been nothing she could do. But possibly, just possibly, Derek could vindicate himself. If the choice was between a haunted Derek and one who had found peace of mind, there was no choice at all.

"I'll help," she said.

Only with the breath he released did Derek realize how much he'd wanted her help—and how unsure of it he'd been. It was a form of commitment. He needed that commitment.

Wrapping his arms around her, he drew her against his tall frame. "Thank you," he whispered.

"When do we start?"

"After the first of the year. After Greer declares his candidacy. He may be the one running, Sabrina, but in the end it'll be our victory."

Sabrina could only pray that he was right.

"He's living there? With you?"

"Uh-huh."

"Sabrina." The deep and disapproving voice of her father bellowed through the telephone, "What in the blazes are you doing?"

"Right now?" Purposely misinterpreting his question, she held the telephone cord aside and twisted to eye the crowded kitchen counter. "Making pumpkin pies."

"What in the blazes are you doing *with McGill?*"

"Mmm, do you really want to know?" she asked a little too softly.

Gebhart Monroe countered with a boom. "Did you actually invite him there?"

Had she invited him there? She'd never issued a formal invitation, but the offer had been between the lines of every letter she'd written. "Yes, I think I did."

"But *why?*"

"Why *not?* I'm not married anymore. I'm not tied to another man. Nor am I a twenty-one-year-old virgin."

Gebhart was silent for just a minute, obviously gathering his composure. In some ways he was remarkably old-fashioned. Sex and his only daughter was one of them. Rather than link the two—or acknowledge that there was or ever had been any relationship between the two—he steered away from the subject. "That isn't the issue here, Sabrina. The issue is the man himself. He's come fresh from prison."

"I know that," she said more seriously. She was grateful her father had chosen to call while Derek was out running.

"Does it make you uneasy?"

"No."

"He killed a man."

"In self-defense."

"He's spent the last two years of his life in the company of the world's lowlife."

"Through no choice of his own."

"But he's done it. And now he's with you. I'm worried, Sabrina."

"I'm a big girl, Dad."

"Age doesn't make you any less vulnerable."

"It does. It makes me a better judge of character than I was five or ten years ago. Believe me, I am in no danger from Derek. If anything, the reverse is true. I'm safer with him here. He's strong, more than capable of protecting me. You were worried about my being alone. You should feel relieved."

"Produce any other man but McGill and I might be."

Sabrina was feeling discouraged—and she hadn't even gotten to the part about telling her father she was in love with Derek. "You don't know him, Dad. . . . Then again," she said with sudden inspiration, "maybe you do. Derek isn't all that different from Bart Slocum, your hero in *Lone Rider*. Bart killed a man—several, actually—but still he was a worthy hero. He killed only when he had no alternative, and he agonized over it even when the victim was the lowest of the low." She was rather proud of the analogy. "Bart did time."

"In a jail. Very different from a modern penitentiary. Do you have any idea what hellholes those are? Yes, I suppose you do, since J. B. says you visited McGill several times. But, please God, to bring that into your home?"

"As I recall, your jail in *Lone Rider* had rats and snakes and a man with something resembling leprosy. But moving beyond that, when Bart was released, he returned to his girlfriend. Did he beat her? Rape her? Spit on her? He certainly did not. He treated her like 'precious porcelain' —I think that was the phrase you used—and he went on to save her life."

"The only reason he had to save her life," Gebhart argued, "was that the villain was after him but shot her by mistake. I'm telling you, if I'd been her father—rather than the guy who wrote the book—I'd have been mighty upset."

"Come on, Dad, you can't condemn Derek simply because of time spent behind bars."

But Gebhart was firm. "I can condemn anyone who threatens my daughter's well-being."

"He's not threatening—"

"Talk with your mother."

"Sabrina," Amanda came on the line. "Your father's right. It's one thing to write a book about the man, quite another to live with him. Is that really necessary?"

Sabrina felt a headache coming on. Her parents' objections to Derek were another indictment to add to the list. It seemed that in their eyes she could do no right. But she refused to cower. "Yes, it's necessary."

"May I ask why?"

"Because I love him."

That brought a heavy silence, followed by a quiet, "You're just saying that for effect, I hope."

"No. It's the truth."

"Oh Lord, Sabrina," Amanda wailed in an unearthly sort of way, "what did I do wrong? First Nicholas Stone. Now Derek McGill. I know that your father and I haven't had the most traditional of marriages—"

"This has nothing to do with you and Dad."

"What did I do wrong?"

"Nothing, Mom. Nothing at all. Just the opposite, in fact. You and Dad are in love. You've always been in love, in *spite* of the unconventional way you live. You've stayed together against the odds. Maybe you've been an inspiration."

Amanda's "Oh Lord!" suggested that she was anything but pleased with the thought, so Sabrina went on.

"You don't *know* Derek. How can you condemn him?"

"I'm imagining what he'll do to your life. Do you honestly think that he's emerged from prison stigma-free? I don't see him working. I haven't read anything in the papers about his being snatched up by one of the networks. There's a reason for that, Sabrina. He evokes negative reactions. He was in a position of power and visibility, and he abused it."

"He acted in self-defense! If he hadn't, he'd have been killed!"

"He shot that man."

"There was a struggle. It was the other man's gun."

"Perhaps. But do you hear yourself? You're defending him. You're bound to defend him. Is that what you want to spend your future doing? Because you'll have to. If Derek Gill lives with you, people are going to ask questions. You'll be as much of a social outcast as he is."

"You know, you're as bad as Dad. Talk about hypocrisy."

"In what way have either your father or I been hypocritical?" Amanda asked indignantly.

"Your books, Mom. Consider Quist. He's great, by the way, but if ever there was the hero as outcast, Quist is it. He's different from the other Dusalonians, different in looks, acts and desires. He broke the rules of the High Command. He alienated the Elite. He lived among the Snaleks for months—talk about lowlife. And still he found his way back, and with the daughter of one of the premier members of the Elite, no less. If Quist could succeed, why not Derek?"

"Quist is fictitious."

"And fiction is largely nothing more than wishful thinking. So why can't you look for the positive in Derek? Why can't you try to make Quist's success real?"

"Because Dusalon is a far cry from Earth. People here are judgmental."

"As they are on Dusalon."

"But *I* control what happens on Dusalon. I don't have such power here, and that's the difference. When you're shunned, I won't be able to help."

"Shunned," Sabrina murmured under her breath. "My God, this is absurd." She raised her voice. "And since when are you—the ultimate nonconformist—so concerned about what other people think?"

"I'm concerned about you, your future, your career. What is it that you want in life, Sabrina?"

"I want a home and a family," Sabrina blurted impulsively.

"And you honestly think Derek McGill can give you that?"

"Actually, I haven't planned that far ahead. Things have been pretty spontaneous where Derek is concerned."

"Aligning yourself with a man like him isn't the best way to make friends and influence people. Putting Nicky in that place was bad enough. This won't help."

Sabrina felt the sting of her mother's words. She had to work harder to keep her voice low and controlled. "If anyone criticizes me for placing Nicky at the Greenhouse, he does so out of ignorance. But since you brought it up, look at it this way. If my putting Nicky 'in that place' was so bad, people will already have come to expect the worst from me, so I won't be surprising anyone by taking up with Derek."

The finality in her tone was not to be missed. Amanda sighed. "We can't change your mind?"

"About Derek? No."

"How about coming out here for Thanksgiving?"

"Thanksgiving is tomorrow. I can't get tickets at this late date."

"Your father could pull some strings."

Oh, yes. He could pull strings. For one round-trip ticket. She could have Thanksgiving dinner with her parents, leaving behind her son and the man she loved.

"Thanks," Sabrina said more sadly, "but no. Not this year."

* * *

Derek awoke late on Thanksgiving morning to find himself alone in Sabrina's big brass bed. He wasn't surprised. A glance at the bedside clock told him that it was nearly eleven-thirty, and he knew that the wonderful smells coming from the kitchen couldn't possibly have been produced if Sabrina had been as lazy as he.

He should get up, he told himself. He should give her a hand. But she'd refused his offers the night before, had specifically told him to sleep late. This was the first Thanksgiving dinner she'd ever made, she said, and he'd gotten the impression that there was a good deal of pride involved in the undertaking. If the smells emanating from the kitchen were any measure, she had just reason for pride.

Stuffed turkey. Sweet potato casserole. Baked apples. He breathed it all in, gave a slow, leonine stretch, then sank back into the sheets and smiled.

This was home with a capital H. This was what he'd missed all those years. This was what he wanted in life, this sense of, yes, belonging. He wanted Sabrina. He wanted a family. And he wanted them right here in Vermont, where the grass was green, the trees lush, the air crisp and clean on cool fall days.

Feeling a sudden urge to be with Sabrina—whether she needed his help or not—he swung up from the bed and reached for the corduroy jeans he'd left lying over the arm of the chair the night before. He'd barely pulled them on when he was paddling barefoot from the room.

The fire in the living room hearth was little more than a glow. He paused to add a log before continuing into the kitchen.

On the threshold, he stopped. Sabrina wasn't there. He turned back for an instant, wondering if he'd passed her in the bathroom, but he hadn't heard either footsteps or the close of a door while he'd lain in bed; the only sounds in the farmhouse were the crackle of the growing fire and the sizzle of the turkey in the oven.

She'd left the coffeepot on, though, and propped against

a nearby mug was a note. "Have gone out to deliver some pies," she'd written in the gentle script he knew so well. "Will be back by one. There's a bowl of cut-up fruit in the refrigerator. Help yourself to that and to coffee, but don't cut into the apricot bread, it's for later. I love you. Sabrina." Tacked on at the bottom was a more hastily written "Happy Thanksgiving."

Smiling, he raised the note to his lips, kissed it lightly, then set it on the counter and filled the mug with coffee. Sipping it slowly, he pondered Sabrina's note. *Have gone out to deliver some pies.* Where, he wondered? She hadn't mentioned anything about it the night before, though he supposed he should have realized that she was baking far more than the two of them could possibly eat. How many pies had she baked? Three? Four? He wasn't sure. Once she'd evicted him from the kitchen, he'd been engrossed in a book.

Wandering into the living room, he stood before the window. It was a gray day, gray in a way that spoke of winter's approach. In past years that would have depressed him. Winter in prison had meant fluctations between rooms that were overheated and those that were drafty, and less yard time all around. Before that, winter had meant the kind of temperamental weather that could screw up a production schedule in no time flat.

Winter here would be different, he knew. It would be snowbound days and snow-silent nights, wood smoke and hot chocolate and the warmth of a hand-sewn quilt. And Sabrina. Sabrina brought thoughts that were gentle and exciting. He basked in them while he finished his coffee, then headed for the shower.

A short time later he was back before the fire wearing a clean pair of cords, a shirt, sweater and loafers. He was freshly shaved and his still-damp hair was combed. He looked pretty good, he had to admit. So where was Sabrina?

Several minutes before one, he heard her car. Jumping from the chair, he started for the window, wavered, turned back toward the chair, stopped. Then, taking a deep breath to steady his pulse, he carefully paced his approach to the kitchen. He entered it just as Sabrina was coming in from outside.

She looked up in surprise, then smiled. "Derek! Sleep well?" Head tucked low again, she turned her back to close the door.

"I missed you," he said. Crossing the floor, he took the coat from her shoulders. It was her cashmere coat, the same one she'd worn that first day at Parkersville the February before. Beneath it she wore a long wool skirt, a sweater and boots. The bulk of the sweater made her look more fragile than ever and heightened his urge to protect her. "How was the driving?"

"Not bad." She opened the oven to check the turkey. "The roads were deserted."

He watched her tug at the drumstick. "That smells fantastic."

"Did you have some fruit?"

"Nah. Thought I'd wait for you."

Closing the oven door, she darted him a fast glance on her way to the refrigerator. "You must be starved."

"Uh-huh."

"The turkey shouldn't be much longer. I didn't have a thermometer—stupid of me, it's the only thing I forgot—but the book says that the bird's done when the leg moves freely, and it just about does."

She was piling the counter with plastic baggies filled with the various fresh vegetables that she'd earlier washed and cut. Her voice was higher than usual, the words coming more quickly, and she wouldn't look at him beyond a fleeting glance here and there.

During one of those glances, Derek had seen that her eyes were unnaturally bright.

Draping her coat over the arm of the meetinghouse bench, he asked softly, "What can I do?"

"Uh"—she was already reaching for a plate and quickly handed it over—"you can put the vegetables here. I'll take care of the dip."

He did as instructed—though, he feared, with far less of an artistic eye that she'd have had herself. In truth, his concern wasn't with the vegetables. It was with Sabrina.

She was looking somber. "Would you like a glass of wine?" he asked.

She broke into a sudden smile when she looked at him and said, "That'd be nice," but the smile faded in the next instant when she went back to preparing the dip.

Derek draped an arm around her shoulders. "Sabrina."

She stopped what she was doing.

"There's no rush on the food."

She bowed her head.

"How was he?"

She ducked her head lower.

By now, Derek knew the telltale signs—the slight hunching of her shoulders, their faint tremor, her refusal to look at him. Wrapping her completely in his arms, he hugged her while she cried softly.

At length, stroking her hair, he said, "I wish you'd let me come."

"It's so painful to see," she whispered on a fragmented breath.

"You shouldn't have to go alone."

"He's my son. My responsibility."

"But I love you. I want it to be my responsibility, too."

"You don't know what you're saying."

"I do." He held her back and bent his head until it was level with hers. His eyes were filled with the urgency that gave his voice a desperate edge. "Marry me, Sabrina. I know it's unfair of me to ask when you're feeling down, but I can't help it. I was sitting here before, waiting for you to come home, and I realized that if I didn't have that to look forward to, I'd be lost. You mean more to me than any other person has ever meant. It's a little humbling to think that I'm not as self-contained as I prided myself on being, but where you're concerned, I'm not. I've never felt this way before. I've never loved a woman before. I've never asked one to marry me, and if you think it doesn't scare me shitless, you're wrong."

Her eyes were moist pools the color of limes. He held them firmly with his own. "I have no right to ask you. I'm unemployed and my prospects of work are lousy right now, and there's the thing with Greer that doesn't thrill you at all, but I'll make it work, Sabrina. I came from nothing once before, and I reached the top. I can do it again. I'll make it all work, so help me God, I will."

He went quiet, and for several minutes their eyes were locked in a volley of silent questions.

"It's a crazy idea," Sabrina whispered.

"Let me do it. Let me fill the void. I want to take care of you."

"That'll be a challenge. I'm a wreck."

"Any worse than me?"

She grinned through her tears. "We are a pair." The grin faded. "I've failed at one marriage already."

"That one fell apart when the going got tough. This one would be starting with tough and doing just fine. We've already seen each other at our worst and the relationship has grown in spite of it. There's nothing to fear." He paused. "What do you say?"

She thought about it for a minute. "My parents will be furious."

"Do you care?"

"Yes."

"Enough to say no?"

"No."

He took her face in his hands. "I love you."

"Me too."

"Think we can make it?"

She nodded.

"Then you'll marry me?"

Again she nodded, this time more vigorously. She didn't know if she was right. She was acting on instinct. She did know that she adored Derek, that she wanted to be with him always, and that maybe, just maybe, her being his wife would make the difference in his plans for revenge.

· *CHAPTER 14* ·

Sabrina and Derek were married on the third of December in the office of a justice of the peace. That night they celebrated over dinner at the Hanover Inn, but they ate alone. They had made no mention of their marriage to family or friends, preferring to keep it private and personal. It wasn't that they weren't in love; anyone looking at them could see that they were. But each had doubts about the wisdom of their marrying at that particular time, and neither felt he wanted his doubts confirmed by a third party, or a fourth or a fifth.

Needing to do something for the sheer frivolity of it, they flew to St. Croix. It was there that Sabrina learned to what extent her husband was an adventurer. He loved sailing, waterskiing and windsurfing, but scuba diving was what truly caught his fancy. He'd never done it before. Neither had Sabrina, for that matter, but in no time she was in all the appropriate gear following Derek and their trained guide through spectacular coral canyons in the sun-warmed Caribbean waters.

In hindsight, Sabrina realized that scuba diving, while requiring a fair amount of guts, was still relatively conventional. Less conventional, and more impulsive, were some of the other things Derek did—like joining in with the native dancers during a beach party, spending an afternoon in a broad hat and bright shirt subbing for a vendor at a thong shop, and awakening Sabrina in the middle of the night, carrying her in his arms to the beach and making love to her in the moonlight.

"We can't *do* this, Derek!" she whispered loudly as he pressed her down to the sand.

The only answer he gave was to bunch her nightgown to her waist.

"Derek, it's a public beach!"

He lifted his hips to free himself from his shorts. His grin gleamed in the moonlight. "It's three in the morning. We're alone."

"This is indecent—ahhhh, Derek—mmmm."

He withdrew, then filled her again. "Feel good?" he asked, his voice thick with sensual satisfaction.

She raised her knees to his hips and met his thrust. "Mmmm."

"Look at it this way." He took a quick breath, then another when the first didn't last long enough to produce a single word. "Anyone chancing upon us will see something beautiful."

Later, when she could think clearly again, Sabrina saw the truth to that. Of course, no one had chanced upon them, so it was fine to be philosophical. But when she was with Derek she felt bold. In fact, what surprised her most was not so much Derek's unorthodoxy but the fact that she loved it. Six months before, she'd have said that the ideal vacation consisted of lying in the sun, reading book after book beneath the shade of the palms and returning to the lushness of a luxury hotel to eat and sleep. That all sounded rather tame to her now. Derek had awakened far more than her sensuality.

Defiance was one word to describe what she felt. Derek and she deserved to have fun. They'd both paid more than their share of dues in the past few years, and she knew that the dues-paying wasn't quite done. They'd gone against the grain, she as a mother, he as an investigative reporter, and their marriage was sure to raise a few eyebrows. But whatever they'd done, they'd done out of conviction.

Or so she told herself during those halcyon days in the sun. And so she told herself when, after ten days, they returned to Vermont.

To say that their life then fell into a pattern was to misrepresent the truth. The pattern was a non-pattern. Sabrina and Derek followed no schedule, simply enjoyed each other from day to day, enjoyed the peace of the farmhouse, enjoyed late nights before the fire, late mornings in bed, long walks over the newly fallen snow. They were lovers playing hooky from the realities of life, and as long as those realities kept their distance, it worked.

Unfortunately, the distance began to diminish as the days passed and the telephone rang with increasing regularity. Sabrina's parents were less than ecstatic about her marriage. Derek's agent wasn't as concerned about the marriage as about Derek's settling in Vermont. Several of Derek's old friends and coworkers, having been recruited by his agent to change his mind, called trying to do just that—to no avail. Maura called wanting to know when she would have a book proposal to deliver to Sabrina's editor. And the Greenhouse called, saying that Nicky really did need to be taken back to his doctors in New York for tests.

Derek wouldn't hear of Sabrina's going alone, and Sabrina was more relieved than she could say. Traveling with Nicky was difficult at best. Having Derek with her, lending physical and emotional support, made a trying two days a bit more bearable.

Derek was humbled by the experience. He'd heard Sabrina's descriptions of life with Nicky, but he hadn't been able to fully comprehend the nature of the demands until he'd had to meet them himself. No amount of special feelings—and he had plenty of those for the child—could blunt the fact that when one took care of Nicky, one had time for precious little else in life.

"I am in awe of you," he told Sabrina during their drive back north. "The incredible patience you must have had all those months, the physical strength alone to continue."

"I did my share of crumbling," she said softly. Nicky was lying against her, asleep. Her own eyes were closed, her cheek resting on his baby-soft hair. "Ask my ex-husband. He'll tell you how wonderful I was."

"He never calls, does he?"

"No."

"You'd think he'd want to know about his son. Will you tell him about this visit?"

She shook her head. "A few more seizures, a few more pills. He won't be interested. No, that's wrong. It's not a matter of interest. He just can't cope with the idea of his son being flawed like this."

Derek took his eyes from the road to dart intermittent glances her way. While her words might have easily been bitter, they weren't. Indeed, there was a serenity to her— the same serenity he remembered from the first time he'd seen her. She'd been holding Nicky then, too. She was a natural mother.

In spite of the fatigue she felt, Sabrina had a difficult time saying good-bye to Nicky at the Greenhouse door. Derek could understand that. He'd had a glimpse of Nicky's smile the night before. He'd felt the tear in his heart, and Nicky wasn't even his.

During the drive back to the farmhouse, Derek held Sabrina close to his side. She was quiet through most of the ride, but she didn't seem strung as tightly as she'd been when she'd returned after seeing Nicky on Thanksgiving day. He wanted to think that his presence made the difference.

When he turned off on the road to the farmhouse, though, he had a moment's sharp fear that his presence was going to make another kind of difference. "We have guests."

Sabrina, too, was peering through the windshield. The light snow that had been falling for the past several hours didn't come close to covering the sleek gray Jaguar that stood by the house.

"Recognize it?" Derek asked. He'd stopped a distance away and was approaching cautiously.

"No." She wouldn't have been concerned, had it not been for the tension in his voice. "How about you?"

He gave a short shake of his head. "A car like that would be hard to forget."

"No burglar would be driving a Jaguar."

But a big shot from New York would, Derek thought. Then he got close enough to decipher Vermont plates through the snow. "One of the transplants you've met?"

She shook her head.

He eased the car slower. "It's a rental."

"I didn't know you could rent Jaguars."

"You can rent just about anything if you have the dough."

She shot an alarmed glance at the house. "Hell, I hope it's not my parents."

"Are they good at picking locks?"

"I wouldn't put it past my dad." She sat back in her seat and remained there even when Derek brought the car to a complete halt.

"Someone's made himself at home. I can smell a fire going."

Sabrina didn't budge.

Grasping the handle of the door, he looked at her. "Coming?"

"Derek, this could be very unpleasant."

"If it's your parents, you mean?"

She gave an apologetic nod.

"Better still," he said, pusing himself from the seat, "stay put." It occurred to him that he'd like to see for himself who was in the farmhouse before Sabrina approached it. Though he suspected that his car had already been heard, he closed the door very quietly. Then, keeping low, he loped toward the house, flattened himself against the clapboard, peered around the window frame.

A minute later he was back leaning into the car. "Tall guy. Long and lean. Blond hair. Wire-rimmed specs."

Sabrina closed her eyes.

"He's wearing a pair of baggy overalls," Derek went on.

"What's he doing?"

"He's sprawled in front of the fire, staring at the flames."

She opened her eyes, muttered. "That's J. B., all right," and climbed out of the car. No sooner had Derek unlocked the front door when she burst through, prepared to do battle. "What are you doing here, J. B.?"

J. B. looked up and stared at her for a long minute before turning his stare on Derek. His expression was blank.

Derek, who'd already heard enough from Sabrina to be more than prepared for her brother, went forward and offered his hand. "Derek McGill," he said.

Sitting up, J. B. shook Derek's hand, then wrapped his arms around his knees.

"J. B.?" Sabrina prodded.

"Thought I'd visit."

"Why?"

J. B.'s stare was as vacant as ever. It was joined by a noncommittal shrug. "I wanted to meet your new husband."

"Mom and Dad sent you."

"They told me to come. I told them to bug off. I came on my own."

Derek snickered at his irreverence and was rewarded by a dirty look from Sabrina, who quickly refocused on her brother. "If you're planning on making life miserable for us, you can get back in that Jaguar and leave."

J. B.'s face split into a sudden grin. "Nice car, isn't it? I've never driven one before." He stopped grinning. "There's a nor'easter forecast. I think you're stuck with me for a while."

She bowed her head and pressed the throbbing spot between her eyes.

Derek, who'd been standing to the side with one hand on his hip, curved that hand around her neck and said very softly, "Want to take some aspirin and lie down for a while? It's been a long two days."

She darted an unsure glance toward her brother.

"I'll keep him company," Derek assured her. "If it's me he's come to meet, we can spare you for a while."

Sabrina knew she was being cowardly, but she didn't care. It *had* been a long two days. She simply wasn't up to dealing with J. B. just yet.

With a look of gratitude—and luck—for Derek, she left the room.

Derek watched her go, then tucked his hands in the pockets of his slacks and turned to J. B. "When did you get here?"

"A few hours ago."

"How did you get in?"

"Window upstairs was open. I climbed the oak and dropped onto the overhang."

Derek thought about that for a minute. "Like the snake did in *Slither*?"

J. B. stared at him soundlessly for a time. "Should I be impressed that you've read me, or dismayed that you identify me with the snake?"

"Impressed."

J. B. didn't acknowledge that one way or another. Derek wondered what he was thinking as he stared, wondering if he was picturing him behind bars. That staring made Derek uneasy. It was like his first day back in New York, when he'd felt that he had every one of his sins and those of his father plastered across his forehead. The past two days had been better, thank God. Between Sabrina's loft and the hospital, he'd only met a few double takes. He could get used to that, he supposed. But J. B. Monroe's endless stare?

Partly annoyed, partly stubborn himself, he stared right back.

That seemed to jar J. B. from his empty reverie. "Where've you two been?"

"New York. Nicky needed to have some tests done there."

"How is he?"

"He's been having more seizures. There's medication for it, but otherwise . . ." He shrugged.

J. B. crinkled his nose to hike up his glasses. "The folks are having a real problem with this."

"With Nicky?"

"With you. And Sabrina. And your marriage."

"Then it's just as well that they're on the West Coast."

"They'll come East. They'll want to see you for themselves."

"What, exactly, will they want to see? I've got everything where it's supposed to be."

"They'll want evidence that you're as bad as they think."

Derek sniffed in a deep breath and looked off toward the window. The snow was coming in great white clumps. Pretty. Too pretty to sully. He shouldn't be faced with J. B. just now. He didn't want the divisiveness in Sabrina's world. But it was there, and it was his to deal with.

"Why did they decide I was bad?" he asked quietly. "Because of the murder? The prison term? My lack of social papers?" He blew out a snort. "Funny, I'd have thought that being a little eccentric themselves, they'd have been more liberal than that."

"They're more conventional than you'd think. And besides, Sabrina's their baby."

"She's over thirty."

"They worry about her."

"So do I," Derek said. He regarded his brother-in-law through sober eyes. "When I first met Sabrina, she was tired and tense, overworked and underappreciated. Lots has happened in her life since then that I can't take any responsibility for, but I do know that since she's been with me she's been better. She eats. She sleeps. She smiles and laughs. She's happy. I make her happy. So how can your parents begrudge me?"

"At this point it's the marriage."

"Me, the marriage—same difference. Sabrina and I didn't have to get married. We could have just lived together. If they're so conservative, they should be relieved."

J. B. stared at him a minute longer, then swiveled toward the fireplace, grabbed the poker and began to push at the burning logs. When he had them rearranged to his satisfaction, he withdrew the poker and studied its forked tip. "It's nice up here."

Derek allowed him the momentary shift of subject mainly because it was so benign. "Sabrina said you'd been up several times."

J. B. frowned at the poker. He turned it once, slowly, completely.

"When do you write?" Derek asked.

"Every few months. Intensively."

Recalling what Sabrina had said about her family's workstyle, Derek believed him. "You're between books now, I take it."

J. B. ran a finger along the tip of the poker. "I was thinking of staying up here for a while. Setting myself up somewhere to write."

"What about your daughters?"

When J. B. looked up, his eyes held something vaguely akin to emotion. "What about them?"

"If you're here, you won't see them much."

"I don't see them much, anyway. They don't like me."

"Come on. All kids like their parents."

"They love them. They may not like them. There's a difference."

Though Derek hadn't thought about it quite that way before, he couldn't argue. He'd despised his parents through most of his childhood, but still there'd been a certain other feeling that he'd been unable to escape. He supposed it was love, a blood-runs-thicker-than-water type of thing. Perhaps that was one of the reasons—albeit a minor one—why he'd been so angry about being set up for murder. His father had paid for his crimes both with his time and his life; it seemed unfair that mud should be slung at his grave.

J. B. was staring at him again, but the stare was less vacant. "Do you and Sabrina plan to have kids?"

Something flared in Derek. His first impulse was to tell J. B. that it was none of his business. Then he paused to consider his own reaction and realized that J. B. had hit a sore spot. "I don't know," he answered cautiously.

"Do you want them?"

"Yeah."

"But she doesn't. She's afraid."

"Given what she's been through, I suppose she has a point."

"That's bullshit. She'd be a terrific mother."

"I think so, too."

"Then have kids."

"She's using birth control, so I can't exactly trick her into it—even if I wanted to, which I don't. She has to be willing to take the chance."

J. B. said nothing to that. He raised the poker, lowered it, raised it, lowered it.

"Are you planning to hit me with that thing?" Derek asked.

J. B. looked up, seeming surprised to find him still there. "Hmmm?"

"The poker." He stepped forward to take a closer look, trying to discover what J. B. found so intriguing. He'd used the poker himself. It was nothing spectacular, just another heavy iron poker. "Do you have plans for it?"

"No."

"Then why were you studying it that way?"

J. B. seemed more puzzled than affronted by Derek's bluntness. "Why do you want to know?"

Derek backed off. "Just curious. I'm a trained inquisitor." It was true, but told only half the story. He sighed. "Maybe if I understand what you're doing, I won't think you're so strange. Frankly, you make me nervous."

Their eyes held. J. B. stared, but Derek stared right back. In the end, J. B. was the one to look away. He lowered his head, pushed himself to his feet and ambled toward the wing chair in the corner of the room. "Should I leave?" he asked without turning.

"Of course not. You're Sabrina's brother. You're welcome here."

"But you're her husband." Slowly he turned. "What are your plans?"

"Plans?"

"Aren't you going back to work?"

"Eventually."

"Here?"

"Possibly."

"How?"

"I haven't quite figured that out yet."

There was a long pause before J. B. said, "Then you're satisfied living off Sabrina for a while?"

Derek's spine grew very straight. "I have never had, nor do I now have any intention of living off Sabrina. If you think I married her for her money, think again. With very little effort, I could probably buy her out."

"You socked it away?"

"I invested it."

"Dad'll be glad to hear that," J. B. said and slumped into the wing chair. He stretched out his legs. "Have any plans for the barn?"

Derek frowned at the non sequitur.

J. B. cocked his head toward the side of the house. "The barn. What are you going to do with it?"

"Use it as a garage," Derek answered, still frowning. "And a workroom. I was thinking of insulating it. Why?"

"I want a corner of it."

"For what?"

"An office."

"You're going to write in the barn?"

With the tiniest shift of his eyebrow, J. B. indicated that he was. "I'll need a Franklin stove, some lanterns and a typewriter. Think Sabrina will mind?"

"I don't know," Derek said. "I suppose not." Then realization dawned. "You want to keep an eye on me, is that it?"

"I want to write a book."

"Why here?"

"Because I like it here."

"How long will it take?"

J. B. gave a one-shouldered shrug. "Two months. Maybe three."

Derek lowered his head and rubbed his neck. He and Sabrina were newlyweds. He wasn't sure he liked the idea of having a chaperon. "Two months," he muttered. He rubbed his neck some more.

"Give me a little more space and I'd have an apartment in the barn. You wouldn't have to see me at all."

"Still, two months is a long time."

"Not to write a book."

"Yeah, but you could make Sabrina miserable."

"Me?" J. B. asked with such innocence that Derek scowled.

"It's her decision," he muttered. "Her farmhouse, her barn her decision. I only pay the bills. You'll have to ask her."

Sabrina couldn't say no. J. B. was her brother. He was a sad figure, very much alone—a fact all the more obvious by contrast to the life she now shared with Derek. When J. B. had visited before, they had been two people alone.

Now things were different. She could afford to be generous.

Not that she gave in without a fight. She made it clear that Derek was no longer on trial, that she loved him, that he was staying. She told J. B. that if he intended to sit and stare and offer nothing more than the occasional acerbic remark, he could just pack up and head back west. And she informed him that he wasn't to create a horror tale about her barn. She loved the barn, the farmhouse, the acreage surrounding it. She found peace there. Not even under the guise of fiction did she want that disturbed.

There was only one other condition she needed met to let J. B. stay. Derek had to approve. When he did, she was actually surprised. She knew he felt uneasy with her brother. But he, too, felt badly for J. B. He, too, was in a mood to be generous. Christmas was nearly there. J. B. was alone. And then, there was a tiny part of Derek that needed to be with family, too. He had none of his own, just Sabrina. He wondered what it would be like to broaden his family base even more.

Sabrina was still worried. She was prepared to find J. B.'s presence a problem, and she told Derek so.

"You're worried that *I'll* find his presence a problem, so you're saying it first," Derek was perceptive enough to point out, "but I'll tell you if it happens, hon. I'll tell you if it bothers me."

Surprisingly, J. B. didn't bother either of them. His presence was unobtrusive. Perhaps he'd taken Sabrina's warnings to heart. Perhaps he'd sensed that Derek could be either friend or foe, depending on his own behavior. Whatever the case, he took over the guest bedroom, which was far enough from the master suite to afford Derek and Sabrina the privacy they wanted. But he did plan to move into the barn, and to that end he accompanied Derek to the building-supply house.

"Ever done this before?" Derek murmured to J. B. as they examined the various insulating materials. He spoke under his breath so as not to be heard by the salesman.

J. B., who was frowning behind his glasses, shook his head. "You?" he whispered back.

"Uh-uh." Derek gnawed on the inside of his mouth. His eye jumped across the room to the wood paneling yet to be chosen. A little bewildered, he returned to the insulation and mumbled to J. B., "The guy says this is the best."

"Looks to be the most expensive," J. B. mumbled back.

"Most expensive isn't always the best."

"Don't you know it."

"Problem is," Derek went on, talking now out of the corner of his mouth, "I don't know much else when it comes to this stuff."

There was nothing vacant about J. B.'s stare. He was eyeing the insulation as though it were truly alien. "A writer isn't supposed to know much else."

"Or a reporter. I flunked shop in high school."

"Me too."

"We need help."

"Professional advice."

"A carpenter."

Of one mind, they turned on their heels and left the store.

They hired a carpenter to advise them on materials and teach them all they didn't know, which was considerable. Fortunately, they'd matured since their high school days. Or maybe it was the motivation factor. Or determination. But they stuck with it and began to see progress.

Sabrina, who visited the barn often, bearing hot drinks and sandwiches, felt as though she were watching a trade-school class. When she dared say as much aloud, she was bombarded with snowballs made of insulation remnants. Laughingly she retreated, but she found herself smiling for a long while after. Turning the barn into livable space was providing a common interest for Derek and J. B., and that pleased her. Derek was engrossed in the project enough not to be thinking about Noel Greer. J. B. was engrossed enough not to be staring off into space. Though communication between them was never overwhelming, that was more because neither was an habitual talker than because they couldn't get along. They did talk when so moved. They did get along. And that gave Sabrina a kind of inner pleasure that she hadn't expected.

* * *

Sabrina spent Christmas morning with Nicky. She was accompanied not only by Derek, but by J. B., which made things easier. For the first time, she didn't dissolve into tears at the visit's end.

During the week that followed, while Derek and J. B. worked diligently on the barn, Sabrina entertained Maura, who had popped in unexpectedly and settled herself in one of the spare bedrooms. Her combination housewarming–wedding gift to Sabrina was, quite fortunately, a futon, which she proceeded to use as a bed in lieu of the floor.

"God forbid J. B. should share the four-poster," she remarked, but playfully. Sabrina knew why.

"You two never did get along."

"That's an understatement. He's a weirdo."

"There are many who'd say the same about you," Sabrina teased. She tipped her head to study Maura's hair. "You've gone darker again."

Maura grinned. "It's working." She'd already told Sabrina about the new man in her life. He was, incredibly enough, the one who'd been looking at her that day when she was at lunch with Sabrina. She'd long since learned that the tie tack had indeed held a diamond and that there were more where that came from.

Well aware that her friend had been sketchy on such specifics as the man's name and occupation, Sabrina had decided that Maura was serious about him but was taking the cautious approach. Sabrina didn't blame her. In some ways, she was pleased by Maura's caution. It showed the maturity that Maura claimed to aim at.

At the moment, though, Maura was looking more mischievous than mature. Lowering her voice, she leaned forward. It was all for effect. She and Sabrina were alone in the second-floor solarium. There was no way the men could overhear their conversation from the barn. "Derek is gorgeous. You didn't tell me that."

"I thought you knew. He was on TV for years."

"Oh yeah, I've seen him on TV, but, Christ, he's even better looking in the flesh." She sat back on one of the large cushions that were strewn about the floor. "Prison obviously didn't do him any harm in that respect. He's aging nicely. Life up here must be agreeing with him."

With several swallows of white wine already under her belt, Sabrina was feeling mellow enough not to pick up on the harm that prison had done Derek. Instead, she finished slicing the Cheddar cheese into small squares, passed one to Maura, popped one into her own mouth. Then she too sat back. "I think so. We're very happy."

"God, I'm glad," Maura said with comical relief. "But I have to say that it amazes me."

"What?"

"That you can be happy up here in the middle of nowhere."

"I'm not in the middle of nowhere. There are other people, and stores and inns and restaurants."

"Still, it ain't New York."

"True," Sabrina conceded with a crooked grin.

"But you were always a city person. What happened?"

"Hard to explain," Sabrina answered, momentarily looking confused. "I'm not sure I would have been ready for this five or ten years ago. Maybe I've grown into it. Maybe circumstance made me ripe for it. . . . Then again," she said, tapping a Wheat Thin against her lip, "I've only been here since September. Maybe by this time next year I'll be starving for New York."

"And Derek? Think he'll last up here?"

The Wheat Thin went into Sabrina's mouth. It crunched between her teeth. She washed it down with her wine, thinking all the while. It wasn't the first thought she'd given the subject. Indeed, brooding might be a more accurate description. "I don't know," she said finally. "He seems happy, but whether he'll get tired of all this . . ." Her words trailed off with a shrug.

Maura didn't pick up on her friend's concern, or if she did she chose not to pursue it. "What about work? Is he thinking of getting back into it?"

"Eventually."

"Back into reporting?"

"I think so."

"But how? Where?"

"I'm not sure he's figured that out yet."

"Then he's not looking for something?"

"Not at the moment."

"His agent is . . ." She squinted with one eye. "Jacobs, isn't it?"

"Uh-huh."

"Is he talking with people?"

"I'm not sure. Originally he wanted Derek to do the talk-show circuit, but Derek refused, and he's stuck by his refusal. Craig calls here every so often, and I don't hear what he's saying; but from Derek's end of the conversation I'd guess that Craig is champing at the bit. Whether he's already looking, though, or whether he's waiting for a green light from Derek, I don't know. I have a feeling it's a combination of the two. Craig's looking, but he hasn't come up with anything that appeals to Derek; and since Derek won't settle for second best, he's prepared to wait it out."

"And in the meantime?"

"In the meantime, he's on vacation."

Maura snorted. "Vacation? Doesn't look to me like he's on vacation. Looks like he's changing professions. Becoming a carpenter."

"Not quite. What he's doing in the barn is for fun. I mean, there's a practical purpose to it, but it's strictly an avocation." She thought for a minute. "It's therapeutic. He needs it."

"Prison was rough?" Maura asked, and was answered by a look that was eloquent in its bluntness. She studied Sabrina for a minute, then placed a Wheat Thin on her tongue and brought it into her mouth as though it were a sacramental wafer. "If I were in his shoes," she mused, "I'd be furious. I'd be wanting to lash out at everyone and everything. I'd feel used and abused. And I'd want revenge. But Derek seems calm. Content. Is that because of this place and your marriage, or has he legitimately accepted what happened?"

Sabrina didn't answer immediately. She thought about the discrepancy between what she wanted to be true and what, in fact, she knew to be true. "I think," she said at last, "that the contentment you see is because of this place and our marriage. He hasn't accepted what happened. I'm not sure he ever will. He was deprived of two years of freedom. His name has been dirtied, his career derailed. There are times"—she lowered her eyes and continued more quietly—"when he's still very angry. Not often—at least I don't think it's often—just from time to time. He tries not to let me see, but I do. It's in his eyes, in his jaw and his hands and his shoulders."

Maura was regarding her strangely. "You sound defeated."

"I would have liked," Sabrina admitted after a moment's consideration, "for our marriage—and me—to have been enough. I keep asking myself what I can do to make it so, but I don't have the answer." She frowned at the bit of wine pooling in the bottom of her glass. "I wanted to be successful at this, and to some extent I guess I have been, but not completely." She looked back at Maura. "I want him to forget the past. But he can't."

"So what's he going to do about it?"

Sabrina wore a painful look on her face but said nothing.

"What are his plans? He won't just sit back and brood. I mean, hell, I don't know the man other than by reputation and the little time I've spent with him here, but he doesn't strike me as the type to live with that kind of anger forever. Seems to me he was a doer. A crusader. The general consensus is that he had balls made of steel. Has he lost them?"

On behalf of her husband, Sabrina was offended by Maura's statement. "He hasn't lost a thing," she said, "but there are right ways and wrong ways to do things. Derek can't just walk out on the street and start hurling accusations."

"Who would he accuse?"

"It's a very long story."

Maura shrugged and tossed her gaze around the room. It was empty except for the pillows, the tray of cheese and crackers, and the two friends. It was a room of endless time and leisure. "I'm game."

Sabrina was initially reluctant. To tell Derek's story

would be to betray his confidence. But as she looked at
Maura—off-the-wall Maura with her newly darkened hair
in stylish disarray, her canary-yellow tunic, royal-blue
tights and sea-green granny boots—something else came
over her. Maura was her best friend and had been so since
they were kids. Over the years they'd shared many intima-
cies. And as far as this one went, Sabrina needed to get it
out. It had been festering inside her since she heard it from
Derek. She wanted another opinion.

Maura had that. "Jesus, what a book," she said, eyes
bright in excitement by the time Sabrina had reached the
end of her tale. "Revenge makes for a great plot."

"I'm not writing it."

"Sure you are. You're a writer. That's your thing."

"I'm also Derek's wife. For now, *that*'s my thing."

"Are you kidding?"

"No."

"Sabrina, these are modern times. You can write *and* be
Derek's wife."

"I know that," Sabrina countered quietly, "but for now
I'm just his wife. Maybe I'm on vacation, too."

"You've been on vacation for three-plus years," Maura
remarked, then qualified herself when Sabrina stiffened.
"Bad word. I know the agony you went through with
Nicky. That was no vacation. How about hiatus—you've
been on a three-plus years' hiatus from writing."

"That's okay."

There was a pause, then Maura said, "So why don't you
get back to it? You have the perfect vehicle."

"I won't use that particular vehicle. Not yet. I told Derek
I wouldn't, and, anyway, he's right. The files are the key."

For a minute Maura looked as though she was ready to
argue further about the writing. Then, wearing a resigned
expression, she said, "If the files exist. It could be a long
shot. I'd think Derek's time would be better spent looking
for proof that Greer put him in jail."

"The fact is," Sabrina said, "that he may never be able
to prove it. His best hope is that if he's able to expose
Greer's dealings with Ballantine, someone will come forward after the fact and shed light on what really happened

with Joey Padilla and that murder trial. Men like Greer make enemies along the way. They have to. There must be people out there who would be more than happy to pound another nail in Noel Greer's coffin. First, though, he has to be discredited. Right now he's too powerful."

Maura was very quiet for several minutes. She ate a cheese cube, then a cracker, then another cheese cube. She finished off her wine, then cocked her head to the side.

"Greer's power is not to be underestimated."

"I know that."

"Isn't Derek worried that he'll be tailed when he goes after those files?" She paused, then stuck on a quick, "Greer knows about the files. You said Derek told him."

Sabrina shifted her gaze to the panels of glass that looked out on the woods surrounding the farmhouse. Life here was so peaceful. Mention of Noel Greer, of Lloyd Ballantine, of the files and revenge stirred a nervous crinkle in her stomach that was very much at odds with that peace.

Unfortunately, the nervous crinkle wasn't about to go away by itself. Again, Sabrina opted to share her fear with Maura, this time in the hope that she could ease it. "I think Derek's hoping that Greer will be too involved with his Senate campaign to bother."

"Isn't that a simplistic approach? If Greer doesn't bother, and if Derek comes up with those files, and if they're as condemning as Derek hopes they'll be, Greer's Senate campaign would be shot to hell."

Sabrina grimaced. "You're not supposed to say that. You're supposed to say Derek is probably right. You're supposed to say that Greer has too much on his mind to worry about Derek, even that Greer is arrogant enough to think that Derek wouldn't dare cross him again. The thought of someone monitoring Derek's activities doesn't thrill me."

Tipping her wineglass to her lips, Maura drained it.

"But I suppose you're right," Sabrina said, feeling discouraged. "Greer is a powerful man. He's the puppeteer pulling the strings. To accomplish what he has already, he's probably utilized a whole cadre of men. One of them could easily be spared to keep tabs on Derek."

Maura gave a sudden frown and seemed momentarily distracted. Then, as quickly as it had come, the frown vanished. "Christ, we're getting morose," she said with a return of her usual ebullience. "There's no need to think about this now, is there? This is supposed to be a festive season."

It was. J. B. and Maura tolerated each other enough to minimize the verbal sparring, and what there was of it was, in its way, entertaining. But that was just the start of their entertainment. As a foursome, Derek, Sabrina, J. B. and Maura spent a day bucking the Christmas-week crowds on the ski slopes, a night gorging on roast duckling at a quaint little inn, another day on snowmobiles, another night at the movies. Sabrina took Maura browsing through the shops she most admired of those she'd discovered since she'd come north. And she cooked. To lavish praise and many a raised glass, she prepared goodies ranging from apple pancakes to veal scallopini to butternut-squash soup to English trifle.

She was pleased with her life. Derek was never far from her side, and she had Maura, her good friend, and J. B., who, with a stretch of the imagination, was beginning to resemble a friend. While she'd been expecting to feel down over the holidays—the first without Nicky—that depression never materialized. And her need for professional accomplishment temporarily took a backseat to her responsibilities as a wife and homemaker.

Two days before New Year's, Maura left to return to New York and to Richard—which was the name she'd finally given for the man she was seeing. Under J. B.'s taunting, she also admitted that he was a businessman; but no amount of taunting, coaxing or pleading—from *any* of them—had produced another word.

New Year's Eve was an experience. Sabrina and Derek had been invited to a party thrown by a pair of writers she'd met when she first moved to Vermont, and they wouldn't hear of leaving J. B. behind. In his own way, he'd truly become part of the family. Beyond that, Sabrina suspected that Derek wanted him along for moral support.

This was to be the first time that Derek had "gone public" since his arrest. It was the first time that he would be standing around making social conversation with people who knew exactly who he was and where he'd been.

"We don't have to go," Sabrina assured him more than once.

But Derek only shook his head. "It's time."

When he said things like that, Sabrina felt a tiny *frisson* of tension, because if it was time for Derek to mix, it would soon be time for more. But she was determined not to let that particular thought ruin her New Years' Eve, and it didn't. Standing back, watching Derek and J. B., she was amused. It was like the blind leading the blind. J. B. was as nervous about the party as Derek. Each became the other's personal crusade.

By the time they returned home in the wee hours, Sabrina was doing the driving. Derek and J. B. weren't drunk, just pleasantly tipsy. It even occurred to her that their lightheadedness wasn't caused by alcohol at all, but by the fact that they'd been received well—either that, or relief that the ordeal was over. In any case, she wasn't taking any chances.

As it happened, Derek had sobered sufficiently by the time they reached the farmhouse to lead Sabrina to their bedroom, take her in his arms and show her how very deep his love was. She half suspected that his New Year's resolution had something to do with that, for he was more hungry than ever for her in the days to come. Her own resolution was more a wish—that this honeymoon at home could go on and on and on.

On the twentieth of January, it ended. That was the day when Noel Greer shocked no one by formally announcing his candidacy for a seat in the United States Senate.

· *CHAPTER 15* ·

Derek spent the twenty-first of January doing some heavy thinking. He had long since mapped out his plan of attack, knew just where to begin his work, but his thoughts ranged ahead, hovering about the various possible weaknesses that had made Lloyd Ballantine corruptible. One of those possibilities would determine the ultimate direction of his search. That direction would be where the danger lay.

Derek didn't want Sabrina subject to danger. She had been by his side when David had called on the phone to alert him to Greer's announcement; she had been by his side when the evening news had replayed the speech. She had made a quiet statement of her intent that if she couldn't fight him, she'd join him.

That scared him a little.

He wanted her help. She was a first-class researcher—organized, thorough and concise in her notes. He'd been through them several times and knew most everything there was to be publicly known about Lloyd Ballantine from his birth to the time he'd joined the Supreme Court. After that, the picture faded. To bring it back into focus, and to learn about those small, personal, non-public items in his biography—that second life, if it existed—would require interviews with the late justice's family, friends and colleagues. If Sabrina conducted such interviews it would openly identify her with Derek's cause. He wasn't ready for that yet.

Nor was he ready for what happened in the early afternoon of the twenty-second of January. Amid dual clouds of misting breath, Ann Fitzgerald and Justin Shagrew appeared on his doorstep like lost puppies from his past. They were swathed in parkas, hats, scarves and gloves, and the little skin that had been left exposed to the subfreezing temperature was ruddy.

Surprised and pleased, if a little puzzled, Derek hauled them inside and introduced them to Sabrina.

"Annie-Fitz and Justin worked with me on many a story," he explained, then gave a skewed grin. "They always were great for showing up just when the pizza did."

Justin held up a hand and vowed in a voice that was slightly slurred by a numb mouth and jaw, "Pure coincidence—and we wouldn't have popped in at lunchtime now if it hadn't been so cold. The cycle doesn't offer much protection. We couldn't bear the thought of sitting on the steps for long, when there were such wonderful smells coming from inside."

Derek shot a glance out the window toward the drive. "I can't believe you came on the Harley."

"I figured," Justin said, "that if the Harley could make it, we could. The windchill factor was something else, though." He looked at his fingers, which were still curled from the handlebars. "They may never be the same."

Sabrina estimated both he and his companion to be in the vicinity of twenty-six or twenty-seven, which meant that they'd started work with Derek fresh from college. They looked clean, and were dressed well, if casually. Ann was petite and seemed shy; Sabrina had the impression she was hiding beneath both the multiple layers of her clothing and the thick mane of sandy hair that, freed now from the heavy wool cap she'd worn for the trip, fell in tight curls to her shoulders. The dark-haired Justin stood taller, wore his layered sweaters loose, his jeans tight, boots to his knees and a tiny gold stud halfway up the curve of his ear. He had a sure smile and made eye contact readily. He struck her as a younger Derek McGill, at first glance the leader of the pair.

"Craig gave you the address?" Derek asked. His initial surprise gone, he was puzzled and slightly wary.

"Reluctantly, and only after we agreed to devote our-selves to getting you back to New York."

"If that's why you're here," Derek said in a light tone that meant serious business, "you're wasting your time."

This time, Justin's smile was surprisingly mature, sur-prisingly understanding. "It's not why we're here."

Derek sought Sabrina's gaze in an instant's silent com-munication before saying, "In that case, it's lentil soup with franks that you smell, and there's plenty, if you'd like to join us. We were just about to eat."

Neither Justin nor Ann was about to refuse. Settling gratefully into mate's chairs around the captain's table in the kitchen, they told of their adventures on the road. At Derek's questioning, they also related what they'd been up to in New York, which, inevitably, brought them to the reason they'd come.

"We need direction," Ann said in a soft, tentative voice. Up to that point, she'd been content to let Justin do most of the talking, which he, in turn, had been more than content to do. But Sabrina had the sudden impression—from what source, she didn't know—that once past her shyness, Annie-Fitz, as Derek fondly called her, was a very bright woman.

Ann went on. "What you used to do at the network was exciting. There's been no one else in the field who can do it quite the same. You had the guts to stand up to Greer, so your stories were a cut above the rest." She darted a timid glance at Sabrina, looked down at the tabletop, then back at Derek and spoke quickly. "If it hadn't been Greer, it would have been someone else. Every network has its self-appointed censor. Unfortunately, that means that some stories are never approached because they are considered too touchy from the start."

She paused to take in a quivery breath. "We're thinking of free-lancing, but we're not sure where to begin. We have story ideas—all those stories that are waiting to be told but have no spokesman without you. We even have contacts. We're good at finding facts when someone tells us where to go, but we have no idea how to pull the whole thing together. We need a mentor." Her eyes flickered, as though she wanted to blink or look away but wouldn't allow herself to do either. "We've chosen you."

Derek studied her long after she'd stopped speaking. Then he said, "You're serious."

"Very."

His expression, which had grown more sober as Ann talked, was close to grim. "If you mean mentor, as in using me for an entree, you're in trouble. My name isn't worth much at this point."

"It is now that Greer's out of the picture."

"Out?" Sabrina asked. "Isn't it the reverse?"

Justin was the one who answered. "Not in our field. As a candidate for the Senate, Greer will have to separate himself from the network. Otherwise, he'll have a conflict of interest."

For some reason, Sabrina hadn't considered that, but in doing so, she realized what a risk Greer was taking. If he resigned his position at the network and then lost the campaign, he'd find himself out in left field. Based on all Derek had told her, she doubted Greer was a man who'd care for that. Which meant that Noel Greer had been pretty sure about winning the election before he'd declared his candidacy. Which meant that if anyone screwed things up, he could well be out for blood.

If Derek was at least in part responsible for that lost campaign, she could begin to understand the satisfaction at stake for him . . . and the risk.

With that in mind, she looked at him. He met her gaze for a dark and knowing moment before turning back to hear what Justin was saying.

"With Greer once removed from the network, his power is suddenly diffused. Sure, his people are still there, and one or another of them may prove to be strong, but nowhere as strong as he was. There are an awful lot of people who were freed by Greer's announcing for office."

Bracing his mug between his hands, Derek adjusted his spine to the curved back of his chair. What Justin and Ann were saying made sense, but more than that, they were two of those who had remained loyal to him. Both had written him when he was in prison. Both had talked with him that day in the studio in New York. He respected and trusted them. And he saw some merit in their personal plans. "This free-lancing of yours," he ventured. "Are you talking television?"

"Possibly," Ann said in a quiet tone. "But we thought it would be easier, from a purely technical point of view, to start with newspapers and magazines and build from there." She sent him an apologetic look. "We're not working with a very broad fund base."

"You don't need one. If you don't have to involve yourselves with filming, the only significant expenses will be travel and phone bills. A typewriter and paper, a word processor if you want one; beyond that, your greatest resource is up here." He tapped his head. His hand fell back to his mug. He squinted into it. "You've totally severed yourselves from the network?"

Justin nodded. "We didn't want to be drafted to work on Greer's campaign."

"Would that have happened?" Sabrina asked.

Derek was the one to say, "You bet."

Ann turned to her. "It had already started—the order was sent around that all staff members were to be there when he announced his candidacy. That was when Justin and I knew it was time to quit. We'd been thinking of doing it for a while. We'd both been increasingly frustrated." She looked at Derek. "After you stopped by last November, things got more tense."

"What do you mean?" Derek asked in a low, still voice.

"You were a living, breathing example of what happened if one didn't toe the line."

Silently Derek held her gaze, willing her to go on. She shot a nervous glance at Justin, then swallowed and faced Derek again, this time with determination. "We know, Derek. We may not know all the details, much less have concrete proof, but we know that Greer had something to do with what happened to you. Everyone at the studio knew it. No one knew quite how he did it, or why, but everyone knew it."

"The antagonism between you two was legendary—" Justin began.

Ann cut in. "But it didn't account for the lengths to which he went to put you away."

"We're not asking that you tell us—"

"Maybe you don't even know—"

"But we wanted to say that we'd be glad to help—"

"If you decide to go after him."

In the profound silence that followed the rapid exchange, Sabrina realized she was holding her breath. She released it slowly and looked from Ann's face to Justin's. Both were focused expectantly on Derek, and Derek was giving nothing away. In a flash, Sabrina was back in Parkersville on the day of her first visit. She recalled sensing a barrier between Derek and her, Derek and the world. The barrier had been shored up by anger and hostility. His thoughts had been his own. He hadn't welcomed any intrusion.

Now, too, there was a barrier, but it was one of caution. While old wounds weren't raw, they were far from healed. Derek seemed suddenly set apart, separate from the rest of them. He was the ex-con, the one who made monthly calls to his parole officer, the one with visible scars for time spent with violent men. He was the intimidator.

They all waited for him to speak. When he did, his tone intimidated only through its utter control. "There was talk at the studio, then?"

After a moment's pause during which Ann accepted that he wouldn't immediately take them up on their offer to help, she answered, "Very little, and that was one of the things that was so odd. There's always talk at the studio— nonsense chatter in the lunchroom, gossip in the halls— but this time there wasn't. It was like no one knew who to trust and who not to."

"We could probably make some pretty good guesses about who was involved," Justin added, "but we have no proof. After years of scrabbling to pay the bills, Johnny Hoddendez was suddenly able to move his family out of the city, but who was to say that the money he used didn't really come from his uncle in Cincinnati, as he said? Word went around that Suzanne Lyons' appointment as an anchorwoman in Charleston came at least in part because she was sleeping with the producer down there—and who could question that?"

Derek's fingers were tight around his mug. His lips were pursed, the muscle in his jaw working to betray his thoughts as he wouldn't do in words.

"He's a tyrant," Ann said, and they all knew she was talking about Greer. "Someone has to stop him."

"I know," Derek muttered, "I know."

"We'll work for you," Justin repeated the offer. "Say the word and we'll do it. Somewhere there has to be proof that he set you up. If not that, there has to be proof that he blackmailed Ned Welnick into resigning as news director, or that he was responsible for sabotaging his major competitor's coverage of the last presidential election, or that he cheated on his income taxes—something, *anything*. I'm not ready to believe that the man is as invulnerable as he thinks."

Ann had come forward in her seat. "But we need direction in that, too. You know what you went through. You have to have suspicions. We'll do the legwork if you tell us where to go."

Derek knew that he should tell them to go straight to hell. They were butting in where they didn't belong. This was *his* hurt, *his* war. And even beyond that, they had no concept of the danger involved. If Sabrina hadn't been sitting right there, he'd have spelled out that danger in living color.

But it probably wouldn't have mattered to Justin and Ann. They were young and zealous. They wouldn't be put off by danger. They'd probably get even angrier on his behalf if they knew all that Greer had done.

"I think," Derek said, taking a tempering breath, "that you're getting ahead of yourselves." He shifted a level gaze from one face to the other. "I thought you came here because you wanted to set up a business."

"We did," Justin said. "Do."

Ann added, "We just thought you could be our first story."

"But I already have a biographer."

Three pairs of eyes turned toward Sabrina, who

promptly shrank into her chair and—holding both hands up, palms out—told Ann and Justin, "He's got me hamstrung, too," which was in some respects a very revealing statement, but one she didn't regret. She looked at Derek, gnawed on her lower lip for a minute before suggesting, "There's the barn."

She thought she was being vague. She thought that Ann and Justin couldn't possibly know what she meant, and therefore Derek could freely decide one way or another. To her chagrin, Ann jumped at her suggestion.

"We'll take it. All we need is a little corner. The thing is, Justin's apartment in the city just went condo, and mine is too small to do anything but sleep in, and we know that we're going to have to find something to use for a home base, but this has all happened really suddenly." She took a quick breath. "If we could use your barn until we get our plans straight—not long, just a few days, maybe a week —that'd be great."

"We've got sleeping bags for warmth," Justin said, "so the barn would be great. Just a roof over our heads while we brainstorm." He looked at Derek and sheepishly amended that to, "While we pick your brain."

Ann turned to Sabrina and said as quickly and quietly as she could, "I know this is a terrible imposition, but we'd work to make it not so. I'll pick up groceries. We'll eat out there. You wouldn't even have to know we're around." She swallowed, then added more meekly, "Except for the time we're . . . picking Derek's brain."

Sabrina thought the idea sounded just fine. She liked having a houseful of people. Not that it was actually the house that was going to be full. She looked at Derek. He was thinking the same thing.

"There's only one problem," he told Justin and Ann.

Justin held up a hand in smooth assurance. "I grew up on a farm in Kansas." He splayed the hand over his chest. "You got animals in that barn, I can handle animals."

"Not exactly animals," Derek said.

"An arguable point," Sabrina murmured.

Leaning close, Derek murmured back, "He's behaving, isn't he?"

"If you call emerging from the barn once a day to sit in a trance at the dinner table behaving . . ."

"He's writing. You said it yourself, that's his style."

"But I thought we'd see a change. He's been better about other things."

"You're looking for miracles."

"Mmm. Maybe."

Derek turned to Justin and Ann. "We have another guest. J. B. Monroe. Ring a bell?"

For a split second, both faces looked stunned. Then, simultaneously—and comically so—they came alive.

"*The* J. B. Monroe?" Justin asked excitedly.

Derek's nod set them off.

"I have read," Justin said, conveying his awe in the separate emphasis he gave each word, "every single one of his fourteen novels."

Ann's eyes were wide. "He's made the *New York Times* list, the *Publishers Weekly* list, two of his books have been made into movies, another one adapted for TV, and another used as the basis for a Saturday morning cartoon show. He's incredibly successful—"

"And he's in your *barn*?"

Derek nodded.

Justin went limp. "I can't believe you put a man like J. B. Monroe in your barn."

"On the other hand," Ann said, "I'm not sure I'd want him in *my* house. His books are too scary for me, and I understand that the man himself is—"

"I feel it only fair," Derek interrupted, "to warn you that J. B. Monroe is my brother-in-law."

Justin straightened. "Your—"

"Brother-in-law?" Ann finished, cheeks flaming. Her eyes flew to Sabrina, who'd been watching in amusement. "I'm sorry. I didn't mean to sound critical. I understand the kind of skill it takes to do what he does. It's just that I . . . I have a vivid imagination . . . I get nightmares . . . so I can't read what he writes."

Sabrina smiled. "No problem there. But J. B. is living in the barn—which is pretty well fixed up, by the way, so there's no danger of your freezing. There are several extra rooms. You're more than welcome to use them as long as you promise not to disturb J. B."

Ann and Justin promised.

It was late that night when Derek finally went to bed. Sabrina had been lying beneath the quilt, waiting for what had seemed an eternity when she finally heard his footsteps. He undressed silently, slid between the sheets and drew her to him. She snuggled against familiar lines to find that while his body was warm, his feet were like ice. He'd obviously sat at the hearth long after the fire died.

"Are you okay?" she whispered.

"Uh-huh," he whispered back.

"You seemed preoccupied when you came in from the barn." He'd gone out much earlier to see that Ann and Justin were settled.

"Just thinking."

Sabrina didn't need to ask about what. It hadn't taken Ann and Justin's arrival to make him think of Noel Greer. The man had become a presence. Sabrina always knew when Derek was thinking of him because his eyes would get angry, his body tense. Increasingly there were spells of tossing and turning during the night. Sometimes Sabrina would awaken to find him standing stark naked before the window, surrounded by the blue glow of the moon's reflection on the snowy landscape. He would look eerie. Forbidding. Like something from one of J. B.'s books. Unwilling to acknowledge the reality of the image, she would turn over and wish it gone, and by morning it was. Until the next time.

It was inevitable that Ann and Justin's arrival intensified his thought.

On the one hand, Sabrina liked Derek's friends. She thought Derek would enjoy being their "mentor" until he decided on the direction he wanted to take, professionally, himself. If, on the other hand, Ann and Justin's presence was going to be an emotional barb in his side, she'd as soon have them leave in the morning.

"Was I right to make the offer?" she asked, referring to the use of the barn.

"Sure. They're nice kids."

They lay silently for a time. Sabrina could tell Derek wasn't sleeping. She was far from sleepy herself, so she asked, "Were they always a pair?"

"They've always been close, like two peas in a pod, but they're not romantically involved."

She raised her head from the pillow of his chest and eyed him through the moonlight. "That's strange. I just assumed they were."

"That," Derek said with a crooked smile, "is because you are a very conventional lady. You see men as sex objects."

The smile relieved her tremendously, so much so that she decided to follow up on the train of thought. Returning her head to his chest, she said, "Well, hell, I'm not blind. Justin is a good-looking man, and Ann is adorable. If they work together and travel together, why aren't they romantically involved?"

"Ann is shy."

"Not with Justin."

"Maybe she isn't looking for involvement with anyone at this point in her life."

"But why not?"

"Maybe she had a bad experience once."

"Maybe the problem isn't with Ann but with Justin. Maybe he's gay."

"Possibly," Derek said without pause.

Sabrina's head bobbed up. "I was only kidding." She studied Derek's face, but it showed no sign of a smile. "Do you really think so?"

"There was always rumor to that effect, and Justin never went out of his way to deny it."

"Did it bother you—working with him?"

"Are you kidding? He's one hell of a researcher and loyal. I always fought to get him on my team. The way I saw it, his sexual preference had no relevance to our work; therefore it was none of my business." He pushed her head down and kissed her lightly on the forehead. "Worried he'll attack J. B.?" he asked, and this time she didn't have to look at his face. She heard the smile that said he was teas-

ing and answered it by rubbing his chest with her hand.
She never tired of touching him.

"Then you don't mind that they're here?" she asked,
suddenly a bit distracted.

"That depends on how long they stay." He turned on his
side to face her and ran his hand from her bare shoulder to
the base of her equally bare spine. "I'm not sure I'm going
to like sharing you so much."

"You won't be sharing me."

"Sure, I will. First J. B., now Justin and Annie-Fitz"—
he nipped her nose—"and here I was hoping that you could
subsist on a diet of me and me alone."

She kissed his chin. "I can."

"But you have so many other people to talk with now.
Don't deny it. I heard you laughing with Ann while you
were making dinner."

"I enjoyed having her there, which is not to say that I
would have chosen her over you, because I wouldn't have
done that. But you were carting wood to the barn, so you
weren't around." She took his chin between her thumb and
forefinger. "I love you, Derek. I enjoy having other people
around, but only if I know that we'll have times like this.
Just the two of us. Quiet, relaxed, peaceful—"

Derek kissed her silent before she could say something
that would make him feel guilty, but the kiss, as always,
affected him, and before long he was seeking more. He
loved her taste and texture. He loved the way she sighed
when he touched her, whimpered when he stroked her,
writhed when he tongued her most sensitive spots. He
loved the way she took command at times, the way she
made love to him with her hands and lips, the way she used
her body, rubbing sleekly, rocking slowly, to drive him
wild. He knew that if he searched the world, he'd never
find another woman to satisfy him as she did. When he
was joined with her, he felt complete. When he brought her
to a climax, he felt victorious. When he reached his own,
he felt that he'd died and come back to life a richer man.

The only problem was that on this night when he came
back to life, he was thinking of Noel Greer. That was when
he knew it was time to act.

* * *

Two days later, Derek and Sabrina were in David Cottrell's office in New York. Actually, they weren't in his office, per se, but in the computer room of his law firm. Derek was at the keyboard of one of the half-dozen computers. Sabrina was in a chair close by his side.

"This," Derek told her, "is LEXIS." He keyed in one cue, waited for new directions to appear on the screen, then keyed in another. "If we had all the time and patience in the world, we would be sitting in the law library poring through yearly volumes of the *Supreme Court Reporter*, but I don't have all the time and patience in the world, so we're doing it this way." He was continuing to type responses to prompts on the screen.

"What are we looking for?" Sabrina asked in a whisper.

"The connection between Ballantine and Greer," Derek said in a voice low enough not to carry beyond their station. "If we theorize that Greer had a personal enough stake in at least one Supreme Court case to warrant his bribing Ballantine, we have to find those cases where Ballantine's might have been the deciding vote."

"How do we do that?"

"LEXIS' memory contains all of the cases decided by the court, along with the date of the decision and the vote, by Justice. We're looking for those decisions made during Lloyd Ballantine's years on the bench in which Ballantine voted with the five-member majority—split decisions, five votes to four, where Ballantine voted with the five." He studied the screen, entered another command on the keyboard.

"Okay," Sabrina conceded. "We'll know if Ballantine voted with the five. But will we know whether his was actually the deciding vote?"

"No. We have no way of knowing that. All we'll know is that Ballantine voted in Greer's favor. You can hardly call it evidence, but it's a start. Particularly..." He faltered, eyes narrowed on the screen, and his words grew distant. "...if we can find more than one case." He took a breath. "Here we go. Got a pencil?"

"Right here."

Derek read the citation by volume, date and page. Sabrina wrote it down, even though it didn't appear to relate to Greer.

"We'll note them all," Derek explained. "If we don't need them, that's fine. On the other hand, if we come up with zip, we may have to look more deeply into those that initially sound improbable."

And so they sat side by side, Derek manipulating the computer, Sabrina compiling a list of cases from those he read off. At one point, when they took a short break, David snagged her in the hall on her way back from the ladies' room.

"How's it goin'?" he asked.

She gave him a feeble half-smile. "Okay, I guess. Not that anything earth-shattering has popped off the screen yet."

"Patience, girl. Patience."

"Mmm, that's what I keep telling myself. Derek doesn't have that much, but compared to me he's loaded."

"Derek has learned patience the hard way. The passage of time today is a drop in the bucket compared to the days, weeks, months he spent locked up just *thinking* of doing what he is now."

"Still, he's incredible."

"Think so, do ya?"

She smiled. "Yes, I do."

"I'm mighty glad to hear that, ma'am, since he thinks pretty much the same about you. But frankly"—he grew more serious—"I'm surprised you're letting him do this."

"Letting him? Do you think I had a choice?"

"You're his wife."

"That's right, his wife, not his keeper."

"Still," he scratched his cheek with a single finger, "I'd have thought that after everything you've been through, you'd prefer a more peaceful life."

"I would. But I fell in love with Derek, and all this somehow came with the package. Derek is determined to see it through. I can't stop him."

"Have you tried?"

"Sure, I have," she said with the kind of quiet serenity

that had drawn Derek to her from the start, "but I gave in because I realized something else—not realized, maybe *accepted* is a better word. Derek *needs* to do this. Right now, he's haunted. There are times when he can push it all to a corner of his mind, but inevitably it comes forward again. He's haunted by the boy he was—growing up as his father's son—and he's haunted by the man Noel Greer would see him be. I wish there were some other way, because revenge is ugly. But he needs to be free. *We* need to be free." She paused, then said sadly, "Many a prison bar isn't made of steel."

David Cottrell stood silently before her for the space of several breaths. Then he let out a whoosh and shook his head in admiration of the woman his friend had been lucky enough to catch.

By midday, Sabrina and Derek had a sizable list of those split-decision cases in which Lloyd Ballantine had voted with the majority. One of those cases concerned Noel Greer and the network he had founded and built and of which he had become chairman of the board.

Citation in hand, Derek went to the volumes on the shelves of David's law library. There he learned that the case was a libel suit that had been decided in Greer's favor with Lloyd Ballantine's vote in support.

While Sabrina was pleased as punch that Derek's theory was proving to have merit, Derek was more cautious. "There should be more," he said, brooding, "if, in fact, Lloyd Ballantine committed suicide. Think about it. Barring some sudden, shocking turn in his life, a man is usually heading downhill for a while before he gets to the drastic point of taking his life. This case was decided four months before Ballantine died—long enough to eliminate sudden shock, not all that long for a real downhill slide. I'll bet the relationship between Ballantine and Greer goes further back."

"To the days before he was on the bench?"

"Possibly."

"Ballantine first came to Washington to serve as attorney general. He'd certainly have had something to offer Greer in that capacity."

Derek frowned, looked down, slowly shook his head. He raised a pained look to Sabrina. "It's right there. I can almost taste it, but it stays on the edge of my memory. It's been that way for so long that I'm not sure I didn't just dream it up to begin with."

"Dream what up?"

"I don't know. That's the problem. Mind spending some time in the library?"

"Of course not."

Some time turned out to be the rest of that day and most of the next, but when they finally finished with the microfilms, Derek had what he needed. Walking briskly, with Sabrina's hand held tightly in his, he led her to the coffee shop where they were to meet the man Derek had spoken with moments earlier on the phone.

Jonathan Sable had been the chief of the antitrust division of the Department of Justice under Attorney General Ballantine. He confirmed what Derek and Sabrina had read—that during his tenure, Noel Greer had been the subject of an antitrust investigation that had been terminated at the intervention of the attorney general. The case against Greer had been strong, Sable claimed. No one had been more surprised—or angry—than he when it had been dropped, and he'd resigned his position soon after. Frankly, he confessed, he was surprised no one had investigated the matter sooner.

Back in Vermont, Derek told Justin and Ann about his search for the Ballantine files. He'd given it much thought, had discussed it with Sabrina. J. B. already knew; it was one of the many things he and Derek had talked about when they'd been working together in the barn. And as for Justin and Ann, Derek knew he could trust them. He wanted their feedback.

Sabrina had another reason for wanting Derek to take Justin and Ann into his confidence. When she thought of feedback, she thought of additional voices telling Derek that he was overstepping the bounds of reason—if, indeed, it ever got to that. In short, she wanted allies.

She knew she had them in Justin and Ann. They hung on

every word Derek said, but then, rather than yessing him, they asked questions. They played devil's advocate, and they could get away with it, since that was largely how brainstorming sessions had been back when they all worked together in New York.

After hours of intermingled talk and thought, they agreed that Derek was headed in the right direction. They agreed that while there was still a possibility that Lloyd Ballantine's support of Noel Greer's causes might have been innocent, Greer had had much, much to lose without that support. They agreed that Greer's nearly violent reaction to Derek's proposed investigation of Ballantine smacked of a cover-up and that if, indeed, Ballantine had accepted a bribe, there had to be a reason. A weakness. Which was how Noel Greer worked. They agreed that the next step to finding the Ballantine files was finding that weakness—and that the first step to finding that weakness was to interview the man's family.

They did not agree on who would do the interviewing. Justin and Ann wanted to help. They could leave right away, they said. They would be relentless but discreet. They would uncover as much about Lloyd Ballantine in his hometown as there was to be uncovered, and they could do it quickly.

Their last argument was the most tempting for Derek. He had already decided to stay in Vermont for at least a week or two before heading out again. For one thing, he didn't want to alert anyone who might be watching his movements that he was hot on a trail. For another, Sabrina was tired. She argued with him on that point, but he could see it. Faint shadows had appeared under her eyes, and she was having more trouble getting up in the morning. He worried that his tossing was keeping her awake during the night, but she denied that it was. He could only conclude that she was feeling the emotional strain of his quest.

Since he wasn't about to give up on the quest, and since she wasn't about to let him pursue it without her, and since he couldn't, just couldn't let Ann and Justin do it for him, his only option was to wait that week or two and see that Sabrina got plenty of rest before continuing.

Yes, he was sorry to lose the time. No, he didn't regret pampering Sabrina. She was his mate, his wife. She was his responsibility, and he took that very seriously—which was easy to do, since he adored her. He knew that if she'd had her druthers, he wouldn't be after the Ballantine files at all. He figured that the least he could do was intersperse his search with more quiet, peaceful times for them both.

So he tried. He tried not to think about Greer, not to listen to televised reports about his campaign, not to follow the coverage in *Time* or *Newsweek*. Instead, he took Sabrina to Boston for two days of laziness in a posh hotel, then brought her home for another two of laziness in and around the farmhouse, then took her to see Nicky, which she'd been wanting to do.

He enjoyed pampering her, and found that as long as he did it with a minimum of fanfare, she enjoyed it, too. It helped that Ann had taken command of the kitchen and was preparing the kind of culinary treats that the tiny kitchen of her closet-of-an-apartment in New York had been unsuited for.

That wasn't all Ann was doing. Under Derek's tutelage, she and Justin had begun work on several of the stories that had interested them. They'd equipped their makeshift barn-office with desks and telephones, and between time spent there and at the college library, they were on their way.

Sabrina worried that J. B. was *in* their way. Each time she ventured to the barn, he was out of his own office and sitting in Ann's. When she asked about the status of his book, he told her to worry about her own, after which point she rarely asked again. She did ask Ann—the two women had developed an easy relationship—about whether J. B. was being a pest and was told with a shy smile that he wasn't.

That was more than Derek could say about Maura, who dropped by for another visit during those two weeks. Derek couldn't quite put his finger on what bothered him about Maura—whether it was the history she and Sabrina shared, or the fact that she took up large chunks of Sabrina's time or that she rarely stopped talking. She was forever asking questions, and that annoyed him. For Sabrina's sake, though, he was always polite. For his own sake, he was always happy to see Maura leave.

When Sabrina got the rest Derek had prescribed for her and still the shadows beneath her eyes didn't disappear, Derek decided that they were related to tension. Knowing the source of that tension and that the only way of relieving it was to solve the Ballantine puzzle, he went ahead and booked two seats on a flight to Chicago.

· *CHAPTER 16* ·

Bernice Ballantine lived in a beautiful Tudor home in the Chicago suburb of Lake Forest. If her late husband had been wanting for money, there was no evidence of it in what he'd left behind. The widow Ballantine was a bona fide member of upper-class society.

Calling her from their hotel soon after he and Sabrina had arrived, Derek set up a meeting for the following day.

"You gave her your real name," Sabrina said after he'd hung up. "Won't that be a tip-off?"

He'd given that earlier thought, knew it would be a recurring problem during the course of his search, but still decided against use of an alias. "One of the things I learned over the years was that the average person isn't tipped off so quickly. He—she, in this case—isn't coming from where you and I are. She doesn't know what's in our minds. Unless Greer has already gotten to her, which I doubt he has or she'd never have allowed for this meeting, Mrs. Ballantine assumes nothing but what I told her—that we're doing an independent story on her late husband and want to ask her some questions—which is, in fact, the truth. The less we lie, the less we risk stumbling over our own deceit."

Sabrina considered that for a minute, then broke into a dazzling smile. "Well put," she said.

"Besides," he added less nobly, "what choice did I have? She'd probably have recognized me anyway."

Bernice Ballantine did recognize him. She commented that she'd watched him many a time, and that she was glad to see him back at work. He did nothing to correct that misperception—which was only indirectly a misperception. He *was* back at work. He was an investigative journalist interviewing a source, in search of information that would send him farther down the road. This was what he'd always done and he did it well. Even aside from the personal stake he had in this particular subject, he felt the thrill of the chase lighten his blood.

Unfortunately, Bernice Ballantine was of little help. She confirmed the standard biographical facts that Sabrina and Derek broached merely for the sake of their cover. She painted a picture of a family man, a devoted husband and father whose primary weakness was a lack of aptitude for mechanical things.

Under Derek's questioning, she said that she'd been proud of her husband, and that though he hadn't been on the bench long enough to make so great an impact as some of the others, he'd taken his job with due gravity. Under Sabrina's questioning, she admitted that she'd never felt completely comfortable living in Washington, which was why she'd returned to Lake Forest as often as she had.

Yes, she felt that the justices were underpaid, but she stressed that she was thinking of some of the others—since, of course, she and her husband had been financially secure. No, she had no knowledge of corruption in the Court. Yes, her husband had on occasion been burdened by the emotional pressures of his work. No, there were no other papers—beyond those already bequeathed to the University of Chicago Library—left behind when he died.

At the conclusion of the interview, she commented that she wished Derek were back at the network. Unable to resist, Derek asked what she thought of Noel Greer's bid for a Senate seat, to which she answered that even if she were a resident of New York, she wouldn't vote for Greer because he was a womanizer, and she couldn't abide infidelity.

"She sounds like the Girl Scout to match her late husband's Boy Scout," Sabrina remarked when they'd returned to the privacy of their rental car.

"Not terribly inspiring," Derek agreed. "Still, it wasn't a total loss. Either I'm a poor judge of character, or that woman was telling the truth. I do believe that she had no knowledge of any misconduct on Ballantine's part."

"Which doesn't mean that there wasn't any. She said that she spent a good deal of time in Lake Forest while her husband was in Washington. That opens the door to all kinds of possibilities."

"They say the wife is always the last to know—"

"Or the first. But not in this case."

"Maybe her daughter is more enlightened."

If Pamela Stanger was more enlightened about misbehavior on the part of her father, she was not about to share it. Married, she lived in a high-rise on Chicago's shoreline, but she refused to meet with Derek and Sabrina there, choosing instead the impersonal conference room of the firm for which she worked as an architect.

Rather formal, though civil, Pamela was a woman of few words. She answered questions as succinctly as possible, volunteering little by way of insightful information. Sabrina found her arrogant; Derek found her defensive. They came away from the meeting, though, sharing an awareness of two things. The first was that Pamela Ballantine did not enjoy talking about her father. The second was that her name, embossed in gold among those of her partners at the entrance to the firm, read "Pamela E. Stanger." There was no B for Ballantine, which was odd. Most women whose fathers had made it to the Supreme Court would be proud as punch of the name. Apparently, this one wasn't.

Peter Ballantine, the late justice's only son, was less tight-lipped than his sister. Though he chose his words with care, a certain cynicism came through. Twice married and twice divorced, he clearly had an ax to grind. Why he had chosen to share his feelings with Sabrina and Derek, they didn't know, but they weren't about to look a gift horse in the mouth.

Quite bluntly he said that while his father had been attentive when he'd been with them, that hadn't been often. Lloyd Ballantine had liked his freedom. By the time his children reached the age of fifteen, they had been enrolled in exclusive boarding schools. As a lawyer practicing out of Chicago, Ballantine had traveled often—leaving his wife behind. As attorney general, he had insisted on keeping the Lake Forest house, and he'd done the same when he was appointed to the Bench, though, theoretically, that appointment was for life.

The separation didn't bother Peter, who had always found his father too much of a goody two-shoes—which was ironic, Peter said, but declined to elaborate. Instead, he went on to say that he felt sorry for his mother. She had deserved better.

When Derek asked him to elaborate on that, Peter sent him a come-on-man-use-your-imagination look that gave Derek and Sabrina the direction they needed.

"Women," Derek announced once they'd raced back to the airport and caught the first flight to Boston. He kept his voice low, his head close to Sabrina's as the plane took off. "We figured it was either booze, drugs, gambling or sex. I suppose sex makes sense." When Sabrina arched a brow his way, he said, "It's the most Boy Scout–type vice of the four."

"Not alcohol?"

"Nah. It's too visible. If you go into a bar and get drunk, people see."

"No one sees a thing if you get drunk at home," Sabrina pointed out.

"Ah, but an alcoholic can't limit his drinking to home. An alcoholic loses control. That's the nature of the beast. He may start at home, but before he knows it, he's drinking at the office, at restaurants, private dinners, parties. Word spreads." He raised his eyes to find the flight attendant, quite appropriately, offering them drinks. Both he and Sabrina settled for Cokes, and as soon as the steward had moved on, he leaned close again. "The same thing is true, to some extent, for both drugs and gambling."

"Drugs, okay. I agree there," Sabrina said after some thought. "Gambling is something else. We've assumed that there was never a money problem, but can we do that? The house in Lake Forest was beautiful, and I'd venture to guess that the townhouse in Washington was, too. There were probably luxury cars and designer clothes—the works. But what if Ballantine was a gambler and had lost just enough money to have everything mortgaged to the hilt?"

"If that was the case, it would have taken more than one or two payoffs from Noel Greer to make things right. And people would have known—bookies, bankers, the executor of Ballantine's estate. Chances are slim that his widow would be living as she is now if Ballantine had come that close to the edge."

"But she said she couldn't abide infidelity. If Ballantine's weakness were women, wouldn't his wife have divorced him?"

"You'd think that, wouldn't you," Derek murmured, momentarily distracted. Then he said more clearly, "That could have been Greer's handle. Ballantine loved women. His wife would have divorced him if she knew. There would have been scandal. Bad press. Tarnish on the badge. Blackmail."

Closing her eyes, Sabrina rested her head back against the seat. "If his weakness was women, and the press never caught on, he must have been very discreet." She opened her eyes to Derek's. "If so, we have our job cut out for us. To be very discreet means to cover one's tracks, and if the tracks are covered, how does one go about locating the women with whom a man who died six years ago may have had affairs? I take it that is what we have to do."

As a writer of nonfiction, Sabrina knew how to do research. There was a fine line, though, between research and investigation. Having crossed it, they were on Derek's turf.

Derek confirmed it. "We have to verify that there were,

in fact, women—and I'm assuming it in the plural, since one woman, a long-standing mistress, would have been far less spectacular in terms of any scandal that Greer might have threatened to create."

Sabrina made a face. "You know, when it comes right down to it, even the idea of legions of women isn't all that scandalous. We're not talking the Dark Ages here. Six years ago, even ten or twelve years ago is well into the sexual revolution. Would the fact of Ballantine's womanizing really been enough to give Greer that powerful a tool?"

"Ballantine was a justice of the Supreme Court. Justices of the Supreme Court are supposed to have whistle-clean images. Ballantine did. He might have been embarrassed to the point of resigning if there'd been a scandal." He took a breath. "Then again, you may be right. That's why we have to find one of those women. At the least she could give us insight into the man at his most vulnerable. At best she could lead us to the files."

"If they exist."

"They exist."

"But why do you think one of his women has them?"

"No one else seems to."

His gray eyes held a challenge, but Sabrina had no better suggestions. "So how do we find the women?"

Releasing his seat belt, Derek stretched. In doing so, he very casually skimmed the faces of the people across from and behind them. The only one who looked at all familiar was the man sitting two rows back. Derek was sure he'd been sitting two rows behind them on the flight out—which said nothing but that a businessman who had the same schedule as they had preferred sitting in front of the wing, as they did.

Settling into his seat again, he said by Sabrina's ear, "Let's assume the scene of the crime to be Washington, since that's where Ballantine was during those lonely times when his wife was in Lake Forest. We know that they had a townhouse on Embassy Row."

"He wouldn't have dared bring a woman there, would he? If he wanted to ensure secrecy, there are other more sensible sites for a tryst. Like a hotel."

Derek nodded his agreement. "It's done all the time. He takes a room under a phony name, makes a call, gives the woman his room number, and she visits him, with the public—and his family—none the wiser. Justices of the Supreme Court don't have the kind of memorable faces that politicians who run for office have. Without their black gowns, they blend into the crowd."

"That could spell trouble for us. Do we try to find the hotel first?" Sabrina asked.

"The woman, I think. A woman."

"But how?"

"Escort services. High-priced call girls. Society prostitutes who know all about discretion. Ballantine probably used a phony name, so we'll have to get a picture to show around." He frowned off into the sky that was getting darker as they headed east. "If this were three years ago, I'd have gone to the studio files and had his picture in a minute."

"It'll take us a little longer than that, but not much," Sabrina said. "One of the biographies I bought had a section with pictures. We could either copy one, or if we're worried about copyright infringements we could just carry the book around."

Derek took her hand. Her fingers seemed more slender than ever. He ran his thumb over the gold band that marked her his. "I knew there was a good reason why I brought you along." He paused, studying her face now. "Feeling okay?"

"Uh-huh."

"You look tired."

"I always look tired."

"You do not. Just lately." He dropped a kiss on her nose. "Beautiful but tired. I'm working you too hard, I think."

She sputtered out a soft laugh. "That's a good one. I haven't done a stitch of hard work in weeks, and you're worrying."

She was right, Derek realized. It was precisely because she hadn't done a stitch of hard work in weeks that he was worrying. He could understand that she was under some strain; he could see her struggling with it at times; but the strain wasn't *that* great—certainly nowhere near the kind she'd had with Nicky. Still, she was tired. If he didn't see an improvement soon, he was going to insist she see a doctor.

They spent another ten days in Vermont before setting out again—partly to give Sabrina time to recoup her energy, and partly to do the same for Derek. He joked that he was feeling his age, but the fact was, the farmhouse had come to represent a haven. Neither the thrill of the chase nor the knowledge that he was working toward the revenge he'd dreamed about for better than two years could totally sustain him—and that came as something of a shock.

He'd thought himself driven. He'd thought, not so long ago, that nailing Noel Greer was critical. He still felt it important, but critical? No. Some things mattered more. Like Sabrina. Like the time he spent with her, the conversation, the laughter, the shared feelings. Like their visits with Nicky. Like the farmhouse.

After only three days in Chicago, he found that the clean air of Vermont, the quiet nights, the sense of security were precious.

Not that those ten days found him idle. He spent hours with Justin and Ann reviewing the progress they'd made, plotting strategy, dictating directions, discussing the basic principles of investigative journalism. With the help of Justin, J. B., a local plumber and an electrician, he shaped the better part of a small kitchen and a second bathroom from the space that remained in the barn.

And he took care of Sabrina when she developed a mild case of the flu, which he guessed accounted for her fatigue. She fought him at first. She wanted to be up and around, supervising what was being done in the barn, baking, even writing—for she had started to write, or, more accurately, make extensive notes on their search for the Ballantine files. When she was beset by intermittent spells of nausea, though, she yielded to Derek's urging and went to bed.

As luck would have it, just when Sabrina was beginning to feel better, her parents flew East for another surprise visit, the first such one since her marriage. That night, lying in bed, she tried to explain her tension.

"There are times when I feel like a coin, with two distinct sides. There's the side represented by Mom and Dad, the side that is creative and artistic and imaginative. I'm a loner on that side, because the kind of work they do—and J. B., too—calls for a solitary existence. Then there's the other side, the one which is me with you up here. It doesn't want a solitary existence. It likes having people in the barn and good smells coming from the kitchen and a fire in the hearth when we're coming home."

She grew quiet for a minute, then said on a mildly plaintive note, "Why do I feel torn like that, Derek? Why can't I simply accept the fact that I'm different from my parents? I have so much *more* then they have, in many ways. But still they make me nervous when they come."

Derek had been nervous himself, far more so than he wanted to acknowledge. He'd been justified in it, he supposed. Amanda and Gebhart Monroe had done little to hide their scrutiny of him. But after an afternoon and an evening of it, he'd grown defiant. To hell with them, he'd decided. If they didn't like him, tough. So he'd dropped all formality and begun to challenge them—subtly, but they'd seen it. Strangely, they'd backed off.

"I'm not sure," Derek began slowly, "that there really are two sides to the coin—or if there are, that they're as different as you think them."

Sabrina tipped her head on his shoulder to study his face in the dim night glow.

"I think," he went on, "that the issue is strength. That's the key. That's what your parents have, it's what you respect. And it's what they're looking for in you, me, us. A commitment to what we want in life."

"I want you. I've never been committed to anything more, but *still* they make me feel like I'm doing something wrong."

Derek didn't respond at first. When he did, it was with a certain sadness. "Maybe it's not your parents, Sabrina. I watched them today, watched them closely. They were wary of me, but other than that, they seemed pretty comfortable here. Maybe it's not them, but you. They represent something you want—or value—in life. When you're with them you miss whatever it is that is missing. Is it the writing?"

Sabrina's first instinct was to argue that Derek's analysis was wrong. But it wasn't. So she said, very softly, apologetically, "Maybe."

"Maybe it's living up here."

"But I love living—"

"Shhh. I know you do. But this isn't New York or San Francisco. You can love living up here but still feel a void."

"That's not it," she said with conviction.

"Is it Nicky?"

"It'll always be Nicky."

"But there's more. What is it, sweetheart?"

"I don't know."

"There is something."

"I don't know."

"There is something."

"I don't *know*."

"Maybe you want something I can't give—"

"No!" She lifted herself above him. "You give me everything, Derek. I love you. I don't want anything else." Her voice died, leaving the vehemently spoken words hanging in the air. A moment later they dropped. A moment after that, she sank back to the bed.

Derek gathered her close, and the strength of their love, the shared warmth, the heat of their passion was enough to push doubts and worries aside for a time. But only for a time. Because things were happening to Sabrina's body that weren't about to stop.

The day after Amanda and Gebhart left, Sabrina and Derek set out for Washington. Derek concentrated on escort services, Sabrina on dating clubs. Together they even visited singles' bars. But after five full days, they came up empty-handed. No one recognized the man in the picture they showed.

Claiming that he needed a breather to think out the next

step, Derek insisted they return to Vermont even when Sabrina protested. He was worried about her. She was thinner than ever and too pale. He knew she wasn't sleeping well because he spent many of his own nights awake.

Something was disturbing her, and he sensed that it went beyond his war with Greer. He was hoping that the farmhouse would allow him enough quiet time with her to worm out the source of that disturbance.

As it happened, he had cause for added disturbance himself. During the flight home, he spotted the same man who had been on their plane to and from Chicago. Possibly a coincidence, he told himself, but that was before he watched the man leave the airplane. Over the years, Derek had found that simple observance of people could often provide information that questions could not. In this case, it was the ease with which the man lifted his briefcase. Derek would have sworn it was empty.

Loath to worry Sabrina with this latest possible twist, he was totally nonchalant in the frequent glances he tossed toward his rearview mirror once they left the airport. He was grateful he'd chosen to fly in and out of Boston, rather than one of the smaller airports nearer the farmhouse; the greater the distance, the more time to lose a tail.

But there was no tail, at least not one that he could see. And when he glanced at Sabrina, he realized that his nonchalance had gone unnoticed. Her mind was miles away.

Later he would wonder why he hadn't asked her there and then what was wrong. He had her alone and unoccupied. She couldn't get up and leave the car or distract herself otherwise—not that she'd ever done that when he'd wanted to talk, but he was anticipating the worst.

In hindsight, he supposed that was why he hadn't asked —precisely because he was anticipating the worst. He didn't doubt for a minute that Sabrina loved him, but that didn't preclude the possibility that she regretted who he was and what he'd involved her in. It was possible to love someone and still want to move in different directions; and he could live with that, as long as the direction she wanted to move in didn't take her away from him.

So, since he wasn't sure he'd like her answers, he didn't

ask. And by the time they arrived at the farmhouse, the opportunity was lost.

Maura was there. That meant nonstop chatter for the remainder of the day, which would have been all right had not the chatter revolved around where Derek and Sabrina had been and what they'd been doing. Derek tried to accept that, as Sabrina's agent, Maura had just cause for interest. Still, he was uncomfortable. Maura annoyed him, it was as simple as that.

Justin, it turned out, was on the road conducting interviews for the story on fraudulence in psychiatry for which Derek had given him the names of several solid contacts. Ann was holding down the office end, though she wasn't doing it alone, since J. B. was a frequent presence in the chair beside her desk. And as it happened, the next morning the barn contingent was augmented even further when three of Derek's past team members—friends of Justin and Ann who'd obviously been tipped off by the pair—arrived intent on joining what they referred to as Derek's Institute for Investigative Journalism. Derek protested that there was no such institute, then proceeded to spend the day discussing story ideas, technique and marketing strategies. When he emerged from the meeting, there was a color on his cheeks that hadn't been there before.

The color faded, though, when Maura took his arm and drew him into the living room that night while Sabrina and the others were talking over the last of three huge pizzas.

"I think I've done something terrible," she said, and he realized that her usual frenetic energy had taken a turn toward agitation. Her eyes were skittish, and there wasn't the slightest hint of the smile that was usually in open possession of her features. "It's about Richard." She paused and frowned, then raised worried eyes. "I'm not sure how to say this."

Derek had trouble mustering much sympathy. In fact, he had trouble believing her. She'd never been at a loss for words before. The best he could do was to remind himself that she was his wife's best friend and bite his tongue.

"Is there—have you ever noticed—" She took a breath and tried again. "Have you ever been aware of—"

"Spit it out, Maura."

"Noel Greer. What you're doing could ruin his career. I'd think he'd do just about anything to make sure you don't succeed."

"Could be," Derek said with caution, momentarily forgetting his personal feelings for Maura as he waited to hear what she had to say.

"In the course of your . . . work . . . on this case, is there a chance that you've been followed?"

Derek felt the beginnings of an awful suspicion tugging at the back of his mind. "Why do you ask?"

She swallowed. "The pictures your friend Jason brought —the ones of him and the others with Greer that Greer had autographed—there was another man in one of them." She clasped her fingers tightly. "It was Richard."

Derek was silent for a minute. "*Your* Richard?"

She nodded.

He couldn't recall a Richard working closely with Greer. "Do you know what he was doing there?"

"No. I knew he was affiliated with one of the networks on an executive level, but he always evaded the specifics. Except when it came to you." Disgusted with herself now, she looked away. "He wanted to talk specifics then, all right. He wanted *me* to talk them to *him*. About *you*."

Back braced against the archway with his hands tucked hard in his pockets, Derek didn't move a muscle. His gaze was dark and direct, commanding her to explain.

"As he told it," she said, "he was with the competition. That was why he wanted to keep tabs on you after you were released from prison. He wanted to know what you were doing with yourself, whether you were angry, vengeful, spiteful, whether you were working or thinking of working. He led me to believe that there was a potential job in it for you, which was why"—her voice wavered— "why I went along."

"He wanted to keep tabs on me," Derek repeated. His voice was cool and as taut as his jaw. "Through you?"

She didn't have to confirm it. Even if her expression hadn't been guilty, he'd have known. It made sense, explained her frequent phone calls and visits, the questions that had so gotten on his nerves. If he hadn't been so busy dealing with the anger of betrayal, he might have been relieved to learn that there was good reason why she'd been such a pest.

Running a hand around the back of his neck, he ground out a low, "I can't believe you did that."

"I didn't realize I was doing anything wrong."

"You're Sabrina's best friend! Is nothing sacred to you?"

"I thought I was helping her out."

"By betraying her confidence? What she told you—what *we* told you—was said in large part in the context of the book Sabrina wants to write. You were here not only as her friend but as her agent. Whatever happened to professional ethics?"

Maura stood her ground, regarding him not in defiance but as one who knew that no argument she gave could excuse what she'd done.

Reading that in her eyes, Derek turned his head away and tried to see it from Greer's point of view. "You had the perfect cover," he said to the window. "Sabrina had said she wanted to write a book and you were her agent." He looked sharply back at Maura. "How much did this Richard of yours know when he first contacted you?"

"Just that Sabrina and I were good friends. He found out the rest while we . . . were getting to know each other."

"You actually dated him," Derek muttered in amazement.

"How was I to know?" she asked in dismay. "What he said sounded goddamned logical to me! It never occurred to me that I was being used—well, maybe once or twice when I felt he was asking too many questions about you and not enough about me, but it passed." She frowned at the floor, ran a palm over the waistband of her jeans, swallowed hard. "I really liked him."

"And he liked you?"

The hand that had been at her waist flew into the air. "Oh yeah, that's what he said. He was going to take me to St. Martin next month. He was going to send clients my way." She sighed and said more quietly, "He was going to bankroll the first of the spas that I told Sabrina about. That was the payoff, I suppose, only I didn't know it was a payoff. I thought he was doing it because he believed in the idea. And because he believed in me." She squeezed her eyes shut for an instant. "Christ, I'm a fool."

Derek was studying her closely. "You really did like him," he said, then asked almost idly, "Richard who?"

"Fraling. Only for all I know, that's not his real name at all."

Fraling. Derek was the one to close his eyes this time. They remained shut for a brief, tight moment. "It's his real name," he said, refocusing on Maura, "only he rarely uses the Richard. The rest of us knew him as Greg. R. Gregory Fraling. I wouldn't call him Greer's right-hand man, because he's too low to the ground for that. He's known for doing the dirty work." Which was perhaps one of the reasons Derek had always detested the man. Fraling stayed behind the scenes. He never soiled his hands, but he did an incredible amount of damage nonetheless. He reminded Derek of his father.

Other than the ghost of a helpless wince, Maura's expression hadn't changed. But she turned and walked toward the window, where she stood with one arm wrapping her waist, the other crossing her chest. It was then that Derek saw through his anger enough to realize that she was hurt. As he thought about it, he guessed she was humiliated as well. For the first time, he felt sympathy for her.

Crossing to where she stood, he said more gently, "He's a bastard, Maura. He's not worth what you're feeling."

She stared silently into the darkness for a minute, and during that time, studying her face, Derek realized that she wasn't a beauty. It was makeup that made the most of her features, playing up some, playing down others. Where that didn't work, her hairstyle took up the slack, and where that didn't work, the flamboyance of her personality took over. Without the flamboyance—and there was certainly none now—the rest lost something almost through a domino effect.

Looking up at him, she said in a measured tone, "He's married, isn't he?"

Derek might have spared her that final pain had Fraling

already been out of the picture. But the man would be expecting to see her when she returned to New York. She had a right to the truth. She needed it.

"Yes. He's married."

She pressed her lips together and nodded. "I had a funny feeling he was. He never spent more than a night or two with me at a time, always said he had to get back to his place in case someone was looking for him. Whenever I told him to leave my number with whoever it was that might be looking, he made a joke about wanting to keep my number to himself, and he followed the joke up with" —she darted a chagrined glance at the ceiling—"well, I never pushed him on it. I never did see his place. He said he liked mine better. The restaurants we went to were always out-of-the-way and dark—he said he couldn't stand the noise of the better-known places. He never took me to the theater or to public functions."

Again she pressed her lips together. Spasms of a frown crossed her brow. "The signs were all there. I should have known. The bitch of it is that I've always loved doing things big and being seen. But with him it was different. I liked the privacy, too. I thought I'd really found the right man."

She was looking sadly off into the night when she asked in a weak voice, "Does he have kids?"

Again Derek debated. Again he yielded. "Four."

"*Four.*" She looked up at him in pained amusement. "Christ, he's a stud—" Her voice broke at that and lost all amusement. "And I am a fucking fool."

"Not a fool, Maura. Just human."

"A fool." She shook her head and breathed a scathing, "Shit!"

"You thought it was for real. You were taken in by a pro. He's a con man, a charmer. That's his job, and he does it well. You aren't the first one to have fallen for his lines, and you won't be the last."

"Now why doesn't that make me feel better?" she bit off sarcastically, then shook her head again and said with remorse, "I'm sorry. You're trying to help. By rights you should be furious at me."

"I'm furious at the situation, which is nothing new, only now there's another person hurt in the mess." And that was, in fact, how he saw it. Quite unexpectedly he found that he was glimpsing not the Maura who was spirited to the point of being dipsy, but one who craved the same kind of love that her best friend had found. Derek supposed that another woman might have betrayed them out of jealousy, but he knew that hadn't been the case with Maura. She had simply wanted to be loved, to be protected, pampered, cared for, and she'd wanted those things enough to overlook warning signs that she might otherwise have seen.

His fingers curved around her shoulder. "I'm sorry you were drawn in."

She shrugged under his hand, then asked in a small voice, "How much damage did I do?"

"Greer knows for sure that we're after Ballantine, but he could have learned that easily enough without you. As for the rest, we haven't gotten anywhere near the files, so what damage there is is minimal."

"Have you been followed?"

Derek told her about the man he'd seen on three of their flights.

Maura was visibly shaken. It was a minute before she'd recovered her composure enough to say, "I really am sorry. If there's danger involved, you have every right to blame me. I know that you never liked me—"

"I never had a chance to get to know you. You were always babbling on and on about *me*."

"Did you suspect me? When you realized you were being followed, you must have wondered about a leak."

"You were—are—Sabrina's best friend. I trusted you."

"And I betrayed you." She turned to him with an urgent expression. "Don't tell Sabrina. Please, Derek, don't tell her. She's all I've got. My parents are gone. I only had a brother, and he's living with the Eskimos in Prudhoe Bay and couldn't give a flying damn where I am or what I'm doing. Sabrina is my family. We have a history. She's the only person in my life that knows anything about the real me, but if she learns what I've done, she'll hate me."

"She'll understand."

But Maura was shaking her head. "She'll be disillusioned. She'll never trust me again. She'll never trust *herself* again." She held up both hands. "And it's not that I don't want to lose her as a client, because I won't mention the book again. If Sabrina brings it up, I'll tell her that I think she'd be better represented by someone else. I'll leave you two alone, I swear I will, and I'll be fine as long as I know that I can call Sabrina sometimes. Or see her once in a while in New York."

Derek closed his hands over hers to still their tremor. "You aren't leaving. Sabrina loves you."

"But I've caused so much trouble."

"If anyone caused it, I did by setting my heart on those files—or Greer did, by stealing two years of my life—or Ballantine did by compromising himself for whatever the reason it ends up to be."

"But I've made things worse. Sabrina will be sick when she finds out."

"*If* she finds out. She doesn't have to. I won't tell her if you don't. But if you pick up unexpectedly and leave, she'll find out, and she'll be doubly sick."

Maura eyed him skeptically. "You can't actually want me to stay."

"Well," he drawled with surprising good humor—given what he'd just learned—"not forever. You were planning to head back to New York anyway in another two days. That sounds about right." His good humor faded. "Maybe your being here will cheer Sabrina up. She's been a little down lately."

"She does look tired."

"Any idea what's bothering her?" he asked with deliberate nonchalance. He felt a little foolish having to ask his wife's best friend something that, as his wife's husband, he should know himself.

With a semblance of her usual flair, Maura put him at ease. "The day Sabrina tells me something before she tells it to you will be the day Gary Hart becomes a monk." She frowned and grew thoughtful. "She may be worried about Nicky. She mentioned that she wanted to get over to see him."

Sabrina had mentioned the same thing to Derek.

"Has he taken a turn for the worse?" Maura asked.

"Not that I know of. I'll have to take her over this week. The thing is that it always upsets her, and there's so little I can do to help. It's a no-win situation. Frustrating as hell."

What was particularly frustrating for Derek was that this time Sabrina insisted on going to visit Nicky alone. She said that she needed to do it and turned down even his offer to act as her chauffeur and sit in the car during her visit.

So his helplessness was compounded. The four hours she was gone were difficult ones for him, and when she returned she was dry-eyed, but quiet and withdrawn. Derek was beginning to think of taking drastic steps to make her talk, when she did so of her own accord.

· *CHAPTER 17* ·

The clock on the bed stand read two thirty-seven, which was three minutes later than it had been the last time Sabrina had looked. She sat up and was still for a while, then quietly freed herself from the quilt and crossed the bedroom to stand at the window.

The night was dark and wet. There was no moon to light the sky, no snow to serve as a reflector. She was half-grateful about the last, since she was wanting desperately to think spring, and rain was a sure sign of that. She'd been feeling chilly lately. She needed the psychological edge that came with the warming of the sun.

There was no psychological edge to be found at the window tonight. The tattoo of rain on the roof seemed somehow disassociated from the pall of darkness that hung heavy and blunt over the yard. Turning from it, she sank into the nearby bentwood rocker, drew her knees up under her nightgown and hugged them close. She rested her cheek on one knee and sat that way for a minute, then turned her head, closed her eyes and propped her chin on the other knee. Then she slowly opened her eyes to look at Derek.

He was sprawled on his back with the quilt pulled to a point just above his waist. One arm was folded beneath his head, bunching that visible part of his chest into a contoured wall of muscle. He often slept that way. She'd initially thought it strange until she realized that Derek often fell asleep thinking—or awoke in the middle of the night and fell *back* to sleep thinking—and since his was a thinking pose, it made sense.

On this night as she looked at him she felt a pulling inside, and without conscious intent, she rose from the rocker and returned to the bed. Folding a leg beneath her, she sat close by his side studying his face. Almost as though she'd willed it, he slowly opened his eyes.

She didn't move.

"Sabrina?" he whispered.

She reached for the hand he had laid on his stomach, and, taking it in both of hers, held it tightly in her lap.

Derek was quickly awake. Something was wrong. There had been times when Sabrina had woken him in the middle of the night with a kiss here, a touch there, one caress leading to another; but there was none of that now, just a desperate kind of clinging to his hand.

Sitting up, he used his free hand to smooth the tangle of hair from her cheeks. "What is it, sweetheart?"

"I'm frightened," she said in a small voice.

"About what?"

"Something's happening. I don't know how it could be happening, but I'm sure it is, and it's scaring me."

He could feel the beat of his blood as it pulsed through his veins, and the hand that had been stroking her hair came to a light rest on the back of her neck. "Tell me what's wrong."

She held his hand tighter. "I think I'm pregnant."

Derek's pulse tripped. He was sure he'd misheard. But

even before he had a chance to ask, she was repeating herself.

"I think I'm pregnant. I don't know how, because I'm using an IUD and it can't come out by itself. It's always worked before, but my body's doing things only a pregnant body does."

Derek stared at her shadowed face for a minute before twisting to switch on the low lamp by the bed. "What things?" he asked when he was facing her again.

"Being tired all the time. And nauseated. That flu I had wasn't the flu. It never developed into anything more than fatigue and nausea—never any fever or chills—and I still have it. My breasts feel tighter, like the skin suddenly doesn't fit what's inside. And I've missed two periods."

"Jesus," Derek breathed. He didn't know whether to be happy or sad, because that depended on which Sabrina was and he couldn't quite figure it out. Then he was distracted looking at her breasts, brushing the back of his fingers against one, finding that it was indeed firmer and wondering why he hadn't noticed sooner. His eyes flew back to her face. "Pregnant?"

Her features wore every one of the fears that had been churning inside her since she'd finally acknowledged the probability. "I've tried to pretend it wasn't so. When I missed my period the first time, I told myself that it was my body's response to all the changes that have happened to me in the last few months—the physical reaction to an emotional upheaval. And for a while I said the same thing about the tiredness, then the nausea. I didn't have either of those with Nicky. But it was so *obvious* when I missed the second time. I'm pregnant, Derek, and I don't know what to do!"

She had begun to tremble. He drew her against him, dragging the quilt up to swaddle them both.

"I imagined all kinds of other things," he said in an unsteady voice that was muffled against her hair. "I imagined that you'd changed your mind about us, or that you were itching to return to New York, or that you'd found a lump somewhere and didn't want me to know. Pregnant— pregnant I can handle."

Her cheek was unnaturally warm against his chest, her hand unnaturally cold on his middle. "Easy for you to say. You haven't been through what I have!"

"I know that."

"Before we were married I told you I couldn't have another child. You knew it. I thought you accepted it."

"I did."

"I can't do it again, Derek. I love you, but I can't do it again."

"Can't or won't?"

"Either. Both."

"Do you want the baby?"

"Yes, I want the baby!" she wailed. "That's why this is so hard!"

Derek felt a slow elation burn its way through his system. Arms tightening around Sabrina, he took a deep breath and commanded himself to speak in a low, calm, confident voice. "It doesn't have to be hard," he said. "The odds are with us. Could be that once you get through this first rough stage, things will be easy as pie and the baby will be perfectly formed and healthy and beautiful and bright."

She pressed her face to his chest. "Oh God."

"Don't you want that?" His voice was husky this time, because the thought of having a baby with Sabrina was affecting him deeply.

"You know I do. It's the only thing that's missing from my life." She raised her head and met his gaze. "We've never talked about that. I'm not sure I've even admitted it to myself before now. It's too painful, because if I start thinking of having a baby and then something happens, I'll be broken. Totally broken."

He took her chin in his hand. "No, you won't. We're in this together. I won't let that happen."

"You don't know what it does—how it feels to have a child of your own flesh condemned like that."

"What happened before was a genetic mistake. It had to do with the biological mix between you and Richard, but I'm not Richard. The biological mix between us is different."

"What am I going to do?" she whispered. Her eyes were large, liquid, pleading.

His fingers slid to cover the pulse at her neck, leaving his thumb behind to prop up her chin. "We need to see a doctor. Do you have faith in yours in New York?"

"Not particularly."

He stroked her jaw with his thumb. "Then I'll find another one. It'll be easy enough. A few phone calls. There has to be someone who specializes in case like these. He can tell us our options. I think there are tests they can run."

"And if they find something wrong?"

"Then we abort." He hugged her close, rocked her gently. "I don't want anything to happen either, Sabrina. Believe me. I wouldn't knowingly put you through that again, any more than I would knowingly put myself through it. We deserve happiness. We've earned it. If there aren't any children in the cards for us, I can be perfectly happy living out my life, just the two of us. But if we can have kids—that's the frosting on the cake. We'd make great kids, Sabrina. The farmhouse was made for them. We have the room, the money and the love."

His voice had dropped to a soothing croon that matched the gentle massage of his hand on her neck. And though the tension remained in her body, it wasn't so acute as it had been moments before. Likewise, her voice was calmer.

"I don't understand how it happened."

He grinned against her temple. "Lots and lots of good, hard lovin'."

"But the IUD—"

"Isn't foolproof. No method of birth control is. Maybe someone's trying to tell us something."

"Divine intervention?"

"Well, we sure as hell wouldn't have done it on our own." He grew quiet thinking about that. "It would be poetic justice in a sense. One fluke of nature giving what another took away."

He let that thought mull in the air for a minute, then said quietly, "You wouldn't let me go with you to see Nicky today."

"I had to work something out in my mind."

"Did you?"

She took a breath against his chest, inhaling his scent for the strength it gave her. "No. I thought I'd see him and tell him he was going to have a little brother or sister, and then somehow he'd give me a sign that it was all right. That he didn't mind, wouldn't be jealous. That he wanted it and was happy."

"Sweetheart . . ."

"He didn't smile for me today. I'm not sure he even recognized me. That hurt."

"Was he fussy?"

"No. Pretty quiet. I held him and talked to him. But something's changing there, too. He's not the same, not my own little boy anymore." Her voice cracked, but she went on. "His body doesn't feel the same. It's getting bigger, heavier. And that baby smell is gone." She swallowed the knot in her throat. "He's more the Greens' than mine. It's like I've lost him completely."

"You haven't. You never will. You're his mother. I'd put money on the fact that when you hold him, he knows. Something in his subconscious clicks. I've seen it, sweetheart. I've seen him fussing, then you pick him up and he quiets down. It'll probably always be that way."

After a minute, she gave a conceding shrug. "But what's happening to me? I feel removed from him."

"Maybe you're needing to make a break. Maybe this is a natural psychological step to help you make that break. Every mother has to let go sooner or later. Every child gets bigger and heavier. No kid goes off to school smelling like baby lotion. If Nicky had been perfectly normal, he'd be in nursery school now, then kindergarten in another year. You'd be letting go, anyway."

He held her silently for several minutes before daring to go on. "You'd also be having a second child, if you hadn't already. And Nicky would be jealous, like most other little big brothers. You can't feel guilty about wanting another child, Sabrina. It's not a question of replacing Nicky, because he'll always have a special place in your heart—and mine, too—and that's how it should be. But he'd want to have a brother or sister. If he could communicate with you, he'd tell you that."

Sabrina's body had grown progressively lax. Now almost at the point of limpness, she was quiet against Derek, letting him share her physical weight just as he'd done the weight that was burdening her mind.

He shifted his head just enough so that he could see her face. "Still here?"

"Mmm."

"Am I making any sense?"

"You always do. But fears aren't always rational. Know what my worst one is?"

He shook his head.

"Failing again. Only this time it would be *you* I'd let down—"

Derek interrupted her to growl, "The only time you let me down is when you say things like that, because it's dumb. Just dumb. You may legitimately feel that way, but it's *dumb*. Do you think you made this child in a vacuum? Did you make Nicky in one? It takes a man and a woman to make a baby. Why in the hell should you blame yourself when a full half of the responsibility is mine? But I won't *take* the blame. Birth defects are genetic mistakes over which we have absolutely no control, and I will not take the blame for something like that. It's insane. Self-defeating."

Only when he finished speaking did he realize that his grip on Sabrina was as harsh as his tone had been. Feeling immediate remorse, he relaxed both, then soothed her by rubbing his hands on her back and saying gently, "I'm sorry, sweetheart. I don't mean to sound angry, but it upsets me when you talk that way. You have courage. That was one of the things I fell in love with. You had the guts to visit me in prison when few other people would. You had the guts to find a proper placement for Nicky when you realized you couldn't handle his care yourself. You had the guts to buy this place and fix it up. And you had the guts to marry me."

"No guts involved there," she murmured. "I'm a sucker for men with dimples."

"I don't have dimples."

"Grooves, then. They're there in your cheeks when you smile a certain way. I like them."

He was pleased to hear that, if a little bemused by the fact that she was thinking of the grooves in his cheeks when they were in the midst of a heavy discussion. At least, he was.

"The issue here, Sabrina, is strength. Inner strength. Courage. When I was behind bars, I had times of utter depression when the only future I could envision for myself was one in which I faded totally into the woodwork. The thing that saved me, I suppose, was my anger, and I do believe that was a strength. I made up my mind that I was going to make it, if for no other reason than to get Greer; and I won't apologize for that, because the alternative was to accept defeat and wither into the corner. I have never in my life been willing to accept defeat."

He paused to let Sabrina comment. When she didn't, he squeezed her lightly. "Are you with me?"

"Mmm," she hummed softly.

"We're scrappers, you and I. When we want something in life, we go after it. What you have to decide is whether you want this baby enough to do that. No test, no doctor is going to be able to tell you conclusively that the baby will be born perfect. They may be able to redefine the odds, but they can't guarantee a thing."

Again he paused. Again Sabrina was silent. This time he drew back and looked down at her. Her eyes were closed, her breathing even. It seemed that, heavy discussion or not, his wife had fallen asleep.

The love he felt for her surged within him, welling up from his heart into his throat until he had to work at a swallow. He reshaped his arms to hold her more gently, more aware than ever that she was to be cherished. Sabrina—and his child. His gaze crept over the gossamer silk of her nightgown to her breasts, then her belly, and again his throat grew tight. If he could have Sabrina . . . *and* a child . . . for a man who a mere year before had been wallowing in the dregs of life it was . . . incredible.

He'd come a long way since then, and it was largely

Sabrina's doing. From the very first, she'd had faith in him. Even when he'd been at his lowest, when he felt every bit the convict, then the ex-convict, she'd treated him like a man worthy of respect. And love. She'd loved him then. She loved him now. And she carried his baby. Not so long ago, he'd have thought himself unworthy of it. By believing in him, Sabrina had made him believe in himself.

Lowering his head over hers, he closed his eyes and hugged her. His arms trembled when he wouldn't let them squeeze her as tightly as they wanted, but he didn't want to wake her. She needed the sleep. He supposed it had something to do with her not sleeping earlier, or the probability that the pregnancy was making demands, or the possibility that, God forbid, she'd found his little speech boring. But what he really wanted to think was that having unburdened herself, having shared the news of her pregnancy after worrying about it alone for so long, she felt better.

Curled in his arms, with her hair wild and her gown caressing her gentle curves, she was the flower child he'd thought her the very first time they'd met. She had come a long way shouldering a heavy load. With it removed, she'd allowed herself to sleep.

Sabrina liked the doctor that Derek found. It was a woman, for one thing, which made Sabrina feel that she would be more understanding of the emotions involved in the situation. For another thing, she spent nearly an hour with them, taking in-depth medical histories, asking question after question of them both, as if she had no other case as important as this.

She pronounced Sabrina seven weeks pregnant. As for how it had happened, she looked from Sabrina to Derek and back, grinned, and said that whatever they did to each other had, apparently, resulted in heightened fertility, which was the most probable explanation for their little quirk of fate. Regarding the IUD itself, she declared that there was more to be risked by attempting to remove it than by leaving it be, and that it would simply deliver itself along with the baby in due course. She felt that amniocen-

tesis was in order, but advised them that not only would
they have to wait until after the first trimester for the test to
be done, but that it would be some weeks after that before
the results came through. Sensing Sabrina's discourage-
ment, she spent the rest of the visit presenting a remarkably
optimistic picture of the chances for the baby to be perfect.

Leaving her office on that positive note, they spent the
afternoon in the Museum of Natural History. There was
something about the antiquity of the place that put things
into perspective. The antiquity and the scope. In comparison, their lives and that of a child they might spawn were
insignificant happenings.

They didn't talk about the baby. They didn't talk about
much, just walked from room to room, sitting occasionally
to rest, arms linked at all times.

That night, looking out over the Hudson from Sabrina's
Manhattan loft after they'd returned from dinner at Lutèce,
Derek said something that captured Sabrina's dilemma in a
nutshell.

"A while ago, you told me that you didn't know who
you were—who you were or where you were going. I like
to think that's changed, but I don't know for sure. Has it?"

She was quiet for several minutes, following the lights
of a barge as it worked its way through the water. "Yes and
no. I'm your wife. As a source of identity, I like that. I'm
going where you're going, where we're going. As for me
as a writer, you know what I want. I'm not there yet. I
won't be until my next book is published, and that may be
a long way off."

"Does it bother you—the delay?"

"No. I thought it would, but it doesn't." She gave him a
tentative smile. "You take up so much of my mind-time
that I haven't an awful lot to spare. Besides, if it bothered
me, I'd do something about it. There are other stories I
could write. The list I started at the beginning of the year
has grown pretty big in the last two months. Some of the
subjects may be passé by the time I get around to doing
anything, but others are timeless. They'll be there, waiting, whenever I'm ready."

Leaning sideways against the glass, Derek took in her

elegance, not for the first time that evening. She wore a red sequined sheath that fell in a straight line to a spot just above her knees. Encased in nylon of the sheerest matching red, her slender legs were perfect for the dress, as were the high-heeled black patent leather shoes she wore. She'd gathered her hair loosely at the top of her head in a style that set off the delicacy of her features even as it played up her onyx earrings and necklace and the overall sophistication of her attire.

But it wasn't only her attire that he admired. It was the alabaster hue of her skin, the translucence of the pink resting high on her cheeks, the luminosity of her pale green eyes. And her scent—he adored her scent. It wasn't slick, spicy or exotic. The jasmine she rubbed into her skin enveloped her in the wispiest fragrant cloud.

She was stunning, he thought. Beside her he felt perfectly plain in his dark suit, dress shirt and polished shoes—the beast to her beauty. And even then she seemed not to notice. She looked at him as though he were a prince.

Some prince. An ex-con. A man out for revenge.

"Who *are* you?" he heard himself whisper in awe.

She didn't take in the awe, or if she did, she was unaffected by it. Her mind was on the question, as it related to the events of that day. "I am," she said with a sad sigh, "a dreamer. I want the pot of gold at the end of the rainbow. But does it exist?" she asked, raising anguished eyes to his. "And if so, what is the price to be paid to reach it?"

There were no answers to her questions, and once back in Vermont, Sabrina found her greatest salvation in work. When she was busy, she didn't think about the pot of gold, didn't think about the baby she wanted so badly but was terrified to bear.

Though he could clearly see what she was doing, Derek was stymied. He could only pamper her so much before she accused him of smothering her. Damned if he did, damned if he didn't—he didn't want to mention the baby lest he bring that look of fear to her eyes, yet in avoiding the subject he let her get away with doing far more work than he wanted her to do.

His friends in the barn didn't help his cause. They had discovered that Sabrina could take their notes and write them up in a fraction of the time they'd have taken, and since she was always there, always willing to work, they took full advantage of her skills.

In that, too, Derek was torn. Sabrina did better when she worked. Her frame of mind was better. She was obviously pleased with what she accomplished. But she got less sleep—absolutely refused to rest during the day—and seemed to subsist on bi-hourly mini-meals of crackers, canned peaches and yogurt.

More than once, Derek called the doctor in New York. Though she assured him that Sabrina was strong and that work wouldn't hurt, particularly since little of it was physical, he continued to worry.

The only time when he felt he had any control over her was when they were working on his case. They had taken to keeping those particular notes and papers in the farmhouse's small second-floor den whose walls were lined with the built-in bookshelves that Sabrina had painstakingly stripped and restained. The room was cozy and private. It was furnished with a long, comfortable leather sofa and a single matching chair, and it was there that they hashed and rehashed the Ballantine matter.

Only there, and under the guise of his own hunger, could Derek ply Sabrina with food. Likewise, under the guise of his own fatigue, he could coax her into napping. And there, more than once, they made love, which was the only time Derek knew for sure what was on her mind.

The Ides of March found Sabrina and Derek in Washington again, this time combing the ranks of the city's private investigators for one who may have been hired by Greer to get concrete proof that Lloyd Ballantine had had at least one extramarital affair.

"If women were Ballantine's weakness," Derek explained, "and Greer used it against him, he'd had to have proof. Something hard and condemning."

From agency to agency they went with Ballantine's picture in hand, but that was still the only picture they'd seen when they returned to Vermont. Derek was far from defeated. He had other avenues to follow and might have done so immediately had he not wanted to give Sabrina a rest. She was still unusually tired and suffering from regular nausea, for which she took nothing. He agreed with her in that, as did the doctor, who hadn't pushed pills other than vitamins. None of them wanted to introduce anything to her system that, in even the remotest possible instance, could cause harm.

They didn't tell anyone that Sabrina was pregnant. If the test turned up a problem, they were prepared to terminate the pregnancy—in which case friends and family would only complicate the issue. Unfortunately, since the test couldn't be run until Sabrina was three months pregnant, which was nearly a month off, and since the results wouldn't be in for nearly six weeks after that, she could well be showing. Fortunately, her wardrobe was filled with long and concealing sweaters, and if that didn't work, she was prepared to take a page from Annie-Fitz's book and dress in multiple loose layers to hide the bulge.

For all practical purposes, nothing in their lives had changed. Wary of making an emotional commitment to a child that might never be, they talked about everything but that; and if there were periods of tension when neither of them would express his fears, they gave themselves no choice but to cope.

Toward the end of March, Maura popped up to visit. Actually, she didn't so much pop up as appear mud-spattered and timid at the door when Derek answered it.

With little more than a raised brow at her timidity and nothing at all to acknowledge the mud—which was inescapable in Vermont in March—Derek reached out, clutched a handful of her sleeve and pulled her in from the wind. Since the night of her confession, he had come to think differently of her. He believed that she'd been legitimately duped. As streetwise as she sounded at times, she was still naive. She didn't know the world as he did. How could she have suspected that she was being used, particularly when she'd fallen for the guy? She'd been hurt, and for that Derek felt partly to blame. So he pulled her into the house, took her coat and bag, gestured for her to leave her muddy boots on the mat, threw an arm around her shoulders and led her in search of Sabrina.

During her three-day stay, she gave Derek only one tense moment. That was when, in the process of general conversation, she mentioned having seen Richard shortly before she came north.

Derek questioned her on it as soon as he got her alone.

At first, she simply grinned. Then she took mercy on him and explained herself. "I thought about it a lot after I left here last time, and I realized that if I suddenly ended the relationship, he'd get suspicious. A slow cooldown was called for. But then, the more I thought about him and about Noel Greer and what they'd done to me—and to you and Sabrina—the more angry I got. So I decided to use Richard right back. . . . He thinks," she said smugly, "that you and Sabrina are hunting down a hot lead in New Orleans."

"New Orleans?" Derek asked, then his mouth began to twitch at the corners. "What made you think of New Orleans?"

"Every year at this time I'm thinking that I've missed Mardi Gras again. That's my kind of party, y'know?"

Having reveled his way through more than one Mardi Gras, Derek knew. He could just imagine Maura there. It *was* her kind of party—so much so that he promised to fix her up with a wild date there the next year, but only if she played it safe with Fraling.

"No more fake leads, or he's apt to punish you for it," Derek warned. "He's a snake of a man. Just ease yourself out of the relationship as comfortably as you can."

Two days later, though, Maura called from New York to give Derek the name of the "exclusive and ultra-discreet" private investigator, the "private investigator's private investigator" who worked out of Arlington, Virginia, the man Fraling had recommended when she'd told him she had a friend who wanted condemning evidence against her husband and his lover.

The detective wasn't as exclusive and ultra-discreet as

Fraling had thought. An easy hundred-dollar bill bought the information that he had indeed once been hired to photograph Lloyd Ballantine in a compromising position. A second hundred produced the pictures, a third the fact that the woman with Ballantine had been married to a congressman. A final hundred produced the woman's name.

Derek and Sabrina felt they'd gotten a bargain.

Without pause they flew on to Tallahassee, where the woman, Janet LaVine, now happily divorced, was living. She was an incredible source. Once assured that her name would never be used, she told of the affair she'd had with Ballantine—afternoons here, evenings there, clandestine meetings that spanned a six-month period and ended not because her husband had found out but because she feared he would. It seemed that Justice Ballantine liked his sex kinky. Blindfolds and handcuffs she hadn't minded, but riding crops left telltale marks on the skin.

Perhaps because she found Derek attractive or because she felt she was educating Sabrina or simply for the power trip of it, she talked on and on. She told of how she had first met Ballantine, how he had carefully guarded their trysts, how he had found no fantasy too wild.

When Derek expressed disbelief, she grew bolder and provided him with the names of others who, if they were willing to talk would verify what she'd said. The "if they were willing to talk" was a critical factor. Nearly all of Ballantine's women had been married. Some still were.

Unfortunately, Janet LaVine knew nothing about corruption on the court, blackmail, or the existence of the Ballantine files.

On the way back to Vermont, speeding along in the Saab at a smooth seventy miles per hour on I-93 north of Boston, Derek had a blowout. The car fishtailed wildly, then veered toward the side of the road. By the time he had guided it into the breakdown lane and stopped, he and Sabrina were badly shaken.

Derek had never had a blowout before. He didn't understand how it had happened. His tires were new and of top quality. They were steel-belted to prevent just such an occurrence. If he didn't know better, he'd have guessed that someone hidden in the woods had used his tire for target practice.

He said nothing to Sabrina about that suspicion.

Even without it, Sabrina was having a rough time. She was finding that no matter how hard she worked or how long the hours, she was still thinking a lot about the baby. She tried not to. She tried to forget that it existed, but her body wouldn't let her. Approaching the three-month mark, she was feeling some relief from the fatigue and the nausea. In its place, she felt fat. She knew she didn't look it, knew that no one could tell, but *she* could. The small, subtle changes were a constant reminder of what lay ahead.

Since she didn't want to think about that, she worked harder. A full-fledged member of the team now, she spent hours working with the others in the barn; and when she wasn't there, she was in the upstairs den or in the kitchen. With the arrival of April, she began planning the vegetable garden that she intended to put in the yard, and there was always another wall to wallpaper or pair of curtains to make in the house.

Sleeping was something she did only when she couldn't keep her eyes open any longer, and if she awoke in the middle of the night unable to fall back to sleep—which happened often—she crept from the bedroom and found something to occupy her mind.

Derek watched and said nothing. Between fear that someone intended him harm and would have no qualms about wiping Sabrina out with him, fear that the names Janet LaVine had given him would lead nowhere, and fear that the Ballantine files didn't exist after all, he was very tense.

He didn't want to upset Sabrina. He didn't want to pressure her. He wanted to give her the kind of strong, silent support she seemed to want.

The trouble was, he'd never been a master of strong, silent support. He'd always been a talker, a doer—particularly when he felt that someone was doing wrong. That was how he felt now with Sabrina, but since he wouldn't let himself say it aloud, the frustration festered.

It was inevitable that at some point he would explode.

· *CHAPTER 18* ·

It had been a long day. Derek had spent part of it with Jason, trying to work out the strategy for a story on the use and misuse of surplus political campaign funds, part of it on the phone trying to contact some of the women whose names Janet LaVine had given him, and part of it trying to connect in some way, shape or form with Sabrina.

He hadn't been particularly successful on any of those fronts. He was tired and testy. Dinner had been a hectic affair, with eight people jumping up and down from the table and four conversations crossing each other—and having finally cleared the farmhouse of everyone but Sabrina and him, he wanted her to sit for a while and relax.

"When I'm done here," she told him as she wiped crumbs from the table, "I'll just load the dishwasher."

He went into the living room, threw himself down on the sofa and waited. After fifteen minutes of brooding that did nothing good for his mood, he strode back to the kitchen to find Sabrina kneeling on the counter. Half of the contents of one upper cabinet was beside her. The other half was pushed every which way on the shelf.

"What are you doing, Sabrina?" he asked.

"I can't find the cinnamon," she answered, shoving aside a box of rice. "I've been looking for it all week. Do you remember using it on toast?"

Derek ran a hand across the back of his neck and looked at the floor as he said, "No, I do not remember using it on toast." He looked at her. "I thought you were finishing up in here."

"Almost done," she said.

Trying his best to be accommodating, he returned to the living room and waited another five minutes.

"Sabrina?" he called.

"Coming," she called back.

He paced the floor, spending a bit more patience with each step. Finally, he whirled on his heel and stormed back into the kitchen. Sabrina had a large bowl cradled in her elbow and was using a long wooden spoon to stir something that looked suspiciously like batter.

"What are you doing?" he asked, making no attempt to hide his annoyance.

She spared him the briefest of glances. "As long as I had everything out, I thought I'd make muffins."

"Muffins."

"Banana."

"Banana muffins."

"You like them for breakfast."

Derek stared at her in disbelief. "You've been up since six this morning. You've worked all day—writing, running to town for food, cooking, writing some more, turning soil in the garden, running back to town for computer paper, changing the sheets on the bed, cleaning up in here —and now that it's nine-thirty at night, you're making banana muffins for breakfast?"

She tipped up her chin. "Is there anything wrong with that?"

It was just the invitation he needed—or perhaps just the goading, since he'd heard a hint of defiance in her tone— because he dropped all pretense of indulgence.

"Yes, there's something wrong with it," he said, hands on his hips, dark brows shelving darker eyes that bore into hers. "You're doing too much, Sabrina. You're pushing yourself ten, twelve, fourteen hours a day without taking a legitimate, do-nothing-but-put-up-your-legs break. Everyone else takes legitimate, do-nothing-but-put-up-your-legs breaks, but by the time they're into that, you're into something else. You're doing too much. It's not healthy."

"Sure it is," Sabrina scoffed, stirring the batter more vigorously.

"You're pregnant. You're supposed to take it easy."

"The doctor said I could do whatever I wanted."

"In moderation. But you don't know the meaning of the word. What in the hell are you doing—auditioning for superwoman of the year?'

She shot him a scowl but kept on stirring.

"Put that thing down," Derek growled, and before she could do it herself, he was across the room, taking the bowl from her arm and depositing it none too gently on the counter.

"Derek—"

"I want to know what you're doing. Are you trying to wear yourself to a frazzle—wear *me* to a frazzle watching you?"

"Of course not."

"Then why are you driving yourself this way?"

"I like keeping busy. I've always kept busy."

"Not like this. Not with this self-inflicted nonstop labor."

"I enjoy it."

"You don't look like you do. You look tense and intense. You blot out everything else but what you're working at."

"That's called concentration."

"It's called neurosis. It's unnatural, given what's happening to your body right now. What is it, Sabrina? Are you daring that baby to miscarry?"

Sabrina was stunned into silence for a minute, but only for that. Something perverse inside her was livid. "What an idiotic thing to say!"

"Is it?" he asked, straightening one long, ropy arm against the counter. "Think about it. Since the doctor confirmed you were pregnant, you've been snowballing—and I'm not talking about your body, because except for your waist and breasts you're thinner than ever. I'm talking about work. Each day you take on a little more, then a little more. You dash from one activity to the next, and I can't believe you get satisfaction from any of them because you don't give yourself the time to sit back and smile."

"I get satisfaction—"

"I know what you're doing, Sabrina. You're running. There's a problem here, and rather than face it you're running. You're terrified of having that test, terrified of having that baby, so you're cramming anything and everything into your day to keep from thinking of how terrified you are. Why can't we sit and discuss it, for God's sake?"

"Maybe because you have other things on your mind," she accused.

"Hold it. There is nothing of higher priority in my mind right now than you and our baby."

"Oh?" She needed to lash back, and she had the means. "Is that why you grab the *Times* first thing each morning and act as though you're thumbing through to get an overall feel for the news before you read the specifics, when I know that all along you're looking for word on Greer? I'm half thinking you want him to fly ahead in the polls so he'll have that much farther to fall when you topple him. But you don't talk with me about that, do you?"

"You don't want to hear. You never liked the idea of what I was doing."

"I accepted it," she said quietly. "I knew that you had to work it out in your own way. So why can't you let me work out my problem *my* own way?"

"Because it's not just *your* problem, and because I don't like the way you're playing Russian roulette. That's my child, too. I want it pampered a little."

Sabrina took a small step back. She braced herself against the counter and tried to look composed. "You think I'm doing a lousy job."

"Sabrina—"

"That's what you're saying. You're telling me that I'm a negligent mother. You disapprove of what I'm doing."

"Yes, I disapprove. You're driving yourself too hard. You're risking your own health and that of the baby. But I *want* that baby, Sabrina."

"And you think I don't?"

"If you do, you have a strange way of showing it."

She threw a hand into the air. "Just because I'm not sitting around with my feet up on the sofa, I'm not pampering this child, therefore I don't want it. That's incredible!"

"Forget the child. Think about you. It's not good for *you* to be pushing yourself—"

"I'm a lousy mother. That's the gist of your accusation. As much as you give lip service to the fact that Nicky's problems weren't my fault, you're not sure. You're afraid I'll do the same thing—"

Her words were cut off when Derek took her shoulders and gave a quick shake. His eyes were dark, the vein at his temple pulsing. "That's wrong! I'd be telling you to take it easy even if you'd had ten other perfectly normal, healthy babies. You're *pregnant*, Sabrina. Pregnant women don't deliberately run themselves into the ground!"

"I'm not doing that."

"No?"

"No. And you can take your hands off me, unless you're planning to shake me again—which would *really* make mockery of your concern for my physical condition."

Only then did Derek realize how his fingers were biting into her skin. Straightening them, he lifted his palms from her shoulders, held up his hands and stepped away. "I think," he said tightly, "that we have a communication problem here. I love you. Yes, I'm worried about your physical condition, but I'm also worried about your emotional state."

Her insecurities crowded in on her. "You think I'm unstable."

"Of course I don't," he muttered. "But face it. You've been through an ordeal with one child and now you're pregnant again. Any woman would be tense. I think that you are under a perfectly understandable strain—"

"And I can't handle it. Is that it? Well, let me tell you something, Derek," she said. "I've handled far worse than this. What makes you think I'll crack? Or is it the macho male viewing the weak, shriveling female?"

Derek glared at her, then drove his fingers through his hair, which fell right back to his forehead. He didn't seem to notice. "Christ, this is amazing. It's getting worse. I try to talk with you, and you twist every word. It's like I'm walking on eggshells around here and every goddamned one of them is cracking." He turned as though to leave, then turned back. "I've been trying to take cues from you. I haven't talked much about the baby or your fears because I haven't wanted to upset you more—okay, maybe I have some fears of my own about the baby, and I don't want to think about them either, but ignoring it is getting us nowhere fast. Because I think about that baby anyway—and I know you do, too—so not discussing it is useless. Maybe we're doing this all wrong. Maybe we should be out walking through baby departments looking at bibs and booties and whatever else parents-to-be look for."

"How can we *do* that," Sabrina cried, "when we don't even know if I'll carry to term? If that test shows something wrong—"

"Goddamnit!" Derek boomed, gray eyes afire with indignation. "*That's* where you're wrong! You are assuming that something's going to be wrong, when the chances are so, so slim of that happening." The frustration he felt was painful, and his expression reflected that. "You say you're a realist, Sabrina, but if that were so, you'd be looking at the statistics and jumping for joy in anticipation of having a healthy baby. The statistics are in our favor, and if statistics aren't real, what *are*? Why in the hell do you look at the dark side?"

Shades of old arguments flickered in and out of her mind. Nick calling her an alarmist. A pessimist. A purveyor of doom. "Maybe," she told Derek in a shaky voice, "that's just the way I am."

"Like hell it is," Derek burst back. "You are a strong, sensible woman, only you've been burned once and now you're so afraid of going all out for happiness and losing it that you're taking chances. Is it superstition? Do you somehow feel that if the baby manages to survive you it'll be strong? Or are you really inviting it to up and abort itself?"

Unable to listen to his words, yet unable to move on legs that felt rubbery, Sabrina lowered her head and covered her ears with her hands. "I don't want to hear this," she mumbled to her chest. "I can't. I didn't ask for this situation. I didn't ask for the anguish a second time through. Damn it, I don't deserve it—" she cried, dropping her hands and raising her head.

But all she saw was Derek's back. Seconds later, the door slammed behind him as he disappeared into the night.

Sabrina waited for two hours. Wandering apprehensively from the kitchen to the living room and back, she waited for Derek to return. With each passing minute of his absence, a hollowness grew inside. An emptiness. An intense feeling of being alone.

Heedless of the fact that it was nearly midnight, she climbed up the stairs and knocked softly on J. B.'s door. She knew he was there; at the end of his book, now, he'd been catching a few hours' sleep in the house each night before returning at dawn to work in the barn. As badly as she felt over disturbing him, she needed to talk with someone close. J. B. was her flesh and blood. He'd forgive her the intrusion.

Quietly, she opened the door and peered into the darkness. "J. B.?" she called softly, unsteadily. "J. B.?"

But it was Ann who rose silently from bed, a waiflike figure in a long flannel gown. Casting a glance back at J. B.'s inert form, she tiptoed to the door.

"Oh God," Sabrina whispered, feeling like an utter fool. "I'm sorry. I hadn't realized—"

Ann put a finger to her lips, turned to grab a shawl from the nearby chair and slipped into the hall, closing the door behind her. "He's really exhausted," she whispered. Taking Sabrina's arm, she led her to the stairs and drew her down onto the top step.

For a minute neither woman spoke as they sat in the half-light from below. Then Ann said, "You didn't know?"

Sabrina, who was surprised enough by what she'd just discovered to escape from her own worries, shook her head. "I should have, I suppose. When he's not working, he's with you."

"I have nightmares, awful nightmares, and when that happens it's worse if I stay in bed, so I get up and walk around." She was talking softly, quickly, a little nervously. "That was how J. B. and I got to talking. Out in the barn in the middle of the night. He has nightmares, too."

"J. B.?" Sabrina asked, startled.

"Well, not so much now, but he used to have them, so he knows what it's like. When he's working, his mind is always on, so he has trouble sleeping. That was why he was up."

"J. B. has nightmares? J. B. always *caused* nightmares. I never knew he had them."

"Terribly, when he was a child." Ann had her arms wrapped around her knees and the shawl wrapped around her arms. She looked pensively toward the bottom of the stairs, then, as though reaching a decison, began to talk very softly and more slowly. "He never told anyone—I take that back—he told his father once, and his father said that nightmares were in the mind and could be easily controlled and that J. B. could do that if he tried. He did try, but the nightmares kept coming."

She smiled sadly, almost apologetically. "They were silly nightmares, one very different from the next. He had an over-fertile imagination with no other outlet. But he was embarrassed. He thought something was wrong with him because he couldn't make them go away, so he kept them to himself, didn't tell anyone. And then he found his own way of coping."

Sabrina didn't have to ask what that was.

"People think him strange," Ann said, turning to face her, "but they don't understand that deep down inside one part of him is still that little boy making stories up out of fear. What's incredible is that he's managed to turn that fear into fame and fortune. He faced the nightmares and used them to his benefit. I respect him for that."

Sabrina hadn't known that J. B. had nightmares!

Ann whispered out a nervous laugh. "I also think I love him, but that's beside the point."

"No, it's not," Sabrina said, feeling something lovely and warm inside. "It's because you love him that you understand him. I love him, but in a different way. He never told me about the nightmares. He never explained why he did what he did. I wish I'd known."

"Would things have been different if you'd known?"

Sabrina considered that, then gave a confused shrug. "I don't know. Maybe I could have helped him somehow.

He's lived through a lot of lonely years. Maybe that wasn't necessary."

"I like to think it was," Ann said, "and I know that sounds cruel, but it shouldn't. J. B. has had to fight a lot of private demons. He's still fighting them, but he's a strong man in his way. A little boy with nightmares, but a strong man. Self-contained, but still needing someone." Her voice fell to a shy whisper. "If it hadn't been for those lonely years, I doubt I'd have climbed from his bed just now." She slanted a timid glance at Sabrina. "Do you know what I mean?"

Sabrina thought she did. Ann was bright and energetic, but an introvert to some extent—as was J. B. Given her interest and aptitude in the kitchen, she was also proving to be something of a homebody, which was perhaps just what J. B. needed. He had met Ann at a point in life when he was realizing that. So good had come from the pain . . . just as Sabrina's relationship with Derek had been forged when they'd both been in hell.

Ann was suddenly looking downstairs. Following her gaze, Sabrina watched Derek step through the front door. He looked up, saw the two women, stopped.

Without a word, Ann stood. She put a hand on Sabrina's shoulder and gave it a gentle squeeze that revealed far more than Sabrina had, then returned soundlessly to J. B.

Alone on her step, Sabrina sat for what seemed an eternity. She watched Derek watch her, ached for him, ached for herself. At the height of their argument, he'd said that he loved her. She hadn't said the words, but she should have, because—looking down at him now, feeling every inch of the distance that separated them—she knew that she loved him and always would. What frightened her most was the knowledge that if it hadn't been for the pain she'd suffered with Nicky, they'd never have met.

He was handsome standing there dressed so incongruously in a leather bomber jacket and sweatpants. With his dark hair disheveled, his jaw shadowed, his eye bracketed by the scar, he was formidable. He was also strong, principled, gentle, amusing and vulnerable in turn. She couldn't conceive of life without him.

Rising from the step, she started down the stairs at a pace that didn't falter until she was sliding her arms around his waist, burying her face against his throat. She felt him complete the circle and sagged a little in relief, but his arms tightened in ready support, as she'd known they would. And then he bent his head and began to nuzzle her cheek until, raising her face, she met his mouth.

His kiss was gentle, but deep and filled with the apology he wasn't offering aloud. Framing her face with his hands, he drew back, then kissed her from another angle, then another. Each kiss was slow, moist, intimate. He used his tongue to enunciate dozens of silent words, none as meaningful as the look he gave her when he held her back for a minute. *I love you*, his eyes said, and then he kissed her again. Her mouth, her chin, her nose, eyes, forehead—he took his turn with each, and when he was done, he gently lifted her in his arms and carried her into the bedroom.

Without a word, he set her down by the side of the bed and tossed the quilt aside. Then he turned to her, caged her face and took her mouth with greater force, greater hunger and need.

Sabrina thrived on all three. She'd been feeling down well before her argument with Derek, and the argument hadn't helped. She knew that she was her own worst enemy. Derek hadn't had to suggest that she was behaving irresponsibly; she'd known it herself, had been feeling guilty about it but helpless to change. Where the baby was concerned, she was ambivalent. She wanted it, she didn't want it. Ambivalence characterized much of what she'd done lately.

There was nothing ambivalent, though, in the love Derek offered. Lips clinging to hers, he shrugged out of his jacket, unbuttoned his shirt and cast it aside, then went for the hem of her sweater. They parted for only the few seconds it took to slip the sweater over her head, then came back together, this time with their bodies bare from the waist up and touching. Hands splayed across her back, Derek worked her in a subtly undulating circle that dragged her breasts—fuller now and more sensitive than usual—against his chest. And all the while he kissed her, moist open-mouth kisses that weakened her knees as surely as his raw, masculine scent drugged her.

She tried to say his name, tried to tell him that she was on fire, that she needed more, but no sound came out. All she could do was tug at the drawstring at his waist with one hand while the other slid down the front of the soft sweatpants to shape his sex.

He moaned, strained closer, cupped her bottom and increased the pressure that way, but it wasn't enough. His breath was coming roughly as he backed her down to the bed.

Sabrina helped him then. Impatient to feel something strong and hard filling the emptiness inside, she untied the drawstring and pushed the sweatpants to his thighs. He did the rest, twisting to free himself without taking his eyes from Sabrina's. Eyes, mouth, hands—something had to be always connecting to compensate for the few hours, just passed, when they'd been apart.

Hands around his neck, Sabrina raised her hips to Derek's tugging at her jeans. She had barely kicked them from her feet when his long frame came down between her legs. Then it was surging up and he was inside. She sighed, arched her back to maximize the sensation of his filling, wrapped her legs around his waist.

For a long time, Derek's hips were still. Only his head moved, guided by Sabrina's hands in his hair. He trailed hot, hungry kisses over her face, down her neck, to her shoulders and upper arms. Then he took her breast into his mouth and drew on it with a firm, strong sucking motion.

To say that his lovemaking was healing was to tell only half the truth. What he healed with his mouth he then inflamed with his hands, and when the rest of his body joined in, Sabrina sizzled.

They made love the way they were—Sabrina warm and giving, defiant and fire-filled, Derek with a streak of gentleness, a streak of challenge, a streak of dark passion that stopped just short of danger. They complemented each other, brought out the deepest, the hottest, the best.

But if there was an added fury to their lovemaking, it was the only sign of where they'd been that night. After

they'd erupted in mind-numbing climax, then slowly returned to awareness, they fell asleep in each other's arms
without a word.

The next day, they left for Cleveland, where another of
Lloyd Ballantine's paramours lived. After telephoning two
who had unequivocally refused to be interviewed, this one
had agreed with caution. Derek hadn't wanted to give her
time to change her mind.

Derek had a qualm or two, namely the safety factor involved in traveling with Sabrina. If, in fact, a sniper had
taken potshots at his car, she was in danger simply by
being with him. He was alert. Even at the farmhouse he
was alert. But there'd been nothing amiss there, and he
saw no sign of a tail on the road. As a precaution, he'd
made their travel arrangements under an alias—which
bothered him only in that his parole officer wouldn't approve. But he felt he had just cause.

More than once he wondered if he was playing his own
form of Russian roulette by taking Sabrina along. But time
was passing, and he needed those files. Only when he had
them in his hand would he be able to tackle the emotional
issue of Sabrina's pregnancy.

Besides, he wanted Sabrina away from the farmhouse
and the many jobs she managed to drum up.

So they flew to Cleveland, where they quickly learned
why Cynthia Conroy had agreed to the meeting. After a
few minutes of introductory chitchat during which she apparently deemed them worthy confidants, Cynthia poured
out a story that rivaled the one told by Janet LaVine.

Cynthia had been married to a career army man assigned
to the Pentagon when she'd interviewed to clerk for Ballantine. She had her law degree. She was qualified. But
something happened during the interview—and it was mutual, she was quick to add. Taking a job elsewhere, she'd
begun meeting Ballantine at odd hours in one hotel or another. He'd excited her. And she had the perfect cover.
Yes, his sexual tastes were a bit unusual, but she'd been
finding her husband boring, so she hadn't minded. If Ballantine was rough sometimes, that was part of the lure.

Knowing who and what he was had always given her a compensatory measure of assurance.

After four months, he'd moved on to another woman. But she'd been hooked. Three months after that, her husband found her in bed with the house painter he'd hired the week before. They separated soon after, then divorced. Since then, the bulk of the money she earned practicing law went to the therapist she saw twice a week.

Cynthia was angry. Eight years after the fact, she was still angry at Lloyd Ballantine, angry at the mess he'd stirred up in her life.

No, she'd never seen nor heard of a set of private files that the man had kept. Nor did she know anything about his having been corrupt. She'd always thought him the epitome of righteousness on the bench. Off the bench, he was something else. The one thing that had amazed her, she said, was that he'd never been exposed as the womanizer he was—pretty remarkable, she claimed, given that he'd fathered an illegitimate daughter.

Like small children hearing the reindeer's hooves on the roof, Derek and Sabrina had trouble containing their excitement after leaving Cynthia Conroy.

"Solid," Derek said as they walked briskly to the car. "It's solid. What more perfect a lever in Greer's hand than an illegitimate child. Women, Ballantine could have denied. They came and went in his life. A child—a child stays. It would be the kind of scandal that no man, no *married* man would want, *least* of all a justice of the United States Supreme Court. If Greer had somehow learned about the child and threatened to expose her existence—which would have led to exposure of the whole sex thing—I'd bet Ballantine would be more than willing to deal." He opened the car done for Sabrina.

"But where are the files?" she asked, slipping into the seat, then looking up at him. "Do you really think the mother would have them?"

"We have nothing to lose by asking," he said. Bracing one hand on the roof of the car and the other on the top of the door, he leaned down. "Ballantine's wife doesn't have them. His kids don't. I've called his law clerks, his secretaries, his partner during the years he was in private practice, those men who were closest to him in the Justice Department—not a one claims to know of the files' existence. That could mean either that they don't exist after all, or that they're hidden away safe and sound."

Straightening, he closed the door, rounded the car and slid behind the wheel. "Think about it. If you'd been Ballantine, if you had a child whose paternity you had to deny, if you felt guilty about that and wanted to do something extra for that child, what better way than to give her a firecracker to beat all firecrackers and let her light it when and if she saw fit? You know what the publishing world is about. Those files would be worth a cool million as the basis for a biography, and what better person to either write or co-write it than one of Ballantine's blood kin?"

Sabrina was still reeling from knowledge of the child. "Do you think Cynthia was on the up-and-up?"

"She knew we'd check things out."

"What if Greer paid her to mislead us?"

"That would mean he's one step ahead of us, and if that were so, we'd have sensed it from some of the others we've spoken with. They'd have been more uneasy. Cynthia would have been more uneasy. But she wasn't uneasy. Just angry. And she volunteered that information. If Greer had paid her, she would have simply acted dumb. But she gave us a name." He frowned. "Why she didn't use it herself to blackmail Ballantine when he dropped her is beyond me."

Sabrina was perhaps more able to understand the female mind. "There's a fine line between hatred and love. She may have despised Ballantine—and still despise him—but adore him a little at the same time."

Derek was perplexed. "Why Ballantine *told* her in the first place is beyond me."

"She said he was really depressed one night. Crying. Maybe he had to tell someone or he'd burst."

Derek sighed. "Certainly does add fuel to the suicide theory—depression, guilt, fear."

They sat for a minute in silent contemplation of the

emotional low required for that. Needing to think more
positively, Sabrina asked, "So we head for Seattle?"

"We head for Seattle." He turned his full attention on
her. "Are you up to it?"

They were getting close. She could feel it. And the more
involved she was, the better she felt. "I'm up for it," she
said with a smile.

In her mid-forties, attractive, petite and soft-spoken,
Gayle Farrell was the least probable-looking candidate for
a kinky sex liaison that Sabrina, for one, would ever have
expected to find. Derek, too, was slightly unbalanced, for
in the well-modulated tone of her voice, the gentleness of
her eyes, the features that radiated a quiet inner strength,
Gayle reminded him of Sabrina.

Still, he conducted himself with the same aplomb that
never failed to amaze Sabrina. She wasn't sure if it was the
eloquence of his eyes, the temptation of his smile, the deep
and flowing timbre of his voice, but something about him
inspired people to talk. She half suspected that, despite
Derek's claim to the contrary, it was the fact that, dressed
in blazer, tie and slacks, he was once again the Derek
McGill of *Outside Insight*, all dashing good looks and
prestige. And talent. As an interviewer, his instincts were
faultless. He knew when to talk softly, when to laugh,
when to tease or prod or accuse or back off.

Much later, Derek was to say that the time had been
right, that Ballantine's death was just distant enough, that
the Janet LaVines, the Cynthia Conroys, the Gayle Farrells
of the world were simply ready to talk and would have
done so regardless of who had been at the door. Sabrina
chose to credit Derek with the coup.

Gayle Farrell felt no anger toward Lloyd Ballantine.
Though she'd been married at the time of the affair and the
marriage had fallen apart soon after, she felt she had
emerged a far stronger woman. On her own, she had taken
a job at a bank and worked her way from teller to vice-
president, something that would never have happened if
she'd been married.

Sabrina and Derek exchanged puzzled glances before

looking back at Gayle. When Derek dared ask about the child, Gayle smiled—that serene smile of hers that reminded Derek so much of Sabrina—and said that she had the best of both worlds, a rewarding career and a wonderful daughter, but that if they wanted to meet Alexis they would either have to wait a month until the semester's end or travel East. It seemed that Lloyd Ballantine's illegitimate child wasn't eight or nine or ten years old, as Derek and Sabrina had expected. Alexis Farrel was nineteen and finishing her freshman year at Yale.

Gayle didn't have the files, of course. If anyone did, Derek and Sabrina reasoned, it was Alexis. So they flew back to Boston, retrieved the Saab and headed for New Haven. They took the shore route, which, though longer, allowed for regular detours that would shake a tail; but there was a dual purpose to it. The shore route was more scenic, more relaxing. With tension building alongside anticipation, Derek needed that as badly as did his pregnant wife.

One of the most incredible things was the physical resemblance between Alexis Farrell and the man in the photograph that Sabrina carried in her large leather shoulder bag. There was no doubt that Lloyd Ballantine had fathered Alexis. Nor did she deny it.

Though every bit as soft-spoken as her mother, Alexis had neither the maturity nor the serenity. She was a serious young woman who walked the campus alone, and she was distinctly wary of Sabrina and Derek.

"I don't understand why you're here," she said. She was leaning against a broad tree trunk in the quadrangle where they'd finally reached her, and looked a little cornered. "No one ever approached me before. No one ever cared who my father was. Why now? Why at all?"

Strangely, while Derek had been perfectly comfortable using a cover in his dealings with the others, he felt a compulsion to go with the truth on this one. "Now, because I've just now learned of your existence. At all, because it needs to be done. We suspect that a very powerful man had illegal dealings with Justice Ballantine. Ballantine's gone, but that man isn't, and he is about to gain even more power unless we learn the truth. The only way we can learn the truth is through a set of files that we were told exists."

"His papers were left to the University of Chicago."

"Those were his official papers. These are different. They detail those illegal dealings."

"Alleged illegal dealings," Alexis said.

Derek stood corrected by the young woman he now saw to be sharp as well as bright. "Alleged illegal dealings. Lloyd Ballantine was your father. You may hate his guts for never having acknowledged you, but he was your father. We have conclusive proof that he led a double life, and everything points to the fact that he committed suicide. If he did that, he had to have cause. Fear of exposure through blackmail would have been a strong enough one to do it."

Alexis hugged the armload of papers she held closer to her chest as she looked from Derek's face to Sabrina's. "But I don't understand why you've come to me. I didn't even know the man was my father until after he died. How can I possibly help you?"

"We thought that your father may have left you those files," Sabrina said.

"Why would he do that?" Alexis asked quickly.

Derek answered in a low, calm voice. "To give you something of value. To make up for all he hadn't done for you during his life."

But Alexis was shaking her head. "I don't know anything about any files, and even if I did, what would possibly be in it for me if I turn them over to you?"

"He was your father. If you hated him, you'd be pleased to see his dark side exposed. If you loved him, you'd want to see the demise of the man who brought him to his knees."

"And what's in it for you?"

It was a minute before Derek answered. "A personal satisfaction that I think, if you try, you can understand," he said. "I'm an investigative journalist. The same man who I believe blackmailed your father was indirectly responsible for a man being killed and directly responsible for my spending two years in prison. I didn't like being there. But I like to think—in my more positive moments—that things like that happen for a purpose. Believe me, I've had trouble finding a purpose for my spending two years in jail—other than to put the fire under me to go after those files."

He paused, eyed her assessingly, tipped his head and challenged her by saying, "You're young. You're idealistic. What if I were to say that my wish is to spare this country another corrupt leader?"

"I'd say," Alexis answered, "that if *you* were young and idealistic, I could buy it; but at your age I'd assume your real interest is revenge."

Stifling a chuckle, Sabrina looked at Derek. "She's a toughie, this one is."

"Yeah," he drawled in the spirit of the thing, "but so am I." He turned back to Alexis. "What do you say? Want to help me spare this country another corrupt leader?"

But Alexis wasn't quite into the spirit of the thing. Again she insisted that she knew nothing of either the files' existence or location. And though, between Derek and Sabrina, they reiterated each of the arguments and made their most poignant pleas, she stuck by her claim.

They knew she was lying. They didn't know how—and maybe it was desperation, because without Alexis Farrell's cooperation they were back at square one—but they knew it. Still, they couldn't tie her to the rack and torture her until she confessed. The best they could do was give her the name of the hotel where they'd be spending the night, then give her their Vermont address, should she want to talk more.

That night, Sabrina and Derek were more discouraged than they'd been since they started their search. They had run into a brick wall in the form of a nineteen-year-old coed, and they weren't sure how best to break through. The only thing they were sure of was that they weren't giving up.

Apparently, Alexis Farrell sensed that. Or maybe it was hatred or love, or a night spent soul-searching. Or maybe she was every bit as young and idealistic as Derek had suggested she was. Whatever the case, she phoned the hotel early the next morning and, shortly before nine, met Derek in the lobby and handed him the Ballantine files.

Neither of them saw the man who folded his paper, rose from his chair and headed for the bank of public phones.

· *CHAPTER 19* ·

The atmosphere at the farmhouse was euphoric. Not only had Derek and Sabrina returned victorious, but the fledgling Institute for Investigative Journalism has sold its first three stories. And to top that, J. B. had finished his book. It was J. B. who formalized the celebration, inviting everyone to be his guest for dinner at a nearby inn, elegant and expensive. And that was only the start of the evening. Later, back in the barn with the precious papers stowed safely away, Derek and Sabrina, J. B., Ann and Justin and the three others who rounded out the crew raised glasses to toast their success.

It was well after midnight when the last of the laughter had faded away and the liquor had taken its toll. Everyone was asleep—except Sabrina, who hadn't had more than half a glass of the stuff. She was wide awake. Her body was at rest, quiet beside Derek's sprawled form, but the motor in her mind wouldn't stop. She was reliving that day, reliving the moment of realization that the files were finally theirs, reliving the excitement of reading them and finding in them evidence against Noel Greer as incriminating as they had hoped.

But her mind didn't stop there. It worked through the writing of the story, worked through the possible markets and the timing of the release. Then, of its own accord, it switched gears and considered the baby. The test was scheduled for the following week, and then the real waiting would begin.

Sabrina thought about J. B.'s courage in fighting his nightmares. She thought about Derek's courage in fighting Noel Greer. And then she thought about something else— what Derek had told Alexis about things happening for a purpose. Nicky's fate was tragic, but did the experience have its up side? Was she a stronger person for it? Was her relationship with Derek stronger, her love for him greater after what she'd been through with Nick? And were the feelings she had—yes, she had them—for the child forming in her belly different from those she'd felt for Nicky? Would she be appreciating this child, treasuring each small sign of growth, savoring each step in its development that much more? Would she be smelling the roses of life, really smelling them for the very first time?

Shaking herself free of those thoughts, she closed her eyes and tried to sleep, but the thoughts returned. Derek . . . J. B. . . . Ann . . . Alexis . . . were they that much bolder than she?

Sensing that sleep was a long way off and needing a diversion, she crept from bed, threw a robe over her nightgown and a shawl over that and left the room without waking Derek. The back door creaked beneath her hand. She left it ajar an she darted across the moonlit path to the barn. Moments later, she returned carrying the Ballantine files.

With the softest beam of light coming over her shoulder, she sat reading them in the den for hours. Periodically, she stopped to jot down notes to herself, but for the most part she simply read and reread, studied and thought. It was nearly three in the morning when her eyes grew too heavy to do more. Locking the file in the cabinet by the desk, she went back to bed.

Shortly before dawn, a loud banging on the bedroom door brought her awake. "Derek! Derek, Sabrina!"

Sabrina was struggling to get her bearings when Derek stirred beside her.

"Wake up, you guys!" Ann yelled, banging harder. "The *barn*'s on fire!"

"Jesus Christ," Derek murmured. After a second's fight with the sheets, he was on his feet and racing to the window. One look and he was back, grabbing for his clothes. "Fire. Holy shit." He hopped on one leg to thrust the other into his cords, then teetered and nearly fell when he reversed the procedure. "Four of them are dead to the world out there."

As wide awake as Derek now, Sabrina yelled, "We're up!" to Ann, then reached for the phone and dialed in the alarm. Derek was out the door by the time she turned back. Grabbing her robe, she pulled it on as she ran after him.

It was arson. Even before the fire marshal declared it so, Derek knew. There had been no slow trail of smoke to alert the sleepers. The fire had started suddenly and burned quickly—with the inferno centered at the front of the barn where the offices were clustered. It was set by a master and had been designed to destroy the papers and files while giving those asleep in the rear rooms chance to escape.

They had escaped. Derek thanked God for that. Justin, Jason, Denice and Bill—all safe, if stunned. The only casualty was J. B. who raced into the barn to rescue his book and any other papers he could reach before the heat had grown too intense and the rafters had threatened to collapse and Derek's hand on the back of his pants had hauled him out. He had been burned where his shoulder had hit a smouldering beam, but other than that he'd been lucky.

The barn itself was a total loss. By the time the engines arrived, it was completely engulfed in flames. The best the firefighters had been able to do was soak the house and the surrounding trees to prevent spread of the flames.

Now, covered with soot and devastated, Derek stood among the charred ruins. It was mid-afternoon. The flames had long since burned themselves out, and what few persistent sparks may have been missed by the firemen's hoses had been doused by the falling rain. It was a gentle rain, an April rain. The air would have smelled of wet earth and growing things had it not been for the overpowering stench of smoke.

The waste of it all tore at him, making him want to scream at the pain he felt. J. B.'s book was singed but intact. One of the reports had been rescued. Everything else was gone. Gone.

All that was left was self-recrimination.

He should have installed a sprinkler system in the barn, or a more elaborate fire alarm. He should have bought a guard dog when he'd suspected Greer was on his trail. He should have purchased the motion sensor he'd seen, the one that automatically tripped floodlights outside at the first sign of movement.

He should have—should have, damn it—copied those files and stashed the originals elsewhere.

But it was too late. No amount of self-recrimination would restore what had been lost. For Ann and Justin, Bill, Jason and Denice, the loss was a minor setback.

For him, it was a major defeat.

Muttering a vile oath, he kicked at the debris by his feet. The barn itself didn't matter. Hell, he'd already thought of buying one of the old Victorian houses in town and shifting the offices there. He'd even thought of converting a second one into apartments for the staff. He wanted privacy for Sabrina and himself. Where teamwork was concerned, enough was enough already.

No, it wasn't the barn that hurt. It was the files.

Dejectedly, he looked around. Sabrina would be back soon. He'd deliberately sent her to the hospital with Ann and J. B. to keep her safely occupied, but she'd be back. He had to get his act together before then, had to know what to say. But what *could* he say?

Hey, don't sweat it, it was only a bunch of papers.

So what was a little extra work on our part—we got to see the country, didn't we?

Okay, so Greer is elected, so what? We've had worse men than him calling the shots.

What's that you say? Revenge? Revenge?

All for nothing. The thought sank deeper and deeper, increasing his torment. All for nothing. It had been his interest in the files that had first roused Greer, his interest in the files that had led to a man's death and to his own trial, conviction and imprisonment. The pain, the fear, the boredom and frustration and fury—all were for nothing. The files were gone.

Squeezing his eyes shut, he bowed his head, pressed his fists to his temples and let out a low, savage sound that filtered into the air and grew mournful as it hung over the ruins of the barn. Slowly it faded. Derek let his fists fall to his sides. He raised his head and opened his eyes to the bleakness he felt.

"My sympathies, McGill," came a voice from behind.

Derek froze. He stared straight ahead, recognizing the voice, refusing to believe that the voice he recognized was there. But just as the charred remains before him weren't about to rematerialize into something useful, so the voice came again.

"It's a terrible loss for your new enterprise, but you'll rebuild. You'll go in different directions, that's all."

Dropping his gaze, Derek took one breath, then another. Then, slowly, he raised his head and turned.

The man he faced was in his fifties, tall and remarkably well built. His skin was as tanned as always, his silver hair—sheltered from the rain by a large black umbrella—as impeccably groomed. He wore the kind of country clothes worn by those who wanted only to look the part, not play it. With his legs planted in a wide stance, his chin set and his mouth slanted smugly, he was as arrogant as ever.

"What are you doing here, Greer?" Derek asked in a low, venomous voice.

Greer was undaunted. He smiled. "News spreads fast. Word of the fire came over the wire just before noon. I said to myself, poor McGill, life hasn't been going his way lately, and I thought that maybe for old times' sake I'd fly up and offer my help." He looked around at the farmhouse, then the lake and the trees. "Nice."

Derek clenched his jaw. "There were people in that barn."

At that Greer did look properly disturbed. "So I heard.

Damn good thing they got out. With your record, you could have been hit for negligent homicide."

"There were people in that barn, innocent people, and you and your torch risked their lives."

"So you think this was arson?" Greer asked conversationally. He scratched his head and looked innocently toward where the fire marshal was sitting in his car taking notes. "Hard thing to solve, arson is. It's one thing if you're in the city and you've got witnesses who saw someone run from the scene just before the fire, but up here—" He gave a rueful shrug. "Up here, no one's around to see, especially just before dawn."

Derek knew he was right. It might be proven that the fire was set, but finding the person who set it would be next to impossible. "Is that why you came? To gloat?"

"Gloat? Because you've had a little misfortune? New York would have been just fine for gloating, if that was what I had in mind." He rocked back on his heels. "You're a good man, McGill." He held up a hand. ". . . have a few weaknesses that need some work, but you're a good man." The hand fell, thumb catching on the side pocket of his down vest. "At one point I was thinking of hiring you to work with me in Washington—you'd make a powerful press secretary—but now that you've put down roots here, it's a moot point. And then there are those weaknesses. You're bullheaded. You always were. Don't know when to yield." He shook his head. "That wouldn't work where I'm going. Politics is the fine art of compromise."

With each reference to the Capital, where Greer had clearly taken for granted he was headed, Derek's fury grew. The only thing to temper it was the utter disbelief he felt at the gall, the *gall* of the man to show up at the scene of his latest crime.

"You know," Derek said, his eyes dark, hard and relentlessly aimed at Greer, "I can pretty much figure out how you did it with Padilla and the trial and all. I can also guess that you weren't thrilled when I was released. You must have thought they'd keep me longer. But what I don't understand is why you didn't just kill me once I got out. A sniper's bullet from a distance aimed not at the tire of my car but at me—wouldn't that have been quicker and cleaner than following me around for months?"

Greer said nothing at first. Then he squatted and poked at the chunks of dark, damp wood at his feet. "I understand you redid the barn yourself. Too bad. That must double your upset about the fire. Of course"—he raised his head and looked Derek sharply in the eye—"so much of the satisfaction is in the doing. It's the project—the planning, the anticipation, the taking of one step at a time."

"But why didn't you go after the files yourself?" Derek asked. "One of your men could have done exactly what I did. That would have been a helluva lot easier."

Without breaking eye contact, Greer straightened. "You don't listen, McGill. That's a definite weakness. You don't listen, you don't hear what's being said."

"I listen. I hear. It's just that I can't believe that this whole . . . charade was performed for the sole purpose of your personal entertainment."

Greer tipped his umbrella to squint toward the thick, lead-hued clouds overhead. "Building and running a megacorporation like mine has taught me many things. I tell you this, McGill, since you seem intent on become an entrepreneur and I see no reason why you shouldn't learn from me. Organization is crucial. You have to be able to divide labor and delegate authority. The duplication of any effort is a waste of time and money."

"In other words," Derek said, wiping rain from his jaw with the sleeve of his jacket, "I was doing it, so why should you. But you knew about the girl. Early on you must have figured she had the files. Still you sat back."

Greer looked off toward the lake. His expression was calm, his tone nonchalant. He might have been chatting about the weather. "A man has to be careful, especially a politician. It's the media. They're out of control nowadays, too damned nosy, too damned conscientious. Everything is seen, noted, reported; and if the politician in question has his sights set on an even higher office, that could spell trouble."

Derek could only think of one "higher office" to which Greer would aspire, and the thought made him sick.

"You're playing a dangerous game, Greer. Okay, I may have lost it this time, but some day, somewhere, it'll catch up with you."

One brow rose and fell in a shrug of unconcern. "I'm cautious."

"No one's that cautious."

"I'm smart."

"You're arrogant. You thrive on manipulating people for the sense of power it gives you."

Slowly, almost absently, Greer panned the farmhouse and its setting. He sniffed, then nodded. "Good-looking place you've got. It really is. Good-looking woman, too."

Derek's spine grew ramrod-straight. A pulse throbbed at his temple, a muscle at his jaw.

Greer sent him a sidelong glance. "Does she know about your background?"

Derek sucked in the inside of his cheek and closed his molars on the moist flesh.

"Tough having to live down a past like that. Doubly tough with a record of your own—speaking of which, I was surprised your parole officer didn't balk at all that traveling. They usually like ex-cons to stay put so they can keep an eye on them." He paused. "You did report the traveling, didn't you?"

Other than the slight, involuntary flare of his nostrils, Derek didn't move.

"Too bad you couldn't get a job back in the city," Greer said. "When I heard you were getting out, I went around, spoke with a few people."

"I'll bet you did," Derek said very slowly.

"I tried to tell them how dedicated you were to your work, but they seemed to feel that hiring a convicted murderer would be an unnecessary risk. And to be honest, they had a point. To take on a man prone to violence, to sink money into a project—"

"I could kill you, Greer."

Greer grinned. "I'll bet you could."

"Get off my property."

"As I hear it, it's your wife's property."

"Get off my land before I strangle you." He was clench-ing and unclenching his hands, itching to do just that.

"Is that a threat?"

"More like a promise," Derek vowed. His hair was wet, falling in spikes on his forehead. His skin was wet, too, and his clothes; but he was oblivious to that. The full force of his concentration was on Greer, who looked for all the world to be enjoying himself.

"Now why doesn't that scare me?" he asked. "Maybe because we've got a pack of witnesses who'd have you pinned to the ground in no time, and because you'd be back in prison on assault charges before you had time to pee, and because once back there, you wouldn't be getting out so quick. The assault of a candidate for the United States Senate is a serious offense." He narrowed his eyes and lowered his voice, goading Derek for everything he was worth. "Come on, McGill, try it. I dare you."

Derek wanted to. The wild look in his eyes attested to it. He wanted to haul back and hit the man so hard that he'd go flying, and then he'd kick him, kick him again and again—just as he'd been kicked that day in the prison shadows—until Greer begged for mercy. And then, only then, would he decide whether he'd let him live.

"What's the matter, McGill?" Greer taunted. "Don't have the guts?"

Derek gave that imaginary body another hard kick. His voice mirrored the force. "I have the guts."

"Then what are you waiting for? You wanted to get me with those files, but you can't." He grinned. "The files are gone, McGill. You're as powerless as ever. What do you say to that?"

Derek didn't say a thing.

So Greer looked around. "Mmm, you've done okay. There really is something to be said for country living. Relaxed and laid-back. A little cottage business, pretty farmhouse, some land. Not bad for second-best."

Derek took a step forward.

"And the wife. Bet she's a hot little thing, getting it on with an ex-con. I heard about those scenes in the prison yard. I heard."

"I could kill you," Derek seethed.

"So why don't you?"

Why didn't he? In the course of a minute's time, he was thinking about his "hot little thing" of a wife, thinking that she was the best thing that had ever happened to him, thinking that he liked country living, liked being relaxed and laid-back, liked having a cottage business, a pretty farmhouse and some land. He was thinking that he liked running on country roads and sculling on the river, that he liked the idea of being near Nicky, and that he had enough story ideas to keep three teams at work. He was thinking that there was nothing second-best about what he had and that he wouldn't change places with Noel Greer for all the money, all the power, all the glory in the world.

Why didn't he kill Greer? With a look of pure disdain, he gathered just enough saliva to spit at his feet. "Because you're...not...worth it," he said and turned to walk away, only to falter when he saw Sabrina standing a dozen feet off. She was looking anxious, a little tired, strangely excited.

Feeling an odd serenity wash over him, he started walking again. When he'd reached her side, he put an arm around her shoulders and started moving her toward the fire marshal's car.

She cast a perplexed glance over her shoulder at an even more perplexed Greer, then said, "Derek, there's something—"

"How's J. B.?"

"Fine. Derek, we didn't—"

"How are *you*?" he asked, searching her face.

"Fine. Derek, what was he doing—"

"He's leaving," Derek said. They'd reached the fire marshal. "Sir, that man," he tossed his head toward Greer, "is trespassing on private property. I would appreciate it if you would call the police for me. I have something more important to do just now."

The fire marshal, who doubled as the town's postmaster and knew and respected Derek as a local, said, "Sure thing, Mr. McGill."

Derek steered Sabrina toward the house. "The most incredible thing just happened."

"With Greer?"

"Uh-huh. He showed up here to rub my face in the fact that the files are lost."

"But—"

He pressed a finger to her lips, then removed it to open the farmhouse door. "I was standing out there, looking around at the mess, wondering how I was ever going to pull my life back together, when he showed up. Then he started in on me, and I thought I'd explode. I honestly, truly came close to smashing him."

They had passed through the kitchen and were nearing the bedroom. Derek had already dropped Sabrina's hand to remove his wet jacket. He hooked it on a doorknob as he passed, then started on the buttons of his shirt.

"But I didn't. And I can live with it, Sabrina. I can live with the loss of those files—"

"You don't—"

"Because *I* know. *I* know the truth. I know what I did and what he did, and I'm the one who'll be able to sleep at night with a clean conscience." Having tossed his shirt on the bed, he ducked into the bathroom for a towel. "Yeah, I'm angry," he said as he emerged rubbing his hair. "I'm angry that he got away with it. I'm angry that he'll win that election, because the people of New York, the people of the country are the losers." He dragged the damp towel over the soot on his face, then abruptly dropped the hand that held the towel and looked Sabrina in the eye. "But I can't live with the anger anymore. I'm tired of it. I have a future, *we* have a future, and I'll be damned if I'll let that anger screw it up."

With deliberate movements, he wiped the soot from the back of his hands. His eyes held conviction. "I did my best. I found those files, and if Joey Padilla is anywhere up there" —he shot a glance skyward—"he knows what happened. I may have been Greer's patsy in that murder, but I paid for my part. I've had enough of the guilt. It's done." He looked down at his hands as he worked the dirt away. "Had I been a chip off the old block, I'd have beaten Greer to a pulp—correction, I'd be looking around now for someone to do it for me. But I'm not. I'm not my old man. I'm me."

He let out the rest of that breath, took another, let it out too. Then, raising his eyes, he said in a voice that was deep and filed with emotion, "I'm free, Sabrina. Free."

Sabrina, who'd been forced to quietly listen to his speech when she realized that he wouldn't let her talk, felt such an intense surge of love and respect that tears came to her eyes. He was free. He was beautiful. He was here.

And she'd thought herself a failure? How could that be? She had a warm home filled with friends and laughter, a gratifying career at her beck and call, a husband she adored and a new baby—*yes, Nicky, a brother or sister*—on the way. A failure? Not possible.

For the first time in her life, she felt she truly knew who she was. No one could write quite the way she could. No one could buy farmhouses, or strip furniture or bake banana muffins quite the way she could. And no one could satisfy Derek quite the way she could.

She had arrived.

Crossing the room on feet that were even lighter than they'd been before, she slid her arms around his waist and pressed her tearstained cheek to his chest. "Love you," she whispered on a broken breath. Then, just as Derek was about to cinch the embrace, she slid from his grasp. "Wait."

"Sabrina . . ."

She was already out the door. He heard her dash up the stairs to the second-floor landing. Her footsteps receded as she ran down the hall. He heard nothing for a minute, then a crescendoing patter as she retraced her steps. When she reappeared at the bedroom door, her cheeks were flushed. Eyes holding his, she approached him slowly, looking pleased, if apprehensive. A foot away she held out the bundle she'd been clutching to her chest.

Derek's eyes widened on the bundle. Then they flew to Sabrina's face in disbelief.

"I couldn't sleep," she explained softly and with a bit of guilt. "Last night. When all was said and done, I was as excited about these as you were, so I got up, took them from the barn and sat up in the den reading them. By the time I was tired, I didn't feel like traipsing back to the barn, so I locked them in the desk and went to bed. Then things happened so fast this morning that I didn't realize what it meant until I was on the way to the hospital with J. B. and Ann. I tried calling, but everyone must have been outside."

Derek continued to stare at her in utter amazement.

"Here." She shoved the files at his belly. "Take them. They make me nervous. When I think what Greer did to try to destroy them, I get a little ill."

Derek cleared his throat. He looked down at the files.

"Take them, Derek," she pleaded.

Hanging the towel over his shoulder, he took the files and tossed them onto the nearby dresser. Then he took Sabrina in his arms, which was the only taking he really wanted to do, and held her as tightly as he dared.

She didn't seem to mind the crush. "Will we write the story?" she asked, her breath soft against his throat.

His arms were trembling. It was a minute before he spoke, and then his voice was hoarse. "First, we call David and tell him what's happened. Then we find the nearest copying place and have two copies made of that file."

"Two?"

"One for a safe-deposit box in town, the other for David's vault." Cupping her head, he held it to his heart. "Then David, you, me, and the original are going straight to Washington. I think the department of justice will be interested in what we have here."

"But what about the newspapers?"

"They'll have to wait. You'll write your book, I'll get my revenge, but all in good time." He went still, reexperiencing that incredible disbelief. "The den. You had them in the den. Christ, I can't believe it!"

Sabrina could hear his smile. Seconds later, when he lifted her face to his, she saw it.

"You are a remarkable woman. Lord, do I love you." He gave her a long, deep, tongue-tangling kiss that left her lightheaded.

"You wouldn't be saying that if the files had burned to a crisp in the barn after all."

"You bet I would. That was what I realized when I was with Greer. The files I can live without." His eyes roamed her face. "You I can't."

A failure? With a man like Derek saying words like that to her? He'd walked away from Greer. Despite the hatred, the fury, the months of plotting revenge, he'd walked away. For her. How could she possibly be a failure, with a victory like that?

Swallowing the emotion that threatened to rob her of speech, she said, "As it happens, you have us both."

Very gently, he kissed the tip of her nose, then her cheek, and there was something about the gentleness—or perhaps the "us both"—that directed Sabrina's thoughts.

"Derek?"

He kissed her chin.

"I want a girl."

He went still for an instant, then, cautiously, raised his head. "You do?"

"Yes."

He inhaled a long, deep breath and closed his eyes in a moment's silent thanks. Then he looked at her and said in a very soft, very caring, very Derek voice, "You do know that it's a little late to be placing special orders. We require a full nine months' lead time on items like these . . ."

Rooting her fingers in his hair, she grinned up at him until her eyes grew misty and her throat knotted. Then, rising on tiptoe, she coiled her arms around his neck and hung on tight.

Returning her hug, Derek basked in her sun, renewed and stronger than ever as it warmed his soul. At that moment, he felt more love, both outgoing and incoming, than he'd have believed possible. And at that moment, he knew they'd made it.